falling

falling

Olivia Liberty

Atlantic Books
LONDON

First published in Great Britain in trade paperback in 2007 by Atlantic Books, an imprint of Grove Atlantic Ltd.

This novel is entirely a work of fiction. The names and characters are the work of the author's imagination. Any resemblance to actual persons, living or dead, is entirely coincidental.

Every effort has been made to trace or contact all copyright-holders. The publishers will be pleased to make good any omissions or rectify any mistakes brought to their attention at the earliest opportunity.

'Pearl's A Singer': words and music by Jerry Leiber and Mike Stoller, Ralph Dino and Mike Sembello. Copyright 1974/1977, Jerry Leiber Music and Mike Stoller Music copyright renewed – all rights reserved – lyrics reproduced by kind permission of Carlin Music Corporation, London, NW1 8BD.

9 8 7 6 5 4 3 2 1

A CIP catalogue record for this book is available from the British Library.

ISBN 978 1 84354 532 3

Designed by Five Twentyfive Ltd

Printed in Great Britain

Atlantic Books
An imprint of Grove Atlantic Ltd
Ormond House
26–27 Boswell Street
London WC1N 3JZ

For my parents

one

The door slammed behind Toby Doubt. There was no sign of Howard so Toby stood for a moment on the step allowing his eyes to adjust to the day. He'd never noticed before that the step was worn, as though a great number of people had passed through here over the years. He'd certainly been through this door often enough – once, twice, sometimes three times – every day, for the three years they'd lived here. Sometimes with Imogen – 'do you have your keys?' – sometimes with Howard, once with a police officer. But mostly he'd done it alone, in the morning, late for work, long after Imogen had left for school.

However, this was the first time, as far as he could remember, that he'd done it traumatized. He examined the hedge: it glittered with debris. A McDonald's milkshake thrust its straw into the sky, below it a green Carlsberg can glinted and a red and yellow Happy Meal. Further into the depths lodged the twist of a gold cigarette box, a brown glass bottle – cough mixture? – a yellow crisp bag, a bottle stained with the remains of something blue. Happy Meal, fags, cough mixture, antifreeze. The key was to put these things in the right order. At the bottom of the hedge, beneath the blackened foliage of last year's growth, stood a white polystyrene cup with a clean bite taken from the rim: a nice cappuccino to finish up. If the hedge hadn't represented a certain sourness in his relationship – 'Toby, I've been asking you for a week, please clear the front garden' – he might have enjoyed the razzle dazzle of this morning's display.

He picked up the briefcase which stood between his boots, the gate swung closed behind him and he crossed between cars to join the Monday morning work force blazing a trail along the pavement towards the station. The plants growing out of the wall quivered and the patina beneath the bench shone like Marmite. Below him a train clattered south. Money to be made. Money to be made. It thundered into the tunnel. There's money to be made!

He joined the queue which stood impatient on the pavement outside 'Steve's Nest'. Ahead of him and above the chug of traffic a man in a pale suit was speaking into his phone: 'And that, Sue, is why...' he turned to look at Toby, white – toothpaste? – crusting the corner of his mouth, 'she's packed her bags and gone over to the other side.' Toby's thoughts turned to Imogen and to her bag, packed and zipped on the red carpet in the hallway. From there they moved to his chest where something cold and sharp lodged in his windpipe. It felt like a large silver whistle stuck in sideways.

Beyond the smeared glass and trays bearing tuna with sweetcorn and neon chicken tikka, Steve, his narrow back looped, was buttering toast. There was no sign of the Bulgarian girl who made the cappuccinos, smiled and told the customers 'nice day'. Beyond Steve, coffee dribbled into a paper cup which rolled on its side. The counter was scattered with lids, empty milk cartons and dirty cutlery. Something clattered to the floor. The Nest was in disarray. Steve twirled the corners of a paper bag, handed it to the wrong customer, he dropped coins, turned to the cappuccino machine, splashed milk, fitted a lid, sprayed his shirt and wiped his nose on his sleeve.

'Large cappuccino, one sugar, two toast granary with Marmite.' The man in the pale suit ordered his breakfast. Imogen hated Marmite.

'Butter?' enquired Steve, a perfect button of frothed milk between his red-rimmed eyes. Steve turned back from the toaster and brushed his hands together. Two of his fingers appeared to be stuck in the same digit of his blue rubber glove. 'Next?' Steve turned his attention to Toby.

He looked like he might have been crying.

'Large cappuccino, one sugar, two granary toast with Marmite please.'

'Butter?' Steve brandished a knife which dripped with yellow and sniffed sharply. He had almost certainly been crying: the underside of his nose glistened.

While the man buttered, Toby wondered whether perhaps there was something, after all, in what Imogen had said: 'I'm telling you,' round eyes ice blue, chin raised, muddy hands emphatic. 'Steve asked the Bulgarian girl to marry him. She told him she needed two months to think about it.' Perhaps the two months were up and the girl had declined his offer. That had been known to happen.

Toby stood on the platform at Kentish Town, his back pressed against the warm brick wall. The toast was in his pocket and the cappuccino in his hand. Two trains clattered one after the other through the station and into the tunnel. Both were packed with standing, moon-faced commuters shuttled in from Luton and St Albans. As each train passed Toby felt its gravitational pull and he pressed his back further into the wall until he could count the indents where the cement held the bricks together. He turned to look at the bridge and the houses above it.

Number 3 Frederick Street stood high above the platform against the clear blue sky. It needed painting. Number 5, belonging to the dentist's wife, was whiter than sugar and Number 1, on the other side, was blue and clean as the sky itself. Number 3 let down the terrace. The wire from the television aerial hung loose across the front and each of its three windows stared out dully through a cataract of grime. Toby wondered if a word existed to describe its colour. Nicotine? Dust? It was a non-colour related somehow to grey. He scanned each window and wondered if Imogen could be in the garden. Perhaps he had merely missed her – an oversight – as she crouched fiddling amongst her burgeoning lettuces before going off to school.

The top of a bobbing head appeared above the wall. In front of the house it disappeared to cross the road and make its way through the gate and up the path to the front door. He would recognize the top of that head anywhere: it was Howard.

A train pulled into the station. It slowed and stopped. There was a collective surge and Toby, hot in his suit, joined the straggle-end of the commuters knotting at the train's doorway. No one got off. He cast a glance over his shoulder. The house was looking beyond him towards the City above which the NatWest Tower fingered the sky. Imogen wasn't in the garden. The house knew it and Toby knew it.

The doors swept closed and the train dragged out of the station. The carriage laboured under the silence of breath and the mass of clean, hot people with a week's work ahead of them. NEWS BULLETIN declared a newspaper inches from Toby's face: A woman, 30, was decapitated when she leant out of a train window as it entered a tunnel in Kent. What kind of bulletin was that? What kind of a woman got decapitated?

'Well, put it this way, Mark,' a moustached man shouted into his phone above the roar of the clattering silence. 'It could not have happened to a nicer person!' Toby rubbed the toe of his brown Blundstone boot against his calf and wondered again what had caused the heart-shaped mark the size of twopence. It was dark like oil, black like blood.

At Farringdon, Toby got off. The platform was infused with soft green light filtered through a roof of arched glass – a serene greenhouse subterranea humming with the meaty whirr of pigeon wings. He sat on a bench. Imogen, Imogen what have you done? You've ripped out my heart and you've gone on the run.

He leant back against the bench and loosened his tie. It constrained his neck and made him more aware of the angular obstruction in his chest. Where the tie had come from he'd no idea. As far as he knew, he'd never owned a tie. It had appeared this morning, milk pink like a dog's tongue, on a coathanger in the wardrobe between the suit and

Imogen's mother's fur coat. He'd worn the suit just once six months ago on 27 December. He'd bought it that same morning on Regent Street in the first day of the sale while Imogen waited on a double yellow line in her mother's Peugeot. She'd been complaining all morning that the car was full of hair – dog hair and her mother's hair – and that she couldn't breathe for swirling skin particles and hair strands. They were on their way to Imogen's mother's funeral and they were late because of Imogen's sudden urge for sex as he struggled with his memory to locate the socks he'd been wearing yesterday. 'Forget the stupid socks, Toby,' Imogen had said as she writhed on the bed and sank her teeth into the mattress. And when Toby came out of the crowded shop to cross the busy road to ask her if a grey suit would be alright, unusually for Imogen, she lost her temper: 'For Christ's sake, Toby, just buy the frigging suit.'

The toast in his pocket was uncomfortably warm. He brought it out and a pigeon landed at his feet. Another arrived. The margarine had made the paper transparent and it reminded him of the lavatory paper with which his mother equipped the bathroom when he was a child. He returned the package to his pocket. The pigeons strutted in circles of disappointment down the platform and away from the bench.

It was hot on the Circle Line and through his trousers Toby felt the seat's upholstery prick the back of his thighs. It was hotter still at South Kensington and by the time he emerged into sunlight, his shirt was entirely stuck to his back. The pavement glittered malevolently. It was, considering the fact that it was before 9 a.m. on 7 June (a date barely beyond spring) unseasonably hot. He stopped in the shade of a building to lift a knee on which to rest the briefcase given to him by Aunt Mercy on the occasion of his leaving school. 'Don't know if you've any use for this,' Aunt Mercy sniffing and lifting it up as though she had no idea what it was for. 'It used to be my father's.' Today, thirteen years later, it was being used for the first time. Shiny catches sprang open to reveal a red satin interior, stained in one corner with a brown blot. Something to do with Aunt Mercy's father. The flouncy pockets were empty. What kind of a businessman came armed without accoutrements?

The letter was in the breast pocket of his suit. White and folded into thirds, it was soft from handling. He unfolded it. MILSON, RANGE & RAFTER appeared in royal blue print across the top of the page above 33 HARRINGTON GARDENS, SW7 1HP. 'Imo' it read. Imo? Imogen, Imo? Toby didn't think so. In slanting hand the letter continued:

> Just ran into the Colonel outside William Hill
> in South Ken. Did'nt know he was a betting
> man? He gave me shocking news. Said U R
> getting married. U sure babe? He gave me
> your adress and told me to write. Don't do it.
> Marry me. Or at least let's do lunch. First Love
> is the only True Love. U know it makes sense.
> Gideon Chancelight (Ur 1st Love!)

Toby refolded the letter and, returning it to his pocket, marvelled not for the first time at the spelling. Gideon Chancelight, First Love, was entirely illiterate. He had discovered the letter, dated 28 April, yesterday in the rosewood roll-top desk amongst gas bills and council tax books and a postcard from Sara in St Moritz. Yes, it was virtually incoherent, however it had shed some light on a problem which had hitherto laboured entirely in darkness.

Toby passed odd numbers on Harrington Gardens – 13, 17, 19, a car shop featuring three shiny BMWs trapped behind glass, 27, 29 and then Milson, Range & Rafter. An art gallery, a second-hand book shop, a riding stable. He had even been willing to consider a bookmaker, but an estate agent? Never. Who ever ran off with an estate agent? The windows were tiled with particulars: Roof Garden; Staff Accommodation; Swimming Pool. Sold. He followed the glass front round a corner and on to a narrow street which doubled back on to Harrington Gardens. Decorated with bright awnings, shop signs swung amongst trees lush with growth; the street looked French. An old man in a suit fidgeted under a striped canopy outside a delicatessen. Drawing on a cigarette, he was preoccupied with neatening the kerb stones. He tapped at them gently with the side of his shoe. Tap, tap. Tap, tap.

Toby pushed open the glass door. A buzz announced his arrival and the door swung shut behind him. A girl, blonde and pink behind a bowl of white tulips, was on the phone. She acknowledged Toby by turning away. With her free hand she pulled closed the neck of her pink cardigan.

'How bad is that? It was like four times, I swear to you. It was once in the middle of lunch, no it was like twice in the middle of lunch. We'd just sat down and I'm like, hello? That is so not normal. So it was like once before we went in...'

Toby coughed and felt the knot of his tie. The girl frowned and turned farther from him. 'Oh yeah, that's right because I remember I'd just gone "Mum, Dad..." and immediately he was like... right, yeah but... Yes. I know all that...'

The office was narrow, a glass corridor camping on the pavement. Four cramped desks were arranged bus-style, one behind the other, against the window. The fifth desk, where the girl sat, faced the door. The office had the veneer of plush respectability: fashionable natural flooring, classical desks, a bookcase, framed photographs of white stucco mansions, yet there was something here that suggested impermanence, a certain theatricality, as though the whole thing could disappear tomorrow. And it wasn't, as Toby had first thought, deserted. In the recesses where the window stopped and darkness encroached sat a monolith of a man. Head in hands he appeared to be asleep at the desk he dwarfed. Gideon Chancelight worn out by Imogen's nocturnal demands. Toby stared but the monster didn't stir.

'And I'm like "Yeah, well, whatever." And my Dad is like…' the girl opened her mouth to smooth something shiny on to her lips. Round and round went the pink finger. '"Er, Daisy, who is this person?" And I'm like "Well, er, look Dad…"' Under the glass desk the girl's thighs were ripe peach-gold. They were solid and smooth and the fine down that covered them glistened in the sunlight. They were netballer's thighs. As though sensing Toby's gaze, the girl pressed them tightly together. Goal shooter's thighs. Where they met ripe flesh dimpled nicely. Panting, breathless, blonde pony tail swishing, a pleated white skirt flaps above thick gym knickers as the girl stands, legs together, to score.

Behind Toby the door buzzed and the girl jabbed a biro in his direction. If Imogen had run off with an estate agent, why shouldn't he? His heart shrivelled under sharp white pain.

The old man who had been outside neatening the pavement wiped small and shiny shoes carefully on the doormat. He looked up and smiled. 'Good morning, sir, and what can we do you for?'

The thin fabric of the man's suit hung loosely from his frame. His soft face was cream-cheese-pale apart from his nose which was red with blood as though he'd been hung upside down. He looked in need of some 'R & R' as Imogen might say. He cocked his head and raised an eyebrow. 'Lettings or sales?'

Toby pulled the letter from his breast pocket and considered the direct approach: 'I am here to enquire after my girlfriend, Imogen Green. Someone at this address' – a glance showed the villain still asleep – 'one Gideon Chancelight has been writing her inappropriate letters and I'm here to find out more.' It didn't sound right. Alternatively there was the Squire's approach: 'Bring on the sodomized son of a bitch. I'll slit his weaselled throat.' That didn't seem appropriate either, here in South Kensington. And anyway the old man looked too frail to withstand such an assault. And the monster? Too large an adversary. Toby cleared his throat.

The man's frown dispersed. 'Gotcha.' A hooked finger clawed the air. He looked Toby down then up and a deep chuckle turned into a phlegmy cough. When he'd recovered: 'It is 9 a.m. on Monday morning and in front of me stands a young man: suit, briefcase, his whole future ahead of him. They don't call me Clouseau for nothing.' He held out his hand. 'In fact they don't call me Clouseau at all. Nigel Harmsworth-Mallett, lettings.'

'Toby Doubt,' said Toby putting his hand in the man's paper dry one.

'We spoke on the phone,' he continued. 'James? John? Wagtail isn't it?' The old man let the names hang in the air, eyes yellowed and watery. He looked away for inspiration. None came and he turned back. 'Nigel Harmsworth-Mallett, lettings. Welcome, well, well.'

'Toby Doubt,' Toby repeated.

'Dote?' The man frowned. 'Well, well, for some reason I was under the impression that you would be descending on us on Tuesday. Ours is not to reason why, well… no matter, the powers that be and all that. Bit of a madhouse here what with all this rain.' He indicated the world beyond the glass, as blue and unconfused as eternity. 'Leaks, rats. An infestation of rats! Lettings, not a good time of year for it. You wouldn't believe the time we've had of it, it has been just one thing after another. Sales is a whole different ball game of course. Well, you're here now, on time, give or take a day or two. You're here, you're ready for action, and everything seems to be in order.'

The soft grey face, creased and misshapen, blinked and nodded while hesitant hands patted change in both pockets of his jacket. 'Well, well.' He shuffled across the brown carpet. 'Well, well, let's see if we can't get Mr Dote up and running.'

Toby followed him past the desks along the length of the office. He stood while the old man sacked a bookcase. His jerking hands shunted aside phone directories, spilt magazines to the floor and flailed before a cascade of cream envelopes. He eventually straightened up holding two files. Squinting he examined their spines. 'Up to a mil above a mil. Chuck?' This was addressed to the estate agent who, slumped, slack-mouthed over his desk, was snoring in the sullen air.

There was no response.

'Earth to Chuck.' Harmsworth-Mallett, birdlike, smiled gently and tapped the side of his head. 'Our friend is not all there.'

'Huh?' Frowning the man raised his fleshy face.

'Chuck, are these files up to date? Are there any other properties Dote needs to familiarize himself with?'

'Dote?' The man frowned and tapped a white card impatiently on his desk. He looked irritably from the old man to Toby.

'Dote. Sales negotiator, Milson, Range & Rafter, commenced at 9 a.m. on Monday 7 June in the year of our Good Lord 2004.'

'Huh?' With some effort the man wheeled back his chair and stood up. He was vast.

'Dote, this is The Chuckler, our representative from across the pond.'

'Chuck Lincoln,' the man held out a meaty hand and regarded Toby steadily. There was a sheen of sweat on his forehead and the hand which engulfed Toby's was fleshy and wet, but Toby took it with relief. Had this man been Gideon Chancelight, Toby would not have fancied his chances.

The old man chuckled. 'The competition.'

Chuck frowned and flopped back in his chair and bent once again over his desk.

'Swings and roundabouts, Chucky, swings and roundabouts.' He patted the American's shoulder and laughed softly as he led Toby to the very back of the office and the last desk. It stood poised in darkness at the mouth of a spiral staircase which sank below the road.

'Your desk, sir.' He wheeled out the chair with a grand flourish of his free hand, waiter-style, files against his chest. Toby sat and put his briefcase upright on the floor beside his chair.

'Have a look at what's cooking,' Harmsworth-Mallett said as he placed blue folders neatly on the desk, 'and we'll get on to more important things, like breakfast.'

Toby opened a file. 'Milson, Range & Rafter,' it read. 'Sales £1,000,000 +.'

'Some of these are on with other agents. We've got agreements with Clark, Kemp... and Sage is it, Chuck? All of them around here except of course John Watford, the King,' he rolled his eyes, 'of South Kensington. Well, we've all been King at one time or another and isn't that the truth, Chuck?'

With thick fingers the American massaged the roll of flesh which bulged above his collar. Harmsworth-Mallett straightened the beige telephone on Toby's desk. Of all the outcomes that Toby had considered, it had never crossed his mind that he might be mistaken for an estate agent and given a job. He cleared his throat. 'Gideon Chancelight?' It did not come out as he'd intended.

The girl on the phone at the front of the office stopped talking and turned towards Toby. Harmsworth-Mallett was so close Toby could identify the alcohol on his breath, was it Drambuie?

Chuck turned sideways to offer Toby his profile.

'Gideon Golden Boy,' the American muttered after some time, his eye cold and pale-lashed as a pig's, 'is on vacation.' The girl resumed talking and Harmsworth-Mallett exhaled.

'Skiing is Mr Chancelight, I believe,' said the old man, patting the back of Toby's chair. 'Right, sir, when you've had a little look at what's on where, so to speak, ha ha,' he tapped the blue folders, 'we'll have a recapitulation of what you'll be requiring. Keys, car – perhaps you have your own? No? No matter, we can offer a lovely little Golf: automatic, air-con, sun roof, etcetera – appointment book, business cards, new shoes...' he made an exaggerated show of looking under Toby's desk. 'And so on and so forth.' He nodded then straightened. 'Breakfast,' he said. 'There's nothing like breakfast to set you up for the day.' Blink,

blink. Smile. 'Cappuccino? Danish?' The old man held out both hands as though Toby had offered money. 'It's on me.'

'I'm good,' the American muttered as the old man passed.

'We know you are, Chuck, we know you are.' Toby watched him shuffle towards the sunlight and the door. It sounded as though he was wearing slippers.

Gideon Chancelight. Skiing.

It was Monday, it was 9.10 and Imogen, along with her class, should be filing into assembly. Probably he should have visited St Hellier's first. He should have disobeyed the Code of the Road and ignored the fact that the first visit is to the gentleman. He should have dealt with Imogen before Gideon. But there was something worrying Toby: it fled from him down the passageways of his mind. He pursued it through a spiral of memory away from horror and down train tracks in and out of darkness through high escarpments dizzy with wild flowers to Victoria Station and the vile bulge of Imogen's red and blue carpet bag packed and ready to go in the hall of the house on Frederick Street. For a moment he had the thing cornered. It shrank black and poisonous against the back wall of his skull. He sprang and for a moment it seemed it was his. Then it swelled and flattened before disintegrating into a bewildering scatter of laughter.

Toby ran a hand across the cool leather top of the desk. He hadn't had a desk since school and then it had been nothing like this. This was a Chesterfield in miniature. It was something for the smaller headmaster. He opened a drawer. Its varnished front moved independently of its base, scattering the contents – coffee cups, the wrapping from a sandwich, a sachet of tomato ketchup clotting translucent at one corner and a mostly empty can of Coke – on to his knee. The Coke can rolled, releasing liquid on to his trousers and clattered lightly to the floor. It disappeared under the desk. Gideon Chancelight, skiing. Toby felt his next move to be not immediately apparent. In front of him the American's jacket stretched a yard across his back.

'Chuck?' He would have been more comfortable with Charles or even Charlie. There was something grotesque about 'Chuck'.

The American turned his head ninety degrees; it seemed as much as he could do. In profile the neck bulged over his too-tight collar and his lower lip hung wet and red. He tapped his foot impatiently and waited for Toby to speak.

'Gideon Chancelight, when is he back?'

The giant's lips twitched. 'Tomorrow? End of the week? Armageddon? Who gives a shit?' The vast head bobbed a few times, thick cropped hair growing straight up at the forehead and trimmed neatly around the ear.

Phones at desks screeched.

'A-Milson-Range-&-Rafter-good-morning. Who? No, sir. Is there anything I can help you with? Right. Uh-huh. Yuh huh. You got it.' Replacing the receiver he sighed, raised his head and circled it on his neck. First one direction and then the other. Toby watched the flesh bulge and disappear and then reappear on the other side.

'Oh brother,' the American said softly. A bone cracked in his neck. 'Monday, Monday, Monday.'

Toby turned the title page of the blue folder.

Prince's Court, Knightsbridge,

it read.

A rare opportunity to purchase this stunning penthouse in the award-winning Prince's Court. Less than a stone's throw from the world's most famous department store, this majestic apartment offers panoramic views across the capital.

He turned the pages. Prince's Court, Queen's Gate, Duke Street, Castle Court, Palace Drive. Residences fit for royalty.

Chuck prodded his phone. 'Hello Mrs York-Jones, Chuck Lincoln, Milson, Range & Rafter – just a quick call re Temple Place as I would reiterate I do not anticipate its being available much longer. Give me a call when you get this and let's hear your thoughts. 7718 7878.

That's 7718 7878.' He replaced the receiver and tapped a pencil on his desk top.

It was 9.25 and had Imogen not absconded with an estate agent she would be filing back into her classroom from assembly in time for her first lesson at 9.30. At least that was when Toby presumed lessons started at St Hellier's. He was ashamed to admit that the timetable he was working from was based on what he remembered of his own school days rather than any knowledge of his girlfriend's. Alternatively, Imogen was waking in a chalet somewhere mountainous and snowy.

When was the last time Imogen had gone skiing? In the three-and-a-half years they'd been together, including the three they'd lived together at Frederick Street, she'd not once gone skiing, or even suggested it as something she'd like to do. Water-skiing, yes, once. One largely unsuccessful occasion somewhere grey in Suffolk when there had been only one wet suit and he'd gone first and peed in it. Why? He couldn't remember but smiled anyway at the memory of Imogen getting into it and stretching it up over pale freckled shoulders: 'Toby, it's all wet in here.' No shit, Imogen, that's why it's called a wet suit.

The door buzzed. Harmsworth-Mallett, hands full, shouldered the glass. It opened and he ground his cigarette into the pavement behind him, flicking it with an elegant back-kick out into the road. Three polystyrene cups balanced in one hand, the other held a plate of croissants on top of the turret. The girl was still on the phone, the old man stood in front of her desk. She didn't appear to have seen him and he leant towards her, hesitant and smiling, his forehead wrinkling apologetically.

'Chloe will you hold on for like one second. Yes?' She looked up.

'Skimmed milk latte? Chocolate on top?' A stage-whisper through a hesitant smile.

She took it and sighed. 'Sorry Chlo – you there?'

And on he came, smiling and blinking. 'One cappuccino, one apricot Danish.' He placed breakfast carefully on Toby's desk. Chuck held a Post-It up above his head.

'What have we here?' With trembling hands Harmsworth-Mallett took it. It stuck to his thumb.

The phones rang. 'Uh, Milson, Range & Rafter?'

Harmsworth-Mallett winked at Toby. 'You have to rise early to answer the phones around here. The fastest draw in the West has our Chuck.' Frowning, he moved the paper towards and then away from his eyes. He shrugged and squinted at the open file on Toby's desk. 'Penthouse at Prince's. A lovely little property and a lovely little deal. One of Mr Chancelight's, one point two. Wham Bam, thank you very much, very nice too. Ten grand in the bank, should take care of the old overdraft.' Air whistled through his teeth. 'Ice to Eskimos. So, rumour has it you come to us from Shayle Nugent... No?' Harmsworth-Mallett, settling himself on to the corner of Toby's desk, seemed only mildly surprised. 'I was sure the boss said Shayles, oh well, where did Mike find you then? McDonald's?' Smile smile. Blink blink. 'What, don't get it?' He reached out to touch Toby's curly hair. 'Ronald McDonald!' He bent over to laugh. 'Well, no matter. Cheap gag. You know how we work here at least.' He wiped a tear from the corner of one watery eye.

Toby had not been likened to Ronald McDonald since school and he was surprised to find that it caused him to feel something like affection for the old man.

'Good Lord. They sent us a rookie. Well I never, well I never did. Presumably you are aware of the fact that you will not be receiving a salary? No weekly, monthly, yearly pay cheque. Just commission on each and every sale. You sell, we shell, as it were. Can be very nice... oh yes indeed. Wolves from doors, early retirement, place in Spain, etcetera.'

Toby followed the old man's gaze beyond the door and across the road to a patch of brightness where the sun glanced off a faded awning.

'Ah, those were the days.' He turned back to Toby. 'And it can be, well, not so nice.' He indicated the American's broad back and lowered his voice. 'Bailiffs, suicide and so on and so forth. Goodbye Jason Townley.' He tapped Toby's desk. 'Goodbye Michelle Lyons. Poor lady didn't last a week. Hello Mr Dote! Wheat from chaff and all that good stuff. Actually, to tell the truth…' he lowered his voice still further and nodded, 'it's been a bit quiet here for two, three months now. Hence your arrival. Shake things up a little.'

'And an address,' Chuck was saying. 'Very good, sir, I will do my best, traffic-permitting. Ciao.' He replaced the receiver and with an air of purpose wheeled back his chair and stood up.

'Chuck?' Harmsworth-Mallett held out the Post-It still stuck to his thumb.

'Mr Baker of Fulham Cross said you would know what it's concerning,' Chuck secured a pen in his breast pocket.

'Indeed I do. Our friend Mr Baker,' Harmsworth-Mallett rolled his eyes, 'has rats. Rats and more rats. Anywhere nice, Chuck?'

'Valuation for a Mr Abdul Senior of Flat 7, Albert Mews, a three-bed basement situated on the Albert Hall side.' The American pushed his chair neatly under his desk and, frowning, straightened it.

'Take Mr Dote. Permit him to see *el maestro* in action.' The old man winked at Toby.

Chuck brushed down each of his shoulders in turn. 'This party is leaving now,' he said unwinding the headpiece from his mobile phone and pushing it into his ear as he headed towards the door.

'Bad news,' Harmsworth-Mallett said, thoughtful. 'Mr Abdul Senior sounds like an Indian gentleman which will translate into all manner of horrors. Do not be disheartened, Mr Dote, if you find yourself confronting green carpets, wallpaper and other unmentionables rendering it impossible to shift. Take your breakfast.' He gestured towards the Danish pastry and the cappuccino.

As Toby stood up an empty sandwich wrapper slid off his knee. The ketchup sachet clung resolutely to his flies. He peeled it off, dropped it under the desk and followed Chuck's bulk out into sunlight.

'Skiing apparently,' Daisy was saying, 'like Wednesday? Apparently with some new bird. Whatever. Skiing? Nice one Gids, whoever goes skiing in June?'

Whoever goes skiing in June? Whoever indeed. Toby wondered how Imogen might like being 'some new bird'. Impatient on the pavement, Chuck was squinting in the sunlight and jangling his car keys. The earpiece of his phone quivered beside his face as he looked Toby up and down, frowning at his boots for a moment before allowing his gaze to return to Toby's crotch where it remained. Toby looked down: the grey fabric was splashed with something.

'Car this way,' said Chuck as he set off down Harrington Gardens, the heels of his shiny shoes moving smartly on the pavement.

As Toby followed he wondered whether perhaps he should have polished his boots and ironed his shirt. He never ironed his shirt. Highwaymen didn't, archivists didn't and nor did Toby Doubt. Actually, it was likely that highwaymen did iron their shirts or at least got someone to do it for them. Perhaps if he'd ironed his shirt, he wouldn't be here now. He'd have finished the book, he'd be a success and the chances were he wouldn't be facing the fact that his girlfriend had left him for an estate agent. Hal Blake aka the Squire: the tragic tale of history's least successful highwayman as told by history's least successful biographer. In fact, that last statement was debatable; in Toby's view there was another candidate for that position. And that was John Lambert III, author of the entirely impenetrable Friends of Beowolf, published 1975 by Bay Tree Press. On the other hand there was no getting away from the fact that John Lambert III – an American one night stand of his mother's and also, as it had turned out, Toby's father – had completed a book and got it published. The thought descended, uninvited, on Toby.

Chuck was bent into an azure Golf to arrange his pinstriped jacket on a coathanger above the back seat. Thick red braces crossed over to frame a sweat-damp blue patch as large as a dinner plate in the centre of his back. Despite this, the straight creases in his sleeves suggested that Chuck was indeed a man who ironed his shirt. He emerged briefly to issue instruction: 'No food inside', before pulling his shirt up at the waist and lowering himself heavily into the car.

Toby filled his mouth with sweet pastry and milky coffee before reluctantly discarding his breakfast on a low wall.

Inside the car a sweat patch showed under Chuck's arm. He rocked in the seat, his hair touching the pale quilted ceiling. Breathing heavily he slotted the key into the ignition and turned it. Toby, lacking air, pushed a button to open the window.

'AC,' said Chuck pushing another to close it. Breathing through his nose he adjusted the mirror, pushed the earpiece of his mobile further into his ear and dropped the hand brake. Heavy on the pedals he reversed out of the space.

Toby sat tall in his seat hoping to find more air near the ceiling and wondered when his relationship had gone wrong. To him it seemed that things had not gone wrong. Perhaps that was the trouble: Toby had been content to continue with life as it was for tomorrow, for the next day and for the rest of it. Clearly, Imogen had not.

Three and a half years ago when he spent the night with Imogen for the first time he'd been as sure of her as he was on the Saturday just past, the last time he saw her. Sure as sure is. Sure as sure can be. As sure as when last summer a much-handled, water-damaged scrap of paper dated 1724 had fallen into his hands. It was a warrant for Harold Blake's death. Hal Blake, aka the Squire, was the most chivalrous, the most romantic and the singularly most dismal highwayman to have ever worked the Great North Road. His failures were legendary until at the age of thirty, betrayed by Jack Scarlett, betrayed by Lady Rose, the Squire was hanged at the Tyburn Gibbet. The scrap of paper was what Toby had been waiting for and he was certain that this was his book to write. Sweating with excitement he'd called Imogen at school. He instructed the secretary to pull her out of class.

'What's happened?' He'd laughed at her voice and told her about the paper. She'd been angry because her mother was ill and she was expecting bad news. This in turn had made Toby angry – that she couldn't be happy for him – which had resulted in him spending that night downstairs on the sofa.

'The trouble is,' his friend Howard had said, offering advice as usual, 'you're writing a book about a loser: the world's *worst* highwayman. What people want is the best. Why don't you give the people what they want and write a book about the world's best highwayman?'

'So. What brings you to Range Rafter?' The American pressed his head back against the headrest and watched the mirror.

What indeed? 'New job,' said Toby, wondering how that sounded.

'No shit.' Chuck flicked his indicator.

'Money,' tried Toby.

'What money?' Chuck started to pull out. He stopped suddenly. 'Cheers mate!' he said in a mock English accent, 'And fuck you too.' After another false start he pulled out behind a white van and accelerated to sit on its tail. 'There ain't no money to be had round here. Who's making any? It sure as shit ain't me.'

'Gideon?'

'Not Gideon. He hasn't sold shit for months. How do you know Gideon?'

'I don't. I've just heard about him.'

'I've just heard about him,' he repeated, mimicking Toby. 'Jesus Christ. Who the fuck is this guy? Superman. Golden Boy Gideon. Gideon this, Gideon that. The guy is a prick.' Chuck slammed on the brakes. The white van was indicating to turn right and as Chuck swerved to avoid it he turned to look hard at the driver.

'A word of advice, friend, never let Golden Boy Gideon anywhere near one of your deals.'

Chuck braked sharply at a zebra crossing. A shrivelled woman with a dog so small it looked as though it was on wheels pattered on tiny feet to pass in front of them. 'Or it ain't gonna be one of your deals. The guy's a snake. In your own time, lady…' The mobile buzzed on the plastic shelf. Chuck snatched it.

'Chuck Lincoln.' He held the mouthpiece against his lips. 'Yeah… seven. I said seven. It will be seven. Yeah… seven.' He dropped the mouthpiece and wiped his forehead. 'Seven-o-fuckin'-clock.' They were running alongside the park's edge now. Railings flitted across scantily clad people. A red setter trotted waving its tail stupidly, a six-foot branch in its mouth.

'The wife,' said Chuck, 'pregnant.'

'Oh.'

'Oh. Yes. Married?'

'No.' A man in orange shorts jumped four feet in the air to claim a frisbee from the sky.

'Hey. Well, that killed that one. "Married?" "No." Just a little more effort required. "No Chuck, I'm not married. I'm divorced, single, engaged to be married." Hell, even gay would suffice. "Married?" "No." Jeeze.' Chuck's tongue darted out to moisten his lips. 'Well I'm married, the wife's pregnant with our first child. Due August. Boy or girl? No idea. Yes I am excited. Excited as hell. We live in Greenwich. It's a nice part of London. We've lived there for two years next month. We've got a nice place. Can see the river from the bathroom window. If you've got a two-foot neck. Holy shit. Big fuckin' deal. I hate this fuckin' country.' He swerved to avoid a car which was reversing into a parking space. He turned on the radio and pushed a CD into the machine. It was the Beatles and Chuck turned up the volume. A bead of sweat cut a haphazard path down the flesh of his cheek.

'Lucy in the sky with diamonds…' He sang savagely, his huge head pressed back against the headrest, his thick arms stretched almost straight in front of him, his hair bent slightly against the ceiling of the car, a million little connectors on the back of a million little dodgem cars.

Mr Abdul Senior, still in his dressing gown, led them into a basement flat oppressive with the smell of damp and aftershave, despite the fact that Mr Senior had clearly not shaved for some days.

'So how long have you been here, Mr Senior?' Chuck, black diary in hand, stood blocking all the light from a window. Toby followed them into the sitting room. 'Good size. Nice and light for a basement. South facing is it?' Chuck stood, pen poised.

Toby lowered himself into a soft white leather chair in the long dark room in front of a large TV which supported a framed photograph of a woman in a mortar board. Toby avoided her scrutiny to stare at the speckled carpet and wonder about turning over a new leaf. If Imogen came back he'd finish the book, he'd clear the hedge, he'd paint the ceiling. The woman in the silver frame looked sceptical, the beginnings of a tense smile at the corners of her mouth. Resting on the arm of the chair was a round white plate holding two biscuits, one half-eaten. Toby picked up a biscuit and bit into it. He'd learn to cook. He'd take up sport. He'd make a mint. He'd stop feeling resentful if she didn't want sex. He closed his eyes to face a memory which told him it was too late. Something had taken place not yesterday but the day before which transgressed acceptable boundaries for relationships. Something terminal which meant Imogen would not be coming back. He opened his eyes. The woman in the mortar board appeared eager to confirm this. She brandished her rolled degree like a truncheon. He took the mug from the circular mat on the table beside the chair. Coffee. Sweet and warm. He bit into the other biscuit.

'The paintwork is obviously a little tired...' Chuck's voice returned to the sitting room, 'in need of some modernization, but the rooms are a good size. I think we should try for...' Toby, straining to hear, stopped crunching the biscuit. 'Bearing in mind that we've got time on our side and bearing in mind there's a good strong market out there... Well, Mr Abdul, we don't want to price ourselves out of the market. Considering the location, I suggest we try for eight fifty. No harm dipping a toe in the water? Let's try for eight fifty and see what comes up. Not what you expected?' Toby could hear the tight smile on Chuck's face. 'Well, not a problem... if you want to try for that... sure... after all, Mr Abdul, it's your apartment. We'll try that. Sure, sure, Mr Senior Abdul... long-shot... but there's no harm trying nine... sure, sure... no problemo. Let's stick it on and see what comes up... very good. I'll call to arrange for someone to come measure up... a few snaps.' Chuck clicked his tongue and mimed taking a photograph. 'OK, Mr Abdul. Thank you for your time. So long as it's convenient, we'll start viewings right away.'

Chuck was waiting outside on the pavement when Toby emerged.

'Total shit hole,' he announced, leading the way to the car. 'Mr Abdul lives in la-la land. Nine my fucking arse. Did you see that crap? The whole place stinks, hasn't been decorated since 1960. He'll be lucky to get seven fifty for it. Prize location, nice size place and it's full of shit. That's right, Mr fuckin' Abdul. Fill it full of shit. The man lives like a pig.' A spray of saliva decorated the steering wheel. While the estate agent readied himself for departure, Toby picked at a white stain on the cuff of his suit. He brought it to his mouth and touched it to his tongue. Yoghurt? Toothpaste? It stuck there and tasted like nothing. Most likely it was milk. Imogen's sister's milk, regurgitated by Imogen's niece at Imogen's mother's funeral on 27 December at the end of last year.

The Firs is full of people. Rufus wags his tale and the winter sun makes long shadows on the unkempt lawn. Under the monkey puzzle tree, the swing seat is just a frame. It's cold, it's Christmas and Toby is holding Imogen's niece while Imogen, Cassie and the Cyclops argue about something. It's about their mother's rosewood roll-top desk.

'Please, not now,' Imogen says. Sour, the baby squawks in Toby's grasp. He can feel its spine, tiny and reptilian, through its white babygrow. He holds it more tightly and watches Imogen, shrunken in dark blue beside Cassie who looms pale and rigid under a stiff black hat. Next to Cassie is Iain, her Scottish, washed-out husband.

'That's Iain with two 'i's,' he says sadly. The Cyclops, Imogen calls him. He has eyes which stare out as though with difficulty from the bottom of a pond.

Beyond Imogen and the child's parents, outside in the garden, is the swing seat beneath the monkey puzzle which in summer wears a faded yellow cushion. It is here that he and Imogen have lain and swung and lain and wondered whether the neighbours' windows are as vacant as they appear.

'Lovely that Anne could spend time with her granddaughter before she passed,' a strong-looking woman with a large face whispers stroking the child's head. 'What's her name?'

Toby squeezes the baby, there's something tight inside it – a bubble of trapped air. As he watches his girlfriend he is aware of a new fear. Perhaps, now that her mother is dead and he is without allies within the Green household, he may not be enough for her any more. His fingers tighten around the tiny rib cage in his hands. The child pukes and Toby wonders how it would be if the baby was his. His daughter. And Imogen's daughter. Perhaps he would be enough for her then. That was before they got engaged.

two

Harrington Gardens was at a standstill. Someone was leaning on their horn. Intermittently others joined in and finally Chuck applied his weight. The problem appeared to be a Range Rover parked on the zebra crossing opposite Milson, Range & Rafter. Two small girls in red and white candy stripes and straw hats stood holding hands on the pavement while a third individual – their mother? – rummaged on the back seat. She didn't hurry to retrieve a tennis racket, a violin case, a lunch box, a pencil case. She loaded up the girls and led them through a wrought iron gate towards the neat grey steps. She stood at the door and, waiting, turned to frown at the traffic. The door opened and closed behind the girls and the woman did not hurry to climb back into the car. Once inside, she turned to reach into the back seat. Sunglasses, seat belt, rear-view mirror. Slowly she moved off, hazards flashing.

'Women,' said Chuck.

'Women,' agreed Toby and, attempting to keep the tone light, continued, 'About women. I hear Gideon's got a new girlfriend.' There was no reply. Toby laughed – a bit of man to man chat, find out what's what etc. 'About five five, blue eyes, curly black hair.'

Slowly Chuck turned to look at him. His face bulged above his collar. He indicated to reverse into a space. 'You what?'

Toby's hands froze on either side of his head: he'd been illustrating Imogen's hair.

The American's mobile buzzed into life.

Toby followed Chuck and words spoken into the American's mobile reached Toby on the warm air. 'I do not, repeat, do not pass a Marks and Spencer's on my way from the office. The route I take. Correction. The only route in existence from South Kensington to Greenwich does not pass a Marks and Spencer's grocery store. Capiche? Jeeze Louise!' Arriving at Milson, Range & Rafter, the American waited for Toby to catch up before nodding sharply, directing him to go ahead. Toby pushed open the door. The office was alive with the whirr of computer equipment. Daisy, still on the phone, was standing to straighten the paper in the printer. With the receiver crammed between her ear and her shoulder, it seemed her conversation was not going well either. A vertical pink line had appeared on her brow: '...about like six? Like that really matters, Chloe. I am going straight from work which finishes at six. It takes like ten minutes to get there so I will be there at like ten past six. OK?' She clicked her fingers in the direction of a stack of red-wrapped reams of paper. Toby picked one off the pile and handed it to her. 'So if I'm going straight from work it's quite likely that I'll be wearing my work stuff, OK?'

Harmsworth-Mallett, also on the phone, raised an eyebrow and jerked his head to indicate a man sitting upright beside the bookcase on a straight-backed chair. He was looking anxiously in Toby's direction.

'Good morning,' said Toby.

'Good morning. I was actually wondering if Gideon was around?' The man bit his lip and looked beyond Toby.

'I am afraid he's skiing.'

'Oh God.' The man looked beyond the window. 'Do you know when he's back?'

Chuck arrived, earpiece dangling from his ear. 'Can I help?'

'I hope so. I was wondering when Gideon's back?' The man looked from Chuck to Toby.

Chuck dropped phone, keys and appointment book on his desk with a certain finality. He sighed. 'We believe Gideon will be back at work on Monday. In the meantime is there anything I can help you with?'

'Well.' The man, hesitant, looked down. 'It's just that we've been dealing with Gideon for a couple of months. He knows exactly our requirements...' He let the sentence tail off.

'If you'll excuse me.' Chuck reached across his desk for the trilling phone. 'Milson, Range & Rafter. Chuck Lincoln speaking.'

Toby did not think he could wait an entire week to confront Gideon. On his desk, a car key on an orange Winnie-the-Pooh key ring lay idle in a pool of sunlight. He picked it up and felt the warm plastic in his palm. When was the last time Toby had a car?

Imogen's father is standing with his back to the table, bow legged as though he's spent his life in the saddle. He's using an electric knife on a joint of beef. 'When,' Lieutenant Colonel John Green is asking above the buzz of the knife, 'did you last have a car, Toby?' This is the first time he and Toby have met and Toby, who has never had a car, is trying to work out why electric knives never caught on. Imogen's hand is on his knee under the table. It's warm and remorseless and through it he can feel her enjoyment.

'Toby's never had a car,' she says. 'He's a poet and is much too poor.'

He takes Imogen's finger and bends it back under the table as far as he can until she twists her shoulder, laughing in pain. Anne returns from the kitchen with potatoes and broccoli and the buzz of the knife is muffled by beef as Lieutenant Colonel John Green digests this information.

'Yeah mate,' said Chuck holding the receiver away from his ear. He held it distastefully at the end of his arm and turned to the man, his mouth twisted. 'Gideon Chancelight for you.'

'I need to speak to Gids,' came Daisy's demand above the churning printer.

The man scanned Chuck's face before taking the proferred receiver.

'Hello? Er, Gideon? It's Peter James. That's right. That's right.' A smile. Relief. 'Exactly. Well unfortunately for us it fell through. The owner took it off the market.' A laugh. 'Tory went ballistic as you can imagine. Anyway it's back to the drawing board. The wedding is six weeks on Saturday. High and dry... my thoughts exactly. Well, to be honest, we're getting a little, um, desperate. In an ideal world we would need to exchange before honeymoon, complete while we're away and move in on our return.' Another laugh. 'Costa Rica, I know... three weeks. I cannot wait.' More smiles. 'Well, minimum three bedrooms. Good-sized drawing room.' Suddenly the man lowered his voice and turned to the window. 'Two. Up to two million.'

The door buzzed as Chuck disappeared into the street – a rogue elephant about to stampede.

'Kensington. Has to be W8. Won't have it any other way.' Peter James nodded and smiled gratefully into the receiver. 'OK, mate. I'm in your hands. Between you and me I think the wedding's off unless we come up with something.'

'Can I speak to Gideon?' Toby held out a hand for the receiver.

The printer had stopped and Daisy, frowning, called down the length of the office, 'I need to speak to Gids.'

'Very good. You've got my mobile? Let's hope it's good news. Alright. Speak then. Cheers.'

'Can I have a word?'

The man glanced at Toby. 'Er, Gideon?' he said hesitantly into the receiver, avoiding Toby's eye. 'Sorry. Lost him.'

'He's on the mobile?' Crossly Daisy punched out a number learnt by heart. Toby, hand outstretched, made his way to the front of the office. Daisy slammed down the phone. 'The mobile's off.'

The man walked to the door through Daisy's black stare. He looked once over his shoulder and was gone.

No Gideon until Monday. Toby's thoughts turned to school. 11 a.m., the end of break-time and now the double slog before lunch.

The car was parked in Palace Gardens. It looked new. Toby got in and adjusted the seat and mirror. It smelt sweetly chemical and it felt good to be in a car. He'd never had a car. Not even his mother had one when he was growing up. 'Bad for the environment,' she would say in the same breath as ringing Aunt Mercy, who lived next door, to arrange a lift out to Tesco's on the ring road where she'd fill a trolley with bleach and tuna and any other environmentally disastrous product she could lay her hands on. He pulled out and accelerated to erase the guilt he felt at the memory of the dogs jumping up around his mother as she struggled to unload the boxes of bottles of gin and Vim outside the terraced house in Cambridge.

As he drove up Queen's Gate towards Hyde Park, he rolled back the sun roof and turned on the radio: Neil Diamond, 'Song Sung Blue. Everybody knows one.' He joined the tail of the serpent of traffic heading north through the park. Shade flitted over his head as he drove under the horse chestnuts and oak trees up towards Marble Arch and the Tyburn Gibbet. Summer in London on a Monday lunch-time, a thousand people unwrapping sandwiches on the grass.

Toby found himself on the Edgware Road, light and dust rising in the heat and above him, through the open roof, stretched the endless blue of a cloudless sky. 'Love me tender,' sang Elvis and Toby turned off to head up through Maida Vale. Beside the road the emerald depths of the canal hung still and deep. Flecks of dust floated slowly on the air above its dappled surface. St John's Wood and all along the outer edge of Regent's Park kept cool in the shade of the chestnuts. Two giraffes swayed yellow and alien in their yard at the zoo, as dazedly they decided how to spend their afternoon. The tented peaks of the aviary were deserted and Toby pushed down on the accelerator to jump the lights and stream through Camden. He swerved to avoid a man in a winter overcoat, his hair a matted beaver's tail across his back. He tooted his horn and in his mirror the man raised a blue can of lager.

Toby took the right-hand fork up Camden Road. St Hellier's and St Anne's. The probability of Toby catching her? High. It was 11.45 a.m. A good forty-five minutes before lunch and, as Daisy had been quick to point out, whoever goes skiing in June? He would slip into her classroom. Sit at the back. Silent, nodding. An impressed inspector from Ofsted. And as the class filed out in grateful obedience, he'd stay behind.

Toby slowed to pull into the lay-by in front of the school gates. The playground was empty, the windows in the squat towers black. He imagined he felt the buzz of imparted knowledge whirring through the building. He got out. Beside the sign St Hellier's and St Anne's, a sturdy padlock held looped chains locking the iron gates. A hand-written note was fastened to the gate: 'Gone skiing. School closed till further notice' he expected to read. Instead it said: 'LORNA: 10.30 a.m. Call main no. and I'll come down and let you in. M.'

The school was ugly. Really ugly. The low-slung concrete buildings that ran the length of the playground were decorated with an outsize checkerboard in dull blue. The taller buildings at either end loomed stained and grey. Despite the fact that the school was less than half a mile from Frederick Street, that Toby had been past it hundreds of times and despite the fact that this was where Imogen spent most of her life, this was the first time that he made a direct connection between this building and Imogen. This lack of interest put another black mark against his name. Imogen on the other hand had been to lunch at the Town Hall. She knew Ted, she knew Judith, she'd met their son Peter and she'd even made it inside Camden Council's Record Room – restricted access only. Of course, Imogen knew everything about the Squire. In fact, second to Toby, she would have been the nation's greatest expert: Born April 1694, London. Hanged, Tyburn Tree, June 1724. A footman from a long line of footmen, to the Stockport family, who had the misfortune to fall in love with his Lordship's wayward daughter, Lady Rose. Imogen knew the date of his first robbery, she knew his weaknesses – 'I'm sorry sir I can see this is causing you some distress, please hop back up and be on your way' – and how successful he became once he took up with the Spaniard, the Great North Road's most feared operative. Imogen knew on what he spent those first ill-gotten gains: lodgings, clothes, Madeira wine and a gold watch for a lady. She knew that he became unstoppable, that Lady Rose became entranced and that the Spaniard became entranced by Lady Rose. And Imogen knew that together they betrayed the Squire: the night was black with rain, Lord Stockport was galloping into town on government business. The Squire astride Phantom outside Best Mangal at the end of Frederick Street, where the Great North Road started, awaited the coach. The Spaniard had provided the tip-off that it was laden with ducats and gems and a nice fat pocket watch. Lord Stockport was ordered out of the coach and into the ditch. He was instructed to deliver. Stockport, however, also acting on a tip-off, was accompanied by two officers of the law. A horse was shot, a mask ripped off.

'Good God man, isn't it our Mr Blake?' was his comment as he came face to face with his own footman. Another firearm was discharged but no one was injured and the Squire was taken, tearful and apologizing profusely, mostly to his dead horse, to Newgate Gaol.

'It's a winner,' proclaimed Imogen some time later (after she'd got over her anger at Toby pulling her from a lesson.) She'd even taken the time one Saturday morning to act the part of Lord Stockport outside Best Mangal: 'Good God man!' she'd exclaimed to Toby's Squire. It would have made a nice change for Imogen, Toby had thought at the time. She frequently and with varied degrees of enthusiasm took the role of Lady Rose Stockport – on the stairs, on the kitchen floor. In the middle of the Squire's unmade bed.

Toby had taken it for granted that she knew about the Squire because the Squire was interesting, just as he'd also taken it for granted that no one, honestly, could be expected to take an interest in the GCSE maths curriculum. He attempted to conjure a name. Any name of any girl that Imogen taught. To his surprise one floated into his mind. Julie Fountain, killed in the Christmas holidays on an estate in Archway by an ice-cream van. Being reversed over by an ice-cream van at Christmas seemed an unlikely end for anyone, let alone a fifteen-year-old girl with the life-affirming name of Julie Fountain. Emboldened by his success Toby turned his attention to Imogen's colleagues. A teacher with whom she ate lunch? The headmaster? Or was it headmistress?

There was of course 'the Hill'. Employed to impart knowledge of something called resistant materials, she'd been at Frederick Street several times. Once quite recently, about two weeks ago, though how she'd fitted through the door he'd no idea. At least twenty-five stone, she'd sat juddering in the garden in the pale May sun, complaining of sensitive skin and jeopardizing a slatted chair he'd laboriously stripped one previous weekend under Imogen's instruction.

Imogen trots up and down delivering food – the Hill is insatiable – and Toby wants to ask as they pass on the stairs, don't you think she's had enough? He doesn't. Instead it's Imogen who whispers, 'Where are you going? Come back outside and talk to Eileen.' Ei-lean? Ei-fat is more like it. He can't stand the guilty way she eats a tiny bit of everything. And later, as Imogen brushes her teeth in the bathroom mirror: 'Today she overheard some Year Nines calling her the Hill.' Toby laughs. Imogen frowns.

'That's cruel.'

'No,' says Toby. 'It's cruel to feed her.'

Toby skips downstairs and into bed. There are crisp new folds of cool white sheets on the bed. Sometimes this happens. Toby loves these days. He basks in the clean bed in anticipation. He can't wait to encompass lithe Imogen with his body. To curl himself around her and feel their perfect fit. She comes in cross and draws the curtains more tightly closed.

'How can you say that? Eileen's ill. She was born with triple the usual number of fat cells.' Toby runs his palm across the cool sheets. He wants to laugh. She sits on the edge of the bed to brush a hand across the sole of her foot. First one and then the other. He imagines he'd recognize those toes anywhere. Even if it was fifty years from now and he came across the feet on their own without that body.

'You don't know what's she's been through,' she says.

True. Thinks Toby. I don't know what she's been through, but I've got a pretty good idea. How about half a million Big Macs, Whoppers and all the apple pies in Christendom?

Imogen keeps her t-shirt and her knickers on and gets in.

'She's lonely.'

Toby wonders how you'd go about getting close to someone who was separated from you always by at least a foot of flesh. He reaches across for Imogen. Intractable and minty, she's looking at the ceiling.

'Take this off.' He pulls at her t-shirt.

Imogen keeps her arms at her sides. 'Life is not the same for everyone. And it's the prejudice of people like you which is responsible for the fact that forty per cent of the people in this country are on antidepressants.'

Forty per cent of people in this country on antidepressants? Did that include the children? Imogen's statistics never cease to astonish him.

'Take this off.'

As Toby drifts off to sleep, his arm dead under an unrelenting Imogen, he hears hooves strike tarmac. Jack Scarlett and the Squire gallop down Kentish Town Road past Auntie Annie's Porter House and the Owl Bookshop. The High Street's 'In Bloom' and hanging baskets swing in the highwaymen's wake as they pound into town for the night shift.

Toby rattled the padlock on the school gate. It occurred to him that perhaps he didn't like the Hill because he was jealous of how protective Imogen was of her. It seemed to him that if it came down to it, Imogen might side with the Hill against him. A woman, frowning, was walking across the playground. Beyond her a man bent to lock a dark green door. The woman arrived at the gate: fuzz of wire-wool hair, jeans pulled up too high, ointment-pink Airtex tucked in. A frumpy, surly high school teacher, Lorna. She looked guilty. Beyond her, 'M' was adjusting his belt as he ambled towards them. It looked as though Lorna and M might have been up to no good.

'Can I help you?' The woman asked.

'I'm looking for Imogen Green.'

'Miss Green?' She frowned as though Toby were a delinquent pupil who had no right to be enquiring after a teacher.

'It's half term,' she said reaching through the gate to fit a key to the padlock. Half term. Of course it was half term. Miss Green was not the type to take a skiing holiday during term time. The teacher was still looking at him unsmiling as she unravelled the chain and pushed the gate open just enough to allow herself out. She stood guarding it as she waited for her boyfriend.

'When does term start?'

'Well, if this week is half term,' her lips smirked slightly in class-room sarcasm, 'then that would suggest that next Monday would be the start of the second half of the summer term.'

M bent to fiddle with the padlock and chain. Toby got back into the car and started the engine. He watched the teachers walk side by side down the hill towards Camden before he pulled out. He was looking forward to telling Imogen that M and Lorna had spent half term rutting in the staff room.

He drove slowly down Frederick Street, following the route Imogen took to work. He didn't even know which side of the road she walked on. He parked on Plantation Road outside the Dragon. He turned off the engine and the digital clock which said 13.13 faded to nothing. He closed his eyes and moved his tongue between his lips.

The earth smell and salt taste of the palm of Imogen's hand spread across his tongue. His teeth scrape across the soft flesh. His cock is constricted as the tip of his tongue sharpens to explore the salt lines and markings and his teeth search for purchase. It's less than a week ago and they're hiding from a clutch of Imogen's pupils in the long evening in the grass on the sweltering heath. She does not like to be seen by them outside school particularly not in the evenings with her boyfriend and a picnic. Shut your mouth Toby Doubt. She presses her hand harder into his mouth and lies across his body to hold him face down on to the spinning earth.

three

When Toby woke the sky was bruised purple and black. It looked like rain. He locked the car and as he walked down Plantation Road he saw that ominous clouds had gathered over the railway line. The back of Number 3 was thick with voluptuous flowers like bunches of grapes grown plump on human flesh. At the top of the house, the bathroom window was shut. Just how he liked it. He closed it. She opened it. She opened it even on winter mornings and filled the room with steam.

As Toby crossed Frederick Street he didn't turn to look at the front of the house. He could feel it though, hot at his back. If she was there then she was there and would still be there when he got back from the shop. And if she was there then she'd be likely to stay longer if he had lager. And if she was back for good it would be nice to have the lager anyway. He refused to look. Instead he examined the railway platform below him. On the St Albans side, a newspaper flapped in the breeze. Two boys sat on the back of a bench, a girl in a short skirt stood smoking in front of them. Toby could see black roots where the yellow hair sprang from her scalp. She was wearing those platform shoes that kept causing Japanese women to fall and die. A night out, a loose paving stone, a trip, a fall. Coma. He wondered if the girl knew she was dicing with death.

The aisles of Mr Cheap Potatoes were brightly lit and empty. Mr Potatoes, who flirted with Imogen – 'I seen you this morning,' two thick fingers, hairy, crossing and recrossing above the counter to demonstrate walking, 'hurrying, hurrying.' White teeth sharp beneath glossy slug of a moustache. 'Where you goin' eh?' – sold him eight cans of Tennant's Super and a packet of Marlboro cigarettes as though he'd never before set eyes on him.

'Bag?' His lips scarcely moved beneath the thick moustache.

Hello Mr Potatoes, Toby wanted to say. Remember me? I've only shopped here every day for three years. Instead he filled the blue plastic bag and said thanks. Cold and reassuringly heavy it bounced against his thigh as he walked past the pub where someone won the lottery once, past the bench that stank of piss, past the newsagent that supplied Imogen with all her local information: shoot-outs, crack raids, rotting bodies discovered in flats. He kept his eyes on the sun, which shone mother-of-pearl behind darkening cloud.

Across the road, the gate to Number 3 swung open and on the doorstep a pile of bones had been assembled. Voodoo. On closer inspection they seemed to be chicken legs arranged in no particular design and the box beside them, red and white striped cardboard advertising Chicken Cottage, suggested lunch. Voodoo or lunch, either way they were an unlikely herald of Imogen's return. He opened the door and, stepping carefully over the bones, went inside.

He closed the door softly and leant against it. There was silence. The red carpet looked threadbare and worn. The walls, dirty and shiny, and the staircase, narrow. Water dripped in a distant basin to punctuate the in and out of his breath. The banisters, stripped pale up to the eighth step, stated plainly that work had been abandoned here. For a moment the hallway was filled with a blast of winter light and the dragon roar of a blow torch.

The hot smell of scorched wood catches in his throat and Imogen, eyes magnified behind goggles borrowed from the science lab, pauses from her work.

Toby dropped both plastic bags at the foot of the stairs. Above him, there was a sudden rumbling of floorboards and Rita appeared on the landing, the white tip of her thick tail flickering. The cat regarded him steadily.

'Hello Rita.' This was probably the first time he'd addressed the cat directly in the year or so it had lived here. Rita crouched, eyes narrowed. Toby put a foot on the first step. The cat's tail twitched. As he reached the landing, the cat arched its back and fled hissing.

Cupboards flapped in the kitchen, a turret of washing-up was piled in the sink and Toby's shoe stuck to the linoleum. A lone plate encrusted with something orange had landed in the middle of the table, under it on the floor the bright blade of a knife shone white. All the windows were closed. Imogen was not at home. The phone pulsed importantly.

'Toby—' his mother started. He erased her mournful voice. 'Toby, Howie…'

He erased eight messages. All starting with 'Toby'. Subdued voices, mostly his mother's, each quieter and more sombre than the last and none the one he wanted to hear. Imogen had not called. Nor had anyone called for her; it was clear she'd been thorough in letting everyone know her plans. Bad news, it seemed, travelled as fast as they, whoever they were, said it did.

Upstairs the bed was unmade and the curtains gaped to show the heavy sky. The scatter of books, the clothes on the floor – the tangled contents of Imogen's chest of drawers – represented much of Toby's activity of yesterday. The wardrobe, however, was tightly closed. Odd considering the state of the room and Imogen's frequent refrain: 'Please, Toby, please. Just sometimes close the wardrobe doors.' He crept across the floorboards careful to avoid the loose one. Past the foot of the bed, past the mantelpiece on which sat the turd-shaped owl which Imogen had made at school. His heart was pounding in his chest. He pressed his ear to the cupboard – the hollow sound of silence. He threw open the door. The cupboard was full of clothes, a mixture of his and hers. He felt along the floor disturbing the cover of shoes. There was no warm body naked in a fur coat. He brought out a box and sat on the bed. Lifting the cardboard lid he found a shoe in tissue paper. A single red suede shoe.

The last time Imogen had been waiting for him in a fret of excitement in the fur coat had been after Christmas.

She comes up behind him to lick his neck, to bite his ear. To rub her breasts against his back. He can feel the heat of her nipples through his shirt. Just let me finish this. Give me five minutes to get the Spaniard and the Squire back to Hampstead Heath and their stash of booty. Just give me five. He climbs the stairs, his head full of plunder and arse-titted carriages. Lady Rose lies in the middle of the bed, the mink coat open around her body. He's the Squire and they make love tenderly. Like this he loves her more than his own need to live. Then he takes her roughly, holding her hands behind her back. She comes straight off. It could be rape for he's Jack Scarlett, he's the Spaniard and night is coming and there's work to do.

Afterwards he stands up and, pencil still in hand, pulls up his trousers. They both laugh when they see the pencil.

It no longer seemed so funny.

He looked at the shoe. If it wasn't for all the dried glue, the shoe might have been beautiful. Alongside it in the box, mysterious shapes of suede and a wooden heel lay loose. The embryonic form of the shoe's mate. Imogen the cobbler halfway through a pair.

The muted doorbell buzzed. Still holding the shoe he pressed his forehead to the window. He could just see the hem of a pale sweatshirt. He pulled up the sash window and leant out. Howie stepped back and looked up.

'Toby.' He looked pale. 'Thank fuck you're here. I was ringing all day yesterday. Where the fuck have you been?' His Adam's apple rode up and down. He seemed angry. 'Thank fuck you're here.' He looked quickly right and then left and then back up at the window. Nice, thought Toby, to see you too.

'How are you?'

How was he? A spectre loomed, a page of memory: he had been drunk, disgraced, vile, humiliated and soiled in borrowed clothes. He had been led home by Howie, a bleating, semi-conscious calf.

'Good thanks. You?'

'Better now. I've been worried to fuck about you. I called the cops.'

Toby laughed. 'You called the cops?' He liked the way that sounded as though they were part of an early evening American TV show. 'Was it *911*? What did the cops say? Are they sending back-up?' He imagined 3 Frederick Street surrounded by US cops, their wide flashing motorbikes propped up on the pavement.

Howard's mouth was open. 'Let me in.' Again his Adam's apple slid quickly up and down his rash-red throat.

'Is there something you wanted to talk about?'

Howard seemed surprised. 'Toby don't be a prick.' He blinked up at the window, his mouth oblong like a distant letter box.

It was strange seeing Howie lost for words.

'Let me in mate.'

'Why?'

'Why?' Howard considered this for a while. 'I need to talk to you. I never should have left you. Let me in. You should not be on your own. I only went home to pick up my sleeping pills. Where were you? I was ringing the bell all night. All day yesterday. This morning. You could have fucking called.' Howard rubbed his neck. When he looked up again he was, it seemed, in control of his anger. 'Look mate I just don't want you to be alone right now.'

What made Howard so certain that Toby was alone? That's what Toby meant when he mentioned to Imogen that Howard annoyed him: his girlfriend had left, ergo Toby was alone. After all where would Toby find another sucker willing to spend time with him?

'I'm not alone.'

'Who's there?' The quick interest of Howard Seaton exposing a lie. Toby smiled. 'Stella.'

Howie, pale and serious. 'Page? Stella Page?'

Toby nodded, enjoying Howard's disbelief. Stella Page.

'Bollocks,' said Howard, the start of a smile on his lips.

'No. She's here,' said Toby. The smile disappeared and Howard seemed to be looking beyond Toby for evidence of the blonde girl.

'Well, say hi to Stella.' He lowered his voice. 'And please call me, Toby. To talk, have some beers. Anything. Just don't shut me out.'

Toby nodded. 'Sure Howie. There is one thing actually,' he said to Howard's retreating form.

Howie turned at the gate to look up.

'That boy you get your cocaine from. Could you give me his number?'

Howie looked nervously at Primrose's house, at the pub on the other side and at the street behind him.

'That won't solve anything. At least if you're calling Amos, let me come in,' lips moving exaggeratedly around the stage-whisper. That was more like Howard. The idea of drugs being taken anywhere in London without Howie – party man supremo – was just not feasible.

'Stella's here. It's not really a good time.' Toby turned to look as Rita padded stiffly into the bedroom.

Howie gazed blankly.

'I'll call you. Hold on. I'm just coming,' this to the treacherous cat on the bed.

Howard, feeling in his pockets for pen and paper, wore clothes – low-slung jeans and hooded top – which would have better suited a fifteen-year-old. 'I'll put the number through the letter box,' he said.

At least Howard would have something for Jane to report to Imogen. Toby Doubt. With Stella Page. In the bedroom. Putting in an order for party drugs. As Toby closed the window, Howie, now on the other side of the road, raised a hand in farewell. Toby pulled the curtains across the window.

He still had Imogen's red shoe in his hand. He lay back on the bed and wondered whether he should call work. They would probably be wondering where he'd got to. He slid a hand down his belly and under the waistband of his trousers to lodge it in the tangle of pubic hair. It afforded some comfort. He thought of Stella. Fifteen years of blonde, blue-eyed Cambridge legend circa 1987. Imogen, hand on hip, glided into his mind. He sat and picked up the phone on her bedside table.

'Archives,' Ted answered. Brusque, pissed off, having to deal with Toby's work on top of his own.

'Ted. Toby.'

'Alright old son. How's it going?' From curt to expansive in half a second.

'Er good.' A pause. Silence.

'So, how can I help?'

'Er, listen Ted. Something's come up, um, family issues, may need to take the week off to sort it out.'

'Nothing serious I hope. The wife alright?'

'Yes. Fine. Look. It shouldn't take too long.'

'Well. You're the boss. To be honest there was some confusion this end anyway. Jane was under the impression that you'd booked the whole week off as part of the surprise. Speaking of the surprise how was it? Nothing too surprising I hope.'

'Surprise?'

'Your weekend. The mysterious surprise. The weekend of love.'

'Oh that. Great.' Toby attempted enthusiasm. With everything that had happened, he'd forgotten about Imogen's 'surprise'. Well he'd had it now and frankly he'd file it firmly under shock.

'Crikey, Lawrence Rickey's just walked in.' Ted lowered his voice. 'Better shoot. Call back in half an hour.' The line clicked dead.

A surprise. What kind of a person would choose that word to describe what she'd done?

Imogen's eyes sparkle as she shaves a pale leg in the bath running her pink flannel over the new smooth skin. 'Toby, I have a surprise planned for the weekend.'

Toby is lying on the stairs as he's started to do recently, head on his hands just inside the bathroom watching as she dips the razor below the water's surface. Steam escapes through the open window. Imogen laughs as she lathers up the other leg. Since Imogen went off sex, Toby is aware that sometimes he is becoming her slave. The Squire has lost his charm and when they do have sex it's Jack Scarlett to whom Lady Rose responds. The dark-skinned, traitorous Spaniard is emerging as the hero.

Toby picked up the phone and dialled her mobile number. The voice said, as he knew it would, 'The mobile number you have called is currently unavailable. Please call later.' It had been saying that over and over ever since she'd left and Toby had started trying to get hold of her.

He climbed up to the little bathroom at the top of the house and lay on the stairs. The bathroom was stagnating with decay. An empty Smirnoff bottle lay beside the bath alongside a heap of unfamiliar clothes, an old man's blue cotton pyjamas. And no Imogen. Laughing and shaving. Shaving and laughing. 'I have a surprise planned for the weekend.'

Toby crawled to his feet and, reaching over the bath, opened the window wide. Purple flowers crowded in to touch his hand. Stung, they retreated, disappointed he wasn't her. The bath was full. He put his hand in the water. Stone death cold.

He lay on the carpet beside the bath, his head beneath the basin. He looked up and wondered if this was an aspect of the house with which Imogen was familiar. He thought it unlikely as he touched the brown stains on the basin's forgotten underbelly. An unexplored Polynesia which spanned the southern hemisphere and wrapped itself around the drainage pipe. Palm trees, rocky outcrops, uncharted waters. A tiny yacht bobbed alone in the middle of a sea. She wouldn't like that. Decades of unseen, slowly seeping, stagnant, London water. He felt a bottle behind his head on the carpet. He lifted it and turned it upside down to his lips. A dribble of vodka reached his tongue. Toby had found himself exactly here, naked and rigor-mortis-stiff in the early hours of the day before yesterday, or was it yesterday? Complete in the knowledge that Imogen was gone. And then it had been some time between Saturday and Sunday when he'd found the letter and had turned the spotlight of suspicion on to Gideon Chancelight. At that point everything had started to make a whole lot more sense.

He got to his feet and slowly made his way downstairs. Past the bedroom where Imogen sits drying between her treacherous toes, down to the kitchen where Imogen stands at the sink smiling fondly, her mind on someone else as she washes the paltry half-handful of carrots she's grown, and downstairs. On the doormat was a narrow slip of torn paper. Scrawled in biro it said 'Amos' and beneath those letters, a string of numbers. Toby picked up the blue plastic bags, heavy with lager, and carried them along the darkening corridor out through the back door and into the garden.

four

The back door wasn't closed and outside it was clear the garden wasn't grieving. In fact it appeared to be revelling in Imogen's absence; its display was celebratory. The row of runner beans, rampant and unruly, bustled greedily about their canes. Parallel rows of lettuces swelled against each other. Roses bundled in their munificence over the wall. He'd never known the garden look so well. It was as though at last, without her constant fiddling, it was rejoicing in just being allowed to be itself.

Imogen crouches, chopping in the flower bed with the side of her trowel, black hair lively in the evening sun, white pants bright beneath her tucked-up summer skirt. And Toby, ten feet above her, watches from the kitchen window. His abandoned manuscript reproaching him from the table.

'Imogen.'

She looks up, frowning, her trowel poised dagger-like. 'How are you getting on?'

Not well. It's like this, Imogen. You are my girlfriend. We live together. And I would like to have sex. Is that really so unreasonable? We haven't fucked for nearly a week and really I'd like to come down there and lay you in that weedless flower bed and fuck you senseless until you've got that good clean black London earth all over your white pants, your arse and definitely in your hair. And then perhaps I'd get on better.

'A cup of tea?'

A cup of tea. Toby's erection deflates against the sink as he fills the kettle under the tap. Coward is what his cock thinks. Coward is about right. However, at this moment Toby doesn't think he could stand to hear her say: 'not now' or 'later' or 'when I've put the carrots in'. With Imogen in the garden Toby is free to fill the kettle how he likes and this is how he likes – through the spout. Water sprays on the floor, it drenches his shirt and a fine jet escapes through the window. He can make the tea exactly how he likes. He can even make it with his eyes closed. The cupboard surprises him by opening the wrong way. Marmite, honey, jam, the clink of sticky jars, the crackle of a bag of rice. Glass bounces off Formica, hits linoleum and rolls. It spills and scatters. Cloves. His hand finds the cylindrical tin. He sets it down beside the stirring kettle and turns towards the sink: one, two, three. The cloves are sharp underfoot. Eyes scrunch tight against the sunlight. Knives skitter on the draining board, a regiment of upright plates and two cups. From their coolness Toby knows that one is thick-lipped yellow and the other fine with a faded blue sailing boat on one side: As Happy As The Day Is Long. The kettle climaxes, cloves stick to Toby's heel. He has tea, kettle, cups. So now the tricky part. As Happy As The Day Is Long.

Toby sat at the wooden table under the green and white Carlsberg umbrella with its fringe of curled tassels. Purple clouds filled the sky. It seemed that night was coming early. He opened a can of lager and wondered what the garden had to celebrate. Imogen's escape made good by train?

The doorbell buzzed. A muted, muffled sound. The bell had been high on the list entitled Things That Need Doing with which Imogen had supplied him when they'd first moved in. He wondered whether things might be different if he'd done something about the bell or indeed about anything on that list. Hooks for coats; chop down the blackthorn; re-tile around the taps in the bathroom; paint the ceilings. He'd done the bedroom and one coat in the kitchen on the end of the broom handle and then standing bent between the units and the ceiling. It had nearly killed him. Still now, three years on, he didn't think his neck was quite the same. And how, realistically, could he have been expected to do the stairs? Sand the floor; erect a curtain rail. For a demi-second he saw himself – a god on a stepladder, white dungarees loose to show toned muscle, taut nipples. Imogen, Mary Magdalen, prostrate on the floor, in a fret of sexual agitation.

The doorbell buzzed again and the memory of the list exhausted him. He'd known, when she'd given it to him, that there was not a hope. He made his way back into the house along the dark corridor to the front door. He opened it. A police officer, short, with a friendly face round as a scone, stood on the step.

'Hello there, officer,' he said. He found he held his can of lager behind his back.

'Good evening,' said the policewoman. Hesitant, concerned even. 'I'm looking for Mr Toby Doubt.' A whisper of a Scottish accent. The walky-talky at her shoulder crackled into life.

'Mr Doubt, I'm afraid, is out,' said Toby enjoying the rhyme.

'Oh.' The policewoman's mouth remained an 'o' as she looked up at him.

'Anything I can do to help?'

'You being…?'

'Tim. I'm Toby's brother, Tim.'

'Ah.' The plastic of her jacket creaked as she reached to turn down the volume on the radio at her shoulder.

'How is Toby doing?' A pleasing furrow of concern marked her brow.

'He's doing OK.'

'Are you expecting him back tonight?'

'Any time. Any time now.'

'Alright to…' the policewoman made a move to come inside.

'Well the thing is,' Toby moved to block her entrance, 'the thing is, officer, he's at his Salsa class. Sometimes they have a drink afterwards. Sometimes they don't. There's just no telling with Toby Doubt.' Another smile.

'Oh.' She took a step back, careful to avoid the chicken bones on the step.

'Was there a message? Anything I should tell him? Friend of his are you?'

'Not exactly,' said the policewoman, the early warmth disappearing. 'Would you give him this and tell him to call into the station to advise that he's received it. The number's there.' She handed over a brown envelope and pointed to a stamp in the corner: 'Headcorn Police Station, Kent,' it read. 'Some personal effects,' she added.

'I certainly will,' said Toby.

'It's important that he calls.'

He watched until the gate had swung shut and she'd crossed the road before closing the door. He wondered when Toby would return from his Salsa class and whether in the meantime he would he mind if he opened his letter. The envelope floated to the carpet. He held a clear plastic bag from which he pulled a folded paper. Wrapped inside was a passport and money. A substantial amount of money. A stack of unfamiliar notes secured with an elastic band. Euros. Enough to leave the country with. 'Toby Lawrence Doubt. 3 Frederick Street, London NW5 2PS. 31 May. Personal Items. Passport, 25 x Euros 20 = Euros 500. 20 x £20 = £400.'

Back in the garden the rain had started. A heavy glob splashed warm as blood off Toby's forehead. He went to the table. Water trickled down between his eyes as he pulled the chair further into the shelter of the Carlsberg umbrella which he and Howie had stolen from outside the Bull and Last on Highgate Hill two summers ago. Or to be more precise, the umbrella which Howie stole and strode down the road with, leaving Toby on the darkness of the heath along the back of the tennis courts and behind the public lavatories until the shouts from the pub had quietened and the coast was clear. He'd arrived home unannounced, to discover Howard and Imogen – 'garage sale' he's telling the gullible teacher – laughing, heads together in the garden as they worked to fit the umbrella into the hole in the middle of the round wooden table which the last inhabitants, moving to a house without a garden, had kindly left behind. Nothing wrong with that *per se*, had it not been for what had happened with Stella Page.

He opened the passport. Toby Lawrence Doubt. The face of a lost man: a person of whom life had got the better.

Toby drank and as he drank he wondered what these 'effects' meant and what the significance of the police officer might be. He drank again and knew they were linked with Howard and Imogen and a certain aspect of his behaviour which had led to the end of that relationship. He wondered where Imogen's passport was. Did you need a passport to go to France? He'd had this conversation with someone recently. Someone had asked him right here in the garden. Imogen's face is pressed up against the trellis amongst the leaves of a rose bush. She's trying to cut thick green string with her teeth. 'Do you need a passport these days to go to France, Tobe?' Sliding front teeth back and forth across the hairy twine. Why would someone want to know that unless a trip to France was imminent? Why hadn't it occurred to him to want to know why Imogen required that information? All Toby had wanted to know was why Imogen wasn't using a knife or scissors to cut the string like any normal person would, as what she was doing now set his own teeth on edge. Where was Imogen's passport?

He took the stairs to the top of the house and into the bedroom. The cat whipped past, its tail as thick as a fox's brush. He emptied Imogen's bedside drawer on to the centre of the unmade bed. Earrings, nail varnish, safety pins, tweezers, a plastic tray of half-gone painkillers, a coffee shop loyalty card. Her pill? The pill? The pill they used to stop them producing a child. He shook the pink and white box: empty. Wherever she was, at least she was being careful. Good careful Imogen. The chest of drawers had already been sacked. There was no sign of her passport.

He jumped the first flight of stairs, flew down the second. The desk was open. It had been Imogen's mother's. Now it was Imogen's. There was some kind of ongoing dispute between Imogen and Cassie regarding the desk. Imogen's disputed rosewood roll-top desk. It was littered with bills – phone bills, water bills, gas and electricity. And it was where he'd found the love letter from Gideon Chancelight. A green piece of paper fluttered to the floor. 'Say No to the Green Wood Estate.' 'No!' shouted Toby. 'No to the Green Wood Estate!' The first drawer bulged with curling photographs. Imogen, a sturdy child on Cassie's knee, Imogen astride a donkey. Imogen, obscure with black curls on a wall beside her mother. A phone book, a Yellow Pages, a book on evening classes in London. That should have been a clue. Anyone knew that the first sign of dissent in a relationship usually comes as evening classes. A tin box of screws, a bunch of keys. A small dusty album filled with papery grey flowers. A jam jar of buttons. A million mismatched forsaken buttons: a collection started by the mother to be continued by the daughter and to be completed when buttons stopped being used. It was apparent that wherever Imogen was, so was her passport. It was also apparent that his own passport, which had been delivered tonight, along with financial compensation, had been delivered for a reason. A reason which would, he did not doubt, become clear in due course.

Back in the bedroom, and by a painstaking process of elimination, Toby ascertained that Imogen's packing was ill-suited to skiing: missing was one white and mostly see-through summer dress, the knickers with cherries on them and ribbons at the hips. Her jeans, the shoes he loved, the ones which she had only allowed him to fuck her in once. Still in the wardrobe was the fur coat (her mother's) and on the shelf above, along with scarves, hats, gloves and every other clothing item intended for snow, the black cashmere rollneck that she was never, not ever, without in winter. Toby pulled it down and held it to his face in an attempt to stave off the obvious: Imogen had packed a bag with seduction in mind. However, as anyone knew, whoever goes skiing in June? Toby squeezed the cashmere against his face and fought against an image of her in the see-through dress – pubic hair and nipples – as she sped down a slope somewhere in the French Alps, the lusty estate agent – 'Let's do lunch!' – in pursuit.

On his way downstairs he picked up the phone and took it outside into the garden. It was raining heavily. Streaks splashed off the crazy paving, bounced off the umbrella. The garden shuddered with delight. Gripping the phone with both hands – you had to be careful with it these days as it was held together by tape following an incident in which he'd thrown it from the kitchen window. Imogen had failed to catch it and the phone had smashed, which was quite obviously his fault. Imogen crossly assembled the pieces of broken plastic and, holding it in both hands to her ear, asked Saffron, whose call had survived the accident, 'Can you hear me? Toby's broken the phone now,' as though this was just the latest in a long line of misdemeanours.

He pushed into the phone the sequence of numbers which Howard had written. With his left hand he held the phone to his ear and with his right extracted a can from one of Mr Cheap Potatoes' bags. He lifted the ring pull.

'This is Toby Doubt. A friend of Howard J. Seaton's. Toby... Yes... Toby. Doubt. I was wondering whether it might be possible to, er, make a purchase.' The words 'hook up' which he'd heard Howard use stuck in his throat. 'Is that right? GCSEs? I didn't know you had those on.' And why should he have known, he wondered, that Amos was doing his GCSEs? He'd only met the boy once: Howie had got him round when Imogen was away with the school on a trip to Rome.

'When the cat's away…' Howie, eager, eyes sparkling, as he dialled Amos.

Well the cat was away alright.

'Wow,' said Toby. 'When's your first exam? Monday? One week today? Half term. Of course it is.' Toby thought back to the half term before his own GCSEs. Standing in the garden trying to learn Latin lesbian poetry. He hadn't done well in GCSEs. Or his A-levels for that matter. Hence the second-rate history degree from the University of East Anglia in Norwich and the eternal disappointment with which his mother had elected to live. He had fallen short of the giddy heights of that great physicist John Doubt, her father, his grandfather and had not taken a First from Cambridge in physics.

'Your first one is geography? Good luck, Amos. And I'm sorry I disturbed you, and by the way, revision is good. I wish I had done more.'

There was a sigh. Then Amos said: 'Yeah man, I figured that.'

Toby put the phone down on the table. He wondered if he did regret the fact he hadn't worked harder at school then decided that as he had no idea what might or might not have happened had he worked harder for his GCSEs and that up until now he'd been quite happy with the life he had – as long as this Imogen situation could be resolved – he probably didn't wish he'd worked harder.

The patter of rain on canvas soothed Toby until he remembered Howard aged sixteen in an orange sleeping bag snoring on his back and taking up the entirety of a two-man tent.

Toby who hasn't slept a wink is tight up against the canvas wall. Everyone knows you should never touch the side of a tent in the rain. Toby shakes Howie awake. He mumbles something in his sleep, rolls his head, moans. He swats at Toby and carries on snoring. Wake up. Move up. It's 1989, post-GCSEs and they're on the edge of a wheat field some miles from Cambridge. Beer cans clatter at the end of Toby's sleeping bag. The land is flat, the barley still green and they've pitched their tent in the middle of an untidy crop circle which they spent most of the night making. And still Howard snores.

Toby drank long from the can on the table in front of him and wondered whether Imogen really had been on a school trip to Rome. Whenever did fifteen-year-old girls go on maths trips to Rome? Perhaps Pythagoras was a Roman? Even so it still seemed unlikely that a class of girls should be taken to the Italian capital to see where the great mathematician bathed.

That night in September with the cocaine and Howard it had never crossed Toby's mind that she might have been lying. And when the cat got back there had been hell to pay: Imogen speechless, cradling the hollowed-out, smiling remains of a marrow in her arms. As large as a thigh and neatly striped in yellow, it had been severed from the mothership and fashioned over lager and cocaine into a cheerful drinking companion by Howard. On Sunday night she'd found it where they'd left it, smiling broadly amongst bottles and ashtrays on the table. Marrow Man – a toothy candlelit, grinning compatriot to the long night's festivities.

The phone rang. Toby recognized his mother's number and let it ring. It stopped before the answerphone cut in. It was much more likely that Imogen had spent that week in the Italian Alps getting together a basic skiing technique. In which case he was glad about Marrow Man.

The phone rang again. Number Withheld. It was Amos.

'Hello, Toby? This is Amos.'

'That's great news. Thanks a lot. And good luck for next week.'

Toby replaced the phone and tried to remember what he could about geography. Considering he'd studied the subject for something like three years it seemed odd that all he could remember was something called Yams and something else called Cassava. He could not recall the name or face of the teacher who'd taught him. Well that was a waste of life, he thought. He raised the blue can in his hand to a rose-bush: 'Good luck Amos,' he said.

The rain was falling more heavily now. Toby moved his chair closer to the table and further under the shelter. Around him the garden heaved and sighed. The roses chattered excitedly, bobbing their heads, dodging raindrops. All the time, they told him, all the time she was out with us, fiddling and tying, digging and planting, she should have been up in the bedroom on the stairs on the kitchen table with you. We didn't need her. The roses shook their heads. The runner beans rat-tled their red flowers in agreement. The lettuces swelled and sighed. And the rain fell. See how we flourish when she isn't here?

'The thing is,' Howie is an authority on all things. On cocaine and music and clothes and life. On sex and shopping and shagging and shoes. Even an authority on Toby and Imogen. 'The thing is mate,' eyeing Imogen's pants through her white dress, 'women are like that. The first two years they go like rabbits. Then it tails off. Between you and me mate, you're lucky to be getting it once a week.'

You're lucky to be getting it once a week.

Howard had said that last weekend at the barbecue. He was contin-uing a conversation that Toby had initiated at least a month previously. What Toby had yet to confide and in fact was unsure whether he actu-ally wished to confide, was that recently, there had been an upturn in his girlfriend's libido and as it happened, just that morning had seen Imogen sated, starfish on the bed. And indeed Toby had felt that it was safe to surmise that his sex life was more or less exactly as he wanted it. Perhaps better.

Rain, black with grease and charcoal, spattered out of the grill and on to the crazy paving. Last weekend the sun was out, the beers ice-cold and Imogen out of reach in her white dress: freckled shoulders and white knickers, going on and on about her wisteria. When was the last time you felt like jumping for joy? Saffron, feet up on the bench, is rolling one of Howie's cigarettes.

Toby turns chicken kebabs on the barbecue. His beer, perched in a flowerpot nailed to the wall is at the perfect height, the girl he loves is wearing the ring he bought her. The complexion of his life is good. His mind turns to this morning and waking to the insistent warmth of Imogen pressed against his groin. It turns then to the exquisite oral administered just before Howie and Jane and Saffron and Charlie, who is dozing on cushions in the sun against the wall, got here. He'd have to say that pretty much now. Now is pretty much the last time he felt like jumping for joy.

The chicken spits and burns his hand, he takes his beer from the flowerpot, a black bee buzzing at its lip.

'It's now.' He turns from his kebabs to tell Saffron. 'I could jump for joy right now,' but she doesn't hear him. She's standing, the half-made cigarette on the ground. She's frowning and rubbing her arm. The trellis above the wall is still shuddering and Saffron's straight arm is bleeding long and red where Rita scratched. She goes inside with Imogen and when she comes back down – from washing it or what- ever they've been doing – the first kebabs are ready and she's no longer interested in when it was that anyone last felt like jumping for joy.

'I don't know why you don't have that cat put down,' she says waiting as Toby turns the food on the barbecue searching for the per- fect vegetable kebab. He puts it on her plate and checks Imogen isn't looking before nodding his absolute and fervent agreement.

The phone rang: a Cambridge number. His mother, again. He took a deep breath. Hello Alison.

'Betsey,' she said. 'Will be any day now. She gets up to pee but then goes straight back to her basket.'

'Right.'

'She's looking at me. Hello Betsey. I think she knows it's you. She sends her love. Yes she does, she sends her love.'

'Right.' Right Alison. That sounds likely.

'So, where are you?'

'I'm in the garden... Yes... Rain... I'm under the umbrella... Yes... I am dry... Yes I am... I'm alright.' I've got an eight pack of Tennant's and several hundred pounds' worth of cocaine on its way. Of course I'm alright. The doorbell rang. 'Of course I'm alright... no... I wasn't there today... that's right... a new job... correct... estate agent. Estate agent... I am an estate agent, Mother... I am alright... I said I am alright... You don't need to... Please don't... I've got someone here... it's Stella... Yes. Stella... An old friend... Stella is here... this is home... I'll come up... yes... next week... there's someone at the door...' He put down the phone and walked out through the rain.

Yes, Mother, she has left. Yes, Mother. You can say her name. It's Imogen. It's Imogen in the garden. It's Imogen with her pants down. It's Imogen astride someone else's cock.

He opened the door to a small boy on a BMX, the wheel of which nosed at the chicken bones on the doorstep. The rain had eased off a little and was now falling in grey streaks. The child was someone Toby had never seen before. The hood of a blue anorak was down over his eyes. Seven thought Toby. Eight, maybe ten years old?

'Eight? Nine? Ten?' he asked.

The child didn't say anything. He leant forward on his handlebars and looked at Toby blankly.

How old are children these days?

'Ten?'

The child regarded Toby steadily. 'Five. Amos said five for two hundred.' Spoken quickly, lips scarcely moving.

It seemed inappropriate to be buying cocaine from an individual on his doorstep out here in the rain, who had not yet reached double figures.

'Do you want to come in?'

The child's hands on the handlebars were shiny wet and, apart from a small oval of face, were the only part of him showing. He looked past Toby into the house and then behind him over his shoulder. In the street another child about his size sat on a similar bike back-pedalling, arm draped affectionately around a streetlamp.

'You're alright,' he said and held out a child's fist, knuckles up. Toby extended his left hand out and closed it around a small polythene bag. He put it into his pocket and pulled out the fold of purple twenties that the police officer had brought.

'Two,' said the child, lips scarcely moving, eyes on the money. 'Two hundred.'

'One, two, three, four...' Toby counted twenties into the child's small hand.

The boy unzipped the anorak and folded the money away into a zip-up pocket on the inside before reversing the bike back down the pathway.

'Tell Amos I said good luck.'

The child wheeled in an arc until he drew alongside his friend. Idly the two meandered side by side along the pavement in the rain. Toby watched them until they were out of sight. He closed the door. The house was still.

The garden was dim. The rain had slacked off. Monday night. Imogen was at her Salsa class in the church hall and when she came home she'd be upset that he'd (a) bought cocaine from an eight-year-old boy (b) interrupted a child from revising for his GCSEs and (c) combined the two.

'You've been ripped off,' perhaps she'd say. Toby laughed at the like-lihood of that.

The orange of the streetlamp beyond Primrose's patio illuminated the garden and Toby sat on the damp chair under the umbrella. The cocaine was wrapped in five separate paper parcels and covered again in cling film. Underneath the plastic the paper was dry. He unfolded one to flatten it on to the table. It was cut from a magazine and showed close-up skin, white and slightly speckled as though recently shaved. The paper was not large enough or the light strong enough to identify the body part. If Toby was to hazard a guess he might say armpit – the bluish bit which was shaved suggested a shadow of concavity. He tasted the cocaine. He was unsure what cocaine should taste like. But this seemed good. He drank some lager. It too was good. The antidote to Imogen. Perhaps he would prescribe himself lager and cocaine until his chest stopped hurting, in other words until either she came back or enough time passed for him no longer to remember who she was.

Next door the French windows on the first floor opened and Primrose appeared in a peach-coloured housecoat. Her hair, fluffy and orange, matched her dressing gown and behind her, the kitchen glowed a homely yellow. She disappeared and returned seconds later holding something above her head. A tray? Toby sat motionless hoping that she wouldn't see him.

'Hello? Is that Toby?'

'Hello Primrose.'

'Not in France then?'

'Not in France. No.' How could I have gone to France without my passport? He would like to know. The thing had been planned, prepared and packaged so that Toby had no chance of following Imogen to France. Now his passport had been returned. He wondered why. And why now?

'I'll stop feeding Rita then.'

'Feeding Rita?' Stupid Toby, the last to know anything.

With a note of impatience: 'Imogen asked me to feed Rita this week. While you were in France. So if you're here, you won't be needing me to feed the cat.' A light laugh, nervous, irritated, as though it was about time Toby took responsibility. Another laugh. This one, brittle on the air, demanded a response. 'Right?'

'I am here,' said Toby standing. 'Imogen has left me. She's in France with someone else.'

Primrose put the hand which wasn't holding the tray to her chest. 'Gosh.' She made a show of swallowing visibly. Toby took comfort from the fact that he wasn't the only one who hadn't seen it coming. Primrose was silent, still. An apricot sentinel over bed-time North London. Toby's thoughts turned to Primrose's own relationship. Scandalous information garnered by Imogen from the newsagent had reached his ears. It was said that Primrose's husband, a philandering dentist, died five years ago in Wandsworth Prison following a conviction for using gas to philander more freely on his patients. Toby thought of Howard's father, of his own father, and wondered what was wrong with men and why they seemed so anti family? Perhaps it was a road that he himself might one day take.

'Gosh, I'm so sorry.' Primrose's sing-song voice. 'Would you like me to carry on feeding Rita?' A generous offer in light of her own catastrophe.

'I think I can manage thank you,' said Toby struggling against the affront that Imogen had asked Primrose above him to feed what was in effect their cat.

'Well. If there's anything I can do.' Primrose paused to shake her head before retreating into her glowing kitchen. Softly she closed the doors.

Perhaps there was something Primrose could do. Perhaps she could tell him exactly what Imogen had said. When Imogen had said it. And when Imogen was planning on coming back. Carefully he unfolded the armpit. He didn't like the bluish hue of its six o'clock shadow. He liked an armpit with a bit of hair. He liked to bury his nose in the smell and softness of Imogen's armpit, in which she allowed the hair to grow a little, sometimes, in winter. He took a card from his pocket. 'Nigel Harmsworth-Mallett' it said. 'Director, Milson, Range & Rafter'. Using the card he separated some cocaine and moved it to the edge of the paper.

The bell of Number 5 chimed prettily behind the neatly-varnished door as warm rain fell softly on to Toby's shoulders. A light went on above the door, illuminating the front garden, an orderly rockery blooming with colour. Primrose, afraid, pressed an eye to the spy hole. 'Who is it?'

I've come to see the dentist. 'It's Toby from next door.'

Clatter of a chain being pulled across, locks being turned. Surprise. 'Hello! What can I do for you?' Primrose stood there in fluffy apricot nightwear. She patted her hair, her face marked with concern.

Toby could feel rain on his forehead.

'What a shock. It's a shock, come in,' she said. 'Come in, it's raining, come upstairs.'

He took off his shoes and followed her along the passage past the dark downstairs room the same as next door which he and Imogen never used. He followed her upstairs on the pale carpet, or more accurately on the strip of thick clear plastic which covered the pale carpet. On his way up he passed strawberries, plums, peaches, grapes, asparagus painted on to plates which ran along the wall to follow the stairs upwards. That last plate struck him as a little out of line. On neither of his other visits had he noticed the vegetable anomaly. He wondered at its significance. After all, there had been times when Imogen's indelicate interest in vegetables, noticeable from the beginning of last year, seemed to have corresponded with her diminishing interest in him. I need to plant carrots, dig potatoes, thin lettuces. He hit the plate with his fist as Primrose's peach form rounded the corner at the top. It clattered pleasantly against the wall. Primrose turned in alarm.

The last time he was here was without Imogen. He'd been coerced into coming to admire the new French windows which opened from the kitchen on to something Primrose called her 'Juliet Balcony'. Too small to stand on, the 'Juliet' was just about large enough to wave from. Primrose, it's superb. I'm going to talk to Imogen, see if we can't get a Juliet too. That way we can both be Juliet and never stuck outside playing Romeo.

The only other time he's been here they came together. They'd been next door a week when Primrose invited them to inspect her interior decorations. Imogen and Toby framed in apricot doorways struggling not to laugh as Primrose bends to swipe an invisible scrap from the cream carpet, then straightens to explain, 'I wanted something warm.'

Toby passed the crucifix at the top of the stairs and the arching frill at the window. Though their laughter was not unkindly meant it seemed unkind now. Here is just lonely Primrose and the ignominy of her husband. If she wanted something warm, why shouldn't she have something warm?

'Sit.' She gestured to a cork stool at a cork breakfast bar. She went to the kettle. 'Hot chocolate?' She lifted the peach-coloured kettle from its tiled mat, removed the lid and carefully turned on the tap. She filled it a little way, turned off the tap and wiped tap, sink, kettle with a folded cloth. She fixed the lid, plugged it in and straightened the kettle on its tile mat. She turned, hands clasped, to Toby.

'You poor soul. You must be all at sixes and sevens. You made such a lovely couple. What on earth happened?' She pushed an apricot wire from her apricot forehead and frowned.

What on earth happened? It wasn't a bad question. Toby could not entirely remember but felt the answer might not reflect well on him.

'Actually I was wondering if you might know something?'

'Me?' She frowned, genuinely puzzled.

'Yes,' said Toby losing patience. 'What she told you when she asked you to feed the cat. When she said she was coming back, where she said she was going and whether it's permanent?' It occurred to him that perhaps the problem was the peach babygrow. Poor Primrose stupid with heat.

'Oh,' said Primrose stripping her mug tree. 'Let's see.' She tore open twin purple sachets and poured both, one in each hand, into the cups. 'It must have been last weekend I saw her. She was in the garden. I was at the balcony.' Primrose pointed with one empty purple packet. The

hand that held the packet shook slightly. 'Imogen was lighting the barbecue,' she said.

If she was lighting the barbecue then that was Sunday eight days ago
and he was still in bed. Dozing, blissful.

'She asked me,' Primrose continued, 'whether I would feed the cat
from the following Saturday until the Saturday after that. I remember,'
Primrose emphasized her triumph with the empty purple sachet,
'because there had been a possibility that I might have been going
down to Bexhill to stay with David and the girls on that first Saturday.'
David was her son, the girls were her grandchildren and Bexhill was
by the sea.

'Did she say where she was staying?'

'Let's see.' Suddenly Primrose turned to Toby. It was apparent that she
was about to impart important information, as her face changed and
her glance slid away. She seemed embarrassed. Guilty almost. 'Look.
I'm sorry. I've got to be honest with you. Imogen asked me not to
mention anything to you about me feeding the cat. I'm so sorry. I just
assumed it was a lovely surprise for you. I'm so sorry. What a terrible
thing to do. I'm so sorry.' She shook her head as she unplugged the
kettle and filled the cups. 'There must be some other explanation. There
must be. I honestly thought she was taking you away for a surprise.'

Primrose stirred first one cup and then the other. Toby watched her
rounded shoulders.

'You made such a lovely couple.' Uncertain, the words faded. She
frowned and laid the teaspoon carefully on a saucer. She shook her
head as though it didn't make sense. 'I just remember thinking. They're
going away to France for a week'.

'For a week?'

'She said not to worry about feeding the cat next Saturday, as
you'd... as she'd be back.'

Saturday was a long way off. And what kind of a girlfriend told your
neighbour she was leaving you? It was unthinkable.

'I'm sorry Toby.'

It was clear now that he'd fly out to France tomorrow. He'd be there waiting for them at their chalet warming his feet at their log fire when they came back from the slopes. Perhaps he'd slit their throats.

'Did she leave an address? A phone number?'

'Let's see.' Primrose was at the cork board on the wall beside the fridge. 'She did actually.' She unpinned a scrap of paper to hand to him. 'Imogen,' it said. Imogen's hurried, excited, capital letter writing. Imogen with her bags already packed. And below it her mobile number. The mobile number you have called is currently unavailable.

The hot chocolate was sickly sweet and he didn't finish it. Primrose came down with him on the plastic-covered stairs. Behind him through the rain he heard her pull the chain across and double lock the door. The light above it went out.

It was raining more softly now – a fuzz of orange haloed the street-lamp. It was late. A man moved away from the hedge, staggering as he zipped his flies. 'Sorry,' he mumbled as he lurched past Toby and up Frederick Street towards St Hellier's where the black trees met above the road.

The door to Number 3 wouldn't open. Toby pushed. Something was blocking it on the other side. He pushed harder and eventually it shuddered over a brown package. He flicked on the light and turned the parcel with his foot. 'Toby', it said. It wasn't her writing. A day of messages and packages none of which contained anything he wanted. He tore the paper. Something heavy bounced off his boot.

Toby read the letter in his hand. 'This is a mobile phone. It is charged up and ready to use. I have put my numbers – mobile, work, home, into the memory. Call me. Howard.'

Toby dropped the note. It fell beside the phone. Control freak, busy-body, Howie.

It was dark in the garden. 'It's raining, Imogen Green,' he said.

'I know it, baby love.'

She was amongst the roses in the darkness at the back where the old mirror was nailed to the wall. Crouched and digging.

'I want to fuck you, Imogen Green.' A schoolboy whine.

'Just let me finish this.'

'I want to fuck you now, Imogen Green.'

Tired. 'So help me finish this.'

The light went out in Primrose's kitchen.

'What are we doing? How long's it going to take?'

'Half as long if you help me.'

'I want to fuck you now, Imogen Green.'

'It will take half as long if you help me.'

He picked up a spade.

'Everything?'

Over her shoulder she smiled. The sweetest girl in the world crouched in the rain in the flower bed. 'Everything Toby Doubt.'

He placed the jacket of his suit over the back of a chair and began with the large tub nearest the back door. He raised the spade high above his shoulder. For a moment he paused, perhaps hoping that Imogen might register the arc his arms made, the vertical spade a parallel with his strong body. With a smooth motion he dropped the spade into the tub at the base of the wide twisted trunk of the wisteria. It cut easily through the earth, his strong arms loose to aid its passage.

five

He watches her as she clatters in and out of tunnels rattling through the sun and shade behind a pink paperback. Her cream trousers stop above her ankle and where her foot disappears inside her shoe, there's a smudge of blue which looks like something someone did with a magic marker in Holloway women's prison. She's told him it's a swallow – if that's a swallow then I'm the Squire – however, he doesn't mind its ugliness because it's part of her. She's wearing trainers, her legs are crossed and the shoe in the air rattles with the movement of the train. It's white and scuffed and while each dent bears testimony to everywhere she's ever been, they won't divulge their secrets to Toby. His eye travels upwards across the tattoo past cream trousers across her green cardigan and up to her face. Although it's mostly hidden behind the book he can read her expression: wrapt concentration. He tries to read the title of the book. He can see the shape of the letters but cannot make sense of them. Sunlight slants across her neck and amongst the freckles on the hard bit below her collar bone and above her breasts a little silver heart, warmed by her own, slides across the skin. She leans to kiss him and he tries to catch the heart in his mouth, metal against tooth. It twinkles with a different light as it slides across, tugging at his understanding. He doesn't know. Instead he focuses on her forehead, the black arch of her eyebrows, the narrow place her nose begins, he focuses on her eyelid, birdlike blue and on her hair, a tangle of independent life. Evening sun flits across her face. Yellow then brown, yellow then brown. Eventually she holds up the book to shield her eye, the rock of semi-precious blue sparkles on her hand.

'What?' She mouths the word although they are alone. Parallel lines score the skin between her eyebrows. 'What?' She chews dry skin on her lip. When he doesn't answer she comes and sits beside him, fitting herself to him. He lets her do this for some time – he would like to know how much she wants to fit. He cups her shoulder in his hand, it fits nicely and reminds him of school and the warmth of a cricket ball. She reads her book. This is how it should be. Together, side by side, both facing the same future.

Toby opened an eye. He wasn't on a train with Imogen. It seemed there had been an accident. He closed the eye and pain spiralled into his neck. He was on his back, outside somewhere and possibly naked. It wasn't raining but that did not mean that things were alright. He was ice-cold and his head rang with the twitter of every bird in North London. Good morning! You'll never guess who I saw! *Avec qui? Vous êtes sûr? Excusez moi! Mais oui!* Pointless, twitter. He opened the eye again. Above him branches pressed against an indeterminate sky. He opened the other eye and wondered what had landed him here. Ladder? Tree? A catastrophic incident of gardening mismanagement? His skull, ice-cold, contracted under his scalp. He touched his thumb and forefinger together. Pain tore down his spine. Accident probably put too naive a spin on this situation. At this stage it would be a fool who ruled out foul play. Name in the frame: Imogen. A traitorous little maths teacher in a green dress. He struggled for air. Gideon Chancelight. The thing grotesque and dark bowled out from a recess of his mind. Toby pursued it and cornered it. Grudgingly it unfolded: it's Imogen and Toby. It's early on and they're in her bed in Highgate tip-toeing their way around virginity stories. Imogen is laughing at Toby aged ten struggling in an empty bath to fit his penis into Melville Johnson's cousin. She stops laughing to hit back with: 'Eighteen after A-levels. In Spain.

My boyfriend at the time. Gideon Chancelight.' Eighteen. Spain. By the pool. He can still hear the apologetic laugh. He presses his nose into her hair. It smells of honey. Gideon. She said. It's Gideon Chancelight. What a stupid name thinks Toby. Now he thought: I'll kill him.

With effort he rolled on to his side. The pain in his neck was crucifying. It was Tuesday and Toby had things to do. He made it to his feet and was pleased to discover that he was not entirely naked. He was still wearing his trousers and boots. He was however in excruciating pain. Neck. Chest. Head. According to Howard the brain can register only a single pain at any one time. Not Toby's brain. His was registering, processing and delivering three very clear messages.

The garden around him hung suspended in the limbo between night and day. Through the non-light it was apparent that whatever had happened to Toby had also happened to the garden. Plants torn up and lifeless covered the ground, lettuces ripped up, lay scattered. The runner beans no longer thrust imperiously towards the sky. It seemed to Toby that he and the garden had been victims of the same vicious little cyclone.

He picked his way across the ripped-up ground and skidded on what might have been a lettuce. He fell. There was a white scream of pain in his knee. Struggling to his feet he saw that he'd knelt on the rake. He pulled it off and steadied himself against a wave of nausea. He made it to the cupboard under the stairs, the door swung open and a cat's carrying case, pink and light, fell out. A jar of spanners clattered after it to scatter on the carpet beside the case in which Rita had arrived. His mission today: to fly out to France and confront his girlfriend. And her boyfriend. Gideon. Virgin-slayer. Chancelight.

Did you need a passport to go to France these days? Of course you did. And thanks to a visit from a kindly police officer, he had his to hand. Did you need cocaine to go to France these days? Of course you did! And thanks to a helpful child on a bike, Toby was equipped to travel. The fly in the ointment, as Imogen might say when she was imitating his mother, was the small matter of her whereabouts. Where did people ski in France in June? Chamonix? Courcheval? Zermatt? Well you can discount that last one, Toby Doubt. He made it to the top of the house with some relief and down on his undamaged knee, plunged his hand through cold bath water to pull the plug. Anyone who's anyone knows Zermatt's in Switzerland.

Courcheval or Chamonix? He struggled to straighten and turn on the hot tap. Outside another day had taken shape.

There were people in possession of the information he required. Saffron had it, Jane had it, the difficulty would be extracting it from either without Imogen getting to hear. An eventuality which might thwart even the best-laid plans. Howie might have known once but would be unlikely to have retained information concerning something other than himself. Toby felt the water. Hot. Too hot. On the other hand it seemed likely that Toby was expected in France. Hence the timely arrival of his passport. He turned on the cold tap, the phone rang. Back downstairs. Each step widened the fissure in his neck. One two one two one two. The floorboards in the bedroom rumbled. On the other side of the equation were those in Gideon's camp. The estate agents. It was unlikely that Harmsworth-Mallett or the American would know much, but then there was Daisy. Daisy certainly knew where Gideon was. He picked up the phone on Imogen's bedside table.

'Hello, er, Toby?' Hesitant, a woman's voice he couldn't place. The bath was running upstairs. 'Sorry to ring so early. It's, er, Eileen.'

'Hello, er, Eileen.'

'Hello.' An uncomfortable laugh. 'Is Imogen there?'

What kind of a question was that?

'She's in the bath.'

'Oh... Um... Sorry. Don't interrupt her. I was just wondering whether she wanted to go for a walk on the heath, er, later on today?' Anxious to have made her thought public like that, breath squeezed from lungs crushed under a good 18 inches of flesh.

'Well, let's see. Imogen. Do you want to go for a walk on the heath, er, later on today?' Toby to the window, curtains half drawn. It had never occurred to him that the Hill could walk. 'She doesn't. No. Sorry.'

'Oh'. The word hung somewhere above Camden as though awaiting a reprieve.

'I'm sorry Eileen. No is her final answer.'

'Right.' Eileen rallied herself.

Toby as a kindly afterthought: 'Actually she's not well. In fact we think she's got TB.' Toby replaced the receiver and on his way upstairs wondered how Eileen might look in the bath. Not a lot of room for water.

He turned off the taps and undid his trousers. They puddled around his ankles. He trod first on one leg, tearing it over his boot, and then on the other. He sat on the bath and took a deep breath before bending to tackle his boots and socks. Odd socks he noted as he sank his body into the water. The question was how to get Daisy on side. As the warmth lapped around his exhausted body it seared his knee and soothed his mind. He saw without much interest that he was still wearing his underpants. With a blue-white toe he turned the hot tap. The key was to get that girl to talk. There was a rumble on the short flight of steps leading up to the bathroom. Coarse and arrogant, Rita, tail twitching, stood in the doorway. The answer had presented itself. Everyone knows that the way to a woman's heart is through a cat. Especially through an ugly pig-dog cat from Battersea Dogs Home. Oh Poor Sweet Kitty Where Are Your Teeth? Toby closed his eyes and wondered what to pack.

The cat was standing against the front door when he came down. It took a disdainful look at Toby and turned away to press one side of its face across the wooden panelling as it walked the door's width. At the hinge it turned neatly to work its way back, drawing the other side of its face across. The cat's eyes were half closed, the white tip of its upright tail flicked with pleasure. Toby watched the animal make four delirious sweeps. He crouched low and stretched out his arms, his palms touching easily the wall on each side of the corridor. Crab-like he made his approach, his breathing hoarse. The cat had stopped and appeared to be listening, ear pressed, to something on the other side of the door. Its eyes were still half closed, as though in ecstasy. Its tail, however, had thickened and was entirely still.

The cat was grotesque. Although they'd lived together for a year, he'd never noticed its size. It sickened him. However, it was the animal's eyes that made Toby stop. The cat turned its broad head, its orange ears pressed against its skull and its eyes gleaming flat with dislike. Slowly the cat raised its chin and opened black lips. Lazy half-closed eyes fixed Toby as the animal unhinged its jaw to show Toby the full horror of its mouth: seven ridged circles of hell guarded by empty, rotten gums. It occurred to Toby that he might crush its skull against the door.

In the instant that he sprang, the cat leapt and crashed into his face, its bullet head bowling into his eye socket. Toby fell backwards and by the time he hit the carpet, he could hear the distant flapping of the cat flap. He sat up to taste blood. He'd bitten the inside of his cheek but it was his eye that ached. He found that he was unable to open it. It felt wet with blood. The cat was long gone.

The queue outside 'Steve's Nest' was even longer than usual. And Toby, in a considerable degree of pain, took his place. His neck was frozen to the left; to look straight ahead caused something significantly greater than discomfort and anything further to the right was entirely out of the question. The pain in his knee was excruciating and the vision in his right eye dim where the cat had collided with him. Late for work, there had been little option but to leave without the animal. In other departments he'd done better; at his feet beside his briefcase stood a smart, tightly packed blue weekend bag. He'd discovered it under the kitchen table. On unzipping it, a yellow plastic snorkel and mask had sprung out and beneath them, folded clothes – blue and white shorts he hadn't worn for several summers, a red tropical shirt Imogen had given him and some other holiday items with which he was only vaguely familiar. The universe seemed decided that he was going on holiday so he'd inserted the cocaine inside the snorkel, and inside the matching mask he'd secured his passport, the Euros, the remaining twenty-pound notes and as an afterthought on his way out, Howie's mobile phone. Whoever had packed for him had chosen an extraordinary selection of clothes. A selection not entirely suited to skiing.

Steve was not having a better day.

'Like I said, mate,' tapping a meat cleaver on the steel counter, 'no cappuccino.'

Discontent rippled down the queue. A women in lilac turned and left.

'Yep?' Steve, eyes drooping with tiredness, held out the meat cleaver smeared with crumbs and the blood of something animal. The nozzle of the cappuccino machine was clogged yellow. Toby wondered whether he might need stitches on his knee, a steak for the eye and a turn in traction for his neck.

'Cappuccino. Two granary toast with Marmite please.'

'No cappuccino.' Steve tapped the knife on the counter.

'Where's the cappuccino girl?' Toby's attempt to raise an arm to indicate the coffee machine failed. Pain seared his neck.

'Bulgaria,' said Steve, eyes dull, cleaver glinting. A boil had emerged on the side of his nose, distending and reddening the feature. 'Just the toast or a hot drink with that?' He jabbed a knife down into the Marmite pot. It seemed that he, like Toby, was in need of a holiday.

'Is she coming back?'

Steve ignored him. The coffee was without a lid and showed a clear yellow film floating on the surface. Toby left it on the counter; it would have hurt too much to reach up to to take it.

Dirty clouds hung low over Kentish Town. Toby stood on the platform and took a deep breath. Marmalade. There was the definite scent of marmalade on the air. Marmalade and foreboding. His briefcase stood upright between brown Blundstone boots and beside it the travelling bag. The round face of last night's police officer floated into his mind to remind him that he'd dreamt of her. A night filled with kindly police officers: Hello Toby Doubt! A solemn man with a moustache. Sit here Mr Doubt. A kindly white-haired officer at a bare table. 'Sorry Mr Doubt. Just a formality.' A lot of forms and a lot of inconsequential questions: 'Won't take a moment.' A gentle hand on his shoulder. A cup of sweet tea in his hand. Date of Birth? Address? Next of kin? Imogen in another room. 'You can't come in here, sir.' And then Howard. Howard with his hooded top, his retro trainers and a bag he wears diagonally across his chest. Grim-faced Howard, his arm around Toby. As usual, he's right at the heart of things.

From somewhere at Toby's feet a mobile phone rang. He unzipped the bag and the screen on the silver mobile flashed orange. Howard it said. Howard calling.

'Howard.'

'You got the phone then.'

'I got the phone.'

A soft laugh. 'The last man in England to use a mobile phone.'

Funny.

'How are you?'

'Good.'

'How is Stella?'

'Good.'

'That must have been strange seeing her after so long. How was she?'

'Good.'

'Same as ever?'

'Same as ever.' Cambridge's fifteen-year-old carnival queen. Perfect.

'Listen mate, I never really apologized for Stella.'

It was true. Howard had never apologized at all in any way for Stella.

But then Howard had never known that Toby had seen him with Stella from the top of the big wheel until a couple of days ago. Still, it was true, he'd never really apologized.

'What are you up to?' He hadn't apologized then and it didn't look as though he was going to apologize now.

I'm on my way to France to find Imogen, kill the boyfriend and bring her back. 'Up to? Oh. Not a lot.'

'Same. Do you want to meet up?'

Same. Same. Same old Howie. What was it that had arrested Howie's development? He'd always maintained that the seminal occurrence in his life had been Mrs Jenkins, Parson's Corner and the see-through tights.

'I can't really.'

'Why, what are you up to?' The roar of traffic somewhere.

You know. No good. A bit of mischief. 'Howard. I was wondering if you might know Imogen's address in France?'

'What address in France?'

'Skiing? Where she's staying?'

'What do you mean?'

'It's fairly straightforward, Howard. Do you have the address?'

'Address, Toby? What address?'

'Don't worry about it. Do you have Saffron's number?'

'Toby?'

'Saffron's number?'

'Jane will have it. I'll get it to you.'

I'll get it to you, as though it was a vital document to be couriered across the capital in need of a signature.

'Toby. I need to talk to you. Today, tonight, I need to come round.'

'Talk? About what?'

'About you, me, life, Imogen. About Friday, about the weekend, about you.'

'Oh?'

'Yes, Toby, yes.'

'Sounds important.'

There was silence and then Howard said: 'I need to see you.'

'I'm going away.'

'Where?'

'Don't worry about it. I'll call you.' Toby pressed the red button on the phone and returned it to the bag. It seemed Howard felt guilty about something. He saw that blood was seeping through the knee of his clean-on canary-coloured trousers. Custard-cream corduroys given to him by Imogen's parents for Christmas, along with a book entitled The Seven Habits of Highly Effective People. Anne had not been up to shopping. And the Colonel being Someone Important in the Army had never been up to shopping. Someone else had been dispatched to shop. The Cyclops? Cassie? That was the year that Imogen received for Christmas from her parents a black Baby Doll Nightgown Ensemble – see-through nightie, see-through dressing gown and black stilettos all trimmed in black ostrich feathers. 'Hurry up with that Toby Stout,' says Imogen, clacking through the kitchen, feathers flailing, holding a wooden spoon. Toby in his too-tight cords unable to get the zip up is sitting on the counter grating cheese to Imogen's specification. He's not sure what he thinks of this – particularly the clacking shoes – and her mother dead just two days.

At least the trousers fitted now. 'Hey,' Toby announced. 'Not so stout now.' He turned his body through 180 degrees until his fused neck was aligned with the bridge and with Frederick Street. The house loomed into sight. It seemed different today. A different house for a different day. 'Hey,' he announced, 'same jacket, new trousers.' 'Nice one,' it seemed to say. 'Nice one, Toby Doubt.' A flat square face loomed at the first-floor window, grim with ginger intent. Watching him on the platform, waiting until he'd gone. Rita. He wondered about going back for it but a train clattered into the station and Toby Doubt, already late, had other matters to attend to.

At Farringdon his bench was occupied by a man in a beige mac. As Toby sat waiting for the Circle Line tube, his bleeding leg stretched straight out in front of him, he saw that the man's feet did not touch the platform. Smooth grey shoes swung inches above it. Perhaps unsettled by the angle of Toby's leg, his face, or the blood at his knee, the man rocked, feet swinging, up the bench away from him. Again the mobile phone rang. The pain caught his breath as he bent to retrieve it.

Through the crackle of poor reception and a roar which suggested the runway at Heathrow: 'It's Saffron.'

'Hello Saffron.'

Words broken by the scream of aircraft taking off.

'Toby.'

'You're at the airport.' On her way to France.

'Toby,' another jumbo took off, 'do you believe in God?'

'What?' Toby blinked at an image of Saffron crossing the tarmac in a padded, zip-up suit, skis over her shoulder.

'Do-you-believe-in-God?'

Toby who required information without alerting suspicions, said 'Yes.'

'I've had a totally religious experience, man!' She sounded excited, her voice mock-Californian and high pitched. 'I don't know what it means,' her voice returned to normal, 'but I dreamt last night,' her words were broken by the roar of something supersonic, 'that Imogen and you and me and someone else I don't know who it was were sitting on the heath, in that place, you know, where we had that picnic with the kite and we were all sitting there and I think it was someone's birthday, Imogen's maybe, and she turned to me and she had this beautiful smile on her face. I can't describe it. Radiant. And just so well ray-dee-ant!' Saffron laughed. 'And behind her was this amazing rainbow that filled the sky and stretched from one end...'

'Saffron.' Toby tried to keep his tone light. 'Where are you flying to?'

A giggle, a hiccup. 'I'm not flying to anywhere. I'm at Haymarket.

On my way to the clinic.'

The roar as a plane took off.

'Toby? I had to speak to you to tell you everything is OK. Imogen is OK. And I love you and life is beautiful.' Again she laughed. 'Alright?'

'Alright.' Said Toby.

'I love you and she loves you and we love you and I love you.' It sounded as though Saffron was crying. 'Oh God, Tobe I love you and I'll see you later.'

'See you later,' Toby echoed.

He placed the phone in the bag face down. Saffron, now muffled, said her goodbyes unobtrusively into the Hawaiian shirt and folded shorts for a few moments before there was silence. Toby's knee hurt. It throbbed with pain. Tears pricked his eyelids. His neck hurt.

Again the phone rang. This time it was Howard.

'Did Saffron get you?' The pair were clearly working in tandem. The best course of action, decided Toby, was to play along until he'd got the measure of this game. 'Good. Now we're coming round tonight. Saffron, Jane and me. So stop all this bollocks about going away.'

'Saffron called to tell me that Imogen loves me,' said Toby.

There was a pause and then Howard: 'Of course she loves you.' He didn't sound as though he believed it.

Toby didn't believe it either.

'Of course she loves you,' repeated Howard wearily as though worn out by Toby and Imogen. 'I'll see you later, mate.' Toby replaced the phone.

So Imogen was Saffron's best friend as Howard was probably Toby's — if men have best friends — as he had been since the day he came to Nareswood and chose to sit next to him. Close by a school bell tolled. The end of break. Time to file back inside. On the other hand had Howard actually chosen to sit next to Toby or was it that the seat next to his was the only one in the whole of 2Y without an occupant? Not that Toby was the least popular boy in the class. It was just that the most unpopular boys, Stuart Hobbs (covered in a crust of eczema) and Gypo (from the Three Hills Estate) sat next to each other. When Howard came, Toby's popularity improved thanks to the fact that Howard's stepfather was manager at the Picture Palace which meant that Toby and Howard were twelve when they saw *Night of the Living Dead*.

The bell tolled more loudly. A man was making his way gravely down the steps, each footfall marked by a toll of the bell he held. A slow, deep, school yard toll. And Toby smells creosote.

He looks down to see a white concave chest and below that the blue trunks that his mother got him with the in-built red belt. He hears the click of their red plastic clasp and acknowledges the truth that before Howard came to Nareswood, Toby had not been so happy at school. Ron they call him, as in Ronald McDonald. Or Tardo as in Bastard because he doesn't have a dad. But on Wednesdays when it's swimming it's Superman, thanks to those trunks. He's in a dark hut with nine other boys. Eight actually. Stuart Hobbs, on account of the eczema, is not allowed to swim. The last time he swam they had to drain the pool.

The boys are wet and wrestling to get their clothes on. It's Poetry next and Mr Root is keen on punctuality. 'Quinquireme of Nineveh from distant Ophir,' says Robert Ashcroft, head thrown back, hand outstretched. 'Rowing home to haven in sunny Palestine.' Someone gives his towel a tug. It's on the floor and Simon Bevan's up on the bench flicking his own towel.

'Gay boy,' says Robert Ashcroft struggling to cover his flapping cock.

Short white socks and neat black shoes clip past in the strip of sunlight beneath the dark wood of the changing room. The girls are already dressed. 'Salty Spanish galleon coming from the Isthmus.'

'Stately,' one of them corrects. It sounds like Louise Pipe.

Toby's towel is small and wet and the bell is getting louder and the only verse he's got down is the last. Dirty British coaster with a salt-caked smoke stack. Butting through the channel in the mad March days. It's been going through his head faster and faster since he got on the bus this morning. With a cargo of Tyne coal, Road rail, pig lead. And still the bell sounds. Firewood, iron-ware and cheap tin trays. He's not sure he can keep it in any longer.

Dirty British coaster with a salt-caked smoke stack. He fits one line with each sound of the bell. Butting through the channel in the mad March days. Boys struggle into shoes, pull bags off hooks. Simon Bevan's first out the door, stuffing a bright seaside towel into his drawstring bag. 'Last one there is a gay lord.' With a cargo of Tyne coal, Road rail, pig lead. 'That's you Superman.' And still the bell tolls. Firewood, iron-ware and cheap tin trays. He grabs his towel and runs. His shoes aren't done up. He tears out into sunlight, water flicking from his hair. And there ahead of him on the path is Chloe March. She walks delicately, feet pointed outwards, neck poised and her dry hair swinging in a high pony tail. Quinquireme of Nineveh from distant Ophir. Toby knows that Chloe March is out of his league. Why doesn't he see, two decades later, that so is Imogen Green? Toby Doubt, Superman, a hollow-chested impostor. He cannot bring himself to overtake Chloe March. He follows her last into the classroom and is made to stand alone at his desk. Red-faced he stutters to recite the only part of the poem he knows, blood pounding in his ears. At the front stands Mr Root. He's ready to blow. Between him and Toby a class of half-turned apple-faced, delighted students.

The man with the bell was making slow progress along the platform. 'Ask and you shall receive,' read uneven black letters across the board at his chest. Larger men shrank behind their newspapers. Ask and you shall receive.

'It sounds like good advice,' Toby told the man in the pale raincoat at the other end of the bench, who did not look up from the newspaper he held to his face.

Well, well. Ours is not to reason why. Toby smiled as Harmsworth-Mallett's voice, rasping and tremulous filled his head.

It was raining at South Kensington. Grey slices of rain sluiced on to the slick pavement. Pedestrians under umbrellas waited to cross. There was a collective movement backwards as a green van, Eden's Horticulture, veered around the corner spraying black water on to the pavement and a collective surge forward as the lights turned red and the traffic stopped. Toby was soaked when he arrived at Milson, Range & Rafter.

'Hey Hey Hey,' Harmsworth-Mallett was coming out of the office. He held the door open and with his free hand clapped Toby on the back. Toby's neck cracked. 'Thought we'd lost you old boy. Cappuccino?'

An exotic pink flower bloomed beside Daisy's ear. Her desk was entirely submerged under paper. She was folding letters and coaxing them into envelopes.

'Daisy?'

She looked up, astounded at being interrupted, hand frozen, fingers inside an envelope.

Toby swallowed, 'I wondered if you liked cats.' Her fingers didn't move. She looked incredulous.

'You wondered like…' shaking her head, 'what?'

'It doesn't matter. I need,' said Toby, 'to fly out to meet Gideon this afternoon.' He looked at his wrist as though consulting a watch.

Daisy, eyes blank and British seaside grey, blinked slowly. The flower behind her ear quivered.

'So?' Slowly she withdrew her fingers from the envelope and brought it to her mouth. Her tongue, pink and muscular, lapped at it. She pressed it closed on the desk in front of her. Ask and you shall receive.

'So. I need you to direct me to his hotel, book me on a flight.' Daisy put down the letter and laughed. Her cheeks flushed. 'Did you think I was like your secretary?' She sat still, her lips parted to show two white teeth.

Toby nodded.

Daisy laughed. She picked up another letter. Suddenly she dropped it, pushed back her chair, stood up and came around her desk pushing past him and out on to the street.

Chuck, tracing the trickle of raindrops on the window with his finger, was muttering angrily into his mobile. The phones screeched out across the office. Toby picked up Daisy's phone. It smelt of Parma violets and shampoo.

'Hello, this is Stavros Dukakis. I saw 15 Kings Reach with you guys last week. I need to see this place again. I'm ten minutes away. Can you run me down there now?'

Chuck's cheeks shone bluish like fine fillet steak as he pressed his mobile to his ear.

'Can you do it?' The voice on the phone was impatient. 'Look. Let me make this simple for you. I intend to buy this apartment. Can you do it yes or no?'

'Yes,' said Toby. The phone in his holiday bag was ringing. He picked up the bag and made his way to his desk. On a square pad of Post-Its he wrote: Gideon. Then he wrote: Stavros, 15 Kings Reach, 10 mins. And then he wondered why everyone was so hostile. Imogen would know. Toby, she'd say. Hun she'd say. She'd sit on his knee and twirl a finger round one of his curls. 'It's not you, Tobe.' She'd tug the curl and kiss his eye. 'It's just one of those days.' He'd scowl at her, he'd jerk away from her hand. 'You know I hate it when you pull my hair.' He wouldn't let her know how much he needed to hear those words.

The phones rang again. He picked up the receiver on his desk. It was dead and the phones rang on. Chuck gestured from his desk: a meaty arm jabbing the air. Toby hobbled to the desk in front of Chuck's. The empty desk with the ringing phone, the desk that belonged to Gideon Chancelight.

'Milson, Range & Rafter.'

'Yes, this is Sergeant. Do you have any news on the St James's Park Tower?'

'No news.'

Toby replaced the receiver and his hand found its way to the cool handle of the drawer in the front of the desk. The place where Americans keep a revolver. The door buzzed and Harmsworth-Mallett appeared with a pyramid of coffee. Toby made it back to his desk ahead of the old man who delivered to Chuck from his precarious balance of refreshments. Chuck turned to him, wild-eyed, ranting into his mobile.

'How can we be expected to have any kind of conversation when you behave like this? Thank you,' as he took a coffee.

Harmsworth-Mallett came on to Toby. He put two white cups, several sachets of sugar and a croissant on a paper plate down on the desk. He raised two hands in surrender.

'You don't write you don't call,' blink blink smile smile. 'Good one last night was it? Good grief whatever happened to your face?'

Toby felt with tentative fingers the swollen area around his eye. 'Rita.'

'Rita? A lady friend gave you a black eye? Well I never.'

'A cat,' said Toby.

Harmsworth-Mallett peeled the lid off his coffee and blew on the dirty scum on its surface. He took a sip and looked heavenward. He tapped the back of Toby's chair. 'Now it seems that, er,' he looked back at the door and lowered his voice, 'that there might have been a little misunderstanding with Daisy. She, er, just to keep you abreast,' he cleared his throat, 'likes to be known as the office manager. Anyway,' he took a sip of coffee. 'Not to worry... weren't to know. Little chat over etcetera, now... onwards and upwards. Ready for some action?'

On account of his neck, Toby's face was locked in Harmsworth-Mallett's direction which the old man seemed to take as an inclination to chat. With a sigh he settled himself on the edge of the desk.

'Shayle Nugent wasn't it?' Another noisy sip. 'Used to work with Peter Shayle. This is going back, oh, donkeys now. I'll bet you didn't know that? Did alright for himself didn't he? Don't suppose he's in much these days Peter Shayle eh? Everything that boy touched turned to gold. Well I say boy... Ha ha... What is he... Late forties now? Early fifties? Still a Hampstead man?' Mallett's face was flecked red with drink. He was drunk now. The drunk in the bar who'll talk to anyone.

'Some you win... some you lose. That man won... and won and won. A natural.' He shook his head and then blew on his coffee. 'A natural like our man over here,' he nodded towards the front of the office. 'Only time I've seen that kind of talent since. Closure. That's what it's all about, closure. Shayle had it, our man Chancelight's got it. Or had it... don't know what's been happening recently. Now you come to mention it's been a quiet couple of months for old Chancelight. Winning streak over? Or just resting?' The old man laughed. 'Watch this space. But the wild card in the pack is Dote. Does Dote have it?' He looked out into the street. The rain was falling steadily and showed no sign of easing. 'Nice weather... for rats.'

Toby laughed and when he felt he had the old man's attention said, 'I need to fly out to France this afternoon to see Gideon.'

Harmsworth-Mallett blinked and blew on his coffee. He took a sip. 'Gracious.'

'The trouble is,' said Toby, 'I'm not sure where exactly he is in France.' A laugh, inspiring what he hoped was confidence. 'I don't even have the name of his hotel.'

'Don't you worry yourself about our Mr Chancelight.' Harmsworth-Mallett took another sip, loud and hot. 'We've all to make our own way in this life.'

The old man's hand, pale and crooked, moved across clumsily to touch Toby's. Toby straightened his fingers and flattened his palm against the green leather of the desk.

'Unfortunately it can't wait.'

'Goodness.' Harmsworth-Mallett's hand, dry and warm, pressed down on Toby's for a moment and then fluttered back to his cup. 'About a property is it? The secret to this game, Mr Dote,' Harmsworth-Mallett lowered his voice to a whisper 'is that nothing is that urgent. Although we like to keep this from the other side...' he thumbed a bobbing umbrella outside the window, 'there is actually very little that can't wait.'

'Actually it's about a mutual friend.'

'A mutual friend. Lovely,' Harmsworth-Mallett smiled. 'I had one of those once – lovely man – lovely that is until I found out he was stepping out with the wife. You know how it is,' he turned to Toby. 'Gave him one of those actually,' indicating Toby's swollen eye. He turned back to the rain on the wind beyond the window. 'And so on and so forth... I say, you're not stepping out with a gentleman's wife are you?'

'I'm not, no.'

The paper on the desk in front of Toby read Stavros. 15 Kings Reach. 10 mins.

'I'm afraid I've messed up, I forgot the car.'

'Forgot the car? Well I never, that really is a first.' Harmsworth-Mallett put his head back and rocked his body laughing gently. It became a cough and he turned away. 'Forgot which car?'

'The car you lent me. Forgot to bring it back.'

'The car I lent you? So where is it? Sold it have you?' When he'd recovered his breath. 'Get a good price for it did you?'

'I've got an appointment at Kings Reach.'

'Lovely place that one. Views down the river as far as Putney. Lovely place. It would look good even in this. That's the kind of place that flies off the proverbial, as it were. Who else has got it? Kemp's is it? You'd do well to check with them it hasn't gone. If it hasn't then I would say you've got a very good chance with that one. A very good chance indeed. A hot cake. Yes indeed.'

Toby felt a bubble of laughter rise from his stomach. It stopped at his chest. He pressed in an attempt to move it on. It stayed where it was, a hot, tight knot.

'I'll tell you what, we'll have a little drink at lunch to celebrate Dote's first sale at Range Rafter.' Harmsworth-Mallett used both hands to trace a banner in the air. 'Drinks on Dote! That's right… marvellous.'

Coffee sloshed on to the desk. 'Buggeration.' The old man felt in his pocket and brought out a pack of tissues. 'Moistened for Your Comfort' they declared in a curl of writing. 'Buggeration,' Mallett repeated, pulling out a tissue with tremulous hands. He polished the desk, his tie dangling limp in front of him. 'So to recapitulate, Dote. You have an appointment at Kings Reach for which you do not have ready transportation.'

'Correct. The car's outside my house in Kentish Town.'

'Kentish Town?' Harmsworth-Mallett replaced the lid on his coffee. 'Kentish Town? What good is that to man or beast? So how are you intending on getting down there?'

'Bus?'

'Bus! You are a card. I'll tell you what. I'll run you down in the Merc.' He stood, rummaged in his pocket and pulled out a set of keys which he threw up and snatched from the air. 'We'll make a morning of it. Be good to see the place.'

The phone rang. Harmsworth-Mallett picked it up. 'Shayle Nugent. I am begging your pardon. Ha ha. Shayle Nugent! I worked there some time ago! Apologies for that. Fast forward about three decades. Milson, Range & Rafter. Hello? Hello? Milson, Range & Rafter?' He looked at the receiver quizzically then held it to his ear. The phones rang on.

Toby limped to Gideon's desk. His knee was seizing up. Chuck, slumped across his desk, moaned slightly. The phone stopped as Toby reached for it.

'Schoolboy error' called Harmsworth-Mallett. 'Never miss a phone call. Miss it and they'll be on to Kemp or Watford or even Shayle Nugent to spend all that lovely lolly. It's fingers on buzzers in this game.' He frowned and picked up Toby's phone. 'I remember when my name was above that door: Milson, Mallett, Rafter it read out there. I'll tell you the story one day if you're interested. I'll tell you about two unscrupulous men named Milson and Rafter who sold old Mallett down the river. I'll tell you about it.' He brought his gaze back from the road outside the window to listen intently into Toby's receiver. 'Your lifeline to the out-side world appears to have been severed. Chuck?' The American didn't move. 'I say, you don't suspect sabotage do you?' His voice became a chuckle which turned to a cough which in turn caused more coffee to spill on Toby's desk. 'I'll get our office manager,' he accentuated the words as though showing Toby how to use them, 'on to it.' He glanced in the direction of Daisy's desk and brightened. 'It's all good fun. For now you can use Mr Chancelight's desk.'

He shuffled up the office and Toby, picking up his briefcase, the hol-iday bag and his cappuccino, followed him: promotion to the desk which stood behind Harmsworth Mallett's own.

'Some say,' said Harmsworth-Mallett with a wink, 'that this is the luckiest desk in the office. Isn't that right, Chuck?'

'Oh brother,' said Chuck, rolling his forehead on the desk.

'Ice to Eskimos,' said Harmsworth-Mallett. He extracted cigarettes from his inside pocket and made his way outside.

Toby sat down. He ran his hands along the desk's leather top. He reached his arms as far as he could and felt the corners furthest from him. He brought his hands down the sides to the near corners. They met at the brass handle of the drawer. He tugged it gently and looked up.

'That's Gid's desk,' said Daisy sharply.

'Ice to Eskimos,' muttered Toby. The hands that touched this handle also touched Imogen.

Daisy, her green skirt seething about her knees, went out to join Mallett. Lodged sideways in the drawer was a heavy black diary. First things first. Besides the book, smaller items in the drawer demanded attention: some pens, a cigarette lighter, a checked handkerchief and a folded square of paper. The lighter showed a woman at the seaside, kneeling on the sand, polka-dot bikini, 1950s breasts, chipped yellow hair piled on top of her head. Along the shoreline it read: 'St Ives'. He unfolded the paper. 'Shawna L. After 4 p.m.' and a phone number. The handkerchief revealed itself as a pair of boxer shorts. The diary was largely empty. Today, Tuesday 8 June, was blank. As was Saturday 5 May (Skiing. France. Imogen). He carried on flicking through it. May, April, March. There was only one entry in the whole book. Under 28 January, in green writing, was written 'My Birthday'. On the inside front cover it said 'Gideon Chancelight. 258 Brompton Road, London'. Toby made a note of the address and the telephone number beneath it. He put it in his pocket. He turned the pages to 10 March. There was no mention of Imogen's thirtieth birthday. Of Toby in the kitchen watching her thin lettuces. The diary made no mention of the tiny rejected threads of leaf laid out like blind rabbits on crazy paving in the weak spring sun. It also made no mention of the ice-blue ring: his giving it, her taking it. He slid the diary back and tried the other drawers. Apart from another pair of boxer shorts and two paperclips, they were empty. He picked up the phone to dial Gideon's number. A dog's howl pierced the office. With some effort he turned. Through impaired vision he made out Chuck, bright red, face scrumpled into a grimace. He was rocking his desk vigorously on its legs. The brass handles rattled against the wood.

'No goddamn sale for three goddamn months. A baby due in six weeks. And now a fucking divorce,' he roared though furious white lips. His hands relaxed and his face hit the desk with a wet slap. His breathing was now coming in sobs. Toby turned back to the phone.

The door buzzed to admit a stocky man, a squat Greek in a navy jacket with shiny brass buttons and buttercup cords as yellow as Toby's own. Toby dialled the number. 'You've reached Gideon Chancelight. Please leave a message and I'll get back to you.'

A confident voice assured that a long succession of deserved happinesses were on their way.

Toby watched as the man shook his umbrella over Harmsworth-Mallett's desk. He flicked his hair, frowned and looked impatiently down the office. Toby held up a finger in what he hoped would signify a request for patience and redialled Gideon's number. 'You've reached Gideon Chancelight. Please leave a message and I'll get back to you.' Blood burned in Toby's cheeks. He replaced the receiver and regarded his hand where it still gripped it. Spidery and freckled, the knuckles showed white. A badly cast B-movie villain against whom the tide has turned. He released the phone, stood and limped towards the door.

'Mr Dukakis?'

Stavros glanced at the heavy watch on his wrist before shaking Toby's hand. A flash of tooth as he turned to push the heavy glass door. 'That's me.'

'Keys.' Toby stood for a moment, soothed by the patter of rain on the roof of the office. Chuck's head was on his desk. It seemed best not to disturb him. Outside there was no sign of Daisy or Mallett.

Stavros pushed at the door irritably and looked at his watch again. 'C'mon man. Busy, busy, busy.'

Toby moved sideways behind Daisy's desk and opened the flat metal cabinet on the wall. Six rows of keys jangled.

'C'mon man. Kings Reach. I want to buy this apartment. Understand? Jesus,' he shook his head and rattled his umbrella, 'it's a wonder you guys sell anything.'

It seemed best, given the circumstances, to let that go. Toby bent to open the top drawer of Daisy's desk – near the surface floated a Polaroid photograph of a smiling Daisy, a shrunken Harmsworth-Mallett and a dark-skinned man in a dark suit with glossy black hair and a smile as white as bone. Gideon Chancelight.

A loud sigh from Stavros and the impatient tapping of his umbrella on the floor brought Toby back to the problem of the keys. Toby put the photograph into his inside pocket. Stavros was examining the American who was now rolling his head from side to side and moaning slightly. The door buzzed and Daisy stood just inside until Stavros realized he was in the way. He moved and her 'thank you' demonstrated clearly that no thanks were meant. Then she saw Toby.

'What are you doing?'

'Looking for keys.'

'What keys?' Twin spots of anger appeared on her cheeks.

'The keys to Kings Reach.'

Daisy waited for him to come out from behind her desk. 'They were never going to be in my drawer.' Without meeting Toby's eye she pulled a piece of paper from behind the cabinet, scanned it and turned holding out a set of keys. 'Like what kind of a prat are you?'

Stavros stood in the doorway putting up his umbrella, his lip curled into something like a smirk. 'Which way?' Again he looked at his watch.

Harmsworth-Mallett was under the awning of the delicatessen. He acknowledged Toby with a nod and tossed the remainder of his cigarette into the gutter. He splashed across the road and into the office.

'At last we are going?' Stavros turned to go.

'My colleague is going to run us down there.' Toby gestured behind him and feeling the man's impatience wondered whether it was usual to inspire such hatred. It hadn't always been like this.

Stavros looked at his watch.

Toby reached inside his jacket to feel the corner of the photograph in his pocket and wondered whether Gideon inspired a similar sort of hatred. He could feel Stavros's gaze – and doubted it.

Harmsworth-Mallet was in the doorway now, struggling into an anorak. 'All set, all set. Look at this weather.' The old man led the way, his hands fluttering to straighten his coat, as the three advanced up Harrington Gardens. The old man, then Stavros and last Toby, who was considering what point there could be in continuing with his life.

The Mercedes was large and probably of the type described as 'executive'. Harmsworth-Mallett put his key in the lock of the boot.

'Locking mechanism's bust. This is the only way to unlock the blasted thing these days.'

Toby opened the passenger door for Stavros. The seat was reclined to horizontal and a strong wave of stale air rolled out, cigarette smoke melded with something more organic, alive even, or, at any rate, recently dead.

'Brollies?' asked Harmsworth-Mallett blinking beside the open boot and gesturing towards the Greek's umbrella. He didn't seem to hear. 'Alright then. Off we go.' He slammed it closed.

Tentatively Stavros got in, wrapping his coat further around him, perhaps for hygiene purposes. He looked with suspicion at the dashboard before reaching out a hand with which to support himself. His other hand held his umbrella, which he planted firmly between his feet.

Toby lowered himself into the back seat behind Harmsworth-Mallett where there was room for his legs.

Harmsworth-Mallett put on his seat belt. He cast a glance at his smartly dressed passenger. 'So, have you been looking long?'

'No,' said Stavros.

'Well, that's good news' said Mallett brightly. He wiped the inside of his windscreen with his sleeve.

Toby pushed a pair of beige socks, damp and worn, on to the floor. They joined a pile of what looked like dirty laundry and a large bottle, brown and empty. Drambuie.

Stavros sat scowling, uncomfortably upright, hand tense on the dashboard.

'I've never known a car go wrong so many times. Hopeless.' Mallett shook his head and still silence reigned. 'Cancer stick?' He took both hands off the wheel to arrange a packet of Silk Cut Extra Mild so that

two cigarettes protruded. 'So, am I to understand this is the first property you've seen?'

'No. I saw this one last week with you guys.' The irritated air of
having to tell this. 'Along with a couple of other places.'

'Same flat? Second viewing. Ah.' Mallett caught Toby's eye in the rear-
view mirror and winked.

'Was it our Gideon Chancelight who showed it? Black hair? Black
Porsche? Black heart? Ha ha. Or was it our large American colleague,
Chuck Lincoln?'

'It was the fat guy in the office. Asleep at his desk.' Stavros's eyes were
caught momentarily by a blonde head on the pavement. Toby was
pleased to note, as the car passed, that, from the other side, the blonde
was male with a thick ginger beard.

'That's our Chucky!'

They were on the King's Road now, the pavement thick with black
umbrellas. At World's End they turned off and headed down towards
the river. A redbrick staggered building loomed like a multistorey car
park at the bottom of the road.

'Kings Reach,' Harmsworth-Mallett announced as they rolled gently
over speed bumps towards it. 'Swimming pool, gym, sauna, 24-hour
security, off-street parking. Wouldn't mind a place here myself.' He
parked on new tarmac beneath a neat row of straight plane trees and
got out.

Stavros also climbed out, put up his umbrella and stood some distance from the car, regarding the monstrous ziggurat.

Toby's door wouldn't open. Harmsworth-Mallett stretched his legs
and seemed in no hurry to help. Stavros turned towards the car,
frowned and turned back. He started walking across the car park. Toby
tapped on the window. The old man made his way to a tree and
steadying himself, hand on trunk, reached into his pocket. He brought
out a mobile phone, squinted at it and put it back in his pocket. His
shoulders sagged and he shook his head. He looked up into the tree's

branches. Toby rapped on the window. The old man turned.

'Good God, man!' He shuffled around to open the door. 'What on earth are you doing in there?'

As Toby struggled to get out, Harmsworth-Mallett pointed to his leg. 'Old war wound?'

Toby looked down to where he indicated. Blood clotted the yellow corduroy at his knee. Toby nodded and Harmsworth-Mallett pinched the flesh on his upper arm.

'Closure,' he hissed and released Toby's arm to arrow his hands vigorously in front of him.

Toby limped across tarmac, through rain, to the glass-roofed entrance.

'Do your stuff, Dote,' echoed out across the car park behind him. Toby turned to see Harmsworth-Mallett back under the tree. He was holding up both fists and jabbing at the air, 'I smell a sale!'

Stavros was already at the lift. The security guard looked up as Toby came in. 'Can I help you?'

Toby stood in front of him. Unless the man had a gun, a return plane ticket to somewhere in France and an address for Imogen, he doubted it. 'Milson, Range & Rafter. For number fifteen.'

Stavros was standing impatiently, the tip of his umbrella lodged in the Call button of the open lift. The doors closed and Stavros exhaled, regarding himself in the mirror. He ran a finger over an eyebrow and turned to Toby. 'The key?' he said eventually.

The words hung in the stillness of the lift. Toby turned them over trying to make sense of them.

'The key, holy crap!' Pronouncing the word 'crep', the Greek snatched the keys from Toby's hand. He selected one and slid it into the lock marked 15 on a panel in the lift. He spent the ascent examining Toby in the mirror. Toby examined himself. His appearance was certainly unusual. His eye was bruised and swollen shut where the cat had knocked him down.

Finally the doors opened, flooding the lift with light. A mobile phone rang close by. They were in an empty room as large as a school hall with windows running the full length. Outside, silver skies swirled above the broad brown river. Stavros's footsteps grew distant on the pale wooden floor until he disappeared through a doorway. The mobile continued to ring. Toby realized it was his own and pulled it from his pocket.

'At last we speak. Toby, John Green here.' The Colonel humouring a cadet. 'How are you?'

'I'm well,' said Toby. 'To what do I owe this honour?'

A pause. Silence. 'Er, well.' The Colonel sounded embarrassed, lost for words even. Make the old man sweat a little. 'I'm telephoning about Friday.' There was a loud squawk followed by a shout of surprised pain and then: 'Bloody bird! Cassie. Catch that bloody bird!'

The Colonel came back on the line. 'Bloody parrot. I don't know why it's got it in for my head, the bloody savage has drawn blood. Toby… Oh Christ, I really am bleeding.'

Toby went to the window. Beneath him the Thames curled around a power station and disappeared west to Putney.

'I'll have to telephone you back.'

The other way, east, was Chelsea Bridge. Toby pushed the steel handle of the window, his thighs pressed against bricks. The disagreeable clack of footsteps heralded Stavros's return. He was holding a calculator in the palm of his hand.

'Asking price one two, correct?'

Toby nodded. He had enjoyed hearing Colonel John Green under attack.

'Any offers?'

Toby shook his head. Stavros examined him for a moment before striding back across the room and through the doorway. Toby leant out of the open window. The rain fell softly and the marshy smell of the river came up to him. Toby pictured the Colonel in disarray, his meticulous white comb-over hanging long and unruly over one ear, blood trickling down his soft pink cheek on to his starched white collar, the African parrot squawking from the curtain rail. Imogen shuddering with laughter with her mother behind her father's back. The Colonel blotting at his head with a fresh handkerchief.

A pleasure cruiser chugged past, its striped canvas covering a full ship of anoraked tourists who'd braved the rain. Its wake drew white diagonals in the milk-chocolate river.

'I don't know why he doesn't just cut it off. It's ridiculous,' says Imogen. 'It's not as if people don't know he's bald.'

'Ssssh,' says her mother, smiling as she puts plates on the table. 'Leave the old man alone.' She clocks her daughter lightly on the head with the last plate.

On the other shore a crane swung out across the water, a black hook dangling. The delayed sound of a ton of gravel being released reached the apartment.

Glass doors opened on to a terrace. Toby slid one across to imagine Imogen tending to her tubs. Would she like it here so far above the earth? He felt in his pocket and brought out the photograph. Harmsworth-Mallett red and drunk, Daisy laughing and looking up at the Spaniard: glossy, slick and insincere. Toby had seen that face before in Imogen's kitchen, before Frederick Street, amongst a collage of Imogen's friends from school.

'Service charge?' said Stavros pushing past Toby and putting up his umbrella.

Below them on the water two gulls bobbed backwards, dragged by the tide. They seemed resigned to their fate as together they grew smaller. The phone in Toby's hand rang.

'Sorry about that. Bloody parrot is out of control. I'm going to have the damn thing shot. Now, about Friday.'

Yes, Friday. Frotting and fucking and free time on Friday.

'I beg your pardon? Yes... well... good... OK...' The Colonel cleared his throat. 'I was wondering if there was anything you wanted to say?'

Toby was sure that there was but right now he was having trouble thinking what it might be. Perhaps it was that nothing gave Imogen more pleasure than when the parrot attacked her father.

'Good... well... think it over and let's touch base tomorrow.'

'OK,' said Toby.

'Good,' said the Colonel. 'Goodbye.'

'The service charge?' Stavros, tapping his foot, raised his chin.

Toby looked out across the river at the whispering silver trees on the other bank. 'There isn't one,' he said. The trees conferred and nodded in agreement.

'One million two hundred thousand?'

Toby nodded.

'I will offer the asking price on the condition that all viewings stop, right now. Understand? Can you telephone now?' Stavros was impatient.

Toby waited for Stavros to put down his umbrella and come back inside before sliding the glass door back across. 'I will call when I get back to the office.'

They drove in silence to Sloane Square. As they passed Peter Jones Stavros said: 'You let me know. Huh?'

Harmsworth-Mallett pulled up outside the tube. Stavros opened the door and got out. He turned once to mime making a phone call before disappearing through the barrier. Harmsworth-Mallett's eyes, watery and veined, sought Toby's in the rear-view.

'Well well' he pulled out, 'looks like there's a new kid on the block. Don't know how Mr Chancelight's going to take the news.' A chuckle then a cough.

Toby spread his hands across his yellow thighs. 'Gideon Chancelight,' he said.

'Skiing I believe, is Mr Chancelight.' Harmsworth-Mallett waited for a crocodile of boys holding hands – red blazers, grey caps, grey socks, unblemished knees – to cross.

'Yes,' said Toby.

'France, I'm told.' Harmsworth-Mallett waited for the last child to arrive safely on the pavement before moving off. He reached for his cigarettes and lit one. Hand on the steering wheel, smoke filled the car.

'Yes,' said Toby.

'Am I my brother's keeper?' The windscreen wipers dragged across the windscreen. 'Odd time of year to go skiing, I must say,' he continued. 'What are we now? June? Much snow in June is there? I wouldn't have thought so. Very odd time to go skiing. Our Greek friend left his brolly.' The old man patted his breast pocket. 'Don't know about you,' as he waited patiently, indicator pulsing, to turn into Harrington Gardens, 'but I could do with a drink.'

Toby followed Harmsworth-Mallett into the office. Daisy was at her desk. 'Chuck,' she indicated the deserted office with a thumb and smirked slightly, 'has taken a mental health break.'

'What on earth is that?'

'He's popped out for a couple of hours to deal with, like, his mental health?' The ring of Daisy's laughter filled the office as she used fingers to arrange speech marks around mental health.

'Shame. Well he's not going to like our news any better. Dote sold Kings Reach. In. Out. Wham, bam and thank you very much. Greek chap. One point two. That's ten grand in the bank, to you sir. Day two, very nice. Should keep the old wife in shoes.' Harmsworth-Mallett smoothed rain-damp hair. 'A mental health break eh? I've never heard of such a thing. Sounds American. Well, each of us has his cross to bear.'

'Oh and, er, Gids is back. He came in to give me this.' Daisy pointed at a teddy bear in a balaclava on skis which stood on her desk. She smiled down at the small knitted creature whose jumper read: 'A Present From Verbier'. 'He'll be in sometime, probably tomorrow.'

'Best get on to our man, see if he'll accept our Greek friend's offer.' Harmsworth-Mallett gave Toby's shoulder a friendly pat.

'By the way,' Daisy addressed Toby. 'Your phone's fixed. Gideon plugged it in for you. And Nigel? Can I have a word?'

If Gideon was back then Imogen was back and France would be a mistake. The animal-like pants of something close reached him. Toby turned. He was alone and the breathing was his own. Someone had moved his briefcase. No longer under Gideon's desk, it was now squarely on his own. The catches were open. He could see Daisy talking to Harmsworth-Mallett under the awning of the deli opposite. The old man was looking at the ground. The phone in Toby's pocket rang.

'Hello, just checking in.' It was Howard. Toby opened the case. The letter was still there, upright in its red silk pouch. 'Where are you?' Daisy, hand on hip, was directing frequent glances in his direction: psychopath with letters, photographs, murder on his mind. Harmsworth-Mallett kept his eyes fixed on the pavement. 'What time are you going to be home?'

'Early,' replied Toby. He felt it was time to be getting back to Frederick Street. Imogen would be needing some of her things. After all, he looked through the rain, the white dress was probably dirty by now and even if it wasn't, it was hardly suitable for this weather – knickers, shampoo, Wellingtons, her umbrella. Toby decided it would be for the best if he was there when she came by to collect.

He clicked the briefcase closed, reached for the holiday bag and left the office. Harmsworth-Mallett looked up from where he stood on the pavement. He saluted Toby briefly. Daisy glowered.

'Appointment,' called Toby to their twin troubled faces. 'And Daisy,' he continued, shouting across the road, 'I was wondering if you wouldn't mind calling in with our Greek friend's offer on Kings Reach.' The blonde's mouth opened, then closed. 'Thanks for that, be seeing you.' He pointed Stavros's umbrella momentarily in their direction and set off through the drizzle to the tube. He tried not to linger on the possibility that Imogen had cut short her trip because she'd realized the error she'd made in running off with the illiterate estate agent. Instead he envisaged Frederick Street: back door wide open, the garden destroyed and, littered with beer cans, cigarette ends and probably some cocaine debris.

The gate to Number 3 was open. The dustbin was on its side and rubbish strewed the front garden. Toby righted the bin and opened the door. Stale light slanted down from the landing on to the red carpet. The hoover roared upstairs across floorboards becoming muffled as it rode across the rug under the table. He leant against the door closing it firmly. I am away for just three days and the whole place is trashed. What are you like Toby? Suddenly there was silence.

'Imogen?'

'Hello?'

He took the stairs unsteadily and threw open the door, which fitted badly. ('Nothing to worry about, wear and tear, you will get that with houses that are 140 years old!')

'Imogen?'

A woman stood in the kitchen. The room smelt of furniture polish. Her dress was grey, she was tall and standing still, a screwed-up duster in her hand. An alien, his wife. Who was this woman? At her feet, Rita looked up from a bowl of milk, eyes dull with resentment. The cat blinked before re-curling its tail around its body and dipping its head back to the bowl.

'Hello, I am so happy that it is you.' Teeth prominent, voice guttural, the woman put a hand on her heart.

Toby did not feel the same. It was Frieda from Lithuania. He'd met her once before but everything he knew about her – which added up to the sum total of everything about which he could not care – came from Imogen. A law degree and a husband who made sandwiches in a factory somewhere near Old Street, and when they first arrived in this country, all of her hair fell out. It looked alright now. If you liked straight hair.

'I was so afraid,' she was laughing. 'These things…' she made jerking gestures with the duster. 'Your face!' she gasped and held her hand to her own eye.

'I thought you were Imogen.'

'Imogen?' She pronounced her name like Imagine. 'Imagine is in holidays in France I think.'

'Have you seen her today?'

'No.' Frieda wrinkled her forehead. 'For one week.' She held up a finger.

'Is she back yet?' Toby pointed at the floor to indicate here and now.

'Back yet? I do not think she is back yet until the weekend.' Rita, bored, stood and mewled up at Frieda. Frieda smiled down fondly until the cat resumed its milk-drinking. She looked again at Toby. 'I think something bad has happened. These things,' she pointed to Imogen's rosewood desk, 'are all over the floor.' She made round gestures in the air with the duster. 'And downstairs and in the bedroom…'

Toby hobbled upstairs. The bed was made and all the clothes picked up. Neat piles of Imogen's underwear plus the contents of her bedside table occupied the bed. He opened the wardrobe. It was all there, the clothes and shoes. But it was the black umbrella hanging from the door handle which told him what he needed to know: she had not been back yet.

Downstairs a spillage of spanners still littered the corridor. Outside, the garden was buried under wreckage. Empty cans scattered the table like fallen skittles, they rolled on the ground amongst the lettuces. The phone, curiously dry in the shelter of the umbrella, rang, as though it had been waiting all day for him to arrive.

'Toby, it's Mum.'

Hello Mum.

'Toby, I'd like to come down tomorrow and stay with you until

Friday,' a pause, 'if that's alright?' Toby wondered whether the meek would inherit the earth and if so, what they would do with it when they got it. 'If that's alright,' she repeated.

He told her that it wasn't, that he was on his way out of the door and that he would 'touch base' with her tomorrow in case there was 'anything she wanted to say'.

The effect was silence. A silence of which Toby took advantage to say goodbye.

Goodbye Alison Doubt. He felt in his pockets. Nothing but a thick purple wad of twenty-pound notes. His briefcase was at the front door. Mud tracked along the corridor could not be helped. He extracted Gideon's number which was stuck to a cold, square package of toast. On his way back to the garden the phone rang again. It was Cassie, Imogen's sister Cassandra.

'Oh you're there,' she said. 'Hi Toby. I was planning on leaving you a message. I thought you'd be at work. It's Cassie. Listen, this is such bad timing, incredibly bad timing but the man who bought Mummy's desk is coming by to collect it on Thursday. I'll come to help. Of course I wouldn't dream of letting a stranger loose in your house. Oh God it's such ghastly timing... '

'Whenever,' said Toby fingering the piece of paper with Gideon's number on it.

'OK great, I told Daddy I thought you'd be OK with it.' Dad, Dad, Daddy-oh!

He dialled the number. 'You've reached Gideon Chancelight. Please leave a message and I'll get back to you.' It was the pause between the 'and' and the 'I' which got to Toby. As though all the world was simple. And... I'll get back to you. A cocky smile, a cheeky dimple, a broken jaw. He took two unopened cans from the table and felt in his pocket for the car keys. He walked back through the house to the front door.

Hold on. Hold on. Not so fast Toby Doubt. Shouldn't there be a note in case she comes by to pick up some things saying that there's nothing to forgive, that he just wants her back? No pressure, just the simple truth? He was up the stairs and through the door before he'd had a chance to change his mind. Frieda jumped back guiltily from the cat which stood regarding him coldly. The pair stared at him. The intruder walked stiffly, trailing earth and lettuce leaves, hampered by the confusion of things in his arms: briefcase, yesterday's toast, the phone, two beers. He deposited his load on the table and took the 'Say No to the Greenwood Estate' paper from the rosewood roll-top desk and, conscious of Frieda and the cat, took an orange pencil and wrote: 'Imogen. I've missed you. Back soon. Toby.' Nothing came out. He turned the pencil in his hand until orange made contact with the paper and tried again. He put the note in the middle of the shining table.

'Downstairs,' said Frieda. 'The garden, what should I do there?'

'Leave downstairs. I'll do it,' said Toby. He took first his briefcase, then the beers, the toast, and the holiday bag from which the yellow snorkel protruded and hobbled awkwardly back downstairs. It hurt so much more going down. 'Imogen. I've missed you. Back soon. Toby.' It could have been written at any time. Last year, or yesterday. Or even on Saturday. Back upstairs, the cat and the witch were as he'd left them – frozen, plotting – and with the pencil that he found he was still holding he added 'Tuesday 3.pm.' to the note.

'Goodbye,' said Frieda. The cat was silent.

six

258 Brompton Road was not what Toby was expecting. For the residence of a Porsche-driving estate agent he had pictured something lofty, along the lines of Kings Reach. Somewhere offering river views, a 24-hour porter and an underground gymnasium. This house overlooked eight lanes of motorway traffic and Toby had driven past it twice at 60 miles per hour through relentless rain, his smashed knee grating above the brake, before managing to slow sufficiently to negotiate the narrow lay-by. His was the only car parked alongside the terrace of six shuddering houses and he the only sign of life besides the fringe of meadow grass which thrust from the eaves and swayed with the traffic. Curiously, at the other end of the lay-by, where it curved to turn back on to the motorway, there seemed to be a public telephone. The receiver was resting in the rain on a black bin-liner neatly knotted and bulging with rubbish.

It did not look like a place in which Imogen would thrive. Behind an oil-black film of carbon monoxide it seemed the windows of number 258 were mirrored. Though why Gideon would have gone to that trouble was anyone's guess; the black from the motorway was more than sufficient to prevent anyone from seeing in. The place was desperate. Toby imagined trying to sell it: 'When Chiswick was a meadow and this was the start of the Great West Road...' The Golf rocked violently as a fleet of lorries thundered past. He tried a different tack: 'Because of this motorway – I'm not saying it's not a blessing, don't get me wrong: Hampshire, Oxfordshire, Dorset, all so accessible – but because of it, the prices have come right down. I take the greatest pleasure in being able to offer you the best of both worlds and a million-pound home for a mere £299,000.' He got out of the car. The rain was softer now. Imogen, here, behind mirrored glass: the Colonel would have a stroke. The place would suit Rita though. Cat flap with direct access on to eight lanes of arterial road.

A light was on in a first-floor window. The bedroom? A lank curtain hung haphazardly across the strip of glass. Imogen would not like that. Imogen liked heavy curtains to block out every shard of light. At least that's what he'd thought, but then again what did Toby really know about Imogen? A scatter of taxi cards littered the doorstep. He pressed the bell. 'Oh hello there. Awful weather. Wondering if Imogen was about?' No sound came, no rumble of feet on the stairs. He pressed the bell again and pushed his ear against the door. The bell's trill died in the silence of an empty space. Perhaps they were 'doing lunch', getting their holiday photographs developed. Or perhaps they were in. Tucked up in bed. He pressed his ear harder against the wood. The house opened up to him – a cavern of silence. No rustle of sheets, no murmur of sex.

Back in the car he unfolded a neat envelope of cocaine. The paper opened to reveal more flesh: soft yellow breast as round as an apple and supporting a pale shiny nipple. He was pretty sure it matched the armpit of yesterday. It was larger and rounder than Imogen's breast, but pleasing nonetheless. He bent to the white powder. Despite the loss of half a can of Tennant's that had sprayed all over the dashboard and the inside of the windscreen and despite the eye-watering pain caused, somewhere near his left eyeball and back teeth, by a supersized white meteor, the drug was quick to take effect, and soon Toby was feeling more optimistic about pretty much everything. Various pains faded. The tight girders around his chest popped as he removed the paper with Gideon's number on it from one pocket and from another a pound coin. He picked a cheerful path through drizzle, avoiding puddles, and lifted the receiver of the public telephone from a soupy pond on top of the tied black bin bag. He shook water from it, brushed something – tomato skin? – from the receiver and held it to his ear. To his surprise he was rewarded with a tone. He dialled Gideon's number. It rang. 'Finally,' said Toby to a purple-necked wood pigeon that regarded him round-eyed from the shelter of a bush, 'something is going my way.'

On the fifth ring, Gideon answered. 'Hello?' His voice competed against the clatter of what sounded like lunch.

'Gideon Chancelight please.'

'Speaking.' This is he. For it is I. Speaking. The pigeon blinked a yellow eye.

And far away on the other side of the table, Imogen's laughter – ecstatic, carefree, expensive – rose above the clatter of fork on plate. 'Gideon speaking. Who is this?'

'Hal Blake here.'

'Yes?'

'I'm calling about Kings Reach, I was wondering whether you were at home.'

'What? Kings Reach? Home?' Gideon Chancelight struggling to make sense of a fairly straightforward sentence. Toby repeated it.

'I'm back in the office tomorrow. Give us a call then.'

'I'm afraid it can't wait. Can I meet up with you?'

'Look. Now's no good. I'm tied up right now.'

Imogen sniggering as she tightened the stockings around his wrists.

'Call me tomorrow in the office.' The phone went dead. The pigeon urged him to call back.

'Hello?' Gideon, terse. The same clatter of lunch.

'This is the Squire,' said Toby. 'Back from the dead and after your blood and you are a dead man.'

'What?'

'I will slit your throat down to your groin and turn you inside out.'

A lull in traffic and Gideon's voice, less sure: 'I know who you are…
and so do the police. Stop calling me.' And the phone went dead. The
pigeon urged Toby to call back. It went direct to voicemail.

On the scrap of paper underneath Gideon's telephone number was
another labelled 'Shawna L. After 4 p.m.' It was probably some time
before that.

'Shawna Lapido,' a woman answered promptly.

'Hello Shawna. I'm sorry to bother you. I'm calling about Gideon
Chancelight.'

'Giddy what? You're going to have to speak up.' Toby heard her
moving around trying to get better reception. A door slammed. 'Hello?
Can you hear me?'

'Hello. Yes, that's better. Is that Shawna Lapido? This is Detective
Police Constable Hal Blake. I've been given your number in connection
with Gideon Chancelight of Milson, Range & Rafter Estate Agents. I was
wondering if you'd be so good as to answer a couple of questions?'

Silence.

'Gideon Chancelight. You do know him?'

'Gideon Chancelight? That estate agent guy?' She was silent for a few
more seconds. 'Why what's happened?'

'Well, that's what we're trying to find out.'

'I don't know him at all. I mean, I met him once. He took me round
a flat a few weeks ago.'

'Do you have any more detail than that? You are perhaps familiar
with his private life?'

'His private life? No, not at all. How did you get my name?'

'It was just one of a number of names and numbers in his diary.
We're slowly making our way through them. Following up leads.
Looking for clues. Making enquiries. You know how these things
work.'

'Oh. OK. Nothing serious then?'

'Not yet. Just one last thing. One line of enquiry we're pursuing is in connection with a woman by the name of Imogen Green. Did you come across her in your dealings with Mr Chancelight?'

'Imogen Green? No,' she sounded doubtful. 'I don't think so. Is she the woman in that office?'

'Black curly hair?'

'No. This one was blonde.'

'Was there anything strange? Anything that stands out in your mind as being a little bit odd?'

There was silence. 'His shoes,' she said suddenly. 'His shoes were a little bit odd. I remember thinking this man drives a Porsche so why are his shoes full of holes. Why doesn't he just get a new pair?'

'Shoes with holes,' wrote Toby on the back of the Post-It. 'Thank you very much, Shawna.'

'Does that help?' So helpful, so polite.

'I think it does Shawna.'

Back in the car, Toby helped himself to a little more cocaine to take the edge off his disappointment. He contemplated his next move. It was remarkable how reasonable people could be when addressed by a police officer. He took the mobile from his pocket. On the fourth ring Gideon answered.

'Hello?'

'Gideon Chancelight?'

'That's me.'

'This is PC Hal Blake.'

'Ah hello, about the nuisance calls is it?'

'Yes and no. First though, I'm afraid I've got a bit of bad news.'

'Oh?'

'I'm afraid so, Mr Chancelight. Your house is on fire.'

'My what?' The lunch-time clatter became distant.

'Your house is on fire.'

'My house?'

'I'm sorry to report that I am standing here with fire engines outside 258 Brompton Road. If you want to save anything you'd better come home at once.'

'Brompton Road? I don't live there any more. I moved out four months ago.' Gideon suddenly suspicious: 'Who is this?'

'PC Hal Blake. Badge number 24579.'

There was silence.

'Hal Blake? Didn't you want to buy a house about ten minutes ago?' The phone went dead.

Toby rang back. The phone went straight to voicemail. He left a message.

'Hal Blake is coming for you. You, my friend, are dead.'

He hung up and stood in the drizzle, his back to the roar of the traffic.

It was Tuesday, it was raining and despite his lack of success, Toby Doubt was in good spirits. He returned to the car, his neck felt better and he scarcely noticed the clotted blood tugging at his knee. And as for the black eye, what black eye? It seemed he'd done as much as he could here. He'd exhausted both his leads. And after all, there was no point waiting in this lay-by if Gideon no longer lived here. He fired up the Golf and released the handbrake. He didn't want to go home. The idea of waiting on the off chance for Imogen – sitting on the third step waiting for the front door to open – crushed his spirit. As he administered more cocaine, his eyes alighted on an unfamiliar set of keys in the corner of the open briefcase.

He pulled out of the lay-by to join the stream of cars heading west towards Hammersmith. He drove carefully round the roundabout and back in the direction of Chelsea and the river, his head inclined towards the empty passenger seat and the railings that ran along the pavement beside the road.

seven

Beneath Kings Reach the tide was out. The river, unrecognizable from the powerful waterway of the morning, was now just a greasy strip running down the middle of the wide grey slouch. Toby sat on the balcony, his legs threaded under the glass balustrade and dangling above the mud. Beneath him three grey geese stood thigh-deep in silt. They were picking their way around shopping trollies and buckets without handles, planks of wood, empty bottles, plastic beer glasses and a million other less identifiable pieces of mostly plastic debris. If it hadn't been for the sharpness of some of those fragments, Toby might have considered slipping from the balcony and into the soft folds.

The rain on his legs shrunk his cords and drew the fabric painfully across the scab on his knee. With some difficulty he threaded his legs back through the slats and stood. He took off his boots. His socks were odd. The short grey one was definitely Imogen's. He might have suggested its partner was under a bed somewhere in Verbier, except for the fact that Imogen's socks never roamed singly. He unzipped the cords and pulled them down. The flesh on his thighs was spongy from rain and he was surprised to see that he wasn't wearing underpants. He ripped the cords over his knee and with them went the scab. The wound started bleeding and his socks were wet. He put his boots back on and threw the cords, inside out, a dead yellow bird, into the apartment behind him. Clack of steel button as they landed in the middle of the shiny floor, slap of damp corduroy. From his briefcase he took the last blue can of lager – PC Harold Blake with work to do – and sat on his case, his damp buttocks sticking to the leather: after all, the last thing you need, Toby Doubt, is piles. PC Hal Blake on a case. On his own case as it happened, on his own briefcase to be precise. He laughed as the rain fell softly on his naked thighs and cooled his knee. The crack as he opened the beer sent a heron flapping into the sky, its wide black wings spread awkwardly against the rain. Toby drank and the bird landed in mud on the other side of the river. The landing was unsteady, as though it had been emergency.

Another bird, black and long-necked stood on a ragged stump of wood that stuck out from the silt. Cormorant, Toby wanted to say. Uncurling its serpent neck, it raised its beak directly into the silver sky. 'Cormorant,' said Toby out loud. From nowhere came Imogen's voice. Shag, she said.

Toby smiled. A shag and some cocaine in the rain. Here above the river. If it wasn't for his neck and the fact that his girlfriend had run off, a shag out here in the rain would be just about perfect. She, in consideration of the wet balcony, might sit on him and he might request that he kept the briefcase under his buttocks. He'd lie back and look up into her clear blue eyes and her skirt would spread up to his chin and down to his knees. He'd close his eyes and allow the cold heart around her neck to slide into his mouth across his teeth against his tongue.

It hurt. Instead Toby made an inventory of his injuries. The catalogue of his misfortune. He started at the top where his head ached. He could feel it bulging around his temples, swelling and receding with his pulse. Inside, thoughts hid from him. The flesh around his eye throbbed. His teeth ached, it hurt to blink and his vision was obscured by flesh and lashes. His mouth was dry as though he hadn't slept and there was a numbness at the back of his throat. Lower down, the fissure in his neck had widened. Cautiously he tried to centre his head. Pain shot into his back. 'You'd want to keep that dry,' came Imogen's voice. 'Warm and dry. Keep it wrapped.' Between his nipples, behind his breast bone, his heart ached tight and hard. The stone that had set-tled there on Saturday meant he couldn't fill his lungs. 'Don't be such a drama queen,' snapped Imogen. Lower down, his balls rested on his briefcase. They were cold and numb and stuck there. He felt numb and sorry all the way down to his knee, which throbbed hotly. Through the gap between the glass and the top of the handrail he peered to examine the wound. He straightened his leg. Three neat puncture wounds from which blood ran thin in the rain. The knee ached. It hurt less when he didn't look. There was some good news though: his feet were warm and toasty in brown Blundstone boots, a head of steam rising from inside them. Good boots these, they'll last a life-time. 'I wish they wouldn't,' said Imogen exploring them with her little foot, toes twisted and bent out of line, the dark crescents of chipped nail varnish like elephant's toes. He couldn't imagine what she had against these boots.

He let his legs dangle again. A gull light enough to stand on the soft mud picked a round-about way to the water's edge. It launched itself and bobbed neat and fat into the still river. Beyond it a blue barge chugged past. Flapping the red and green dragon of Wales, the boat forged west towards Putney and Wales, the man at its helm noble in a straight-brimmed hat.

'It's a long way,' Toby shouted. The boat's wash slapped against the shore erasing the birds' footprints and licking clean the orange tip of a traffic cone.

Toby wondered if things might have been different if he hadn't worn these shoes. If he'd worn shoes that Imogen had approved. He wondered what kind of shoes she'd have liked him to have worn: girls' silver trainers like the ones Howard wore? Shiny little shoes like Harmsworth-Mallett's? Relationships, he knew, were about compro-mise. Toby's heart ached. Don't be such a baby, Toby Doubt. People leave people all the time and all the time people get over it. But this came so silently, without warning. Without a notice period. If someone's leaving don't they throw things? Scream? Sleep in another room? Slam doors? Aren't there arguments? Late night phone calls? People don't just steal away in the night leaving clothes, runner beans and their cat. Wasn't it customary to write a note? 'Like living with a baby,' she said when he left the front door open. 'You what?' when he overflowed the bath. 'Why is it always me who takes the rubbish out?' Her voice rose in his mind, becoming more desperate: 'please let the bath out', 'don't leave towels on the floor', 'put the washing on', 'take the washing out', 'wash up', 'pick up clothes', 'lock the door'. He put his head in his hands and the tirade continued: 'your memory', 'always me', 'sick of it'. Two crows dive-bombed a heron. They flew screeching and squawking in ragged circles around it. Co-ordinated, they dropped from the sky, beaks first, spiralling like bombers.

That was surely just the difference between his way and hers. It wasn't as though he never tidied up. Sometimes he spent a whole day on the house. From top to bottom, bucket and mop, dustpan and brush. Well, once he had, anyway. And besides, she always forgave him, sat on his knee, wound her hands through his hair, reached across for him in the night. His way and her way.

And again she's on that train. Soft lips together, light and shade sliding over her face, down across her straight freckled nose over her soft lips. She puts her book, face down astride the blue checked seat. She stands. His hand falls from the warmth of her shoulder. She brushes down the cream trousers. She straightens the green cardigan. She stretches her arms above her head. She smiles. 'Adder's tongue, self heal, crow's foot,' she says. 'Dove's tail, crane's bill, lover's knot.' She picks up the book, she goes to the window. Toby can see the outline of her knickers under her cream trousers. She stands on her toes in white trainers to reach the clips at the top of the window. She bites her lip and turns to frown at Toby. Suddenly it screeches open all the way down and she puts out her head. Now it's Toby's turn to frown. With the rattle of the train and the roar of the wind he can hardly hear what she's saying – plague's bill, devil's tooth, death's claw.

A man's voice reached him from inside the apartment: 'This one they finished a year ago… It's actually Kenworth Partners who did The Spire next to Canary Wharf.' The slam of a door, shoes on shiny wooden floor. 'They won an award for this. It's the first building… What's this?' Toby turned to see a man in a navy suit bending to pick up his yellow cords. A woman appeared beside him. 'Trousers… hmm… a little bit unusual.' He laughed nervously and put them over his arm. 'Wet trousers, very odd indeed, well, moving swiftly on… it's the first design scheme to combine… ' The man jumped visibly when he saw Toby struggling to his feet on the balcony. He put a hand to the red tie at his chest.

It seemed to Toby that it took forever for him to get to his feet. His scrotum stuck to the leather case, his boot wedged under the balcony, his knee grated on the glass. He snatched his briefcase and behind it, moved to the open glass doors, blood trickling down his shin.

'Excuse me,' said the man in the suit, the cords hanging limp from his arm. 'I'm sorry to disturb you, sir. Er… Jonathan Malone, Fawcett, Sage.' Frowning, nervous, he looked uncertain. The woman was backing away.

'You must be an estate agent.' Toby smiled broadly.

'Yes. Fawcett, Sage. Jonathan Malone. We were told the flat was empty.' The estate agent looked nervously from Toby to the woman, gesturing around the room with his free arm.

'Blake,' said Toby, transferring his briefcase into his left hand and holding out his right. 'Harold Blake.'

The estate agent made no move.

'The flat's no longer on the market,' continued Toby cheerfully. 'It was sold this morning.'

'I understood there'd been an offer made,' stammered the man. He must have been little more than twenty. 'But I didn't know that we were no longer under instruction.'

'Yes. Offer accepted, deal done. So, er, thanks for coming.' Toby smiled. His lips were numb. Speak the estate agent's language. 'No more instruction.'

'My apologies. These must be, er, yours?' Hesitantly Jonathan Malone held out the trousers, his eyes fixed on Toby's.

'Thanks. And so sorry you've had a wasted trip.' Smiling, sympathetic.

'Not at all. We'll, er, show ourselves out.'

The woman scuttled to the door. She turned for one last look at Hal Blake. The estate agent shook his head slightly as the door closed behind them.

Outside the river was quiet. The crows and the heron had disappeared and it looked as though the river was filling up again. Toby struggled out of his boots and back into the cords. Stiff and cold they skinned his knee and chafed his thighs. He zipped them and squatted to finish his beer. He rubbed a spot of cocaine into his gums before closing up his briefcase.

It was dusk by the time he pulled into Frederick Street. Mr Cheap Potatoes had lit the Christmas lights which provided year-round illumination for his Grocery and Convenience Store, and the Builder's Arms was flesh-full of standing men. There was a parking space outside the house. And a neatly wrapped package stood on the doorstep, secure in two plastic bags, silver foil and a Tupperware box. It was warm and smelt of food. He could hear the cat scrabbling frantically at the letter box on the other side. The telephone was ringing.

He stood in the little hallway. Rita watched him steadily from the dimness of the third stair. The house felt cold: unloved and unlived in. He shut the door behind him.

'Imogen,' he shouted up the stairs. Perhaps if he acted normally so would she. With his thumbnail he picked a scrap of paint she'd missed from the knob at the bottom of the banister. The food in the package smelt homely and warm, lasagna perhaps, but still the house was cold. The cat sniffed the air a few times then picked its way past him, around the bottom of the stairs and along the corridor towards the garden. The phone stopped ringing and Toby went upstairs. He deposited his briefcase on the table. The phone rang again. Toby continued upstairs.

The montage of photographs was in the cupboard beside the airing cupboard on the landing at the foot of the small flight of stairs that led up to the bathroom. Somehow he'd known it was here. It was at the back of a stack of things, which included an old map of Surrey, a mirror and one of Imogen's dead relations' unfinished paintings of the sea. Toby brought it out. In one corner the glass was smashed and a photograph peeled outwards, dogeared and fading. He took the whole thing downstairs into the kitchen and put it face down on the shiny polished table. It had been on the wall in Imogen's kitchen in Highgate. He'd seen it a thousand times. Imogen after A-levels in Spain with all her friends from sixth form in Surrey. Saffron and Anna and whoever that girl was who looked like a psychopath in every photograph and Gideon. Big deal, he'd looked at it a hundred times. Now, however, Toby needed time. He took a beer from the fridge and opened the briefcase. He brought out the package of cocaine and flattened it out on to the clean worktop beside the kettle. The square of paper with the yellow apple breast. From the briefcase he pulled another floating square of magazine. It showed the armpit and the reciprocal curve of the other breast. He slid the papers together and wondered when he'd have the face. There was something familiar about the body. He had a feeling that he'd know the face: plump lips pink and parted slightly, slick with gloss. Wet teeth showing between them as a shiny finger moved around and around trailing oil. The finger moved more urgently. A pink tongue flicked out and the finger changed direction. Purposeful and probing it left a sticky trail. Toby groaned and scoured the kitchen for something with which to take the coke. A square of paper came to hand: Hi, it said. 'Next week some new Cif for bathroom please we are almost empty' followed by a smiley face, and then 'Frieda'. Toby rolled the note and snorted a good amount of cocaine. The distant buzz of the doorbell. He wiped his nose and on his way past the table turned the montage face up. One step at a time.

He opened the front door. Standing on the doorstep, juddering underneath a huge green umbrella, stood the Hill. Mauve blouse, trembling bosom, bunch of red and purple flowers in her dimpled hand.

'Hello.' Heavy forehead bearing down on shifty eyes, she looked uncomfortable. Toby felt that she did not like him. 'I've brought some anemones for Imogen,' she said and held out the flowers and a mauve envelope which matched her blouse.

'Why don't you come in,' he held the door wide.

The Hill hesitated: 'Are you sure she's well enough?'

There wasn't space for the Hill to pass in the narrow corridor while he was standing there so he backed off until he was at the foot of the stairs. He watched her awkwardness as she closed the front door and he listened to her breathing as she followed him upstairs. She followed him into the kitchen and took a scarf of purple silk from around her neck and stood uncomfortably.

'Sit down,' said Toby. She sat in a wicker chair at the head of the table, her flesh spilling over the sides. It creaked and sagged and groaned and cracked as she bent to examine the photographic montage in front of her. The phone rang.

'Would you like a beer?'

The Hill looked worriedly in the direction of the phone and back at Toby. She bit her lip until suddenly her face cleared. 'Yes, thanks, that would be great.'

'Toby, babe, it's Saff,' Saffron's chakra-balanced voice came soft through the answerphone. 'I'm here with Jane and Howie and we're on our way up to Kentish Town. There's been some kind of a fire at Camden Tube but we're all OK and we're on our way. Hope you're OK and we'll be seeing you in a little while. Oh. It's Saffron.'

Toby put a beer and a glass on the table in front of the Hill. As a gesture of goodwill he pulled the ring pull. She turned the can around. 'Tennant's,' she said.

Toby disappeared into the part of the kitchen where the sink was, the kettle and the cocaine. He leant over it with Frieda's note.

'So how is she?' the Hill asked.

Toby came back wiping his nose. 'She's OK.'

'Any chance of… ' The Hill pointed with a finger several times at the ceiling.

'Asleep,' said Toby. 'Will be now until tomorrow.'

'Oh.' The Hill frowned.

Toby wondered when he'd become so adept at lying. I love you because you pathologically cannot tell a lie, was what Imogen said. Perhaps it was her love that had kept him truthful.

'I'm so ignorant,' said the Hill. 'What exactly is Tuberculosis? It's not as serious as it sounds is it?'

'No,' said Toby. 'It's just a heavy cold. Some kind of infection in the lung. All it means is that you sleep a lot.'

'Oh.' The Hill looked sceptical. 'Poor Imogen. It's typical to come down with something like that on the first day of the holidays. What happened to you by the way?'

Toby didn't know what she meant.

'Your face.' The Hill moved her hand across her own.

'Oh,' said Toby. He sat in the chair next to hers. He put his hand to his eye. He'd got used to the fact that his vision was impaired by flesh and eyelashes. 'Rita' he said. 'The cat and I, er, had a run-in this morning.'

'How did the cat come off?' The Hill had covered her mouth with her white hand. Behind it, it seemed she might have been smiling.

'Fine I think,' said Toby. 'And look at this.' He straightened his leg. The blood stain on his trousers was now black. 'This one particularly hurts.' He rubbed his leg above the knee. 'I knelt on the rake. And this,' he put his hand to his chest, 'this is crushing me.'

'Ouch.' The Hill was smirking openly now. 'All today?'

'All this morning before I went to work.'

'Sounds like a bad day.' The Hill's pale chin wobbled. 'I'd have gone: Nope,' she held out two hands, white and fine, and shook her head, 'sorry but this day is not for me. Back to bed!'

'Look at this,' said Toby drawing his chair as close as he could to the montage without encroaching on the Hill's bulk.

'I was,' she said. She moved the montage across the table towards him and leant a little in the opposite direction.

'Spot the cunt,' muttered Toby.

'I beg your pardon?' The Hill turned, her face folding into her chin. She laughed and turned back to the montage. 'I recognize Imogen. I love the hair. She should go short again, it really suits her... but then again, anything would suit Imogen.' She sighed and slid a dimpled finger across a photograph of Imogen and Saffron and the Psychopath in sunglasses. 'But I don't know any of these others.' She came back to a photograph of Saffron. 'That's not Saffron is it?' She laughed. 'When are these from?'

'Do you want some cocaine?' asked Toby.

'Cocaine? God I haven't had that for ages.' She looked delighted. Toby went through into the kitchen and came back with the paper breast and the cocaine in the palm of his hand. He put it down on the table. Toby was glad that she hadn't used her glass. She was drinking straight from the can as he was.

'What should I do?' the Hill put down her drink. 'Should I,' her voice changed, deep and throaty and faux American, 'rack up some lines?'

Toby nodded. 'I'll do the beers.'

'Should I close the blind?'

Toby watched from the kitchen as the Hill rummaged in a small green bag which had been lost amongst her layers and folds. She emerged with a card and popped closed the bag. 'Alright to do it on this?' She wiped a hand across the montage of photographs.

The phone rang. Toby studied the Hill bent over the glass, the clack of her credit card, her neat hand moving at double quick time.

'Hello Toby,' a gravel deep voice crackled through the kitchen. 'It's Aunt Mercy, I'm leaving you a message to give you lots of love.' There was a pause in which a dog barked. 'Psssssst! Betsey! Quiet! Lots of love Toby. I'm thinking of you.' And the answerphone clicked off.

'Oh bless!' The Hill caught her breath and looked over her shoulder in the direction of the phone and then at Toby. She ran a finger up the side of her credit card and licked it. 'That's such a nice thing to do. Just leave a message saying Lots of Love. And what a groovy name. Mercy. I've never heard that before. Aunt Mercy. It sounds straight out of Agatha Christie.'

'She's not actually my aunt.' Toby came back with beers. 'She's my mother's girlfriend.' He sat down again.

'Really?' The Hill raised an eyebrow and rattled her card on the glass.

Yes really. Some people are fat. Some people are dishonest and some people favour same sex relationships.

'Yes really. They've been together a long time and when I was growing up they thought that it would be easier for me, school etc, if I called her Aunt Mercy.'

The Hill nodded sympathetically, hand poised above the coke.

'As opposed to Dad,' he went on.

She laughed.

The lines in front of her were numerous and neat and Toby was pleased to see that a heap of the rest of the cocaine covered Gideon's grinning face.

'Nice,' said the Hill holding up the paper which showed the round yellow breast. 'Nice bit of breast. No head. No brain. Just tit! Like it!' She turned to Toby. 'You obviously buy your cocaine off a classy individual. So where's your dad?'

'My dad,' said Toby handing over Frieda's note.

'Hi. Next week some new Cif for bathroom please we are almost empty. Frieda,' the Hill read and re-rolled it. 'I think it was better when they called it Jif. Don't you? So. Where's your dad?' Delicately she held the rolled note to her nose and bent to the photographic montage.

'America' said Toby. 'Massachusetts, I think. He was a one night stand of my mother's. Probably the only time she's ever been with a man. He's American, some kind of academic who specializes in Medieval Literature, Beowolf, that kind of thing. He visited Cambridge in 1973, met my mother, fertilized one of her eggs and went home.'

The Hill handed the paper to Toby. 'You've never met him?'

'No.'

'No urge?' Rubbing her nose.

'I've thought about it, but I can't see the point. He doesn't know I exist and what would be the point of telling him now? Howard – a friend – and I planned a trip a few years ago. He tracked down John Lambert III to Amherst College in Massachusetts where he was teaching Anglo-Saxon Literature. He even rang the college to find out how old he was.'

'And how old was he?'

'The right age for love in 1973.'

'John Lambert III. What happened to the other two?' The Hill sat back in her chair, thick black lashes around eyes almost as pale as Imogen's.

'Killed by fathers of despoiled virgins. Howard got me his book: *Friends of Beowolf*.' Toby laughed. 'It's unreadable. I think Beowolf was the only real friend John Lambert III ever had.'

'Does that mean you're John Lambert IV?'

'I suppose it does.'

'So what happened to the trip to meet him?'

Toby looked out of the window. 'I couldn't work out what I was going to say: Hello daddy, I am your son. Let's get something to eat! Then Howard found cheap tickets to Acapulco so we went there instead.'

'You know nothing at all about him?'

'Not a lot. And what I do know has so far been sufficient.'

'That's so sad.' She sniffed. 'I think I'd definitely want to meet him. Just to see what kind of a person he is. You might have tons more brothers and sisters. Alright to have another?' The Hill was poised above the montage still holding the rolled note.

'Mind you don't have a heart attack,' said Toby wondering how he would handle such an event.

The Hill, rolled note poised in her hand, head on one side, turned to him, lips a different shape. 'That's not a very nice thing to say.'

'I didn't mean it like that,' Toby said.

'Glad to hear it, Goldilocks,' said the Hill. Laughing, she bent over the montage. She sat straight and rubbed her nose. 'I was born,' she said, 'with three times the normal number of fat cells.' She lifted her head and rubbed her nose again. Suddenly she gasped and froze. Violently she leant back in the chair, her hand clutched to her chest. She was struggling for breath. Toby jumped to his feet, hands limp at his sides.

The Hill laughed and sat back in her chair. 'So, do you think you'll ever meet him? Your father?'

Toby sat down, his own hand clutched to his heart which was leaping in his chest. 'Howard brings it up periodically, he really wants to meet him. I'm much more interested in meeting Howard's father.' His hand was shaking and he sloshed beer on his shirt.

'Steady,' the Hill smirked.

'The last time Howard saw his dad he was eleven and his father, Martin, was standing in the road outside their house in Sheffield with his leg in plaster surrounded by police. Howard watched from the front door as the police handcuffed him and put him in the back of the van. I think he might have seen him once since. He was in prison for two years: Trespassing and Lewd Conduct. Howard's dad was a peeping Tom. The most prolific, I believe, that Sheffield had ever seen.'

'A what?'

'A peeping Tom. Watches people having sex. Preferably up ladders. At night.'

The Hill covered the montage with both hands to protect the cocaine from her laughter. 'You are not serious.'

'Every night when Howard was in bed, Martin the window cleaner would go out with his ladder and climb up to bedroom windows all over the city on the off chance of finding people at it.'

Her mouth disappeared into her face. The chair squeaked.

'Apparently he'd been doing it for years. Howard remembers his father as a man permanently cut and bruised and bandaged. He was always falling off ladders, being pushed, punched. I felt sorry for Howard's mum. She thought he was working late.'

The Hill was crying with laughter. The chair creaked and juddered. 'I've never heard of such a thing. That's men for you. Can you imagine a woman doing that for kicks? A peeping what?'

'Tom. The night he was arrested he was up his ladder outside a house on some estate in Sheffield. The man saw him at the window: "What the bloody hell d'you think you're doing, bloody pervert?" A poor imitation of Howard's impression of a Sheffield accent. 'The man pushed him and Martin fell twenty feet on to gravel. Still holding his penis. Or his "Peter", as Howie tells it. He was arrested, taken to hospital, put in plaster and before his leg was dry he'd escaped. The police picked him up at home.'

The Hill was flushed with pleasure. 'Does Howard see him now?'

'No. His mother moved to Cambridge, changed her name, remarried and refused to see him when he got out.'

'Harsh.'

'Yes. Howard did speak to him once. A few years ago. No mention was made of the lewd conduct.'

'Bless,' said the Hill and wiped a tear from her pale cheek.

'More beer?'

The Hill nodded. 'So… when's the wedding?'

The wedding. Toby bent inside the fridge. A yellow light lit up a single egg, a pint of milk clearly separated into something thicker at the bottom and water at the top. The top shelf bowed with beer. He stood up.

'We haven't set a date.'

'I have a feeling Imogen would like a Christmas wedding. Hint. Hint.' The Hill's eyes glinted. 'Do you mind if I smoke one of your cigarettes? I just have a feeling that Imogen might have found the perfect dress for a Christmas wedding. That's all I'm going to say.' She laughed and Toby handed her the lager.

A Christmas wedding. A sleigh pulled by reindeer through an enchanted Surrey snowscape. Or better still up and down the Alps cutting through the swirl of a perfect blizzard.

'A Christmas wedding?' he asked. 'Or just a wedding in the snow?'

'Either, I guess.' The Hill smiled and ran a finger neatly across the glass, collecting stray bits of white. 'I just know there's a little something that has, shall we say, caught Imogen's eye and let's just say it's made for snow.'

The conversation was beginning to depress Toby and his eyes fell on the central photograph in the montage in which Gideon stood, under a light dusting of white powder, shirt undone, cigarette in the corner of his mouth, eyes squinting against the sun. Jack Scarlett. Liar, traitor, murderer, dead man. Toby put a finger on his face.

'Who is that?' The Hill tapped a forefinger on the glass. 'I noticed him before but didn't want to say. Just in case. Imogen's ex or something. But he's not bad.'

The doorbell rang.

'Should I cover this?' The Hill's mouth was open.

Downstairs the house was dark and dim. It reminded him that Imogen had left, as though he needed reminding. He opened the door. It was Howard. Howard with beers in a bag and behind him Jane and Saffron. The girls held hands and Toby detected a degree of reluctance in his visitors which would not have been here had Imogen answered the door.

'Dark in here. Hello mate, glad you're in. Can we come up?' Howard kissed Toby.

'Toby.' Jane kissed him and then came Saffron bobbing her yellow head. They all kissed him. They all followed him upstairs. Toby, still feeling the place on his arm where Jane had squeezed, listened. Bottles and cans in bags, shoes and breathing and the stomp of all their feet. Howard was saying something about a fire at Camden Tube. In the kitchen the light was bright and the Hill sat illuminated at the table. She made a move to get up. She didn't get far.

'This is...' Toby couldn't remember the Hill's name. He was hoping she'd supply it. She just sat there like a smiling peach. 'This is Miss Hill,' he said in the end. 'She teaches resistant materials with Imogen and this is Jane, Saffron and Howard.'

'Eileen,' said the Hill gaily. 'Is this the Howard?'

'What's this?' Howard, eyes on the cocaine, pulled out a chair.

'Yes, this is the Howard. We were talking about our fathers. Yours and mine,' said Toby.

'Fascinating,' said Eileen with a smirk.

Howard stiffened. He looked down at the table.

'Hi Eileen,' said Saffron, making use of the silence and bending to kiss her. 'How are you?'

'Pretty good thanks,' said Eileen looking anxiously at Howard. She suspected she'd been indiscreet. 'Shame about Imogen isn't it?' She looked up and wrinkled her nose.

Saffron straightened. She looked at the Hill in wonder. And then at Howard.

'Beers?' said Toby from the kitchen.

Jane sat beside Howard. She put a hand on his arm. He got up and went into the kitchen.

'You're off your tits.'

Toby stood and closed the fridge.

'And what the fuck happened to your face?'

'One of those days,' said Toby.

'What days? What happened?' Howard had his hands on his hips. Like someone's father. Like Imogen's father. Hold on old chap, that really isn't on. Now just hold on one minute.

Saffron came into the kitchen. She stood at the window and looked out. She covered her mouth with her hand.

'The garden,' she said. In the orange illuminations the ripped-up garden looked post-nuclear. 'Toby. What happened to the garden?'

Howard joined her at the window.

'Toby?'

'Redesign,' he said and opened a cupboard in search of glasses. Imogen's long-stemmed, jewel-encrusted antique set seemed entirely appropriate.

Saffron pushed the back of her hand into her mouth. The garden was making quite an impact and Toby was pleased about that. Saffron and Howard versus Toby. It seemed he'd won that round. Howard put his arm around her shoulders. Jane, from her upright position at the table, looked over, concerned. It seemed she too wanted to come to the window. Let her come thought Toby. The Hill's chair crackled.

'Why don't you have some coke,' Toby told Saffron and Howard. 'It'll make you feel better. It makes me feel much better.'

Howard sighed. 'Not now thank you,' as though Toby was in Howard's house and Howard wanted to go to bed.

Toby opened a can of Tennant's and the Hill approached, arranging her purple scarf around her neck.

'I'd better be getting back now,' she said, her eyes flickering nervously between Saffron and Howard. Their backs to the window, they both regarded her with what might have been hostility. 'But thanks for the drinks and send my love to the patient.' It seemed she couldn't get out fast enough.

'What patient?' Howie asked when the kitchen door had closed behind her.

'How should I know?' said Toby making his way to the table. 'Help yourself to beers.'

Toby sat beside Jane. 'How are you Jane?'

'So so,' said Jane holding up a wavering hand. 'But it's you we're worried about.' She closed then opened brown cow eyes.

'Would you like some coke? I know I would.' Toby reached across and pulled the picture with the cocaine on it towards him.

Jane mouthed something to Howard and Saffron in the kitchen. Toby bent over the cocaine. 'He's off his head,' said Howard coming over to the table. 'You both should go. I'll stay here with him.'

'Let's all stay' said Saffron.

'Coke?' asked Toby sliding the collage across the table to where she stood on the other side.

She smiled and shook her blonde head. She looked down. 'Oh my God.' Sweeping cocaine from Gideon's face. 'Where did you find this?' Laughing she turned the picture around. She tapped her own face in a silver wig. Her expression changed and her finger moved to Imogen. Imogen with her short hair, her slight smile. And then the finger moved to Gideon with his air guitar. 'Prat,' she said affectionately. Again her finger went to Imogen's face. She turned away and gulped in air.

'I think you should go.' Gently Howard touched Saffron's arm.

Toby laughed. 'I think you should all go.'

The suggestion was followed by whispering, some collaboration, an unbearable look from Saffron, a kiss from Jane, more whispering outside the door and footsteps on the stairs.

There was a finality in the front door closing. A slam and a thud.

A sickening thud. And everything was in darkness, there was nothing but black. The clatter of a train thundering through a tunnel, and darkness, and then light.

Footsteps on the stairs and Howard returned to the kitchen. He came and sat next to Toby. He seemed to be waiting for him to speak. A sigh. The creak of a chair. If he wasn't going to bring up Saturday night then neither was Toby.

'So,' said Howard.

'So,' said Toby.

'So,' said Howard. 'How are you?'

'I am as you see me.' Toby lifted blue cans on the table looking for one with beer in it. He rolled the note and bent to the cocaine. Howard put a hand on Toby's wrist.

'That isn't going to help.'

'Help what?'

'You.'

Toby laughed. 'Help me what?'

'It's not going to *solve* anything.' Howard stressed the word solve and used his hand for further emphasis.

'What's to solve?'

'Toby,' said Howard.

'Howard,' said Toby

'Let's go to bed.'

'You go to bed if that's what you want.' Two decades of friendship and nothing to say. 'Two decades of friendship and nothing to say,' said Toby.

'I love you,' said Howard and Toby saw that he was upset and felt guilty. Then he felt embarrassed.

'What happened?' The words came out more harshly than he'd intended.

'What happened?' There was not a line on Howard's pale face.

Toby swallowed. 'On Saturday.'

Howard looked like a man dying of thirst. He panted for air.

He brushed his hair back from his face. 'We came back here,' he said eventually. 'Don't you remember? We came back here.'

'I do remember,' said Toby.

'We came back here. We bought some vodka. You were wearing those dodgy blue things.'

'Nursing home pyjamas,' said Toby.

Howard laughed. 'The nursing home pyjamas.'

'Where are my clothes?'

'They kept them. We came back here with the vodka. You had a bath, we drank the vodka and you told me that you knew about me and Stella Page.'

'I knew about you and Stella Page,' said Toby. 'I saw you from the top of the big wheel. I loved Stella Page,' said Toby.

'I know,' said Howard.

'How could you do it then?'

Hands held out, palms upwards as though waiting for the answer to fall into them. It didn't come. 'I don't know, mate. Jesus, I don't know. You don't know anything when you're fifteen.'

'You knew how I felt about her.'

'I know,' Howard sniffed.

'Have you done it with Imogen?'

Howard, horrified. 'No, I have not.' He put a hand on Toby's. 'No mate. I haven't.' He pressed down and said more quietly. 'I haven't. So we came back here and drank the vodka in the bathroom and talked about Stella Page. And then I took a cab to pick up the sleeping pills. I was gone less than twenty minutes and when I got back you must have been asleep. You didn't answer the door or the phone, all night and all day. I shouldn't have left,' said Howie.

'It's OK,' said Toby.

'It's OK now,' said Howard. 'Let's go to bed.'

'OK,' said Toby.

When Howard had set the alarm and was on his back gently snoring on her side of the bed, Toby went downstairs. He caught up with Imogen outside. The skies were entirely dark and the little garden was half lit with orange from the street light which towered over the wall. While Rita, crouched noisily over the dish, got to grips with the lasagna, Toby and Imogen dealt with the garden.

Haw haw haw rasped the saw as it ate its way through the gnarled grey trunk of the wisteria. Haw haw haw Toby laughed as he noted the rhythm with which the serrations splintered the wood. The saw sang, confident of victory. Toby allowed his arm and then his body to become an extension of the the blade. Haw haw haw sang Imogen as she crouched to pick out another puzzle piece of crazy concrete paving. Toby watched Imogen's reflection in the mirror. White nightie wet with rain and muddied at the hem, knots of spine, stegosaurus-prominent, flourescent orange. Sharp knees bent and her hair a rain-wet knot of dripping rats' tails. Imogen. Bottom lip between her teeth, a child making mud pies. My muddy little Imogen.

The trunk tightened around the saw and Toby found he could not move it in either direction. The silence jarred the rhythm of the garden. He looked up and saw the dark foliage which ran up the brickwork. The gnarled trunk and branches clinging to the side of the house. The big, luxuriant, purple flowers moonish in the darkness. He reached up with his hand to touch one. Ripe and heavy it fell softly into his palm.

Toby Doubt laughed as he surveyed the garden and the fourteen or so jobs that were currently on the go. A merry-go-round of jobs. His laughter made him excited and he twanged the saw in the trunk. Under the umbrella he opened another beer and helped himself to some cocaine. His spirits soared and excited laughter bubbled in his throat.

'It's you and me babe,' he sang to the garden as he looked around for something new to try. It was then that he remembered the chain saw.

eight

It was Wednesday and windy and Primrose, in bulging fly-eye sun-glasses, closed her front door. She bent to double lock and triple lock it, the hem of her peach-coloured shirt lifting on the breeze. From somewhere inside the house, an alarm beeped.

She jumped when she saw Toby leaning against his own front door. 'Oh good Lord!' Hand on heart. 'You startled me.'

'Good morning.'

'Good morning to you too. How are you today?' Chin lifted, defiant helmet of apricot hair bending in the wind. 'Did you get the lasagna I left?' She gestured towards Toby's feet and the pink 'Voyager' that contained Rita and now stood where the lasagna had last night. Inconsolable, the cat mewled and moaned and patrolled the case.

'Yes, thank you, I did.'

'Oh good, because I rang and there was no reply and I'd already made it and I didn't know whether to just leave it and I didn't know when you would be getting in... Who have you got there? Is that Rita?' Primrose removed her sunglasses to see better. The gold scarf knotted at her neck, tugged at by the air, floated out behind her. An elderly air hostess missing her trolley.

'Yes.'

'Vet?'

'Yes.'

'All alright?' Frowning.

'Yes.'

She put her sunglasses back on. 'Well I'm off to sell my ties.' She paused, cleared her throat and waited until Toby said: 'Ties?'

'Yes, ties.' Nimbly she picked her way across her rockery to come to the fence which separated the gardens. From a plastic bag she pulled a coathanger arranged with a neat spread of plastic-wrapped ties.

Toby picked his way through the crisp packets and newspapers and plastic bags.

'What happened to your eye?' Primrose draped ties over her arm for examination. They were red and gold and blue and at the bottom where the fabric widened there seemed to be various shapes added in mostly flesh-coloured paint. Behind him the cat yowled.

'Very nice' said Toby. Twin reflections nodded warped and insincere in her glasses.

'It's Seth,' said Primrose looking from Toby to the ties. 'I subscribe to the Teachings of Seth and he advises that adversity is a gift and only from adversity comes fulfilment of the self.' Again his twin reflections bobbed. 'My husband died. I was left with well, not a vast amount of money, and, a lot of well...' she smiled and thrust out her arm 'ties. I could have sunk into a depression, sold the house, given up. Instead,' she lifted her chin 'I've updated John's silk ties using fabric paint and have put to good use a creative talent which I thought was dead and buried at school!' She paused to giggle: a nervous, brief gurgle. 'And in doing that I've had great fun! I've given these ties a new lease of life and if all goes to plan, they'll go some way to making me some rainy-day money. I sell these for £20 each.' She lifted a blue one for Toby to examine. It appeared to have been customized with what might have been a peach-coloured penis. 'I've only sold one so far,' said Primrose, a frown momentarily clouding her face. 'To John's partner Dr Harbert. I don't suppose you...'

'Oh,' Toby felt in his pockets and brought out a roll of purple twenties. Meanwhile Primrose removed the blue tie from the hanger.

Toby handed a twenty-pound note over the fence. The tie in plastic crackled in the wind.

'Great,' said Primrose, chin raised and unevenly spotted in peach-coloured make-up.

'Great,' said Toby taking the tie.

'Now I've sold two. I'm off to the Dental Association's Annual Conference.' She waved the ties as she picked her way back across the rockery and down her path. 'Wish me luck.'

'Good luck,' said Toby.

Carefully she closed the gate behind her, checked the latch was in place and, waving once, disappeared down Frederick Street in the direction of the lights and the pedestrian crossing.

Toby waited until she was out of sight before folding the tie into his pocket and picking up the unwieldy pink Voyager. The day was blustery. The sky was blue but littered with bubbles of high cloud, like the one obscuring the sun. However, there was activity in the sky and Toby was confident that the clouds would disperse, the sun would come out and June would continue as June was meant to: breezy and optimistic.

On the physical side of things, his neck was much better and his black eye was just that: there was none of that face restructuring swelling of yesterday. As far as his outfit went, a night spent in bed and woken promptly by Howard's alarm meant he was up early enough to polish his boots – the stain shaped like a heart was still there but somehow he'd become attached to it – and overall they shone nicely on the platform. He'd even taken Imogen's hairbrush to his suit and had managed to remove most of the mud – a few spatters clung to his ankles but nothing that anyone who wasn't looking for it would notice – and despite the fact that Steve's Nest was dark and deserted, Toby could not help feeling that the Closed sign which hung at the window was a herald of better times to come: Steve on his triumphant return from Bulgaria, holding his bride ahead of him in the saddle.

And this morning, Toby had Rita, a savage animal caged in pink plastic. The cat was meowing resentfully despite the effort to which he'd gone: its cage was furnished with towels, cushions and a liberal scattering of Frisk Biscuits. Still Rita moaned.

At Farringdon, Toby put the cage on the bench between him and a blonde woman with a round belly who was filing her nails. 'Poor baby,' the woman said bending to peer at Rita through the pink plastic mesh, and then gently to Toby, 'Boy or girl?'

As if he either knew or cared: 'Neutered,' replied Toby.

The woman frowned. 'Hello pussy.' She tried to touch Rita through the grille. 'Hello pussy. Hello catty. Hello kitty. What's your name?'

As if she could answer that one. 'Rita,' sighed Toby.

'Hello little one. Hello Rita. Hello gorgeous. Yes baby. It's alright girlie. Yes Rita. Hello gorgeous. Yes baby.'

Toby closed his eyes against the cat's yowls and the woman's noises. Her accusation was quiet when it came but nonetheless levelled at Toby – 'Ouch! She scratched me' – as though somehow it was his fault.

At South Kensington the sky was a deep blue. He emerged into sunlight and Rita, perhaps relieved to be back above ground, cried more softly. She was sitting upright at one end of the case, which made carrying awkward.

At Milson, Range & Rafter a cluster of men clogged the doorway. Shattered glass glinted green on the pavement and two men wearing white gloves held upright a large sheet of glass. 'Mind your backs,' said a third, and Toby and his pink case were allowed through into the office. Inside his feet crunched on glass. Daisy's desk was empty – a possibility Toby had not considered. He'd been counting on a grand entrance.

'Business as usual, Mr Dote.' Harmsworth-Mallett was holding the receiver of his phone. He smiled and blinked. 'Keep your shoes on and I think we'll get through this. Good night last night?' He replaced the receiver. 'Nice big celebration was it?'

Toby nodded.

'Good. Good. We're getting a smart new door today. Ha ha. Now who doesn't like a smart new door eh?'

Toby nodded. Who indeed?

'Good good. Good good.' Harmsworth-Mallett put a finger to his lips and with his thumb indicated the recesses of the office behind him.

Toby followed the direction of the old man's thumb. Chuck appeared to have been involved in some kind of accident. Stitches ran down the centre of his forehead and his arm was in plaster. Awkwardly, he turned in his chair to punch numbers into his phone with his functional hand. He finished and picked the receiver off the desk.

'Mr John Batson please. Chuck Lincoln, Milson, Range & Rafter.'

Harmsworth-Mallett whispered: 'Hier soir, notre ami, Chuck. Minor, er, disagreement one might say, ahem, with the, er... avec la porte.' He mouthed the French and his hands fluttered excitedly around his phone. He frowned. 'Le or la porte?'

Toby tried to recall yesterday. Chuck and work and yesterday. He couldn't even recall what day it was yesterday.

'Lower, lower, lower, lower' said the man in dusty jeans who was crouched in the doorway guiding the new glass door on to its hinges. 'Hold it. Up a bit up a bit. Up a bit. Up a bit more.'

The glass was an inch thick. It would take, thought Toby, a fairly major minor disagreement to have an impact on a door like that. Harmsworth-Mallett seemed to read his mind. He turned to glance at Chuck who was still on the phone and turned back to mime a head-butt action, then smoothed his hair. Chuck finished his call.

Harmsworth-Mallett coughed and with trembling hands squared a folder on his desk. 'We don't have all the details in as yet. So...' in an unnatural voice, 'what are you going to shift for us today Mr Dote? Brunei's place on Holland Park Avenue? Twenty-five million. Would probably settle for twenty though. Been on the market long enough. Eh Chuck? What do you say?' He turned in his chair, blinking and smiling. Chuck was looking out of the window and didn't appear to have heard. Harmsworth-Mallett shrugged. He tapped his finger not unkindly on his temple.

'The important thing is to include him,' he mouthed the words exaggeratedly, bloodless lips, blue-banded earthworms, stretching across darker teeth. 'Brunei's place is not to, er, everyone's taste. Vulgar some might say. I prefer the word opulent. The Sulton of Brunei's taste in furnishings lies at the, shall we say, more *ornate* end of the spectrum. Well, well. And who do we have here?' Harmsworth-Mallett got to his feet dabbing his mouth with a handkerchief. Rita, lodged in the corner of the cage, whined disconsolately.

'Rita.'

'Hello Rita. Welcome to Milson, Range & Rafter. I do hope you enjoy your visit.' He made a small bow and extended a hand. The cat shrank from the gesture.

'She's not herself,' Toby apologized.

'We none of us are. We none of us are.' Harmsworth-Mallett straightened his papers decisively.

Chuck's head had been stapled together with thick white stitches and the flesh on either side was green and troubled. He was staring, unfocused, at the street beyond the window. Rita mewled and as Toby passed, Chuck turned to him, his face creased with hatred. 'Prick,' he said. A bubble of white spit on the American's lower lip burst. His eyes burning, he lifted the middle finger of his unharmed hand and held it still and white-knuckled in front of his face.

Rita wouldn't fit under the desk so Toby put her nearby in a shaft of sunlight which slanted between particulars in the window. He would deal with the problem of Daisy and the cat later. As Harmsworth-Mallett might have said, he'd cross that bridge as and when.

The cat's moans were soon masked by the roar of a hoover. Beyond Chuck, Toby watched a man in blue overalls, frowning, as he ran the vacuum over and back over the carpet. He crouched to lift the door-mat and with his free hand took a brush to the awkward corners of the office, flicking out glass fragments as his other hand worked the hoover. Toby had never seen an individual so adept at cleaning. He wondered whether this man vacuumed at home. He certainly looked at home with a vacuum. Perhaps this was the task of men everywhere. Like mowing and washing the car. Men's work. He pictured the Spaniard, hoovering; then Harmsworth-Mallett, Silk Cut in the corner of his mouth as he eased his hoover into tricky corners; Howard with the latest model; Chuck in a temper slamming his machine into the skirting board. Toby had done it once at Frederick Street when he'd been clearing up a bag of sugar which he'd spilt on the kitchen floor. He'd spent a not inconsiderable amount of time searching for the hoover. Imogen, outraged, had refused to tell him where it was. 'We have lived here for more than two years and you don't even know where we keep the hoover.'

The wardrobe, the cupboard next to the airing cupboard, the cupboard in the kitchen, behind doors. Finally he caught up with it amongst the pots of paint and varnish the last owners had left behind, under the stairs. Imogen had thought it important enough to tell everyone about it. Her mother in hospital, weighed down by sheets, managing a smile. The Colonel, holding a plastic cup of water in the corridor outside: 'Er Toby. Just wanted to say,' a tear wiped from an old blue eye, 'I know you've been a brick to Imogen through her mother's illness.' A brick who doesn't hoover. Jane: 'Useless.' Howie: 'Good man!' Saffron: 'Typical.' His own mother, defensive: 'Toby's never had much time for housework.' And nor for that matter had Alison Doubt. Up and down the wooden stairs of the house in Cambridge large balls of dust and dog hair bounced. Toby wondered whether John Lambert III, if he'd stuck around, would have hoovered.

The hoover stopped and the man wound in the cord, admiring his handiwork. The silence pounded against Toby's eardrums. It seemed that real men hoovered. In front of him Chuck fingered his forehead.

Rita meowed and the shrill of the telephones took precedence. Chuck made no move.

'Milson, Range & Rafter.'

'Fiona Green.' A female voice, imperious – the Queen. 'Is this sales?'

'Yes.' Toby was at least certain of that.

'I need to sell my apartment in Kensington. Can you come and do a valuation?'

'Now?'

'Today is no good. Tomorrow?'

Mrs Green's flat was in Kensington Court and had two bedrooms, two bathrooms, a roof terrace complete with table, chairs and 'brand-new parasol job' which she was willing to offer with the property, if a suitable price could be agreed upon. The drawing room was south-facing, the dining room, large, the kitchen, new, and the whole property, recently decorated. Mrs Green wanted the flat exchanged, completed and sold by mid-August. And, pending a valuation of course, she was willing to make Milson, Range & Rafter the sole agent, for which she would be delighted to pay 3 per cent. Milson, Range & Rafter had been recommended to her by her downstairs neighbour Edwin Stack who was something to do with the Albert Hall and who had bought his flat most satisfactorily through someone called – a pause while she consulted her notes – Gideon Chancelight. Was Gideon still there and did he know Edwin Stack?

'My name is Toby Doubt, Sales Negotiator, Milson, Range & Rafter. What time would suit?'

In front of him Chuck lowed, swaying his heavy head from side to side.

Toby replaced the receiver and opened his briefcase. It appeared to contain toast – several grey-wrapped rounds – one blue lager can, empty, but dribbling slightly, and cocaine. Toby found three neat packages of cocaine. He took Gideon's letter from a sconced pocket. 'Just ran into the Colonel outside William Hill in South Ken... He gave me your adress and told me to write.' A brick to his daughter while his wife was dying. But still not good enough for marriage. 'First Love is the only True Love.' He wondered if that could be true. Melville Johnson's cousin aged ten in Mrs Johnson's ensuite, standing on the lavatory with her skirt up, matter of fact, resigned to Toby's investigation. Maybe he should write a letter. Let's do lunch. Melville Johnson's cousin a thirty-year-old woman packing a suitcase, leaving a family. Perhaps that was what was wrong with the world. People just weren't with the right people. Gideon and Imogen had started a chain reaction that would set the world to rights. Melville Johnson's cousin, a woman now, skirt up, knickers round her ankles. Melville Johnson's cousin's husband going through the phone book in his home town. Imogen on a train crossing the country, her face hidden by a book as she thunders in and out of sun towards Gideon. Toby refolded the letter and returned it to the briefcase. He brought out a hard packet of toast and unfolded the grease-proof paper. Knowing his luck, Melville Johnson's cousin was probably dead. He closed the briefcase with twin snaps, laid it on the desk and placed the toast on top.

Chuck barked, a harsh unexpected sound, like a seal at the zoo. Toby looked up, his fingers working to unwrap the toast. Daisy all ringlets and dimples in a flouncing floral skirt, a coffee in each hand, was picking her pretty way amongst workmen. One crouched to look up her skirt, another rested on his haunches and the man with the hoover stood to attention to allow her into the office. She looked like a girl who'd go giddy over a cat. Behind her a dark man, sharp in a navy suit said something to her. She threw back her head to laugh. The Spaniard. Jack Scarlett. His black hair fell diagonally across his forehead and shone blue in the sunlight. He pushed it off his face and turned to say something to the man crouched at the door's hinges who looked up to laugh.

'Stop it Gids.' Flushed, Daisy turned back.

'Messages, Mr Chancelight.' Harmsworth-Mallett held out an

upturned hand, on each finger of his hand stuck a square Post-It. Gideon placed a cappuccino in front of him and peeled off the messages one by one. He glanced at them and strode the length of the office, right hand outstretched. One two three strides. The office rumbled. Toby stood up. Rita was complaining. Shut up, he commanded the cat silently.

'Toby Doubt,' said Toby holding out his hand.

'Gideon Chancelight.' The hand was warm. Dry, large. 'No one told me it was bring your pet to work day.'

Rita wailed.

'Congratulations on Kings Reach,' he said, showing two rows of neat white teeth. A scatter of freckles on a straight nose. 'We should have a drink to celebrate. Welcome to Range & Rafter. Good to have some competition.' As he turned the vents in his jacket flashed peacock blue. 'Eh what, Chucky Egg?' The American shrank from the hand that ruffled his hair.

Rita moaned and Toby looked at the orange animal through the pink plastic mesh and wondered why he'd brought it. Gideon was here – here now in the same room, hidden behind the bulk of the American, but he was here.

The office hummed with activity. Harmsworth-Mallett was on the phone: leaks, rats, withheld deposits. Daisy's printer churned out pages and men on both sides of the new door bent to squeeze oil on to hinges, to wipe fingerprints from the glass. Daisy smiled and sparkled. Chuck wrote urgently. A warrant for Toby's death. And Rita, distraught in the Voyager, whimpered. There was no need for it now. He kicked the cage. For a moment the cat was silent.

In that silence a golden croissant arced high above the desks, its twin points spiralling in the sunlight. Above and beyond the American's fuming bulk two brown hands reached into the office air to shepherd it, a flash of sky blue at each cuff. A safe pair of hands.

Daisy dimpled, wriggling in her chair. 'Nice catch, Gids.'

'Daze.' Toby could hear the smile. 'You don't fuck about with a man's breakfast.'

Toby took Rita downstairs. He thought perhaps she'd like it down there. He knew at any rate that he would prefer it if the cat was down there. The spiral stairs pinged with each step and the basement rose to meet him. He fumbled for a light switch. A low-watt bulb buzzed from the ceiling and in the gloom he made his way to a table marked with dark rings circling a kettle. Beside the kettle an old sandwich and a carton of milk swelled amongst empty brown bottles. In the far corner of the room, amongst damp boxes and a collection of redundant computers, lay the curl of what looked like a recently abandoned sleeping bag. The carpet, brown and swollen, rose and fell, a fetid sea. It was the kind of place in which a person might die. He put Rita on the table beside the milk and allowed his mind to be overrun by unwelcome images: Imogen and the Spaniard through Mrs Johnson's bedroom in the bathroom with the Tampax and the sanitary towels in the cupboard in Spain by the pool after A-levels. It was some time before Toby's erection had subsided sufficiently for him to go back upstairs.

'There you are.' Gideon, dazzling in the thin bright air stood beside Toby's desk. 'Anything on this morning?' Even teeth, white enough to advertise apples. 'No point sitting here festering. I've got a viewing, the penthouse at Palace Mansions.' A halo of blue hovered at the crown of his black head. 'Been up there yet?'

Toby blinked.

'Worth a look; if you've got nothing else on you might as well come along.' He looked at his watch. 'Twenty minutes good with you? I would take you, Chuckley.' The American was cooling his forehead on the window. 'Sadly there's just no room in the back for a big man like you.'

Gideon stood in front of Daisy's desk. She was on the phone, bright-eyed and upright, hand playing girlishly with the cord. 'There's like loads of us going up there. There's Gids.' Both hands on her desk, the

Spaniard leant towards her, the vent in his jacket parted to show Toby the powerful round of his buttock. She wriggled with pleasure and turned away from him laughing. 'There's Ed, there's Charlie. There's like me of course. Just come… I've got to go, see you later.' She replaced the receiver and stood up. She took a cardigan from the back of her chair and came out from behind her desk putting it on. Together she and Gideon went out into the sunlight, Gideon tugging at a lock of the blonde's hair, the sentries on the door hushed with quiet respect.

Toby finished unwrapping the package that rested on his briefcase. He bit into the toast. It was hard and salty. He re-wrapped it and opened the case. He stacked it on top of the other identical packages of toast in one corner. He rolled the beer can against the stack. One yellow apple breast on a square piece of paper surfaced. He picked it up to lick it clean of white traces. A man – dark suit, red tie – stood watching him from between properties on the other side of the window. Toby turned to face him and turning the paper over, continued to lick it, enjoying the bitterness against his tongue. The man's eyes met Toby's above the yellow breast. His eyes widened and he moved off. Chuck was on the phone and beyond the new door, which was installed on its hinges now, he could see Harmsworth-Mallett across the road under the awning of the deli, smoking.

The door buzzed to admit the man. Dark suit, red tie, undercover cop. He stood uncertainly, he looked at his watch, looked briefly at Toby and blushed. Toby shut his briefcase and stood up. Cautiously the man approached. He looked from side to side.

'Hello,' he said. 'Er, James Wagtail. I'm, er…'

Interested in cocaine? Here to search the briefcase?

'Can I help?' asked Toby.

'Yes, er, I'm here for Nigel Harmsworth-Mallett.' He looked around the office. 'Or Gideon Chancelight.'

'Can I help?' said Toby.

'Nigel?' The man raised his eyebrows.

'That's the name.'

'Er, hello. James Wagtail. We spoke on the phone.'

'That's right. That's right.'

'OK then.' The man blushed further and looked about him. 'Um. Where should I sit?' He seemed to be avoiding Toby's eye.

'Sit?'

'Yes, er, I'm due to be starting work here today.' A laugh and again he looked around him, as if for somewhere to lay his briefcase. 'Sales.'

'Shayle Nugent wasn't it?' asked Toby. Before the man could reply Toby cleared his throat. 'Unfortunately there has been a misunderstanding. We're not expecting you,' Toby turned the pages of his empty appointment book, 'until Monday of next week.'

'Oh. But I spoke to Mike and he said...'

'I'm afraid Mike made a mistake. We'll see you next Monday. 9 a.m. 21 June. In the meantime, enjoy the sun.' He smiled in what he hoped was a decisive way. He could see Gideon across the road and Harmsworth-Mallett and snapped closed his briefcase.

'OK...' The man hesitated as though waiting for a second opinion.

Toby swung the briefcase off the desk. 'So sorry you've had a wasted trip.'

The man turned to leave.

The black Porsche was knee-deep in rubble. Maps, cups, bottles and stained scraps of paper. Gideon bailed some of it into the cramped back seat, the vents in his jacket flashing kingfisher, his socks a matching iridescence. He left the door open and went around to the driver's seat.

Toby lowered himself in and put on his seat belt. His foot stuck to the carpet on a ball of chewing gum. Imogen travelling knee-deep in rubbish too enraptured to care. Gideon beside her, a love furnace, consuming fuel, sandwiches, cappuccinos, chocolate. Tossing the debris at her ankles.

Frowning, Gideon looked over. 'It's a karzy in here. Sorry.'

He pulled out into the stream of traffic heading east. With a square brown hand he reached over and opened the glove compartment. He fitted the stereo and sat back.

'So.' He looked over at Toby, a frank examination. Straight brown nose, long-lashed dragon-green eyes. He changed gear. Strong thighs. 'So,' he said again. He seemed troubled, as though he needed to speak. Toby would let him. He examined the road ahead and tried not to picture Imogen's knickers between this man's teeth.

'So, this guy walks into the shop about twenty minutes ago,' began Gideon.

Toby pushed his back farther into the leather seat and wondered how he felt about being told a joke by this man. He watched Gideon's brown hand go to various knobs on the dashboard, then hover in front of air vents to monitor the rush of cool air. He became aware that Gideon was waiting for him to speak. 'Who's there?'

'What? I saw you talking to him – suit, red tie, dark hair. Twenty minutes ago I saw you speaking to him in the office. Who was he?'

'I don't know,' said Toby.

From the way Gideon turned to look at him, it seemed that he suspected Toby wasn't telling the truth.

'He didn't give his name,' said Toby.

'Didn't or wouldn't?'

'Wouldn't,' agreed Toby.

'Did he ask for me?'

'He did,' said Toby.

'Christ.' Gideon swallowed. 'And it wasn't about a property?'

'It wasn't about a property.' Toby resisted the urge to fold his arms. He could see sweat on Gideon's forehead.

'What did you tell him?'

'I told him that you were out.'

'Good lad. Good lad. Christ Almighty.' Gideon ran a hand through his hair. 'When did you say I was back?'

'I said I didn't know. Problem?' asked Toby.

'Oh yeah. Problem,' said Gideon. 'If that was who I think it was. Christ on a bike.' He blew upwards under his hair. He turned to look at Toby, teeth showing. 'Major fucking problem. But thanks for dealing with it. Sounds like you've bought me a morning. What happened to the eye by the way? Surely not Mr Chuckles Lincoln?' He laughed.

'No, not Chuckles Lincoln.'

'I hear you two are not best buddies. Harmsworth-Mallett tells me you reached melt-down on day one. Congrats. It took me the best part of a month.' He laughed. 'That eye must have hurt.' He passed a hand across his own and turned back to the road.

Toby nodded. 'It did. How was skiing?'

'Skiing?' Gideon turned the radio on. He frowned. 'More of a dirty weekend which spilled over. I was in Verbier, but it was more of a hot tub kind of weekend. Not a lot of snow,' he laughed. 'You know how it is...' Another frank examination. Summing up, ascertaining. Did Toby know how it was? 'I'm paying for it now though.' Gideon worked strong brown fingers to tune the radio. 'I am wrecked. Something to do with champagne at high altitudes.' When he'd found what he was looking for he turned up the volume.

'Hurry down while stocks last. Croydon, Sidcup, New Malden. Pay absolutely nothing for twelve months. The Sofa City. Make home the place you want to be.'

Gideon pulled a pack of Marlboro Lights from his pocket and felt around for a lighter. He untucked his shirt with a brown hand and, frowning to look down, pulled the tartan waistband of his underpants out. He snapped the elastic. His stomach was as hard and brown as his hand and a snarl of black hair licked upwards towards his belly button which sat, neat and contented, lord of all this muscle. He drove with the unlighted cigarette in his mouth, his hand half inside his underpants, as though it was a comfort and Toby wasn't there. 'Christ,' he said occasionally, shaking his head.

Imogen taking her champagne at high altitudes. Glass in her hand, toes in a hot tub somewhere in the mountains in an off season ski resort.

The car hovered at a zebra crossing while a blonde girl in pale jeans and a white cowboy hat sashayed across the road. She was drinking a coffee and idly Gideon watched her progress. From nowhere she smiled and waved and changed course to bear down on the Porsche.

'Hello stranger.' Smiling through Gideon's open window, her voice was deep. 'I thought it was you. Long time no see and all that. How've you been keeping?' With one hand she held the car still.

'Oh, hi there.' Gideon pulled his hand abruptly from his pants and sat upright, as though he'd been pulled over for speeding, he swallowed, checked his mirror and turned back to her. 'How are you?'

'Good, thanks.' Smile, smile. The woman moved the cowboy hat back on her head. 'How about you?'

'Good,' said Gideon.

'Haven't seen you in a while.'

'I've been away,' said Gideon.

'For six months?' The woman, blue eyes round, winked at Toby. 'Just kidding. Let's get together. Go out. Something. I'd like that.'

'Do you mind if I bring my boyfriend? This is Toby.'

'What?' said Toby.

'Boyfriend?' asked the woman bending to the window and looking across at him. She raised her eyebrows. 'Nice choice.'

Gideon put his hand firmly on Toby's thigh.

'Hold this for me would you?' she said handing her coffee through the window. Gideon took it and the woman rummaged in a tasselled shoulder bag. 'Here's my card. And don't lose it this time.' She smiled at him, took back her coffee and blinked at Toby. Gideon accelerated over the zebra crossing.

'Yikes.' Toby could feel the heat of each of Gideon's fingers still on his thigh. 'Jesus Fuck and anyone else out there who can help.' Gideon threw the card high into the air through his open window. It fluttered into the road behind them. 'You should be locked up,' he shouted. And when he'd recovered his breath: 'That sick individual is a man waiting for the operation.' The engine roared and behind them the road disappeared into a bend. 'He took me back to his place. Jesus wept... I did not let him touch me, I swear to God. Oh Jesus wept... I need a light.' The cigarette was back in his mouth and he was fumbling under the handbrake. Toby checked his pockets. To his surprise he pulled out a lighter. It said St Ives across it beneath the picture of a bikini-clad woman.

Imogen kneeling in her bikini on a towel down by the sea. On a sandy enclave in a rocky part of the beach which is not as deserted as they'd thought. She is helpless with laughter flat out on a towel, as Toby crouches naked nearby behind a rock hoping that the wholesome and fully-clothed family of four holding buckets and spades will come no further.

He held the flame to Gideon's cigarette and they both jumped as his mobile phone rang. Gideon checked it before answering. 'Juicy Lucy, can I call you in five?' He threw the phone back on to the dashboard and turned the radio up to sing along. When there were no words, he was content to whistle out of the side of his mouth.

Sunlight flitted between trees and the song faded. Toby turned the lighter over and over in his hand.

Imogen helpless with laughter makes no move to help. She doesn't pass him a towel or his shirt or his shorts. He's there crouching, a naked ape behind the rocks and the family is upon him. It can't look good. 'Sorry,' says the man, turning abruptly. The woman cuts a brisk course in a different direction, urging the children to follow. They scuttle after her looking over their shoulders at the bending wild man.

Imogen, fists buried in the sand, is still helpess with laughter.

'Folks, we're halfway through the week' the radio announced. Gideon turned the volume down.

'If you ain't got nothing to say, don't say nothing at all. So where were you before? Am I right in thinking Shayle Nugent had something to do with it?'

'Before?' asked Toby.

'Before Range & Rafter. Life before Range & Rafter. Can there be such a thing?' Gideon snapped shut the ashtray.

'In Kentish Town.'

The hands moving on the steering wheel were strong and brown and capable. Safe hands, sticky with sweat, they stuck to the leather. They were hands that knew their way around other people's bodies. Hands that knew their way around Imogen's body.

'Camden way?'

Toby nodded.

'Estate agent?'

Toby shook his head. 'Highwayman.'

'Is that right? Good money?'

'Not as good as this.'

Gideon hunched down over the steering wheel to laugh. 'Same game though. Where did you keep your horse?'

nine

Palace Mansions stood tall enough to block out the sun. Set back from the street it glowered behind a brow of heavy white stucco. While Toby wrestled with the chewing gum and the car's carpet somewhere under the rubbish, Gideon stood on the clean marble step examining a bunch of keys. Who would spit out chewing gum on the floor of a Porsche? That's the kind of thing that Imogen would accuse him of doing. It offered a degree of comfort to know that she would come up against the same thing here in Gideon's Porsche.

'Problem?'

Toby got out, slammed the door and rubbed the sole of his shoe on the pavement.

Gideon frowned and pulled his phone from his inside pocket. 'What now? Hello?... Daisy, Daisy give me your answer true. I'm half crazy all for the love of you. I can't afford a carriage...' Toby heard the blonde girl's laughter. 'Oh Daze, look,' Gideon imitating her voice, 'I don't like know about tonight. I'll come for one but like can I do the whole night? Just not sure babe. Listen. Catch up later. We've got a house to sell?'

Humming, Gideon squinted at the keys. 'Good little flat this one. Not sure about the buyers though. He's fine, but her?' He looked up the street and whistled. 'Not the full ticket.' He chose a key, put it in the lock and pushed open the heavy door. The porter was reading a magazine.

'Morning, squire,' said Gideon, heels sounding smartly on marble.

Too late, the man looked up. Gideon had already passed and was leading the way through the building past the grand staircase which stood at the centre and swept upwards through a broad well of light. Gideon stopped at a pair of brass lifts on the other side of the stairs. He ran a finger across the top of the button and examined it.

'Nicely looked after. If you're paying two-mil plus you want the place nice. Communal parts and all that. In fact, for two-mil plus you want the works. 24-hour porter who knows your name, hands you your letters, calls you a cab, orders you pizza. Probably not that one.' Gideon didn't bother to lower his voice. 'You'd want someone nicely turned out. Someone trustworthy, personable. English for starters. Or a Pole. The Poles are good little workers. But preferably English.' His gaze travelled to the corners of the lobby. An elaborate table on gold legs supported a large arrangement of flowers which loomed thick and artificial-looking. Gideon nodded his approval. 'It's the little things like that which make a deal.'

While the lift rose to the top floor, Gideon rested his head against the mirror. 'Now, if it was him on his own,' the words came out distorted as he pulled back to examine his chin. 'Not a problem. A pleasure doing business, sir.' He picked off something with a thumb-nail. He straightened, smiled and held a bunch of keys out to his own reflection. 'An absolute pleasure, sir. Here are your keys. And here is my commission: eighteen grand. Very nice. Thank you very much indeed.' He bowed to himself as the bell clanged and the doors opened. They emerged into light. An intricate black and white marble floor shone beneath the elaborate glass dome that crowned the building. The stairwell was wide and oval, its sweeping black banister spiralling gracefully into yellow dimness. Toby leant over. The marble floor of the foyer a hundred feet below looked pale and soft as marshmallow. Gideon joined him, hands on the rail. 'Whoah! Wouldn't like to go over that.'

Toby wondered about lifting the Spaniard's legs and watching him float, arms, legs, fingers outstretched.

'Nice stairs. Now I'd like to talk you through the game plan.' Gideon pushed himself off the banister to lead the way to a door set within a golden triumphal arch. Fluted pilasters ran the height on either side. 'Solid gold,' muttered Gideon fitting a key and flicking hair out of his eyes. 'Now, I'm going to level with you.' He turned, hand still at the lock. 'I have been at Milson, Range for fourteen months. During those fourteen months I have sold precisely fourteen properties. That, my friend, is an average of one property a month. In short, I am the engine that drives the machine. The premier estate agent in West London. Now you, my friend,' his voice a quickening mutter as again he bent to the lock, 'are fresh off the boat. Am I right?' He straightened, smiled at Toby and examined the keys in his hand. 'It's a fucking gold door.'

He focused on the lock again. 'Now don't get me wrong. You've had a success. You've made yourself 10 K. It's not bad. But do you have the clients, the contacts, the drive to follow through: bang bang bang sale sale sale?' The lock turned and Gideon frowned at the bunch, looking for another key. 'I've been talking to Mallett and I my friend have had an idea. We – that's you and me in English – team up for these next few months. I share clients, contacts, deals with you. And everything we sell, bang bang bang, we split fifty-fifty. What do you say?'

Toby didn't know what to say.

'This, my friend, is a once in a lifetime opportunity. The opportunity to ride with El Maestro.'

To ride with El Maestro. 1720, the Spaniard to Lord Stockport's footman. 'Son? You need to learn the ropes. How's about we team up for a couple of months? Ride together? Split the profits?'

'I'm interested,' said Toby. 'However, you're sure El Maestro is accurate?'

'Say again?'

'I said,' repeated Toby, 'isn't El Maestro a little inaccurate considering the fact that you haven't sold anything in four months?'

'You what?' Gideon straightened abruptly.

'The talk is...' Toby cleared his throat, 'that you, my friend, are finished.'

'What? Who said that?' Sharp white teeth.

'Everyone's talking about it. Chuck, Daisy, Mallett.'

'What?'

'That you're on your way out. That's why they brought me in. That's why they're bringing that new guy Wagtail in next week.'

'That is bullshit,' said Gideon. 'Prince's Court, I sold that April. End of April.'

Toby shook his head. 'Everyone is saying you've lost your touch. On your way out. Finito.' He folded his arms.

'I'll show you fucking finito.' Turning back to the door Gideon pushed a key into the top lock. 'When did any of those fuckers sell anything?' Biting his lip, he rattled the key in the lock, 'Mallett? Twenty years ago? The Chucklehead has made one sale this year. I took home 150 K last year. Not one of those fuckers has ever come close to a whiff of that kind of cash. Finito my arse. What I offer to you my friend is this, take it or leave it, a fifty-fifty partnership. Unless of course you fancy your chances and want to go solo, no contacts, no leads, no clients. I offer you two months. We clean up West London starting here.' He pushed a third key into a low lock. 'We sell this flat together. Right here, right now we strip these fuckers of the two million they're willing to part with. Are you reading me?' The Spaniard to the Squire. The highwayman to the footman.

'We split the commission – all eighteen grand of it – fifty-fifty. What do you say? Christ am I hungover? Do we have a deal?'

'We have a deal,' said Toby.

'Finito my arse.' Gideon turned to Toby and for the second time, they shook hands. The heavy door swung open and Gideon felt inside for a light switch. 'After you, sir.' He held out a hand.

They found themselves in a square room. Generous but windowless, it was carpeted in pale cream which lapped at each wall. The four walls were clad in soft gold mirror and in the centre of each wall stood a golden door below an identical gold-leaf pediment. In the middle of the ceiling – vaulted, cathedral-like in the same peach-coloured mirror – hung a vast chandelier. Light, refracted through a thousand glass jewels into endless mirrors, made an infinite forest of honey rainbows. And in the middle, Toby and Gideon.

'Well hello…' Gideon turned slowly. 'According to Arab wisdom, this is the Vestibule of Truth.'

Toby turned until the front door was indistinguishable from the other doors and he felt a curious sense of being unable to identify the door at which they'd entered. Air seemed scarce. He watched their reflections revolve around each other. The Spaniard: immaculate and broad-shouldered suggesting sex and success and money, his blue shirt and yellow tie a dazzle amongst rainbows. And Toby: loops of hair wayward above a flapping suit, unhealthy, asymmetrical, unhappy. A suggestion of mud caked his ankle. There was no contest. It was the Spaniard. Every time.

'The Vestibule of Truth,' said Gideon. 'It's said that whoever looks into these mirrors will eventually see the truth.'

'I've seen it,' said Toby.

'Anything nice?' Gideon tapped at the mirror. 'Two-way. What d'you reckon? Dirty bastard.'

'Close your eyes,' said Toby, his breathing thick.

Gideon looked at his watch. 'Another time.'

'We'll sell this flat if you close your eyes.' Toby's heart was pounding. He would crack his bird-egg skull here before the witness of their infinite reflections.

Gideon looked at Toby. 'Is that a promise?'

'That is a promise. Close your eyes.'

'Whooah. Get off me freak!' Gideon held both hands out in mock alarm as Toby came towards him. 'I'll scream.'

'Trust me,' said Toby.

Gideon, faux camp, sighed. 'If it means a sale.' He checked his watch again. 'Quickly then.' He closed his eyes and stood still in the centre of the room. His red lips were parted slightly.

Toby held him by the shoulders. The Spaniard was, by Toby's estimation, two or so inches shorter than him. A six-foot Spaniard, broad and lean and lithe and strong, the perfect height for a man. Gideon licked his bottom lip. It glistened where his tongue went. His nose was freckled like Imogen's, the skin under his eyes was dark as though he hadn't had enough sleep, and on his chin, a red mark where a spot had been. Toby watched a pulse twitch beneath olive skin at his temple. He felt Gideon's breath on his face and smelt his deodorant. 'Hurry up,' he said, his lips moving smartly around the words and Toby smelt something else. Beneath the soap and the cigarettes and mint it throbbed at a lower frequency, demanding his attention. He screwed his eyes tight against Imogen's laughter. Roughly he turned the man by his shoulders.

'Whoah.'

Once twice three times.

'Steady on old boy.'

He felt his breath blend with Gideon's and his own expression in the mirror flashed occasionally, teeth gritted against Imogen. Head thrown back, tits jouncing, her laughter rang in his ears. Gideon was panting, his tie a lick of gold streaming to keep up.

'Enough already.' Gideon's lower lip hung loose, his eyes opened briefly.

Toby turned the Spaniard more quickly, gripping his shoulders roughly. In the mirror above their heads he watched the kaleidoscope flashes amongst the fragments of chandelier, the hem of jacket, Gideon's feet clumsy, turning to keep up with his body. Faster. The Spaniard vanished in the ceiling. A blur turning to white light. Gideon laughing, Toby laughing, Imogen greedy for her orgasm, teeth bared urging him on. Toby let go. Gideon staggered. Eyes shut he crouched, shirt untucked, one arm in front, the other behind. He swayed and staggered, fell across the room, his feet sidestepping to land hard with a thud against one of the doors. He sank slowly to the floor. A businessman, drunk, gone down on the tube. Toby laughed and felt that he also had collided with a wall. His head flopped forward and he was sick. A thin brown froth glided down the white door to puddle on the pale carpet. Imogen's laughter faded to silence.

From somewhere close by Gideon groaned. 'What the fuck was that noise? Did you puke?'

Toby was aware of movement on the other side of the room. 'Jesus Christ.' Gideon was standing over him. Toby heard his own laughter. 'Jesus Christ, you fucking puked, you arse. Fuck a duck. Jesus.' Toby reached up to the hand which hovered in front of his face. His shoulder hurt where Gideon yanked. 'Get up. You've got to clean that shit up pronto – they'll be here any second.' Suddenly the hand was dropped and his arm fell hard on to his body. Again he heard his own laughter. Nearby a door opened and closed and Toby became aware that he was alone in the room. He lifted his head and managed to locate a door handle. Using that he made it to his feet. He opened a door. A regiment of wire coathangers rattled with breezy consternation. His reflection, white, concerned, followed his progress around the room. The next door swung open to allow a rush of cold air. The hall shone, blinding white and above it on the other side of the glass dome, a circus of white clouds raced through the blue sky. The third door opened into another hallway, the light switch shone beguilingly gold. He flipped it and mock candles flickered orange against faux marble walls. He ran a hand over the painted veins. A Gothic castle demanding exploration. The door swished shut behind him. Toby's feet whispered on the carpet until he held curled brass handles of double doors. He flung both wide.

The room sighed with pleasure at being found. Exquisite rainbows littered the floor which ran tens of metres towards windows stretching the room's breadth. On the ceiling fat white cherubs blasted trumpets to dance around each chandelier. The sun peered through diamond panes beyond which the tops of the hushed trees bowed in supplication.

Toby stood on the threshold.. Somewhere behind him a mobile trilled. He held his breath. It rang unanswered, then stopped. The floor bounced slightly as he stepped on it. He tiptoed past marble fireplaces and made his way to the windows: mock-Tudor hinged squares with shiny gold-leaf handles. As he reached for a golden handle, he became aware that someone was in the room with him. He tried to steady his breath. It was coming ragged and fast. Afraid, he felt the skin on his face tighten. Wondering if this was the moment when someone died, he turned slowly to see Gideon.

'Kitchen that-a-way,' the estate agent said quietly thumbing the corridor behind him.

'On my way,' said Toby moving past him out of the room. The square mirrored hallway was pungent with vomit. He opened the door opposite, another corridor ending in double doors which this time opened on to a kitchen. Cold and empty, a black marble sink stood under a window. On the chiselled draining board stood two cups: brown and pedestrian, upside down. They were cups for cleaning ladies, estate agents' cups. Interlopers in the bare splendour of the apartment. He filled one from gold dolphins which frolicked above the sink, and drank. He wondered about Gideon Chancelight and about Imogen and about the best course of action.

'Fuck a duck.' Gideon was crouched in the corridor bending to the space between the carpet and the door. Biting his lip he was attempting to shunt something into that space to hold the door open. His mobile phone was ringing. 'Pass that to me,' he snapped, hands struggling with the door. He paused to pull open his jacket. The lining shone peacock blue. The phone's top was just visible above the pocket which was decorated with gold embroidery which read Gieves & Hawkes, Savile Row.

'Hello?' Toby's voice sounded false in the mirrored room. Imogen wanting to know what time Gideon's home and whether they're in or out tonight and if they're in what would he say to one of her fish pies. 'Hello, Imogen.'

Gideon, outraged, held out his hand for the phone, his other held the door open. Toby passed it to him. 'Give me that... Hello? Lucy... Listen babe in the middle of something right now can I call you?' He threw the phone on the carpet. 'We are way off target on that commission. Help me out here.' He turned back to the door and bit his lip again to give his attention to whatever it was he was trying to cram under the door. He gave one final shove and sat back to watch the door drag across the carpet and close. 'Fuck it,' he said. 'Got to open this door up. Listen, mate, have you cleaned that puke up yet?' He turned to have a look. 'What have you been doing? They are about to arrive. Jesus. Bog roll, cleaning stuff. Use your head. Just clean that shit up.'

Toby smiled slightly.

Gideon frowned and reached for his mobile. He squinted at it: 'Fuck a duck. They'll be here now.' He smoothed his hair. 'We need to open the windows, open the doors. Mate, just deal with the puke.'

Unsteadily, Toby went through into the room which thronged with cherubs. He went to the window. It opened easily and he leant out. Beyond the dazzle of Prince Albert on his throne, the park stretched green and rich and far enough to show the earth's curve. Marble Arch and the Tyburn Gibbet were hidden by the earth's roundness. The Squire was already in the Spaniard's thrall.

'Right. I have a plan.' Gideon, dynamic, efficient, strode across the room to stop at something large and red and low to the floor. He crouched down, his tie lapping at the pale boards. 'Give us a hand old boy.' Gideon strained against its weight. The object seemed to be some kind of an outsized foot carved from red stone and resting on a breeze-block-sized lump of the same.

'Jesus. Give myself a hernia. Come on!' Gideon, teeth gritted looked up at Toby, his forehead furrowed with effort.

The foot wore a simple sandal, the kind of shoe a man of the desert might wear. However, it was the size of the foot that was unsettling. The big toe standing erect from the others was as wide as a fist and as long as a banana, its flat nail a shield against the sun.

'What is it?'

'A foot, fucker.' Gideon strained to move it.

Toby envisaged its owner having it sent over from somewhere hot. Dubai perhaps, a little reminder of the desert: 'And one of those feet. Get me one of those perky feet!'

'Are you going to help?' Gideon's arms hung limp, his tie, lifeless on the floor.

'Do what?' Toby looked around.

'Cover the puke bozo. You push I pull.'

Toby crouched to put his hands against the stump of ankle. He knelt and pushed on the stub with the flat of his hands. Above him Gideon strained, pulling at the block. A drop of his sweat splashed on to the foot. Toby sat, back against the wall, the soles of his boots against the object's Achilles tendon. Gideon crouched opposite to clasp the sprightly toe in both hands. Knuckles white, he wrenched at the foot in time with Toby's strains.

'Now, let's have this muthafucka,' Gideon commanded through gritted teeth. There was a snap and the estate agent flipped on to his back and skittered across the shiny floor. A dropped tortoise. Toby saw the underside of his shiny shoes. Sole gone, a hole the size of a marble and a flash of dirt-coloured, once-blue sock. His head hit the wooden floor. There was silence – Gideon lay motionless. Toby was standing, the monolithic foot in his hands three foot above that symmetrical face, those straight white teeth. Whoops. Sorry. And Gideon's head a blueberry burst all over the pale floor. Gideon sat up, legs crossed childishly in front of him. He opened his hand and in it lay the toe: a large red turd in the palm of his hand.

'Muthafucka.' He wrapped a fist around the toe, met Toby's eye and laughed. He stood up and, frowning, dusted down his suit.

The missing toe lent the foot an air of dignity that had previously been lacking. Like Venus without her arms.

'One thing after another this morning.'

The doorbell rang, an expensive chime.

'Muthafuckas.' Eyes wild, Gideon coaxed the toe into the pocket of his trousers. He straightened his tie and with dexterous brown fingers, tightened the knot. 'Fuckit Fuckit Fuckit. You will have to stand over the puke until I tell you to move. Fuckit.' Turning his cuffs he led the way. They arrived in the Vestibule of Truth and the doorbell chimed again. Gideon took Toby by the shoulders and reversed him up against the door. 'Do not move until I give the signal.' Gideon took two deep breaths, examined Toby's position and felt in his inside pocket. He brought out a small brown bottle, unscrewed the top and shook out four white pills. He handed two to Toby and took his, screwing up his face against them. Two white pills lay in the centre of Toby's palm.

'Beta blockers. Steady the old ticker. Help with panic attacks.'

Toby swallowed both, gagging against their dryness. Gideon straightened Toby's tie, lightly rearranged a curl on his forehead. 'Leave him to me. I want you to work the woman.' He took a deep breath and opened the front door.

'Hello hello. How are you both?'

'In a hurry,' came a woman's voice.

'Hello Gideon. Good of you to sort this out for us at such short notice,' came the man, embarrassed, laughing lightly.

'Come in,' Gideon stood back.

The woman, who was expensively dressed in cream and leather, came into the Vestibule of Truth on high-heeled boots. The man followed like a resigned teenage son. She jumped when she saw Toby. She looked him up and down. Her eyes lingered for a moment on his boots.

'Hello,' said Toby. Her glance swept up again and she turned away.

'This is my colleague, Toby Doubt. Victoria, Peter.'

Peter held out his hand, hesitated when Toby made no move and finally came over to where Toby stood. 'Good to see you again,' he said. 'You were in the office yesterday when I called by? No?'

'Great. Now,' Gideon opened the door which led out of the Vestibule of Truth and lowered his voice, 'this apartment is, er, shall we say... a little bit special? Arabian prince... '

'Before we go any further.' The woman held out a hand on which a large diamond glittered. 'Does it fulfil our criteria?'

'Tory, I'm sure by now Gideon knows exactly... '

'Peter,' the woman's voice overrode his. 'I'm fed up of wasted trips to see dingy flats with pokey drawing rooms.'

'Absolutely. Tory's got a good point,' continued Gideon impatient at the open door. 'As I was saying, this particular Arabian prince took too many wives unfortunately, the oil ran dry, the old King lost his temper and ordered his son back to the kingdom. And that is why, my friends, he's looking for a very quick sale. Hence the bargain.'

The woman rolled her eyes. 'It stinks,' she announced, her eyes resting on Toby. Gideon gestured for them to come through into the corridor.

'That smell is frankincense,' he said. 'Quite pungent isn't it? Good airing and it'll be gone. Some people love it. Some hate it.' The corridor flickered beguilingly with the fake candlelight. 'I know I love it.'

'Disgusting.'

'As we leave this room I should probably tell you that it's called the Hall of Mirrors. It dispels bad energy and ensures that anyone entering the house is cured of all bad karma.' Gideon smiled. Victoria tossed her hair.

'Well it obviously didn't do much for the Arabian prince,' she retorted.

'Let's do the ballroom, come back to the dining room, kitchen, study and on into the sleeping quarters. Does that work for you? After you.' Candles shimmered across marble and Peter followed Victoria into the corridor. 'Cunt,' muttered Gideon into Toby's ear.

'Nice wide corridor, guest cloak— Excuse me... ' Gideon swept ahead to slide open a mock marble door. 'Taps, imported gold... just a bit of fun.' Water sounded in a basin.

'Imported gold?' snorted Victoria. 'As opposed to the home-grown variety panned in our very own Thames?' Peter did not meet her glare. She flipped her hair across her head and, buttocks sliding under butter-soft cashmere, went to the double doors.

'Fantastic!' Peter laughed as light flooded the corridor and the ball-room was revealed. Victoria — like a little goat up on its hind legs — trotted across the floor while Peter gazed at the ceiling. Gideon strode after them.

'Fantastic cherubs, they look Italian.'

'French actually. I have it on fairly good authority, though don't quote me on it, that these have been lifted directly from the King's bed-room at Versailles. They're quite special aren't they? Symmetrical fire-places.' Gideon, twin barrels on each hand cocked, indicated identical grates.

Something approximating a smile appeared on Tory's glossy lips. 'This would do for a party.' The smile shrivelled and the hands went back into her pockets. 'I hate the windows.'

'Great view though,' said Gideon striding over towards them.

'The floor is so Ikea.'

'The leather sofa here, the chair here.' Peter arranged his furniture.

Victoria frowned at the ceiling: 'The leather won't work in here.' She trotted towards double doors at the far end of the room and there was silence as she disappeared through them and then her voice came, fainter now: 'Needs decorating.'

'Why don't you, er, accompany Victoria?' came Gideon's suggestion to Toby.

Obediently, he went through open doors into a thickly carpeted turquoise forest thronging with golden birds of paradise. Behind him Gideon was saying: 'Kensington Roof Gardens… never forget it… bite-size burgers, bundles of fries, mini milkshake vodka shots. Best canapes I ever had.'

Victoria was in the kitchen. She was frowning at the taps: 'Monstrous.' Toby pulled himself up on to the unit in the centre of the room. She turned to look him up and down: an insubordinate butler. His heels swung against the counter as he wondered about requesting she give him her engagement ring. Perhaps she'd refuse. In which case he'd have to cut off her finger. 'Outlandish bitch,' he rolled the words around his tongue. 'Sodomized whore of Satan.' She might swallow it rather than hand it over. He'd then have to slit her open and feel around inside her gullet until he located the diamond. Or more likely, she'd swallow it and he, being the Squire, would ask her how she was feeling and whether she'd like a glass of water. It would probably be better to leave something like this to a professional. The Spaniard for example would know how to encourage her to hand over the ring.

'Is that the way you sell flats?' The words came down the length of her pale nose.

Toby waited until her heels had stopped clicking on the slate before telling her: 'Properties sell themselves.'

'Is that right?' she said. 'I'm sure your boss wouldn't be very happy to hear you say that.'

Toby laughed. 'He's not my boss, we're partners.'

'You're a partner?' Victoria raised her eyebrows. 'And you believe that properties sell themselves?'

'It's our philosophy at Milson, Range & Rafter that a property will sell itself. And if it doesn't then there's something wrong with it.' He finished and watched her.

'It's disgusting to sit up there.' She turned away. 'It's unhygienic.'

Toby jumped off the unit. 'It would seem that I have misjudged the situation,' he said. 'I had you down as someone who forms their own opinion as to whether something is worth buying or not, rather than relying on the patter of a salesman.' He opened the door that led from the kitchen. Victoria, hands in her pockets, came through into a room in which there were more sinks and another cooker.

'This,' said Toby, 'is the secondary kitchen, crafted from finest Welsh slate. Four lorry loads were brought down from Aberystwyth. In fact, these two kitchens cleared an entire quarry and Wales is less grey as a result. Now, in this small room is everything you could possibly need for cleaning a majestic flat such as this. Washing machine: the very finest in Japanese technology offering cycles we've only ever dreamt of here in the West.' He opened a cupboard and an ironing board flopped down.

'Obviously this is a room in which a woman such as yourself,' he bowed to Victoria, 'would rarely find herself. This would be the preserve of maid and butler.' Toby tried to return the ironing board to the cupboard. He failed. Instead he leant against it, his back to the idea of Imogen astride it, face pressed sideways into its padded surface.

'In this single, modest room is everything a maid could ever wish for.'

Hands in pockets, outraged, Victoria looked at him.

Behind them Toby could hear Gideon jocular in the kitchen: 'I've never been a fan of islands or whatever they're called. I'd rip all this out and throw down a farmhouse table. Sturdy, rustic. Simple. Cosy kitchen suppers and all that malarkey.'

Toby opened the door at the other side of the room and they were back in the carpeted corridor, the faux candles twinkling gamely.

'After you.'

Stiffly Victoria went out.

'Exquisite marbling,' said Toby. 'This was not a man to scrimp on life's little luxuries.' He decided that if these walls were life's little luxuries he did not have a problem with being a man who scrimped on them.

'OK,' Victoria said. 'Point taken. Thank you very much – enough of the commentary.' She flapped him away with a hand.

He followed her into a large square room which was dominated by a vast Viking ship of a bed that curved up at both ends, shiny and embossed with gold.

'Fit for a prince,' supplied Toby.

'Prince of Darkness,' said Victoria rummaging in her bag. 'What kind of a person sleeps on something like this?' She photographed it with her mobile phone.

'No photographs,' said Toby. 'And it's a princess who sleeps on a bed like this.' He examined the crest on the headboard. It was a gold, three-dimensional rendering of what might have been the pyramids.

'And this would be staying would it?' She looked up. Above the bed on the ceiling was an identically shaped mirror. Oval and gold-tinted, it stared, unblinking, down.

Toby looked up at their reflections. Her pale coat, the bag over her shoulder, the dark roots beginning to show at the parting in her hair. And on the other side of the bed, his own. He imagined them working together to put a sheet across the mattress. He blinked and saw Imogen struggling with the sheet alone. Victoria swept her hair across her head and walked to open a door. She disappeared.

It drove Imogen insane that he was never there to help with the sheets. 'At least put the pillow cases on,' she'd shout upstairs to the bathroom as he sank bubbling beneath the water.

'Cooling off chamber,' said Toby following Victoria. 'For when you have a fight… '

'Dressing room,' said Victoria coldly, snapping off the light. Her laughter rang out: 'Hideous.'

Toby followed her into a bathroom, black and gold to match the bed. Walls and ceiling were gold mirror, the floor was slate and the room was dominated by a black and gold jacuzzi sunk below the floor. A bank of three black basins – seashell shaped and flecked with gold –

lined one wall.

'His and his and hers,' said Toby.

'What? Look at the lavs. How extraordinary!' The diamond flashed imperiously on her hand. 'Grotesque. I've got to get Pete in to see this.' She clipped back the way they'd come.

How could he have imagined that Imogen would be happy with the shabby little house in Kentish Town when this was available to women? Jacuzzis and ballrooms, chandeliers and diamonds. Exhausted, Toby sat on a bidet. What do you think, Imo? Keep the bed or get a new one? Blood pounded against his skull. He put his head in his hands. There were footsteps and then Victoria's voice in the bedroom. 'This has to be seen to be believed.' Toby stood up as she appeared.

'Priceless,' said Victoria. 'Come on, Pete.' And then to Toby: 'How long has it been on the market?'

'One day,' said Toby.

'Any other interest?'

'A writer and his wife,' said Toby. 'She, like you, asked about the bed.'

'And? Did they make an offer?' Impatient, Victoria tossed her hair.

'I'm afraid I can't... '

'Off the record.'

'Off the record, yes they did.'

'Come on. More detail! What was it and was it accepted?' Victoria's eyes glittered.

'I am not at liberty to say,' said Toby. 'But what I can tell you is that the offer, while very competitive, was just below the asking price. We're waiting for the Old King to get back to us.'

'So it hasn't been accepted. Pete?' Victoria left the room and Toby sank back on to the bidet.

Gideon came into the bathroom. He frowned when he saw Toby. 'You feeling alright?' They could hear Victoria's voice in the bedroom.

Gideon patted Toby's shoulder as he looked around at the black and gold opulence. 'Fuck me.' He eyed the jacuzzi: 'We could have some fun in here. Couple of chicks, some chilled fizz. Nice bit of Neil Diamond.' Bending, he turned on the tap. 'Oh yeah baby, we got hot.'

'And the bathroom.' Victoria's diamond flashed in several mirrors, her heels clicked on the floor, her body asserted itself under the fluid lines of her coat and Gideon turned off the tap and straightened. 'Jacuzzi, Pete. Jacuzzi.'

Peter faced its sunken majesty, looking in his suit as though he'd never been naked. 'Wow, this is great.' It seemed Peter might have been referring to Victoria's improved spirits rather than to the bath.

'We'd have to get rid of the bed. Obviously. Can you imagine your mother's face? Or Piers and Candace?' Her eyes were sparkling. 'Actually we should keep it in the guest bedroom. Can you imagine? Come.' She rattled his sleeve. 'Let's see the other bedrooms. With a little imagination... ' she smiled at her reflection.

Peter's smile was apologetic and directed at Gideon as he was dragged sidestepping out. Her voice receded into the corridor and Gideon sat on the loo next to Toby's bidet.

'Synchronized dumps for the closer couple.' He adjusted his tie. 'Nice work on the offer, you devious fucker. And nice work on the witch. How did you sweeten her up? Give her a little bit of... ' Gideon whistled and cranked his arm which ended in a balled fist. 'You alright?' He slapped Toby's thigh. 'Remember. I need you in position on the way out. Perhaps you should assume it now? Feet together, against the door, cheerful smile.'

Gideon checked his watch and stood up. He touched his toes, bouncing as his hands rose and fell above the floor. He stood straight and circled his head first one way and then the other and, whistling faintly, followed the direction the couple had taken.

Back in the Porsche Gideon waited for Peter and Victoria to reverse out of the space in their shiny-black Range Rover.

'Right,' he said. He opened his appointment diary, licked his thumb, turned to the back page and dialled a number. 'Jonathan Quick. I'll hold.' Again Gideon licked his thumb. He scraped it across a mark on his trousers until it disappeared.

'Jonathan Quick, Gideon Chancelight, Milson Range Rafter.' A pause while Jonathan Quick digested this information. Gideon rubbed the thumb across the plastic of the dashboard.

'Regarding Palace Mansions. Just shown it to a client who would like to make an offer. Two. That's right. Two million pounds. Cash. Ready to move. You have my numbers. Peter... ' Gideon flicked through the diary. 'Peter James is the purchaser. I repeat, Peter James. Cheers Jonathan. As soon as.' Gideon closed his phone, handed the diary to Toby, checked his mirror and pulled out.

'Ain't life grand?'

ten

'Well it's been quite a morning. And it looks like we might have shifted Caesar's Palace as long as our friend the Sheik 'n' Bake plays along.' Gideon, uncomfortable in his seat, put his hand between his legs, adjusted his underpants and returned it to the gear stick. 'And if that's the case, my friend, not wishing to jump the gun etcetera but woo hoo that's my cash situation solved. I've been thinking...' Gideon's hand, strong and brown, landed on the gear stick again. 'How does a sixty-six-thirty-three split sound?' He turned to Toby. 'Peter James is my contact. You heard the man. He was unwilling – that's right unwilling – to deal with anyone else. I set it up, put the Palace and Pedro James together. And you.' He irritated the gear stick beneath his palm. 'All you did was almost fuck it up with that puke-a-roo when we arrived.'

The lights were red at South Kensington. Still uncomfortable, Gideon writhed in his seat to feel in the pocket of his trousers. He leant back, head braced against the leather headrest. He straightened his legs and bit his bottom lip. The lights changed and someone hooted. Gideon brought out the oversized red toe. It rolled on his palm in the air between the seats.

'I forgot about you.' He smiled at it fondly and put it in the tray beneath the handbrake and moved off towards the office.

'So' he turned to Toby. 'sixty-six-thirty-three? What do you say? Fair?'

Toby was wondering about the effect of champagne at high altitudes.

'OK… OK.' Gideon fumbled in his pocket for his cigarettes. 'OK. You're right. You sorted out old Sour Chops. Fuck me, the woman would curdle milk. Fifty-fifty. Nine grand each. You OK with that?' Gideon looked over. 'I should imagine you are OK with that. Nine grand for fifteen minutes' sweet talk and a natural way with women. You good with all women?'

Gideon turned to Toby. Toby didn't understand the question. Gideon turned back to the road and Toby examined his profile: the nose was straight, perfectly straight and cut away into a short curve before swelling into a full top lip.

'You good with all women or just the ones who inhabit the area up their own backsides?'

Toby's thumbnail was dirty; black with something like tar. He picked at it and felt Gideon's gaze on his face.

'Hello, earth to Toby. Women. Any good with them?'

Toby, mouth dry, arranged his face in an approximation of concern. 'Woman trouble is it?' he asked looking straight ahead. Like someone's father, or like a woman's calcified husband talking about her menstrual cycle. Women's trouble. Trouble with women. The kind of thing the Colonel might say. Tempted to laugh, he examined the back of the red van in front: 'Trafic' it declared in italic writing. A spelling mistake or just an economical way for vans to classify themselves? Why use two where one will do?

'Yep, woman trouble pretty much sums it up.' A humourless laugh and Gideon fumbled with his pack of cigarettes. He put one between his lips. 'I, my friend, am arse-deep in woman trouble.' He thrust his hand down beside his seat.

Arse-deep or neck-deep? 'Oh? What's the problem?' Man to man. A friendly bit of interest. Acid rising in Toby's chest.

'The problem is… ' Gideon felt with his hand down the other side of the seat. 'Got a light?'

Impatient, Toby searched in his pocket. For the second time that day, he brought out the lighter showing a blonde, kneeling Imogen with cantilevered breasts.

'Cheers.' Gideon lowered the window and pulled open the ashtray. 'The problem is… ' he laughed and ran the hand that held the cigarette through his hair. 'I can't even say it. The problem is… ' Gideon glanced at Toby. 'You're sweating.'

Toby touched his forehead.

'The problem is this… oh, sweet Jesus.' Gideon dragged audibly on the cigarette and exhaled. 'There's this girl. She's pregnant. She says it's mine, she's moved into my place and her husband is trying to kill me. That in a nutshell is it.'

Oh. 'Right,' said Toby.

'No shit,' agreed Gideon.

'She's pregnant?'

'Six weeks gone.'

'And it's yours?'

'Do you think this would be a problem if it wasn't?'

Gideon explored his upper lip with his tongue. Toby wondered about slamming his fist into the flesh under his jaw. He wondered about the part of Gideon's tongue that protruded between his teeth and about whether, if it dropped into the valley between his thighs, it would be recognizable as the tip of Gideon's tongue.

'Oh yes,' said Gideon. 'I ran into this girl a couple of months ago. I've sort of known her a while. Anyway she comes back to my place. Drinks, a smoke, some Neil Diamond and a shag for old time's sake. So…' Gideon tapped his cigarette on the car door. 'Turns out she's married. Great. Lucky guy. Nice to see you and goodbye. You'd think. But no. Oh no, baby. Cut to now. She's left the husband, she's trying to move in with me, she's having my baby, she washed my lucky shorts and… I'm looking forward to getting put in hospital by her ex. What the fuck?' He turned to Toby.

Toby tried to move his lips around words. None came. Husband?

That was news.

'Gobsmacked? You and me both, mate.' Gideon laughed and put a hand to his forehead. 'This husband is some kind of gangster. On top of that, he's not a happy camper. There have been death threats, phone calls: you're dead, I'm going to burn your house down, I know where you live. I'll kill your mother. The guy is psychotic and apparently never goes out without a monkey wrench. The-guy-never-goes-out-without-a-fucking-monkey-wrench.' Gideon laughed and tore at his fringe.

'As if I don't have enough going on what with this baby and now a psycho with a spanner.' He checked his rear-view mirror. 'Apparently he's been inside before and now he knows where I work. He's that fucker you saw this morning asking for me – suit, tie, monkey wrench. Fuck me backwards.' Gideon was running a hand faster and faster through his hair.

'I have got to convince her to go the abortion route… how am I going to do that? The silly cow washed my lucky shorts.' Gideon turned to look. 'She washed my lucky shorts. I wore them every day for more than a year and every single sale I did at Range Rafter I wore my luckies. Those shorts netted me in excess of 150 K. Bitch washed them.' He dipped inside his trousers and pulled up the tartan waistband of his underpants. 'These ain't the same,' he said. 'They're running on twenty-six days.'

Toby's life had unfolded on to a new vista. A new landscape had opened up and here was a new set of facts demanding organization and assimilation: he was a psychopath and Imogen was pregnant and they were married. He supposed he could accept the first.

'Where's she living?'

'Apart from when she's at mine which is way too much of the time? Fuck knows. Somewhere in Fulham.'

Fulham? Not Saffron. Not Jane and Howard. But Cassie and Iain. Cassie and Iain lived in Fulham near the Hurlingham Club. 'Sister,' said Toby.

'Pardon?'

'Do you love her?' Lips fumbling with words.

'Love her? Do I love her? What planet are you from? I can't stand the fucking sight of her. She's on the phone, she's in the flat, she's having my child. Her hair is all over the fucking bath.' The Spaniard retched. 'I can't stand the fucking sight of her.' He lit a cigarette from the sharp end of the one he was smoking. 'Epic,' he said and threw it from the window.

Imogen on her back with the Spaniard on top. No more contraceptive pill. Just Imogen and the Spaniard and the baby they've made.

'Look out.'

Gideon slammed on the brakes and the car squealed across the road skimming the rear lights of 'Trafic' which was attempting to park. He looked in the rear-view mirror and whistled.

A cloud of black smoke hung heavy across the road behind them. A woman with a pram on the pavement stood frozen in fear.

'Fuck a duck.' Gideon was laughing. 'Love her? Do I love her? Are you out of your mind? The slag washed my lucky shorts. Her husband is about to kill me and now she's having my fucking baby.'

The lighter was warm and wide in Toby's hand. He turned it. A baby in that belly. It seemed ridiculous. Perhaps the child was his. After all, pregnancy made women do strange things: eat coal, shoplift, swallow lighted matches. Some even took taxis home to addresses they hadn't lived at for a decade, back to boyfriends they hadn't seen for fifteen years.

'What's wrong with you?' asked Gideon.

'Is the baby definitely yours?'

'Don't know. Could be. Don't know.' Gideon slumped, defeated, head against the steering wheel. 'Don't trust the cow; however, I reckon I'm pretty potent.' He brightened momentarily and then slumped over the steering wheel again. 'The bad news is that apparently the psychopath never shagged her. Now I'm beginning to know why.'

'Rubbish.'

'What?'

A footprint on the black dashboard in front of the passenger seat in Gideon's car showed a swirl of rubber patterns. The sole of Imogen's white trainer.

'Of course he shagged her,' Toby said, outraged. 'I can't believe she told you that.'

'Exactly my point.' Gideon tapped the steering wheel with the back of his hand. 'My point exactly. She tells me that he's boring, broke and bad in bed. Not to mention the other downer: the man is a psychopath. So, like you say, why the fuck did she marry him? Not my fucking problem. Someone is telling porkies here. The point is they were married, they shagged like rabbits, the baby's his. However I'm a much better catch. I'm rich, I'm gorgeous, I drive this little beauty,' he patted the dashboard, 'and I don't need a monkey wrench to get a bit of respect around here.'

Gideon's mobile phone rang. He jumped.

'Hello? Yep. Oh Jonathan, hi… That is indeed good news. I'll call my people now, get things moving. A-sap. Cheers. Speak later. Ciao.'

He closed the phone. 'That's a deal, partner. Our Sheik 'n' Bake wants to do business. That's nine Gs each.' Gideon grinned at Toby, thumped his arm and accelerated loudly up the bus lane. 'We're in the money. We're in the money. We're in the money.'

'Do you think she might go back to the husband?'

'Eh?'

'The husband. Do you think she might go back to him?'

'Who?' Gideon impatient, was bemused.

Toby took a breath. 'The pregnant girl.'

'Eh?' Gideon looked at Toby. 'You're one odd mother. We've just cleared eighteen grand and you're wondering about "the pregnant girl".'

His imitation of Toby was not unkind and Toby let it go. Besides he had other things to think about. Broke? Boring? Bad in bed? The three Bs. Whichever way you looked at it – and there was no easy way to look at it – Imogen had gone because he was broke, bad in bed and boring. Each sounded fairly terminal when it came to reasons for leaving people.

'Fuck me you've had a good week,' said Gideon. 'Nineteen K and its only day three. I don't believe you've never sold houses before. The way you worked that chopsy slag "Oh Peter those chandeliers are a bit Ikea!" You, my son, are gifted.'

Gideon cruised past the office looking for somewhere to park. Harmsworth-Mallett was standing smoking in the sunlight. He saw the Porsche and lifted a thumb. Up, down, up, down, up, down. Gideon rolled down his window to give Harmsworth-Mallett a thumbs-up. The old man smiled and performed an elaborate bow, cigarette spiralling in his hand. He finished with a flourish and cupping his hands around his mouth called: 'See you down at the Fox.'

'Don't you love the guy? You want to hear about woman trouble?' Gideon whistled. 'His wife kicks him out and for the past two months he's been living in his car. At least he's got a Merc.' Gideon reversed the Porsche into the space. 'It's going to be tight in here.'

Chuck remained at his desk, bandaged and morose, drawing obscure symbols of dark intent on the window while Gideon and Toby followed Daisy and Harmsworth-Mallett down to the Curious Fox.

'The Golden Boys. Here they come.' Harmsworth-Mallett was standing at the bar, smoking. 'What are you having?' Blink blink smile smile. The man looked at peace, shiny shoe perched on brass footrest.

'Toby Doubt,' said Gideon clapping him on the back. 'Odd fucker but one hell of a way with the ladies.'

'Is that so sir?' Harmsworth-Mallett said to Toby, eyebrows working overtime. 'G and T for Daisy.' With a trembling hand he pushed a short glass with a slice of lemon buzzing inside towards Toby and pointed past him with his cigarette.

Pristine in pink and white in the yellowed interior of the Fox, Daisy was at a long wooden table examining her mobile phone. Toby carried the drink, shoes sounding hollow on wooden floorboards. Behind him Harmsworth-Mallett sang: 'Goldfinger. The men with the Midas Touch...'

Daisy stiffened as Toby placed the drink in front of her. As he sat she zipped her handbag in such a way as to accuse him of theft as her eyes sought Gideon at the bar. She put her phone on the table, took a sip from her drink and smiled at something she wasn't going to share. Toby looked at his feet. One of the legs of his mud-spattered trousers had ridden up to show his ankle. A sorry spindle of leg which tapered before disappearing into a large brown boot. A milk-white broom handle scrubby with ginger hair. Broke. Bad in bed. Boring. How could he blame Lady Rose Stockport for choosing the Spaniard? Next to him Daisy examined the pink tassels on her scarf.

'Hello Daisy.'

'What?' She frowned and dropped the scarf. She picked up her drink.

'Stella.' Gideon sloshed a pint on to the table in front of Toby. Beyond him Harmsworth-Mallett in a haze of smoke stood smiling at the flashing fruit machine.

Daisy squirmed and dimpled. 'Hey Gids.'

'Hey Daze,' he replied, pulling out the stool opposite Toby. 'And how is Lazy Daisy?'

'I'm not lazy.' Little girl voice, shiny-lipped pout. 'I have mailed 247 letters this morning.'

'Who's the lucky man?' Gideon turned to Toby: 'Last month Mr Eric Larkspear of 18 Emperor's Gate called to say that despite 200 letters through his door, he was still uninterested in selling his property though Range Rafter.'

'Hey!' Daisy, mock sullen, reached across the table and lightly slapped Gideon's arm. 'It was 18 Queen's Court and anyway it wasn't my fault, I was hungover.'

'A toast,' said Gideon holding up his pint.

A splatter of coins sounded from the fruit machine. Harmsworth-Mallett moved his cigarette from one hand to the other.

'Most people would be, like, grateful to get any letters at all. Let alone 200.' Daisy held out her glass.

'To Palace Mansions.' Gideon touched his pint to Toby's. As an afterthought he touched Daisy's.

'You and me... ' Lowered voice, conspiratorial, coaster up on its side, Gideon leant across the table: 'I reckon we've got sales sewn up.'

Daisy sighed and sat back.

'We get rid of Chuck and work the two-pronged attack all across West London.' He tapped the coaster on the table. 'We'll sell Kemp, Sage, Watson right out of the market and take a million each, three years, what do you say?'

Daisy tapped her phone on the table.

Toby didn't know what to say. Three years sounded like a long time. It sounded like the kind of time in which a marriage, divorce and a death might take place.

'We'll clean up West London.'

'By the way.' Daisy flicked her pink scarf over one shoulder. Gideon lifted the cardboard coaster from the table and looked up at her from under his fringe. 'What's that cat doing in the basement?'

'What cat?' Gideon sat back in his chair and, wiping his lips, put the coaster on the table and his glass on top.

'It's mine.'

Daisy turned her attention to Toby. 'Sorry we can't have it down there. Health and safety. We're not allowed animals in the office.'

'Chill Daze.'

'I'm allergic to cats.'

'From all the way downstairs?' Gideon showed white teeth.

'Whatever. I wanted to warn you anyway as Mike is like coming in this afternoon.' The statement rose at the end to leave 'afternoon' hanging, a trigger for hysteria.

'Mike?' Gideon laughed. 'Magic Mike Range. The man who hasn't shifted a property in a decade. What's he going to say about it? This man,' he pointed to Toby as he drank, 'has made Magic Mike seventy grand in two days. Do you really think he's going to kick off about a cat in a cage downstairs?'

Harmsworth-Mallett shuffled his way to a place at the table. He placed a short glass of what might have been whisky carefully on a coaster in front of him and crossed thin legs tightly. His suit was shiny at the cuffs. 'How does it feel to rule the world?' He quivered in the stale afternoon.

Daisy sighed and pulled both ends of the pink scarf until it tightened around her neck. She rolled her eyes and stuck out her tongue. Toby wondered if the fabric might be strong enough to pull until her head came off.

'Pretty good old man. Pretty good. And how's the wild and wacky world of lettings?'

'Rats, leaks, more rats.' Harmsworth-Mallett turned a short glass in tremulous hands. 'A ruptured boiler. A broken sash window. A hornets' nest. A leak from upstairs. I need a right-hand man. Oh, and now mice.' A sigh and a dewy smile. 'Mr Edward Lawson of Emperor's Gate called this morning to report mice.' Mallett's eyes drifted beyond Daisy through dusty glass on to the road somewhere outside. 'These things are sent to try us.'

'Send in the cat.' Gideon nodded to Toby. 'And what's the scoop on the Chuckler?'

'The Chuckler? Sadly our friend from across the pond is a little worse for wear and tear. His feelings have been rather hurt by our Mr Dote.' Harmsworth-Mallett lit another cigarette. 'It would seem he rather thought of Kings Reach as his sale. And the Greek,' he puffed on the cigarette, exhaled, looked at the tip and puffed again, 'as his client. And the commission, you see, as his commission.'

'That old story.' Gideon rolled his eyes.

'What exactly happened?' Daisy frowned her contempt. 'I'm sorry, but you don't, like, break down the front door do you? I don't know if I feel comfortable working in the same office as someone that violent.' She shuddered elaborately.

'So what exactly happened?' Gideon tipped his stool.

'I'm not entirely sure. I was working late... the key was in the door but I had it locked. I was downstairs sorting a few things out...' Harmsworth-Mallett coughed and turned his glass. 'Keeping up to date on the accounts. I heard the door rattle... to tell the truth... '

'What time was it?' Gideon interrupted.

'Oh, er, late.' Harmsworth-Mallett, guilty, blinking into his pint. 'There was this almighty crack. I went upstairs and there was glass everywhere, and Chuck, dear old Chuck, was face down, half inside the office, half outside on the pavement. Glass, blood, his head was quite split open and he was shouting all kinds of things: Theft... Kings Reach... Dote. Turned the air quite blue.' He laughed as his fluttering hands came at last to rest on his glass. 'It seems Dote was the straw that broke the proverbial.' He sighed and went on.

'I called an ambulance. Chuck went off to Charing Cross and I enjoyed a coffee with the police. And this morning as though nothing had happened and it was any other Wednesday, he arrived at work. On time.'

Daisy looked at Toby, her eyes flat grey. 'So was Kings Reach, like, *his deal?*'

Gideon laughed. 'All's fair in this game Daze.'

'It seems he'd shown our Greek friend the property on a previous occasion,' said Harmsworth-Mallett. 'However, when our Greek came into the office yesterday, Chuck was asleep and it was Dote who took him down there.'

'So it *was* his,' asserted Daisy, nodding, looking from Gideon to the old man and back.

'No,' said Gideon. 'Anyone can show a property. Selling it is where the skill is.'

'Someone should at least have woken Chuck up.' Daisy examined the lemon in her glass.

'Yeah right.'

'I believe you are not entirely to blame.' Harmsworth-Mallett reached across the table to touch Toby's arm. 'There were other things contributing to our friend's, er, upset shall we say? Domestic troubles I believe. All is not well at the ranch. So to speak. That, my friend, can make anyone crack.' He laughed humourlessly.

'Anyway,' Daisy trimmed a fingernail on her teeth, 'he should still be fired for breaking down the door.'

'Women eh?' Harmsworth-Mallett said, emboldened by whisky. 'Whatever happened to the milk of human kindness?'

'The man should be fired.' Daisy appealed to Gideon. 'So it's right is it that that he should get away with breaking down the office and then just be allowed to, like, come to work, as though absolutely nothing has happened? What's he going to do next? Like suicide bomb it?'

'What's Mike's take on it?' Gideon ignored her.

'Ah Mike. Mike is not best pleased with having to fork out a thousand pounds for a new door. However, on the back of Kings Reach,' a nod at Toby, 'and now Palace Mansions he's not doing too badly.' Harmsworth-Mallett looked into his glass. Eventually he said: 'Accidents will happen.'

Daisy snorted. 'If that was an accident then I'm the Queen.'

'Daisy, you know you are,' said Gideon.

Daisy seemed unsure how to take Gideon's remark. She blushed, avoided Gideon's eye, examined her nail and smiled.

'The Chuckler has not sold a property since...' Gideon said to Harmsworth-Mallett, 'Duchess Walk.' Gideon gazed into the middle distance. 'March. Four grand. That's four months without earning. He's crap at sales. You need help on lettings. You should have Mike move him over to help you out with the rats. Get him on a salary. He's been here long enough to know how things work. Toby and I have got sales sewn up.' Gideon drained his glass. 'With his attitude he's giving our operation a bad name. Another one?' Gideon stood. 'That solves his problem, his wife's problem, your rat problem and your problem.' He held his glass out towards Daisy and closing one eye, examined her through it before turning to go to the bar.

Harmsworth-Mallett nodded gently into his own glass. 'Do you know I think the boy might be right.'

'How does it solve my problem?' Daisy wanted to know.

The pavement that led back to the office glittered. While Gideon outlined a strategy for shifting Flat 17 in Queen's Wharf, Chelsea, to Mr Solomon, a man who was, by all accounts, eager to buy, Toby was thinking about Rita. His head made clear by the beer, he'd realized that the cat may serve a purpose after all. As they passed Luigi's, Gideon waved at the dark-haired waitress who, polishing glasses behind the counter, lit up with a smile. Toby turned to the Spaniard:

'Gideon, I need a favour.'

'For you partner, anything,' he said looking at Toby with deep green insincerity.

'I'm sorry to ask you this, but I'm pretty desperate.' Pretty desperate about summed things up.

An expression of concern marked the Spaniard's forehead: 'We can't have that.' Smiling, he squinted into the sun.

Toby took a breath. 'I'm having some work done on my house. And the cat, Rita, has to be out for a couple of days. I was wondering whether you might be able to have it at your place for a couple of nights. Just until the plastering's finished... '

Gideon frowned. 'I've never had a cat. What do you do with them?'

'Food, water. I've got all that with me. It's easy. I'm sure, er, the pregnant girl,' Toby cleared his throat, 'will know how to look after it.'

'I don't have a garden. Where do they go to the toilet?'

'Don't worry about that. They don't really go that much.'

Gideon looked doubtful.

'I know,' said Toby. 'You can persuade the girl to have an abortion by promising her a cat.'

'You reckon?' Gideon looked sceptical. 'Anything's worth a try.' He clapped Toby on the shoulder.

'Thanks,' said Toby. He smiled and held open the new office door for Gideon.

eleven

It was dark outside and there were too many people around the table in the Fox. Toby couldn't breathe for the string of numbers repeating in his head. Oh double seven double four double nine. Oh double seven double four double nine. There was Daisy and Harmsworth-Mallett and Gideon. There was Mike Range, a girl in yellow and a girl in blue and a girl with a necklace of pearls around her neck. The Spaniard stood to drink his pint of Stella, the focus of all their happy faces: 'And I'm on my back... ' The girl in blue laughed. 'And this fucking toe,' Gideon's eyes widened, 'is nesting in the palm of my fucking hand.' He lifted a hand as though weighted with it. 'So I've got this priceless Ottoman antique nesting in my hand. The doorbell rings and that fucker Doubt is just standing there with puke dripping down his face... '

Girl in pearls turned to look. Blue girl laughed: 'Like gross!' Yellow girl drank and Daisy put a hand through her hair: 'You are such a prat Gids.'

'Do not say any more.' One hand up, Magic Mike Range was laughing, his moustache stretched above his open mouth, his game-show face crinkling tangerine orange. 'Enough. I do not wish to hear any more.' He brought his glass to his mouth and drank. 'Do not tell me any more. Toby I am relying on you to keep this man under control. Capiche?'

'Is your cat OK?' The yellow girl asked Gideon. 'Should we cover it?'

The pink Voyager was on the table behind Gideon and the music was loud enough to mask the cat's misery.

'Shall I cover it with my jacket?' The girl in yellow extricated herself from the table to be near the Spaniard.

Oh double seven double four double nine. Oh double seven double four double nine. Eight three four. The number as it happened had been the wrong number but still it went round inside Toby's head. The Spaniard was surrounded. Even Magic Mike was not immune to him. Brown and glittering and ripe like a nut he was telling another story.

'So this fortune teller is saying to me – she's looking down at these cards on the table – your run of prosperity is about to dry up old son unless you forge a solid partnership with a new guy who will be coming into the office. You might have doubts about this guy at first,' Gideon gestured to Toby and laughed, 'however, you must make a solid partnership and you will both do very well out of it. The old hag was right so far... ' Gideon drank. 'Especially about the doubts.' Gideon laughed. 'Toby Doubt, get it?'

Oh double seven double four double nine. Toby gave this number to the policeman. The policeman has asked him for a number, not any number. The right number. Leaning forward intently, pen poised above policeman's notebook. This is the number that Toby knows. It's oh double seven double four double nine.

'Poor bastard,' says the police constable coming back into the room a moment later.

'Poor bastard,' says the police officer looking down at the notepad.

'The poor bastard,' says the kindly police officer. 'It's the girl's number.'

'Poor bastard,' says the police officer. 'He's given me the girl's number. I can hear it ringing.'

'You're weird,' said Daisy coming over to collect a packet of Marlboro Lights which was on the table beside Toby. 'You're so weird. You've been staring at Gideon all night.' She went back to where she'd been standing by the fruit machine near Harmsworth-Mallett and turned again to examine Toby. She shook her head and lit a cigarette. She pulled Gideon to one side. The girl in yellow looked bereft. The girl in pearls followed them with her eyes. The group was sad without him. Magic Mike said something to Pearls and Blue and Yellow. They nodded but their hungry eyes were on Daisy and the Spaniard. Daisy was whispering in his ear. Suddenly Gideon burst out laughing. His brown face split to show white teeth. He drank, swallowed and laughed again. Everyone laughed. Gideon put his pint on top of the fruit machine. Harmsworth-Mallett looked up briefly.

'Of course I know that Toby fancies me,' said Gideon. He came over to run an arm along Toby's shoulders. 'This man is in love with me.' He clicked his pint against Toby's which was on the table. 'And who can blame him?' Blue laughed and Pearls laughed and Yellow laughed. Mike smiled and looked genially from Toby to Gideon. Daisy did not laugh. Gideon bent to kiss Toby on his forehead. His lips were soft and wet.

Toby was hot. He stood.

'Where are you going?'

'I should be getting back.'

'Have you got the hump?' Gideon asked.

Pearls laughed. Daisy watched closely.

'No,' said Toby.

'Sorry about calling you a fucker. It was a joke. Required for the story.'

'That's fine. What about the cat?'

'What about it?'

'Still OK to take it?'

'Still OK to take it.' Gideon clinked his glass against Toby's, which had an inch of lager left in it. 'Be seeing you and here's to Palace Mansions.'

Toby lifted his glass and drank the last of his pint.

twelve

Mr Cheap Potatoes was down on all fours when Toby came in. He frowned and with some effort, stood. He rubbed his knees. A doll-pink streak of taramasalata was splattered across the grey linoleum and a matching diagonal streaked his thigh.

'You be careful.' Frowning he pointed at the floor before making his way behind the counter where he pretended to dust batteries.

Toby examined the alcohol. Super, Extra, Special. He chose Special Brew, paid Mr Cheap and went home. Past the hot mouth of the tube, past the pub where they won the lottery, past the row of dishevelled men on the bench. They were singing something Irish. The furious one touched his hat. Toby saluted, crossed the road and opened his front door.

The house was silent. No Rita spitting vitriol from the stairs. That was good. It was about time Rita pulled her weight. After all, and as he'd told the cat, it wasn't just him that Imogen had abandoned. He collected the scatter of letters from the mat. Two bills, one envelope for a P. Robinson Esq. and something mauve and addressed in blue biro to Mr Toby Doubt. He turned the letter over and put his thumb into the corner. A small, dark shape in the middle of the carpet drew his attention. He bent forwards to see a tiny vole on the dark red pile, its white hands folded in death, its eyelids blue. There was no Imogen to save a shrew. There was no cat now either. That was good.

The envelope fluttered to the floor leaving behind a card embossed with a raised and colourful heart shape done out in flowers. 'In Sympathy' read a curl of gold. And inside: 'Dear Toby' in tight blue biro. 'When someone you love becomes a memory.' And in the former twirl of gold: 'The memory becomes a treasure.' Again the biro: 'Thinking of you at this time, Hazel.' Hazel? Hazel. Imogen's parents' next door neighbour in Surrey. Hazel. He stood the card astride the tiny shrew and wondered when its memory would become a treasure. Soon he hoped.

The back door was open. Toby stood in the doorway and felt something like surprise that the area hadn't been cordoned off. It was clearly a disaster zone, a police-monitored crime scene. A sea of ripped-up, torn-out plants rose around the wooden table. Smashed pots, trees, evergreens, hardy perennials, trailing shrubs, bushes blown apart. The little Christmas tree that Imogen brought in and out each December was ripped, white flesh jagged, from its roots. This was the work of a vicious little tornado. Toby picked his way across the wreckage to the table, counting the various tools he recognized: two forks, one spade, a hoe, a saw. A trellis clung haphazardly to the wall. The rake took a half-hearted swipe at his face and with a sigh sank on to an upturned plastic seed tray. Toby sat heavily at the table and made room for the new gold beers amongst the clutter: empty blue cans, a coffee cup, something unidentifiable and yellow in tin foil. He leant back and looked up at Imogen's beloved tree. It still clung lustily to the house, arranging the bustle of unfurling leaves and purple flowers prettily around the windows. The chain saw lay abandoned on the paving next to the trunk. Its orange flex was still attached through the back door to the house. Despite the fact he could see daylight through its trunk, the tree had not, it seemed, noticed it was dead. How long would it take to get up to speed? Another day? Two days? A week? Just how long did plants take to get with the programme? He smiled at its stupid optimism.

'Hello?' It was Primrose, hesitant at her French windows above the carnage. She was wearing electric blue: more Queen than Juliet.

'Did you enjoy the lasagna?' She was eying the Tupperware box on the table in front of him.

Rain-soaked, ripped tin foil. Massacred by the greedy cat, the remains of a lasagna.

'Yes, thank you.'

'Your garden... ' she looked embarrassed.

'A bit of a mess.'

'I was wondering... '

'Having a total overhaul. A redesign.'

'Yes. I was wondering if there was anything you, uh, didn't want. It seems such a shame to let it all die. Well, they've got a welcome home here.' She swallowed and surveyed her own plot.

'Take anything you want.'

'Well not now. I've got to go out.' Looking down at her outfit. A preposterous suggestion.

'Tomorrow, the next day, whenever suits.'

'Well. I've still got your key. Seems a shame to let those roses die.' Removing an imaginary speck from her royal blue lapel she began to close the windows. 'By the way, aren't you going to ask me how I got on at the annual conference?'

'I was just coming on to that,' said Toby.

'I sold five ties,' she said and stood smiling, awaiting applause.

It sounded, to Toby's ears anyway, thin when it came. Despite that, Primrose bowed before closing the doors. Toby heard the key turn in the lock.

He opened his briefcase and removed a small package of cocaine and wondered briefly whether Primrose had been complicit in her husband's dental crime. Nurse Prim holding the gas while the lusty dentist busied himself under patients' skirts. He declared her innocent, released her from his enquiries and unwrapped the tiny paper with trembling hands. Three new red scores marked his hand. Rita's parting shot as he'd gripped the cat by its neck in order to get his rolled-up note into the tiny barrel at its collar. He'd spent a taxing afternoon composing the note. The challenge had been to let Imogen know that Gideon perhaps was not good life-partner material, that he, Toby, would bring up the child whether or not it was his, that he wanted her back, missed her, loved her, forgave her. To let her know that he was now rich, much less boring and resolved to master any technique under the sun to become better – the best – in bed. To convey all that, whilst maintaining his dignity, on a piece of paper the size of a postage stamp had proved difficult. In the end, with all the distractions, the phone, the hatred emanating from Chuck, Gideon's air punching and Harmsworth-Mallett's request that Toby 'meet the boss' – as he stood, hands behind his back to introduce Mike Range, the moustacheoed, orange-faced, key jangling proprietor of Milson, Range & Rafter, he wrote 'Imogen. Phone home. Desperate. Toby.' And now all that was left was to wait for the chicken to come home to roost.

The cocaine was hard, packed into a small, pale square. He flattened the paper on to the table and moved the powder, using a biro, to its edge. The picture showed a square of belly. Smooth and round and the same yellow as the breasts. He knew it was a belly because towards one edge of the paper was a belly button, neat and deep. He turned the paper until it was upright. He had an urge to see her face. He felt angry that he had been denied it thus far.

He put his feet up on the table and drank. Gideon with Rita on the back seat of the Porsche. He was singing along to the radio and the cat was belting out the chorus as they drove across London towards a pregnant Imogen. She opened the door and there she stood, fat in front, Imogen. He was having difficulty picturing Imogen without her garden. How did she spend her evenings? Spread-eagled on the bed, chewing gum, leafing through a magazine, awaiting the Spaniard? He came in, she dropped the magazine, blew a pink bubble and moved awkwardly to get up off the bed, one hand on her swollen belly. The

Spaniard put down the Voyager, said, 'I've brought you a surprise.' Imogen's face. Rita's face. 'Oh my God. That's my cat.' Gideon, shock. Imogen, shock. Rita, shock. Toby smiled. The phone was ringing. Right on cue. He bounced off the wall at the bottom of the banister and took the stairs. Three at a time. One two three strides. Turn the corner. One stride. And he was grabbing the receiver.

'Hello?' It's Imogen. I made a mistake, she's saying. I miss you. I'm so glad you sent Rita with that message. I thought you'd never forgive me. Hormones. The baby's yours. I love you. Of course I never slept with him etc.'

'Toby.' It was Howard. Howard James Seaton of the overlong hair styled like the Monkees, the persistent taste in music everyone else grew out of and the important early-morning pitch to Alcron.

'Hello Howie.'

'I'm glad you're in. I came round earlier but you were out.'

'Right.' In out.

'Not using the mobile any more? I'm on my way round. If that's alright.'

'I'm on my way out.'

'Out where?'

Toby tired of always having to make excuses, wondered why he couldn't just tell him he didn't want him here. His fingers closed around something in his pocket. It crackled.

'I'm going out with Primrose.'

'Primrose?'

'Primrose, the next door neighbour.'

'The next door neighbour who molested all those people?'

'That was her husband.'

'Oh yes sorry… *that* Primrose?'

'That Primrose.'

'Why?'

Toby pulled the cellophane-wrapped tie from his pocket. 'Seth,' he told Howie. 'We subscribe to the teachings of Seth and Seth says that adversity is a gift and only through adversity do we achieve fulfilment of the self.'

'Right,' said Howard. 'When will you be back?'

'Late,' said Toby.

'Don't suppose I could, er, come along?'

It occurred to Toby that perhaps Imogen might be trying to get through.

'Listen Howard. Primrose is at the door. I'll call you as soon as I'm back.'

'I'm worried about you mate... '

Toby replaced the receiver.

Upstairs the answerphone was chocka with messages: the light flashed constantly. Since when had he got to be so popular?

'Toby... it's Mum... please call me.'

'Toby, it's Mum... I'm worried.'

'Toby, it's Jane. No need to call back. I'm just ringing to say I. Love. You.'

'It's Howie.'

'It's Mum.'

'It's Howie.'

Delete.

'Toby. It's Cassie.'

Hello Cassie.

'I'm here with Daddy... ' the voice paused while a child wailed in the background. 'Just to let you know that Iain and I are coming down on Thursday with the guy to pick up the desk. We're expecting to see you. Also, Daddy wanted me to tell you that Imogen isn't here yet. Apparently there's been a delay as... ' Here the voice changed slightly, 'she's too messed up.' A gurgle, a gasp: 'Hush baby. Mummy's on the phone. So... ' A deep breath, 'hope we'll see you tomorrow otherwise don't worry we'll just let ourselves in... '

Too messed up. Fuck messed up. Toby opened the window behind the sink. He looked at the arched spout which was the tap and considered bending to bite down on that cool metal. To break his teeth on the pipe. Fuck messed up. He slammed shut the window. A sweet splintering of wood. He opened it again. He'd bite down on that spout until his teeth were shattered in their gums.

He turned his thoughts to the cat and to Imogen. Perhaps they were not yet united. Any number of things could have happened. Gideon delayed at the Fox. Another drink with Daisy, with Mike and Pearls and Yellow and Blue. Another with Harmsworth-Mallett to celebrate the sale of Palace Mansions. Perhaps Gideon had forgotten Rita, left her mewling amongst the spilt beer and cigarette ends. Or perhaps Imogen had not arrived yet. Too messed up, having a quiet drink with Saffron, refusing wine. 'Actually,' quiet voice, large confidence: 'I'm pregnant.' His stomach flipped. Life without Toby. And so much life. A baby growing inside her. 'Yes,' she said with the ring halfway down her finger. To have and to hold, for better, for worse. Well this was worse and the bitch lied.

Outside nothing stirred. Toby picked his way to the table. He considered throwing the rose bushes over the fence into Primrose's garden. He studied the complicated horticultural tangle and decided it would be difficult to effect. Boring. Broke. Bad in bed. It was the bad in bed bit that hurt most. After all, wasn't it him who had embarked on the heroic search for her non-existent G-spot. The pillow wet with her gurgling laughter as she rolled her head from side to side, eyes scrunched up, delectable hint of double chin. He'd already decided that the G-spot was a conspiracy invented by women to reinforce the inadequacies of men.

However, there's something irresistible about Imogen when she's scrunched up laughing like that. Now here's Imogen, her face on a pillow he doesn't recognize, beneath Gideon and his heat-seeking missile of a cock which is headed directly for her G-spot.

He picked up the lasagna and threw it over the wall. It cleared the trellis easily, spattering him with rain-diluted cheese. It hit Primrose's garden with a satisfying clatter as plastic skittered across concrete. Bad in bed. She hadn't always thought that. 'Mmmmm,' she sometimes said. 'Oh Toby. Mmmm.' Her voice fading into breath and heat. Her eyes dark with lust.

There have also been times when Imogen is insatiable. He's home from work. The house is silent. Even Rita's out. It feels as though no one's been here for a century. 'Imogen?' he calls up the stairs. There is no response. There's no one in the garden. She's not in the bath. 'Imogen?' He walks into the bedroom kicking off his shoes. Lizard tongue of arm flicks out of the wardrobe to grab his shirt. A heaving heap of fur pulls him inside. Off balance, Toby falls through cupboard air bitter with the cardboard smell of unworn clothes. He lands on a jumble of shoes and amongst them at the bottom of the wardrobe is something animal: it's Imogen naked inside a moth-eaten fur coat. Begging for a blind, sticky cupboard fuck. Afterwards it's him who sits cross-legged in the old fur coat while warm Imogen lies head in his lap rearranging shoes underneath her buttocks. Looking up her eyes gleam softly in the dim cupboard.

'This wardrobe is strictly no-smoking.'

'What about with the door open?'

Broke, boring, bad in bed. Sometimes she liked him to pull her hair when she came. 'Harder. Toby. Pull. My. Hair.'

The phone was ringing. Toby wasn't sure he wanted to speak to her now. 'I'll pull your hair for you,' he muttered. 'I'll pull it off.'

Again he collided with the wall at the bottom of the stairs. Boots screeched across floorboards and he was gasping for air.

'Hello?'

'Toby, it's Mum.' Heavy, there was the weight of everything in that voice.

'Hello Mum.' Toby tries to match it depth for depth of misery. No wonder John Lambert III never stuck around. Imagine a life weighted with all that misery. To have and to hold, for better for worse. No wonder Aunt Mercy bought the house next door. Imagine waking every morning to peer down into that pit of despond.

'I wanted to talk about Friday.' A voice trapped against its will inside a being it wished would die.

'Friday?'

'Yes love, Friday.' Yes Love, Friday. As though Sorrow was coming for the weekend.

'Yes.'

'I'd like to come to yours tomorrow night if that's alright. Unless you were planning on going down early.' If that was what it took to stop his mother then yes he was going down early.

'I'm going down early.'

'Oh, not to worry. I understand. I thought you might... I think you should. I'll go direct. OK Toby.'

'OK Mum.'

'I'll see you Toby.'

'See you.'

'I love you Toby.'

'Goodbye Mum.' Toby replaced the phone. He could not remember his mother telling him she loved him. For some reason it hurt. He went downstairs.

The front door was open. Someone had been in while he was upstairs. The gate was shut but pregnant with information. The bin was overturned but come to think of it, hadn't it been like that earlier? Who had a key? Why, Imogen. Imogen had a key. And then he remembered Primrose. Primrose in royal blue with a brooch on her lapel: 'I still have your key.' Her hair moving united as she bobbed her head. Silently he closed the front door and leant against it listening. Silence. The drip of a tap and his own ragged breath. He waited until it had steadied then tiptoed to the garden. One two one two along the edges of the corridor where nothing creaked.

The garden was as he'd left it. Empty. Just one fat robin standing on the Christmas tree beadily cataloguing the wreckage. He turned and a face caught his eye at the window on the half-landing halfway up the stairs. A flash of white, a moon face floating upstairs. His heart was at his throat when he sprinted along the corridor, feet spread wide against each wall.

He took the stairs and the whole house groaned. He leapt the fourth step and stuck to the edges where the creaks weren't. The kitchen glowed streetlamp-orange. He stood for a moment on the landing to catch his breath. He tiptoed into the room: empty. He hit a bad board and the creak reverberated around the house. He'd blown it. He pounded up the remaining flight of stairs. He bent to the bedroom door. He heard its silence and left hand on top of right he held the cold clear handle. He turned it slower than the speed of sound. Imogen in the cupboard held her breath. Imogen Green underwater champion. She was good that girl, but so was he. She waited, sharp knees up against sharp chin. He felt the silent sniggers as she held her breath, a cup of tea cooling between the soles of her feet. He opened the bedroom door a crack. Slowly, slowly. Breathing through his mouth he surveyed the room. She was good this girl. The curtains at the window were untouched, open. They hung as though made of stone. We haven't, they sang, we haven't been touched for a thousand years. The bed wore a knot of duvet. Don't know, it swore, don't know on the Holy Bible what it is you're talking about. The drawer in Imogen's bedside table was open an inch. Toby suppressed a smile and, creeping around the loose floorboard, made his silent way towards the wardrobe. He'd give the bitch a heart attack.

It had been dark for some time when Toby found her. She was in the garden. She shone white as pearl, her ghost nightdress luminous in the dark. She was crouched in mud where crazy paving used to be, picking with her nails at a jagged triangular piece. And Toby felt as tired as the earth. As tired as time. The chair's legs splayed under his weight, his head lolled forward. In time he reached on to the table and felt for an unopened can. It was nighttime. It chilled and fizzed enthusiastically as he opened it. He watched Imogen. She hadn't even turned around yet. He took the presence of the fridge-fresh beers as a sign that she'd been expecting him. He regarded the garden. She'd done a good job. The bushes and plants were piled against the back wall and on top of them, in the night, the little Christmas tree. The seedling trays were stacked neatly and the garden tools were assembled near the back door. Like with like. A pile of jagged slices of concrete was growing beside her. She had now picked a hole in the paving about a metre square. Teeth showing white on her bottom lip, she rocked back and forth to dislodge a large slab. While Imogen focused on the task, Toby fortified himself with beer and cocaine. Surreptitiously he watched her in the large mirror against the back wall. A busy little ghost with a night's work ahead. He leant to the cocaine on the square of paper. And as he did, he became aware that the figure was no longer absorbed in its work. He looked up and in the mirror his eyes met Imogen's. Pale, unblinking. Toby froze, his hand covered the cocaine.

Imogen smiled. A smile that spread slowly across her face and widened to show her teeth. White and animal. Her hands still around the jagged triangle of concrete. He swallowed. Her nightdress shimmered.

'Imogen,' he tried to say. His face was wet. His chest ached.

She watched.

'Imogen.' He tried again. Silently her reflection laughed, stood. It brushed earth from its hands and went, shaking its head, into the house. Toby was afraid to follow. Instead, he allowed the tears to roll down his face. With shaking hands he raised the paper to his lips and emptied the bitter contents on to his tongue. He washed it down with the beer and stood to take up where Imogen had left off. He bent to the large piece of paving. Too heavy to lift he rolled it across the garden's rubble and towards her pile, which stood against the white-washed wall.

thirteen

It was 9.10 on Thursday morning and Toby was late for work when he closed the front door. Despite the fact that everything seemed to be in order in the front garden – the two black bins stood upright, side by side – a number of things were troubling him. First the fact that he'd had to prescribe himself a small amount of cocaine before leaving the house. This did not bode well for the day ahead. Nor, if he'd brought himself to think about it, for the rest of his life. Second, the fact that, for reasons currently obscure to him, he had sought out the monkey wrench amongst the jumble of spanners and screwdrivers on the carpet by the back door and had put it in his briefcase to take to work. His third worry centred on Imogen and the fact that she hadn't called. This was something which had troubled him periodically throughout the night: at 3.41 a.m., 4.03 a.m., 4.27 a.m. and at 5.39 a.m. – already, by this time, light – he'd gone downstairs to check the answerphone. The fact that she hadn't called had in turn spawned a host of worries concerning what might or might not have happened as far as she was concerned, as far as the cat was concerned and what might happen when he arrived at the office.

Another anxiety centred on his clothes. Today he was wearing a puff-sleeved cream blouse taken from Imogen's chest of drawers. Over it he wore the jacket of his suit, which hid, he hoped, the fact that he was dressed, somewhat badly, as the woman who had left him.

The car was outside the house. He took the parking ticket from the windscreen and went to unlock it. It was already unlocked. Despite his various difficulties, it was Toby's fifth worry which was the most troubling. It was too unpalatable to contemplate.

'Good morning!' Primrose, majestic in cherry blossom pink, appeared at her door. The flowers in her rockery shuddered as she shut it behind her. 'We've got to stop meeting like this!' Sunlight glinted off her sunglasses as she bent to double lock the door.

Toby, who was inclined to agree with her, checked behind the seats for vagrants or murderers who might have spent the night, before lowering himself into the car. Sweating, he put his seat belt on. The tight seams of the shirt cut into the flesh under his arms. 'A problem halved is a problem shared,' he said as he opened the sun roof and wondered whether there was anyone on this earth with whom he'd be willing to share this particular problem. The sun blazed through the roof on to the crown of his head – a beam of heat and light to explode his skull and scatter the arching sky with brain and bone and worries. A thousand jewelled sun dogs.

He joined the traffic heading south towards Camden and felt with joy the strengthening wisp of smoke winding from the top of his head into the pale sky. Why, he wondered as he helped himself to a little cocaine from the navel in the belly on the open envelope of paper on his lap, were there never any new cars on Kentish Town Road? The van in front looked as though it had been rough-roaded across the Sahara and the car in front of that was held together with knotted string and piled high with rags and bones. The queue of battered traffic snaked half a mile and disappeared around the corner into Camden.

Toby turned on the radio. Elkie Brooks was putting her all into it. 'Pearl's a singer. She stands when she plays the piano... ' It occurred to Toby that standing to play the piano was altogether an unlikely thing for someone called Pearl to do. Pearl would surely be inclined to sit modestly in her front room in some Welsh town somewhere in order to sound out a tune. Standing to play the piano was more in line with something a guy might do. Someone attention-seeking, pleased with themselves. Probably in a white suit. Elton John for instance might stand to play the piano. Howie would stand to play the piano. Or Gideon. Toby swallowed. Gideon Chancelight. Sweat pricked the skin under his eyes.

Toby was alongside the newsagent. He had moved little more than twenty metres and beyond the snake of people holding newspapers, waiting to pay, Toby could see the woman who supplied Imogen with all of her information. Behind the counter her headscarf shone white like the Virgin Mary's. She would certainly know something about him and Imogen. Toby wondered about parking the car and going in; however, he was afraid of what she might have to say.

It was 9.18 and the flow of traffic was so slow as to be imperceptible. It seemed that the traffic was refusing to move until Toby confronted the memory that sang and danced and which he sought to avoid. 'Pearl's a singer,' and there stood Elton John standing to play the piano. He wore an obscene suit, it was white with tiny diamonds sewn on to it. Something more appropriate perhaps for figure-skating. The odd wire of hair showed above the suit at Elton's back and every outline of the singer's broad body was visible. Toby licked his finger and dabbed it in the cocaine. He rubbed it on his gums. The memory receded and Toby relaxed. It was just a dream. People dream about things every night: about dying, killing, about having sex with their mothers. It didn't mean that they were dead, murderers, or actually shagging their mothers. He had woken at 8.56 a.m. in bed, with, despite the broken nature of his night, warm feelings of contentment and security. With a smile on his face, his face in the pillow and his penis softening against the mattress, he'd pieced together a memory and from that had identified the source of his contentment. From there the smile had dissolved.

'The long and the short of the matter is,' he told Elton who was half-turned, smile splitting his greedy orange face, as he pumped at the piano keys, 'I dreamt that Gideon Chancelight... ' Sweat pricked at his upper lip and Elton paused from the chorus, hands in mid air, a look of bemusement crinkling his musical face. 'That Gideon Chancelight...' He swallowed loudly. 'That I had Gideon Chancelight's... that Gideon Chancelight was... that we were... lovers.' Toby finished, defeated. As if 'lovers' came close to describing the carnage about which he'd dreamt.

A knowing smile spread across Elton's face. He turned back and pumped the piano. 'Pearl's a singer.'

'The first wet dream I've had since I was fifteen years old,' shouted Toby at the singer's broad back. 'And it was about Gideon fucking Chancelight.'

Elton ignored him, choosing instead to throw his entire body behind the chorus as he belted out the words: 'That's not any old man, that's the man who's fucking my girlfriend.' From the way his leotard-suit strained at his body, particularly at the lascivious crack between his buttocks, it was clear that Elton was smiling. The traffic dispersed and soon Toby was in Regent's Park with not another car in sight.

Despite the fact that he was an hour late, Toby was in no hurry to arrive. He parked on Queensgate. He was regretting playing the Rita card. It had not provoked the response he'd wanted. Indeed it had pro-voked no response at all. As he dawdled along the street he considered the various scenarios which might have taken place. The most likely was the most uncomfortable: Imogen, delighted to be reunited with Rita, is just that. Delighted. End of story. She'd been wondering how to get the cat, and here, out of the blue, complete with carrying case, was the cat. Do not look a gift horse in the mouth. A man in a suit holding Imogen's dark blue mobile phone stepped into the road. He watched Toby through narrowed eyes waiting for him to pass. Had she checked the cat's collar? 'Imogen. Phone Home. Desperate. Toby.' He hoped she hadn't. Desperate, in the cold light of this day, was not an attractive characteristic and was probably something that had contributed to her leaving in the first place.

Of course, inevitably she would look the gift horse in the mouth and a conversation would follow. She'd ask Gideon where he got the cat. He'd say Toby, the new guy at work. Curly orange hair, he'd elaborate, questing pink face, a mole. Shock on Imogen's face. Shock on Gideon's face. Gideon would know that he was dealing with a psychopath, Imogen would know just how 'desperate' Toby was. And Rita would know, if the cat had any imagination at all, that it had just a few hours to live. A man up a stepladder beside a hanging basket obscene with pink flowers waited until Toby had passed before emptying Imogen's green plastic watering can into it. Water sloshed on to the pavement. The man whistled. And Toby wondered why everything this morning was conspiring to twist the knife.

If there was any kind of justice in the universe Gideon would have put the cat on top of the car while he kissed Daisy goodbye, spoke to Mike, finished a phone call, put his jacket in the boot. He would have driven off at speed and Rita would now be lying on the other side of a hedge somewhere, missing in action. This would also explain why Imogen hadn't called. 'Listen mate.' Gideon at his desk. 'Bad news I'm afraid. It's about the cat... '

Dazzling sunlight glanced off the new glass door. Focusing on the idea of the Voyager on its side somewhere secluded, Toby pushed it open. Daisy looked up and froze, hand mid-way between desk and mouth. Harmsworth-Mallett replaced the receiver of his phone and looked Toby up and down. Gideon's desk was empty.

'Gideon not with you?' Harmsworth-Mallett looked past Toby into the street, head cocked. Toby felt blood fill his face.

'Daisy and I thought the two of you might have spent the night together as it were, heh heh, celebrating and what have you.'

There was a new light in Daisy's eye, her cheeks were flushed. Lips too tight, her glance slid away.

'I was going to say it's not every day you clear ten grand but with you – heh heh,' Harmsworth-Mallett continued, 'that's exactly what it is. Out with Gideon were you?'

Toby, face hot, opened his mouth to speak.

'We're yet to see Mr Chancelight this morning.' Toby's tongue stuck to the roof of his mouth.

'Guilty,' Harmsworth-Mallett proclaimed.

'Er, Gids called earlier.' Daisy's voice was strange, muted as it came out from the hot smirk of her disobedient lips. Her glance darted across Harmsworth-Mallett, across Toby. 'He's sorting something out, er, um, a domestic something, apparently.' Her small laugh was followed by some unnecessary rummaging in a drawer.

A domestic something apparently. So Daisy knew. The polyester blouse stuck to Toby's spine and under his arms it sawed at his flesh. It was flaying him alive.

'He'll be along in a little while.'

Domestic something. Domestic something big and bad and terminal. Toby could feel it coming.

'Messages, heh, heh.' Harmsworth-Mallett with a Post-It fluttering on his thumb. 'You're off the hook.' White of eye desperate with red veins. 'For now.'

The Post-It read 'Mrs Green 0207 089 6777'. Toby stuck it to his briefcase. It occurred to him that life could not be so unkind and it occurred to him that perhaps, downstairs, there might be a chance...

He took the spiral stairs briskly and descended into the basement. Once on the soft carpet he didn't wait for his eyes to adjust but made his way to where he knew the table was. He skidded on a plastic bag and as the kettle and coffee rings and newspapers came into view, he saw that the cat was gone. He climbed the steps. Gideon, Imogen, Rita and one psychopath: he saw that he'd played entirely into their hands. As he emerged into the daylight of the office, Daisy averted her eyes. There was nothing to do but wait. He sat at his desk. He placed his briefcase in front of him. He slid twin gold buttons across until gold latches sprang open. He lifted the leather lid. The air was cooler in the case and smelt of Marmite. He touched the monkey wrench, which shone dully amongst the paper fragments of girl and the wrapped toast. It was cool. He felt its weight in his hand.

'Cappuccino?' Harmsworth-Mallet, standing, smiling.

'I'll come with you and get some toast,' said Daisy smiling, smoothing down her skirt.

Toby wheeled back his chair and stood, monkey wrench in hand, to pass Chuck who was bent double under his desk. He looked like a maharajah's elephant with an elaborate green leather seat on its back. Toby resisted the urge to mount the desk and ride the estate agent out on to the street to lead a charge down Harrington Gardens. Instead, silently and squarely he placed the monkey wrench on Gideon's desk. He would know what it meant. The phones rang. Chuck reappeared red faced and frowning.

'Milson, Range & Rafter... And who shall I say is calling? If you'll hold the line Mrs Green. Putting you right through.' The phone on Toby's desk rang. There was no Mrs Green. Toby knew that. Everyone knew that. Mrs Green had died at Christmas. Hairless and colourless, he'd even seen her in an urn.

Returning to his desk he picked up the phone: 'Hello?'

'This is Mrs Green. I'm afraid there's been an appalling mix-up my end. I'm afraid eleven o'clock no longer suits. Sorry to be a perfect bore but could you make it any earlier?'

It didn't sound like Mrs Green. Harmsworth Mallett, hands occupied with coffee, was negotiating the door.

'Green. Mrs Green. As in the colour. Is that Toby Doubt? Look here. All I need to know is can you get here any earlier?'

'When?'

'As soon as. Any time between now and half past ten.'

Silence.

'Look, is it possible? That's all I need to know.'

'Right.' Toby took a deep breath — elongated nose, round greedy eyes, a pale anteater reflected in the gold latch of his case.

Is that Toby Doubt? Is that Milson, Range & Rafter? Am I Mrs Green? The questions were not as straightforward as they sounded.

'What time can I expect you?'

'In fifteen minutes.'

'Very good. 18 Kensington Court.' There was a click as she replaced the receiver.

Toby stood and felt sweat, cold on hot skin, trickle down his spine. He picked up his briefcase and walked towards the door. The sweat under his arms stung his skinless flesh. The feeling was not altogether unpleasant.

'Where is Kensington Court?'

Harmsworth-Mallett was licking the plastic lid of a cappuccino. 'Kensington Court? Down by the Stonemason's?' The old man looked around for verification. There was a smudge of chocolate on the end of his swollen nose. Daisy didn't seem to hear. She was eating toast and smiling fondly at a magazine open on her desk. Mallett turned to enlist Chuck's help.

'Down by the Stonemason's Arms. Pretty sure it's that white new-build. Backs on to the Stonemason's? Is it Chuck?' Chuck picked up the phone and punched out a number.

'Yes,' blinked Mallett. 'It's down by the Stonemason's.' He blew on his coffee. 'That's right. I knew it was down there. Milson, Range & Rafter,' he answered the phone holding out a hand to silence Toby. 'Good morning Suki, bear with me while I find out.' He put the phone on the desk and made his way to the bookshelf. He bent and fiddled with some papers and in his unhurried way, returned to his desk, sat down and picked up the phone. 'Hello Suki. You're in luck my dear. We've got plenty. Oh enough to pave the streets of Kensington and probably some left over to pave Chelsea too and having done that there's probably enough to do Albert Bridge, and once we're on that side of the river I don't see why we...'

Toby picked up his briefcase and pushed out on to the street.

He flagged a cab.

'You're having a laugh.' The driver indicated a white building beside the school. Kensington Court: a black wrought-iron gate rose ten foot into the skies and, as though London was populated with human beings eager to scale it, the top was crowned with a spangle of razor wire. Through the bars flourished a Kensington utopia of hanging baskets beset with butterflies.

Toby pressed the bell marked 18, his face wet with sweat. Breathing through his mouth, his nose bubbled uselessly. Hayfever, asthma, too much cocaine. The gate buzzed open and Toby stood amongst the tropical vegetation. Mrs Green, risen again, with words to say to Toby Doubt. The door of Number 18 was already open. Hello long time no see. Forgive me sometimes I took your daughter for granted but I love her need her want her I'm just a selfish man forgive me please and send her back I'll love her make her happy for the rest of my life.

A woman bent to restrain a Jack Russell by its blue collar. The hound of hell. Black hair set in waves, the bending figure was short and squat: Anne Green on her knees. She screamed when she saw Toby. She released the dog. Toby screamed. You aren't Mrs Green. Stump-legged impostor. She screamed again. The dog trotted to a palm tree and lifted a leg. Blood splashed on to Toby's shirt.

'Fuck a duck,' said Gideon getting out of the Porsche. He slammed the door and flicked black hair out of his eyes.

'Man alive,' he said and, directing his key at the car, locked it.

'Fuck a duck,' he said again as he mounted the pavement and drew level with Toby outside Chico's Patisserie. Gideon, like Toby, was holding his appointment book in one hand. 'What the fuck happened to you?'

'Shirt. Too tight.' Toby could feel the blood bubbling from his nose as he spoke.

'Christ on a bike.' Gideon squinted through the tinted windows of the car, patted his breast pocket, slipped his car keys into his trousers and, placing a hand just below Toby's shoulder blades, pushed him through the glass doors. Blood splashed on the doormat. The office was deserted except for Daisy who was on the phone. She gagged and replaced the receiver. Swivelling 180 degrees in her chair she bent towards the wall choking.

'Downstairs,' said Gideon directing Toby towards the back of the office. 'Trouble with a vendor,' he offered. Daisy whose head had disappeared inside her shell-pink t-shirt made a muffled choking sound. Gideon kept his hand on Toby's back as he steered him down the spiral stairs. A warm cloud of mildew engulfed them. 'This way.'

The bathroom was lit by a dim skylight in the pavement above. Toby regarded himself in the speckled mirror: A faded silhouette. Gideon pulled the light cord and a man of horror stepped forward. The shirt was soaked red. His face was slick with blood. Toby heard Gideon's steps ping ping ping back up the spiral stairs and smiled. His teeth were yellow and he felt already-drying blood crack on his skin. He opened his mouth wide and watched as flecks floated into the basin. He heard conversation upstairs – Gideon and Daisy – the blonde's voice rising in flirtatious excitement. Gideon's laughter stirred the air. Toby put both hands on the basin and felt it rock unsteadily on the wall. His eyes stared out at him dull and defeated from somewhere in the mirror. Upstairs, suddenly, there was silence. He turned on both taps. Ping ping ping and, eyes wide, Gideon appeared in the doorway. He held up the monkey wrench.

'Jesus Christ. Who the fuck brought this in?'

Toby held the basin with both hands. It felt cool.

'Did you see him?'

He watched Gideon in the mirror.

'This is a warning. A warning. But Jesus Christ, of what? Did you see this on my desk?' He looked down at the metal in his hand. 'Jesus, fuck, when do you think he brought it in? Fuck where's Mallet?' The stairs pinged on the way up and pinged on the way down. 'Jesus Christ what the fuck do I do – my life is in danger.' He threw something blue on to the floor. Toby picked it up, a t-shirt. 'Where the fuck is Mallett? Oh and this.' A green plastic box landed at his feet, a First Aid kit.

Toby waited until he heard Gideon and Daisy talking upstairs before taking off his jacket. The seams of the shirt bit deeper into the twin wounds under each arm. He dropped the jacket to the floor and delayed looking in the mirror. He was afraid that his arms were severed, hanging to his torso by a last thread of skin. When he did turn he was surprised to see that the cream puff sleeves were completely clean. The blood was confined to his face and the shirt's front. He lifted his arms. The shirt was damp, but there was no stain. He unbuttoned it and peeled it from his body. He lifted his arms again. He circled them twice in each direction. He put the plug in, filled the sink and submerged his face in cold water. He pressed his nose to the bottom of the basin. Through open eyes he saw the water darken with blood. How, he wanted to know, could she allow him to go through this? How could she sit, pregnant, waiting for the rest of her life, while his fell apart? As though he and she, the past four years and Frederick Street had never happened?

There was a time before he knew her when he'd had a kite on a beach in Norfolk. He was with his mother and Aunt Mercy who had driven them here all the way from Cambridge to see the dead whale. They'd walked around it bent against the wind through sand spongy with blood. And the whale had been insignificant against the sky, insignificant against the beach. This huge lump of swollen putrefaction. There was nothing that had made this whale a whale here now in that mountain of rotting flesh. Except for one thing. The only thing that suggested that this slippery mound had ever been alive: its silver cock, five feet long, flopped out, languishing on the beach. Wide rivers of fish blood diluted with water were returning to the sea. He closed his eyes and felt the wind on his face and saw the kite's tail bob bob bob in the endless white sky. He saw Aunt Mercy, he saw his mother, hands over noses and mouths, trudging downwind of the carcass. In the car, going home, Aunt Mercy and his mother: 'Eighty foot or seventy. At least'; 'I couldn't see its eyes'; 'Poor soul. Whatever must it have been thinking'. The thing of interest – surely its penis, which was the same length give or take an inch or two as ten-year-old Toby – was the thing they didn't mention. Conspicuous by its absence it was this that alerted Toby to the fact that he was missing something in his life. Not just from this trip. But from everything. Then he thought it must have been his father. Later he discovered that it was Imogen. Imogen with her foraging fingers, her strong thighs. Hand in hand they stand before the whale admiring all five feet of its cock as the blood makes its patient journey back to the ocean. He unwound the window in the back seat and through his mouth took a deep gulp of air. Toby choked, hit the back of his head on the taps. Blood and water sprayed through his nose, over the mirror, wall, floor. He coughed and bent choking. Ping ping ping. There was blood everywhere. Ping ping fast feet on the steps.

'What the fuck... '

Still choking, Gideon steered him from the sink.

'Sit here on the toilet.' The seat was up. 'What the fuck do I do? Mallet didn't see anyone. Daisy didn't see anyone. Chuck didn't see anyone. You didn't see anyone did you? The police say it's not an emergency.' He was crouched on the floor, dark head in his hand holding himself steady with the other on Toby's knee. 'How the fuck does he know my desk? Fuck! And worse, how did he manage to get in here without anyone, not one single one of you wankers, seeing? What the fuck are you all? Blind?'

Toby was having trouble breathing. Each breath came in a harsh sob His nose was blocked but tears ran freely from his eyes.

'Jesus you are messed up. You're soaked. Where's Daisy's shirt? Come on I need your help.' Gideon grabbed a green towel from the rail and put it over Toby's shoulders. It was damp. He put a hand on Toby's shoulder. It was warm and solid. 'Come on.' Gideon crouched on the floor in front of him. 'Put the shirt on and we'll go next door and sort you out with some fresh kit. We've got to get out of this office.'

'When I was ten,' Toby took the shirt. 'My mother and her girlfriend took me to a beach in Norfolk to see a dead sperm whale. It was sixty foot long. It was rotting on the sand... '

Gideon turned from washing his hands. 'Whooah. Rewind... your mother and her girlfriend?'

'My mother and her girlfriend took me to a beach... '

'Hello, your mother is a lesbian?'

'Not the kind of lesbian you're thinking of. Anyway, this whale was rotting in the sand... '

'What kind of lesbian am I thinking of?' Gideon drying his hands on the green towel.

'The kind you usually think of? Lipstick, hot pants? I don't know.'

'What other kind is there?'

Toby considered for a moment, not without affection, the way his mother moved sideways around the kitchen table, Aunt Mercy's wicker basket of gin and sherry, her turf account, Betsey. The way Aunt Mercy and Alison Doubt watched the racing and the way they shouted at the small TV.

'Gideon,' Daisy's voice came from upstairs.

'What the fuck is that? He's back. The fucker is back.' Gideon slammed closed the bathroom door, locked it and leant against it.

'Gideon.' They could still hear her calling.

'Tell the fucker I'm out tell the fucker I'm out. Tell the fucker I'm out,' Gideon muttered under his breath as he pushed his weight against the bathroom door and shook his head, fists clenched at his sides. 'Just tell the fucker I'm out.'

They both heard footsteps on the stairs and Daisy's voice, scared, worried: 'Gideon?'

'Go away go away go away. Help me out here,' Gideon muttered angrily. 'Lean on this door you useless fucker.' Toby got to his feet.

'Gids?' Gideon jumped away from the door as the girl rapped against it. 'Gids are you in there? I've got like the police on the phone – they want to ask you some stuff?'

Gideon unlocked the door and opened it. 'Is there anyone else up there?'

The stairs pinged on their way up.

Toby stood. He looked in the mirror. He put his head back. A shotgun's twin barrels clotted red. He let the water out, rinsed the basin and filled it with clean water. He used the towel to clean the blood from his chest and his hands. He wiped the walls and the mirror where blood had sprayed. He pulled the t-shirt over his head. It was small: a child's top. He heard Gideon upstairs and pulled the shirt down over his body. It had white letters on the front – LIFEGUARD – and didn't stretch down as far as his trousers. He held it down as he slowly climbed the stairs. He felt exhausted. Gideon was on the phone at Toby's desk. He was standing as close to the staircase mouth as the card would allow.

'I'll hold.' He lifted a finger in Toby's direction. Toby sat in the upright chair beside the bookcase. He watched Chuck in profile as he bobbed his head from side to side.

'Rats rats rats,' he said and picked up the phone. 'Michael Honduras? Chuck Lincoln, Range Rafter. I'm calling about your little, uh, rat problem at... that's right... just to say that someone from Sanitize will be calling you directly to fix up a time. It is non-toxic, entirely safe for dogs, cats, humans, children. All pets. Yes, that's right sir. Not a problem... all in the line of duty.'

'Doody,' repeated Toby. 'The line of Doody.'

The door buzzed and Harmsworth-Mallett came in with five poly-styrene cups on a tray. He threw his cigarette into the road. 'Cappuccinos,' he announced. 'Daisy.' He put one on her desk. She turned the cup round and round and looked up smiling.

'Thank you,' she said.

'Chuck.' Harmsworth-Mallett placed a cup in front of the American.

'Thanking you sir,' said Chuck looking up. 'I've sorted old Honduras's rats out.'

'Good on you, Chuck.' Then Harmsworth-Mallett shuffled to Toby's desk. He gave a coffee to Gideon who nodded shortly.

'No sir... you are not hearing me. Like I said, this *is* an emergency...'

The old man came to Toby where he sat against the wall beside the bookcase. 'Cappuccino old boy,' he said and with tremulous hands held the tray in front of Toby. Toby took one, the old man took the other and then bent to lean the tray against the bookcase. He straightened up to examine Toby tenderly.

'What's all this about then?' His hands one underneath the other, palms up, supporting his coffee. 'What's going on here?' Eyes blood-shot beneath unruly brows.

Toby, bewildered: 'On where?'

'All this blood. They're all worried about you.' He nodded gently about the office. Daisy stirring sugar into her coffee, smiled dreamily into its depths. Chuck whistled lightly, the headpiece of his hands-free jangling at his ear. Gideon, one foot on Toby's chair was shouting into the receiver: 'No I am not safe here... no he's not here right now... well obviously he has been here... yes recently... a monkey wrench... Christ on a bike, a large spanner with an adjustable head! Jesus... '

'So, what happened eh?' Harmsworth-Mallett patted his palm clumsily on Toby's shoulder. He looked at the back of the hand that held his coffee. It was flecked with dried blood. Toby didn't know what had happened. He tried to think but unruly and disconnected information leapt about his mind. The answer to the question wasn't there.

'Should we take a little trip to casualty?'

Gideon was shouting: 'So you want me to call another number...

Fulham Road Police Station, let me get a pen... '

Mallett laughed gently. 'Been overdoing it have we? My father did that. And one day his liver burst. Just like that.' He shook his head, looked down at the desk and laughed again. 'One day overdoing it, next day dead.'

'It's your fault if I die so... thanks a lot for your help.' Gideon slammed down the phone and peeled the lid off from his coffee. He frisbeed it into the air. It fluttered for a moment deciding what to do and then put on an extra spurt to land on top of the bookcase. 'Cunt,' he said and stood slurping his cappuccino. 'The police say it's not an emergency. Got to get away from this office. I'll take our friend next door and get him sorted with some fresh kit.' Gideon wiped foamed milk from his mouth.

'Next door?' asked the old man.

'Auntie Rose and her emporium of suits.'

'Good idea,' nodded Harmsworth-Mallett. 'Let him finish his coffee.'

'It's only a nosebleed,' said Gideon.

'He doesn't look well.'

'You're alright.' Gideon bent down to Toby who drank the sweet coffee. 'Bring it with you. Let's go.'

'Let him be.'

The door buzzed. Gideon, spilling coffee, sprang behind Harmsworth-Mallett. A large woman rolled in, pregnant and tall, holding car keys. She stood filling the doorway. Chuck got to his feet. He turned to Harmsworth-Mallett.

'The wife.' He blushed and looked away, a sweating ham. 'Alright to take five?' His thumb indicated Harrington Gardens.

'Minutes yes. Days no!'

The wife laughed perhaps at what she supposed was the boss's joke.

Outside on the pavement they watched as Chuck put a tentative arm around her.

'Sweet,' said Harmsworth-Mallett.

'Large,' said Gideon.

'How are you feeling?' Harmsworth-Mallett asked Toby, greenish and close, his face studded with dry patches and scabs.

'Ready?' asked Gideon.

Toby got to his feet.

'Bye,' said Daisy. She blushed and looked away. 'Back to front,' she muttered. Toby turned to see her drawing a hand across her chest.

He went out into sunlight. A Jaguar was manoeuvring into the space outside the florist, the man from the delicatessen was winding the pole to lower the blue striped awning.

'This way,' said Gideon and slid behind Toby as they set off past Luigi's. The man behind the counter waved. Gideon raised a hand. He stopped in the shade of red canvas. SUITS YOU read the sign showing a peeling picture of a 1920s man in top hat and tails. A sign in the window read TAROT READINGS, TUES, WEDS, THURS.

'I fucked up last night.' Gideon pushed open the door, which chimed with the same ding dong as Alison's house in Cambridge. 'I stayed at Daisy's.'

He went in, Toby followed. A heavy rack of ties fluttered as the door closed. A cave padded thickly with suits, it stank of all the men who'd ever worn them.

'How can I make it any clearer?' Gideon wiped his brow. 'I stayed at Daisy's last night.'

'Hello dear.' A small woman behind the counter under a heavy fringe of ties slid a pair of trousers up a hanger. Her hair, a cluster of gold bubbles, must have been a wig. 'Dear, dear, dear what have you been up to?'

'Hello Aunt Rose, how are you? I was wondering whether you could sort my friend out?' The old lady peered through the gloom over the top of her glasses. 'What's he after?' The chain jiggled at her neck.

'The man is after the works — suit, shirt, tie... I fucked up, mate, I shagged Daisy last night.' Toby opened his mouth to breathe better.

'Don't see why not,' said the woman. She hung the trousers on a rack behind her and unhurriedly lifted an old-fashioned hatch to step out into the shop.

'Why are you laughing?' Gideon asked, angry.

Aunt Rose examined Gideon in his navy wool suit. 'I remember that fellow,' she said and brushed a fleck from his lapel. 'Treating you alright?'

'Does the job.'

'What size are you?' Rose, chin raised, addressed Toby. '42?'

Toby nodded.

The woman looked at Gideon. His head was in his hands. 'Oh God. Oh God. It was a mistake. I've fucked up. Oh fuck.'

'Is that right dear?' Aunt Rose walked around Toby once, tape measure hanging round her neck. 'I'll find something for your friend and then I'll read your cards. How's that? Now what colour in the suit?'

'Dark; grey, blue, black,' said Gideon. 'I need good news today. What a fuck-up.'

Aunt Rose moved to a double rack thick with dark suits. They swung as she used a hook to bring one down. And then another. And then another. She handed one after the other on the end of her pole to Gideon.

'Oh Christ I don't remember a lot about it… we left the pub and walked round to Daisy's. I was definitely in with the flatmate and then… '

Aunt Rose took the jacket from one of the hangers Gideon was holding. She handed it to Toby.

'The flatmate went to bed. Oh Christ.'

Toby put the jacket on over his t-shirt. Rose moved behind him to straighten the shoulders. She moved him to a long looking glass. The jacket was long and slim-fitting. To Toby's mind he looked like a New Romantic.

'And I woke up this morning. First thing I saw was this fucking teddy bear in a pink dress. What the fuck am I going to do?'

'A nice fit,' she said. Toby could see the curls at the top of her wig moving in the glass above his shoulder as she pulled at the fabric.

'Marry her,' said Toby.

'Waist?' She pulled trousers from the hanger and held them up against him. 'Try them.' She turned away.

'And now I've got monkey wrench closing in. How the fuck can I deal with this? You could try to help.' Gideon fingered a tie.

Toby's trousers wouldn't come off over his boots. He stumbled into a swinging rack of waistcoats. He couldn't help laughing. The waistcoats swung to disperse a bitter tang, the smell of toil and disappointment.

'You've got to try to help.' Gideon stood in front of a mirror, the tie around his neck.

Toby knew he'd need to help himself before he could even begin to help Gideon. A start, he thought, would be to take off his boots and then he'd manage the trousers. He pulled a dark curtain across.

'Help me,' said Gideon.

'I will.' In odd socks Toby looked down to see that he was wearing tight and pale underpants that he didn't think were his. Somewhere on the other side of the curtain he could hear the murmur of Aunt Rose's voice.

'The young man is a taurus. Watch out for him as he is not what he seems and needs to be treated with caution.'

'And what about the monkey wrench?' Gideon sounded desperate. Toby sat down to listen.

'The tower,' came Aunt Rose.

'And?'

'It means a new beginning.'

'Why all the flames and all those people burning to death?'

Toby could hear Aunt Rose laughing, he reached for the navy

blue trousers. They smelt as though they'd been given to a man by his mother for his first job at the sausage factory, or on the garage forecourt.

Toby stood. He came out from behind the curtain. Gideon was sitting with his back to him at a small table opposite Aunt Rose.

'And what about the baby?' he was asking. 'What about the fucking baby?'

Aunt Rose noticed Toby. She got to her feet. 'How does it feel?'

'Fine,' said Toby.

'Shoes, shirt, tie?' She bent, short legs straightening under a swinging rack of suits and emerged with a pair of black shoes in each hand.

Gideon turned. 'Take a pair of lucky shoes.' He lifted a foot off the ground. 'Don't know what I'd do without mine.' Despondently he leant to flick something off the toe.

'And a shirt?' asked Aunt Rose.

Back behind the curtain Toby sat down to take off the jacket. He looked at the lucky shoes and saw he had them on the wrong feet.

'And what about the baby?' Gideon asked again. Toby heard cards being dealt out one by one.

'The baby is your child,' said Aunt Rose. 'She's a little girl.'

'What about the abortion?'

'What abortion?' A gurgle of Aunt Rose's laughter. 'There is no abortion.'

'Jesus Christ.'

From the pocket of the jacket he'd been wearing earlier came the tie that Primrose had made. The dentist's tie. Blue silk and customized by Primrose with a fleshy pink ejaculating cock.

Gideon leant across the table to tug at Toby's tie. They were in Luigi's and Gideon was sitting furthest from the window, against the wall and out of sight.

'What the fuck is that?'

'It's for good luck,' said Toby.

'I'll be having that then.' Gideon loosened his own tie and pulled it off.

Toby unknotted the blue tie and handed it to Gideon who set about arranging it around his neck. He stood and with a quick glance outside turned back to straighten it in the mirror. Gideon turned to Toby, fingers cocked and aimed in Toby's direction.

'Shepherd's pie times two. By the way... ' Uncharacteristic furrows marked Gideon's brow. 'Been meaning to ask you... are you a taurus?'

Toby shook his head.

The furrows dispersed. 'Great, mate. Great. Keep an eye out for old Spanner Boy.' He clapped Toby's shoulder and made his way to the counter.

Toby watched the girl at the till, with cups on the fingers of each hand, put back her head to laugh. Gideon held up the blue tie. In the mirror behind her, a flash of Gideon's white teeth. That length of pale throat. So the baby was Gideon's. Toby supposed it would have been too easy if the baby had been his.

'Wake up.' Gideon sat heavily at the table. 'Can't afford to have you sleeping on the job. We've got two shepherd's pies in the microwave. That's three minutes for you to talk me through what happened. And don't give me that "nothing" bullshit.' Gideon helped himself to a piece of bread, dipped it into a saucer of olive oil, bit into it and used the remainder to point at Toby's nose. 'Come on. I might look incredibly youthful; however, I was not born yesterday. Whose wife are you shagging?' Gideon winked. 'Black eye one day, broken nose the next, I'm not a complete wanker.' His chin glistened with oil.

Toby felt unwell: 'I'm not shagging anyone's wife. Someone's shagging my girlfriend.'

Gideon deep in thought mopped up the remainder of the oil. 'Hmm. I don't get it. Someone's shagging your girlfriend and you get a black eye and then you get your nose broken. How does that work?

The guy found out she's no good?' Gideon laughed.

Toby laughed.

'Jesus Christ!' Gideon pressed his entire body against the back wall of the cafe. Toby turned to see Daisy walking past. She glanced in. 'Jesus Christ help me out here. Is she coming in?' A hoarse whisper. Daisy had passed and Toby shook his head. 'Did she see us? Jesus Christ, thank God.' He lifted the blue tie and kissed Primrose's painted efforts. 'Sweet Jesus. Praise the Lord for the lucky tie.'

Gideon held his empty cup in the direction of the counter and the waitress. 'Coffee please,' he mouthed the words and winked. 'Daisy.' Gideon replaced his cup on his saucer. 'I can't believe I shagged Daisy.' He slapped his head. 'Fool fool fool, Chancelight. What have I done?' He put his head in his hands. The waitress arrived holding a jug of coffee. She smiled quizzically at Toby and looked at Gideon's slumped form. He sat up.

'Hello babe. Coffee, lovely,' and waited until the waitress had filled his cup and had moved off. 'I can't believe I did it.' He was turning the saucer which had held the olive oil under his finger. It whirred round and round on the marble table. 'I don't know how it happened. A drink at the Fox. Back to Daisy's and the next thing I know,' Gideon was talking quietly to the dish – a spinning blur – beneath his finger. 'I wake up in her bed. Oh, mate.'

Gideon released the saucer which spun into the air, hit a mirror and smashed on the floor. Other diners looked up from their lunch.

Lunch arrived and Gideon unwrapped his knife and fork.

'How's Rita?' asked Toby.

'Rita?' Gideon frowned blowing air through his full mouth. 'Hot.'

'The cat.'

'Oh. The cat. It's good. It's at Daisy's actually. She let it out and gave it some milk. Listen. I've got an idea.' The estate agent loaded his mouth with mashed potato. He looked around and wiped his lips before leaning in towards Toby. 'Got plans for tonight? Someone is shagging your girlfriend, I am being stalked by a psychopath, I've just fucked the secretary, I'm having a baby, we made nine grand each yesterday, my instincts tell me we should have some fun. You up for it old boy?'

fourteen

Toby was sitting in the passenger seat of Gideon's Porsche. It was parked in a bus stop outside Marks & Spencer on Kensington High Street. Gideon was somewhere inside the shop and Toby was listening to Elvis Presley's 'Love Letters' and wondering when it was that he'd last had sex with someone other than Imogen. 'The only way to get over your girlfriend,' Gideon had said picking a spot on the side of his nose in the rear-view mirror, 'is to fuck someone else pronto. Get it?' Toby thought he did get it but wasn't entirely convinced that was the answer. He couldn't imagine reaching for a body other than Imogen's. So he closed his eyes and reached for Imogen. She knelt within the lazy circle of his open legs in the middle of their bed.

From where he is he can reach any part of her easily. It seems she has things other than him on her mind: she's swatting his hands away as she rattles on about some man she knows who throws seeds out of a train window every day on his way to work and over the years has planted the most prolific and rarest wild flower garden the country has ever seen and through which he travels day in day out to and from his work at St Hellier's and St Anne's. He's been doing it for years says Imogen as she grips his wrist and forces his attention from between her legs. Wild burr. Sweet breast. Lamb's tooth. It's not the first time that this man and his seeds have invaded Toby's mind. Who is he?

Gideon emerged from automatic doors on a crest of pastel-dressed women. Violet and lime and strawberry ice cream. 'Fuck off,' he told the bus driver who was gesticulating from his open window, and lowered himself into the car.

'Something for the ladies.' He threw a green and white bag on to the back seat. 'Three pack of white cotton shorts. Small.' He stuck his arm out of the window and pulled out. 'Small makes the package look so much more.' His hand, now in front of him, held an imaginary bunch of grapes.

'Do you know anyone who throws seeds out of the train window on his way to work?'

'You what?' Gideon looked over at Toby. 'Now, the beach.' He drove in the middle of the road on the tail of the car in front and scraped the car along the kerb as he brought it to a halt on a single yellow line outside a shop lit neon: The Fake Beach. Gideon got out. He came around to Toby's door: 'Rays.'

'What?'

Gideon leant into the car: 'It's like this mate. There's two birds in the pub. One is fat and forty. The other is twenty, a goddess. If seven minutes once a week means you get the goddess every time, what kind of twat wouldn't do it?' Gideon straightened. Toby undid his seat belt and got out. Gideon slammed the car door, the Porsche rocked.

The girl behind the counter knew Gideon. 'Alright?'

'Hey babe.'

She pushed back heavy dark hair from a glowing face before flattening two dull pieces-of-eight on to the counter. There had to be more where those came from: The Ducats, bitch! A beaded curtain scattered and re-formed and Toby followed Gideon into the back of the shop and a row of numbered cubicles.

'Keep your pants on.' Gideon opened the door to Number 7. 'Don't want an incident with the old schnozzle.'

Toby laughed, almost naked in a plastic blue tube deafened by the roar of a fake sun. He looked down at his body. Blue and damp and speckled and scrubby with patches of orange hair and the pair of strange tight pants. They looked like women's pants. Here he was working up a sweat upright in the Fake Beach. Imogen would laugh: 'You what?' She'd tell Saffron. His mother would looked bemused. Mercy might laugh. But Imogen would laugh until she cried.

He'd tell her: 'It's like this babe. There's two chicks in the pub. One is fat and forty...' And again he was with Imogen on the train rattling through the wild flowers on the high escarpments.

'It's the only place in England,' says Imogen turning from the window, 'where the onyx orchid grows.'

The plastic sun roared, the tube dripped with other people's sweat and Toby picked up his book on Newgate Gaol. Didn't your mother ever tell you never to stick your head out of the window of a moving train? He puts the book down and wonders if she'll see the orchid – after all they must be doing seventy at least.

Ten minutes later, hot and wet with sweat – the suit stuck to Toby's skin – they were back in the car. Rod Stewart's 'Baby Jane' came on and Gideon lit a cigarette. 'Looking good.' He turned the radio up and pulled out the ashtray. He lowered his window. 'Now these girls...' He threw his cigarette out of the window and swung on to the Brompton Road, 'Priscilla and her mate are good as gold. Good as gold and up for anything.' He turned to Toby and nodded, white teeth showing. They were heading west into pink sky and a sun which hung low enough to be looked at.

'How do you know them?' Toby was awkward in the closeness of the car. Under his clothes – someone else's clothes – his body felt like melting wax.

Gideon looked over. 'Perhaps we should have limited you to three minutes on the tanner.'

Toby put a hand to his nose.

Gideon laughed. 'You live and learn. Your one is Priscilla's mate, you got that?'

Toby's nose was hot and sore.

Gideon pulled a tiny leather book from his inside pocket which he dropped between Toby's thighs. 'Da book of lurve,' he said and worried the top of the gear stick with his palm, waiting for pedestrians to cross.

Toby allowed the black book to remain there in the valley between his legs. He looked at his legs encased in someone else's trousers. The alien shoes, the strange shirt, Gideon's tie. He picked up the book. It was fat with use.

'Priscilla and some other female… check, June the what is it? Tenth? Eleventh?'

Toby opened the diary and Gideon swung the Porsche on to the Fulham Road. Each page was a scrawl of hieroglyphics and phone numbers, a festival of sexual accomplishments: Sylvie, Dawn, Anna. Different colours, names, numbers. There was scarcely a date which wasn't crammed with his rapturous scrawl. Toby fanned through it in search of Imogen. How often had they seen each other while she was still at Frederick Street?

'Thursday 10 June. 11 June?' Gideon was getting impatient. 'What's the date today? I met her two weeks ago, Friday, club in Camden, blonde, nice tits.'

On Thursday 10 June beneath a row of navy type which read 'Full Moon', Gideon had written: 'Pamela + 1' and then a mobile number.

'Pamela?'

'Pamela. That's it. What have I been saying? Priscilla? Christ on a bike. Don't want to fuck it up before we've even started.'

The first streetlamp flicked on. Toby was glad that it was early summer – the promise of something on its way – and not autumn which spelt the end of everything. He wondered how long it would take Imogen to get over Gideon once she had this small notebook in her hands. He imagined it would take about as long as it was taking

Toby to get over her: for ever. He looked across at Gideon. It was wrong to take someone's girlfriend, impregnate them and not even want them. Toby needed to punish Gideon. However, he wasn't at this moment certain of what the correct punishment should be. Gideon's phone rang. He pulled it from his pocket, glanced at it and widened his eyes. 'Yikes,' and then 'hello?' Imogen. Toby held his breath. 'Daisy. How are you doing? Listen babe can I give you a buzz back? I'm with Toby. He's having some kind of a breakdown.' Gideon looked over as he changed gear, he stuck out his tongue. 'Yeah. It's really bad.' He lowered his voice: 'I think he's schizoid.' Gideon searched for his cigarettes. They were between his thighs. 'Of course I'm being careful, Daze.' He laughed as he put one between his lips. He turned to Toby, eyes alight with pleasure. 'No it hadn't occurred to me that the monkey wrench had anything to do with him,' he said through lips clenched from holding the cigarette whilst talking. 'Though now you come to mention it, he was the only person in the office at the time. Yes I will be careful. You're right.' Bored of the conversation now and wanting to light his cigarette, he said, 'Listen babe can I call you as soon as I've tamed the beast... OK... gotcha... will do... ciao.' He closed the phone and swerved to avoid a bicycle. 'She says you're Monkey Wrench.'

Toby laughed, Gideon laughed and parked the car on a single yellow line outside a bar called the Windmill. Above the letters a green neon windmill flashed, yellow sails whirling. 'Daze,' he said. 'Sweet girl.' And laughing, shook his head.

Toby opened the door. It scraped across the pavement.

'Mate,' said Gideon.

Toby turned.

'The book of lurve, man.' Gideon clicked his fingers.

Toby opened his palm. Gideon picked up the small leather book and got out of the car. He held it to his heart. 'Don't want that getting into the wrong hands,' he said and put it in his inside pocket.

Toby followed Gideon over a chain-mail bridge which trembled under their weight. A troll in a bow tie let them pass.

The room was largely empty and dimly lit. A pale steel bar snaked its length and lights, heavy and pendulous, hung low over small tables. It was the kind of place to which Toby never went. Two women, one blonde, one dark, sat on either side of a round table. Two pairs of identically crossed brown legs, two identical glasses of champagne, they looked up as Gideon and Toby came in. Their eyes lingered on Gideon. Pamela plus one? Gideon shook his head. Another table was colonized by a group of men. Gangsters at the top of the tree here to discuss division of spoils. Gideon's phone rang. 'Dark rum and Coke, thanks.' He flipped it open.

From the polo-necked, pockmarked barman, Toby ordered the rum and Coke and a pint of Stella. In the tilted mirror, behind the man's head, he watched Gideon. Happy to hear from someone, surprised, pleased: 'It has been a long time… oh, same old same old… ' as he strutted the length of the bar, the hand that didn't hold the phone raking through his hair.

'No pints,' said the barman – Scottish, blank-faced, hands spread on the steel top in front of him.

'A Stella?' Toby watched the mirror.

'No Stella.'

Gideon was walking head down back towards Toby. The mirror showed a mood change: smile gone, his mouth opened and closed to receive bad news. Someone ill or dying. Dead perhaps. Accident? Gunshot? 'No… When?' He turned again and walked, head down.

'No Stella,' repeated the barman, fingernails rapping impatient on steel. 'Lager?'

'Beck's, San Miguel, Budweiser… ' the fingernails didn't stop.

'See you there… yeah mate… of course… quarter to… see you then… yeah… thanks for letting me know. Tomorrow then… a quarter to… bye… see you there.' Gideon shut up his phone and sat on the barstool beside Toby. He picked up the dark rum and Coke, fresh and sparkling with bubbles on the inside, a slice of lemon, condensation on the outside. With his tanned hand he held two straws aside to raise it to his lips. Primrose's tie hung limp as he examined the drink. Tilting the glass towards him he shut one eye to squint into the dark depths.

'Friend from school,' he said and swirled the straws quickly around the glass. He pulled them out suddenly and laid them on the bar. He took another mouthful. 'Friend from school,' he gestured with a thumb to the area in the bar where he had been on the phone and, frowning, crunched ice. His eyebrows came down in a momentary frown. 'Friend from school Adam called to say ex-girlfriend. First girl-friend. First love. Adam called to say she, er, died.' Gideon frowned and lifted his glass, his little finger stuck out. 'Decapitated.' He put the glass down on the bar and took a sharp breath. He drew a finger across his throat. 'Head came off. Christ alive.' His hand returned to his glass and he turned it, clinking the ice cubes against the sides. 'Head knocked off.' Gideon brought a slow motion fist to the side of his head. 'Like that,' he said. His head moved slightly with the fake blow. 'Kerpow.'

Gideon crunched ice. He picked up the straws and put them back in his glass. He swirled the drink. 'Train. Kent. Head out window. Tunnel. Kerpow.' He clapped his hands together hard and frowned. 'De-fuckin'-capitated. Same again. Dark rum and Coke and,' he pointed at Toby's bottle of San Miguel, untouched beside its clean glass, 'one of them. Head smashed all over her boyfriend. Nice one... He's lost the plot. Barking fucking mad. Getting married everything. How the fuck does that happen?' He turned to Toby. 'Fucking decapitated.'

Train. Tunnel. Kent. Didn't your mother ever tell you not to stick your head out of the window of a moving train?

'She was thirty wasn't she?' said Toby. 'I saw it in the paper.'

'De-fuckin'-capitated.' Gideon drummed his mobile softly on the bar. 'Funeral tomorrow.' Toby shook his head.

'Head knocked off.'

'No.' Toby laughed gently. 'Everyone's got a head.' He tried to imagine a person without a head. A man in a dark suit appeared. Navy blue, like the one he was wearing, but this one was pinstriped, smart. In place of a head he had a short stump, like a child's drawing of a ham bone: red surrounding a circle of white. Holding a smart black briefcase in his left hand and, moving brightly from person to person, held out his right hand to pump enthusiastically the hands of those he met. 'Good afternoon. Good afternoon.' An enthusiastic, indiscriminate, stupid little ham bone.

'Everyone's got a head.'

'That's what I'd have thought.' Gideon put a pack of Marlboro Lights on the bar in front of him. On top of them he placed matches, corners flush together. He brought them over to the edge of the bar and lined the edges up with that. He frowned down at them feeling the three edges flush. His hair fell over his eyes.

'Poor babe,' he said softly. Gently he pushed the cigarettes away. The matches skittered lightly across the bar.

He took a deep breath. 'Funeral Friday eleven o'clock.' Gideon looked towards the door, tapped his foot against the rung of the stool. Quietly he whispered: 'Head or no head. That girl gave great head: first blow job I ever had.' He smiled and blinked rapidly. And bent to rest his forehead on the cool metal bar. Toby's hand hovered over one of his shoulder blades. Conscious of the barman's eyes on him he let it drop to connect with sinew and muscle and somewhere under that, breath and lungs and grief. In the distance beyond Gideon two women made their way over the bridge. The one in front had short, stiff white hair and a thick ginger coat reminiscent of Rita's. She was laughing. The other was shorter with black hair and a white coat. She held both rails as she crossed and looked, unlike her friend, as though she'd been trying on her mother's shoes. Blonde made it ashore and straightened her pink dress across her breasts. Between them something sparkled on a chain. The other girl bent just inside the door. She took off her shoe and leaving her pale leg dangling above the floor, tapped it against the palm of her hand. Behind her, four men came over the bridge. They looked like American fighter pilots. The last, Undercover Cop Action Man in jeans and black rollneck, cast a swivel-eyed glance around the room, before stepping up behind the girl now bending to put her shoe back on. Crudely, he thrust twice, before making his way, at the centre of the now-laughing group of men, to the bar.

The girl stood and awkwardly adjusted her bag. She was flushed from bending. Meanwhile blonde was clambering on to the stool beside Gideon. She ordered 'two gin and slims with ice and lemon,' and Toby could see that the round black beauty spot above her lip had been painted on. She was, he decided, Pamela.

Gideon remained immobile, head on the bar. Plus One came over and, looking uncomfortable, struggled up on to the stool beside Pamela. They looked at each other and laughed. Pamela turned and caught Toby's eye – cornflower blue and insolent – and looked away sharply. The drinks arrived and she picked one up and sucked through a black straw, blinking steadily and leaning towards her glass, her mouth a cherry-red 'o'.

Keeping his head low Gideon peeled the soft white square from under his glass and blew his nose on it. Cautiously, under his arm, he looked to where Toby indicated. He turned back and nodded. 'Let's do this.' And jumping off the barstool led the way across the room to the table where the two girls now sat, bobbing and nodding and smoking cigarettes. He kissed the blonde on the cheek. And moved around to kiss the girl with dark hair.

'This is my friend and colleague Toby and I think champagne is in order.' Gideon slid on to the bench beside Pamela.

'Hayfever like me.' Pamela sniffed and indicated Gideon's eyes. 'Were you at the bar?' She gestured with a white-tipped nail and eventually put the nail to her mouth to indicate confusion.

The other girl was called Colette. She smelt of soap and had nice white teeth with a gap between the front two and drank her gin with a steady sort of sincerity.

'Been away?' she asked.

'No,' said Toby.

'That from here then?' He liked her voice, schoolgirl-ish and London. And he liked the way she raised her chin when she'd finished speaking. As though challenging him to disagree. 'The sunburn,' she said and touched her own nose.

Dumbly Toby brought a hand to his face. This skin on his nose felt crisp and hot, sunburned. 'It happened earlier,' he said.

'Today?' She frowned. 'Have you seen the weather?'

It was dark outside now and Toby couldn't see the weather. He tried to remember how it was.

'It feels more like snow.' Her eyes brown, unflinching, regarded him steadily over the rim of her glass. Younger than Imogen. Quite a lot younger. Quite a lot shorter. And quite a lot rounder too.

'So. You work with er... ?' She looked at Gideon.

'Gideon.'

'Gideon.'

'Yes.'

'Estate agent?'

'Yes.'

'So, er, sell many properties?' She smiled, mostly to herself.

He nodded. 'A few.'

She picked up her glass and looked around the bar. 'Office round here?'

Toby nodded.

'Live round here?'

Toby shook his head.

'Where do you live then?'

'Kentish Town.'

She nodded. 'I'm from North London.'

'Whereabouts?'

'Highgate.'

'Do you know Warminster Road?'

She looked blank. Toby looked at Gideon. He was holding Pamela's hand and was making no effort to disguise the fact that it was her breasts which interested him. She didn't seem to mind and adjusted the pink dress so they rose and swelled like cantaloupes.

He turned back to Colette. The urge to take her soap-clean hand and tell her everything that had happened, that was happening, that Gideon was with Imogen, that he'd sold two houses and that apparently he needed to fuck her in order for everything to be alright was almost overwhelming. He sensed that this girl might be able to help.

'What?' She held her drink at chin level and started to laugh. 'I thought you were going to say something.'

The pockmarked barman brought over a bottle of champagne. He turned away to open it and Pamela's eyes glittered as she watched him. Bottle braced on his thigh, he bit his lip to ease out the cork and she bit hers in anticipation.

Colette put a cigarette between her lips. Toby felt in his pockets and brought out a lighter. 'St Ives' it said.

'My nan lives in St Ives,' said Colette turning it over in his palm. She lit her cigarette and examined the lighter. 'Well, just outside, Carbis Bay do you know it?'

Toby shook his head. He was searching for the words with which to enlist this woman's help. 'Looks like Pamela,' he said pointing to the picture of the 1950s bikini-clad pin-up kneeling on the chipped sea shore.

Colette rolled her eyes. 'Yes it could be Pam.' She looked over at her friend, turned back and lowered her voice. 'Let's cut the crap' she said. The savagery of her words surprised him. 'You would rather be with Pam. I'd rather be with him,' she pointed at Gideon. 'They'd rather be with each other. So. You're stuck with me and I'm stuck with you.' She laid both hands palm up on the table and smiled. She looked sweet when she smiled. He smiled back.

'I wouldn't rather be with Pam.'

Colette picked up her glass. He watched her pale throat as she swallowed. She laughed. 'Well I'd rather be with him. Porsche, millions of pounds.' She put back her head and laughed.

'Excuse me kids.' Gideon held up a sparkling yellow glass. 'A toast.'

'Hear, hear,' declared Colette.

'A toast,' said Gideon. 'To Pamela and Kirsty.'

All four glasses clinked. 'Kirsty,' said Colette. 'I like it.'

'I love bubbles,' said Pamela, the orange coat draped across her shoulders, her half-closed eyes daring anyone not to want to fuck her.

When they left, Pamela went first, coat worn actress-style across her shoulders. Gideon crossed the bridge just behind her, his right hand dangling car keys against her buttocks. London. June. Colder than it should have been. Toby followed Colette. The plan was to continue drinking in the bar at the Intercontinental where Gideon knew the manager.

Pamela folded into the back seat of the Porsche. Short pink dress, split-peach buttocks outlined clearly. Gideon drew sharply on a cigarette. Pamela moved along inside the car shuffling down the seat, her bare thighs tight together. Colette was stuck between the front seat and the car's frame. She was trying to force her way through on to the back seat. Hips crushed, she pulled out and went at it again. One shoe fell into the darkness between the pavement and the road. Colette angled her hips against the car to re-try. Gideon, serious, picked up the shoe. A slash of black against his upturned hand. The bouncers on the pavement watched. Colette reversed out for the third time. Pamela began pulling at Colette. 'Hurry up,' she said.

Once inside Colette turned with some difficulty to sit, red-faced, hands in lap. A fully rigged ship in a bottle. Sombrely Gideon passed the shoe inside. Pamela snatched it. The bouncers turned away to hide their laughter. One dragged his foot across the pavement to extinguish a cigarette – a zip of gold. Gideon slammed the car door. Toby would have liked to have spared Colette that.

'Totty in the back,' said Gideon throwing his own cigarette to the ground and striding across the front of the car. As the Porsche slid off towards Knightsbridge the bouncers no longer bothered to hide their laughter.

'Hungry?' asked Gideon.

'So so,' said Pamela, eyes glittering in the back seat.

Colette was silent. Toby watched her in the side mirror. She was looking out on to the pavement, hands, palms up, crossed in her lap.

'I have a plan, people,' said Gideon. 'People, I have a plan.' He shifted the car into third to roar through the changing lights by Harrods, swing up towards the park and double back in the direction of Kensington.

There was muffled laughter from the back seat. Colette had found the Marks & Spencer's bag. Toby watched her shudder as she opened up the box and held out a pair of white shorts to Pamela. Pamela, determined not to laugh, was looking out of the window. Toby smiled. Curiously, on the radio, Rod Stewart was still singing 'Baby Jane'.

Palace Mansions was dark except for the light that shone from the entrance hall. Two tired shrubs stood balding in square boxes on either side of the front door. They seemed uncertain as to whether they were alive. Toby didn't remember seeing them the last time they were here. Gideon turned off the engine and cut the lights. Toby got out and bent to move his seat as far forward as it would go. The girls got out and stood shivering on the pavement. Pamela put her coat on, her arms bent delicately behind her as though someone else was helping her into it.

'I love that.' Tentatively Colette stroked Pamela's orange arm. 'Where's it from again?'

'D'you like?' Pamela was distracted.

Gideon opened the boot and lifted out a bottle of champagne. Pamela took it and looked across the road and into the velvet depths of Hyde Park, her pale chin lifted. He brought out another bottle which he handed to Colette and then two more which he gave to Toby. 'Office supplies. Perk of the job. Lights, camera and… action. Ready for some?' Toby nodded. Gideon smiled. Behind the boot he made a fist. He looked at Toby's hand. Toby raised it and also made a fist against which Gideon pushed.

'Happy days,' said Gideon. He smiled and slammed shut the boot and walked to the entrance of Palace Mansions. He tapped on the glass door with his car key. A buzz and the door opened.

The porter dropped his paper, removed his feet from the desk and bounced forward in his chair. 'Good evening, sir,' to Gideon. He examined Pamela.

'Have you got numbers of takeaways round here?' Gideon asked.

The porter nodded until the flesh on his chin jangled.

'What d'you girls fancy? Indian? Thai? Chinese?'

Pamela wrinkled her nose. 'Anything,' she said graciously and with an elaborate shudder held her coat across her chest.

The man handed over a selection of shiny leaflets, his eyes still on Pamela.

'Cheers,' Gideon held out his hand for the bottle of champagne Pamela was holding and led the way to the lift.

'Is this your place?' she asked.

'A friend's,' said Gideon, leaning behind her to summon the lift.

'Is your friend in?'

'Sadly,' said Gideon, 'he's on safari.'

It was close in the lift. The end of a day in early summer and the beginning of a night. Cigarette smoke and perfume. Toby remembered the cocaine in his pocket and his spirit sang. 'We need beers,' he said.

Gideon nodded. 'We've done one better: champagne old boy!'

The lift clanged five, six, seven. Toby hoped the lift would go up for ever.

'You're naughty,' said Pamela to Gideon. Colette was looking at her shoes.

They stopped with a jolt at floor eight. Toby held his breath as the doors opened. He shivered with excitement. 'We need beers,' he repeated.

Gideon, who wasn't really listening, nodded and led the way to the gold-framed door.

Still Colette wasn't smiling. Toby desperately wanted her to smile. Behind her the elegant oval of the stairwell fell away. 'Colette.' She looked at him. He could hardly say her name he was so excited. 'Colette.' He held her by the wrist and pulled her to the wrought-iron balustrade. She was watching her friend. Pamela was standing in the ornate doorway. Breasts pushed out, head on one side, hands supporting a green bottle. Gideon, sorting through a bunch of keys, held one out. She made no move to stand aside and Gideon put the key to the lock, his face an inch from her breasts. A flicker of pink tongue fondled the silver pendant between them. Imogen's pendant. Gideon's tongue. Newly-weds on the first night of their honeymoon.

'Oh God,' muttered Colette, hands in her pockets. Laughter bubbled up inside Toby. I love you, he wanted to say for some reason.

'Beautiful,' he announced instead to the marble eight majestic floors below.

'Would you look at that?' Colette's gaze remained unflinching on Gideon and her friend.

The door to the flat opened and Gideon and Pamela disappeared inside. The interior glowed warmly. Grabbing Colette by the wrist Toby pulled her into the hallway. He closed the front door. The chandelier hung gold in the mirrored ceiling. And a million shards of light were reflected and re-reflected along with infinite aspects of Colette and Toby.

'Ow,' said Colette. Toby let go and the girl rubbed her wrist.

'Close your eyes.'

She laughed. 'Yeah right.' Toby liked the way she did that little nod. Her black hair bounced.

'Close your eyes.'

'My mother always said: "Colette? Strange man, strange place, middle of the night, be good and do exactly what he says, especially if it starts with close your eyes".'

Surprised, Toby laughed. 'I want to show you something.'

'How can you show me anything with my eyes closed?'

How indeed? Sweet Colette, both eyes open, a wintry smile on her lips. Gently Toby held her shoulders. He looked at her mouth. Cherry red and shiny. Sweet and tight at the corners where it disappeared into smooth cheek. He looked again at her lips. He wondered about running the tip of his tongue across them. From left to right in the groove where they joined. Sweet he guessed. Sweet and sticky and cherry wet. He allowed his knuckles to gently brush her pale neck. He looked up at the ceiling at her reflection. Her white coat swirled open, her black hair split by a blue-white line. His own arm reaching across to her. The floor sparkled snow white.

Toby let his arm drop as he took the wrap of cocaine from his inside pocket. Carefully he held it on the palm of his left hand and with his right, delicately opened out the paper. He held it to Colette. He was upset to see it showed a portion of golden thigh and strip of dark, neat-trimmed bush. What could she think? At least the paper stopped just above the part where it could have got obscene. At least the woman didn't have a face. Colette looked from the paper in his hands to his face. He licked his finger and dabbed it lightly on the paper and held it under his nose. Again he held it out to her.

'No thanks,' said Colette. 'I don't do drugs.'

'Oh.' Toby brought his finger to his mouth and sucked the remaining powder over the surface of his tongue. Colette watched him. 'Let's go,' he said and opened the door that led into the ballroom. Gideon had passed this way already: the mock candles flickered enticingly.

'Like it,' said Colette and led the way towards the light that glowed under the door ahead. She reached it and, hesitating, turned to Toby. She fumbled for both handles. The heavy doors opened and before them was the ballroom. The length of the room, unfettered by furniture, glowed soft orange. The twin chandeliers shone dimly and manicured flames licked neatly at both hearths. Toby followed her and allowed the doors to close behind them. Colette turned sharply at the sound.

'Well?' asked Toby holding his arms wide as he surveyed the vast space. He wanted to open the window to breathe in the fresh night air of the park but was conscious that Colette might be cold.

Colette surveyed the room. 'Your friend doesn't have much stuff.' She was taking off her shoes.

'He doesn't like stuff.'

Colette's eye fell on the one item in the room – the foot-shaped breeze block. 'That's it?'

'That's it.' Without the big toe, the foot appeared almost important. An important piece of pre-history.

'If I had only one thing, I don't think I'd choose that. I think I'd have a couch, a really comfy couch. Or an aquarium.' She rubbed her toes. 'Or a plasma screen.' She wriggled the toes – each was as round as she was. 'I never wear heels. I'm more of a trainers girl,' she said and put her shoes neatly alongside the concrete foot.

Toby took off his own shoes. He looked at his socks. Odd. The light blue sock on his left foot belonged to Imogen. It had a splash of blood across the ankle. He wondered how that could have happened. He wondered what she'd say. 'Toby.' A frown, a scowl. She might even throw it away.

'Odd socks!' Colette seemed delighted by the discovery. She tiptoed in the flickering light towards the window. Calves bluish and round, she reached the window and turned to whisper: 'Can I open this?'

Toby nodded. He held his breath until he felt the night chill across his cheek. The stale emptiness of the room parted to allow the inquisitive intrusion of the sharp night. Colette leant out of the window, her white coat stuck out stiff behind her. 'It's so cold tonight. It feels like snow,' she said to the darkness.

The door opened and Gideon came in. He was naked except for a pair of wet white shorts which did nothing to hide black pubic hair and the long shape of his pale penis. They made, as he'd said they would, the package look so much more. His body was brown, his nipples neat and his chest almost hairless. His legs by contrast were dark with hair. From his mouth a cigarette drooped and from his hand, an open bottle of champagne. His feet left splashy prints across the wooden floor. He handed the bottle to Toby.

'Get your chops round that old son,' he said and flicked water out of his hair.

'Swimming pool?' Colette asked, brown eyes round.

Gideon laughed. 'Hot tub, sweet thing. Come and get in.' He assessed her briefly. 'Pam's already in.'

Toby handed the bottle to Colette. She looked around the bare room. 'Glasses?'

Toby shook his head. She brought the bottle to her lips and drank. Gideon watched her. She drank thirstily and, bringing the bottle down, looked from Gideon to Toby. She handed it to Gideon. He drank and handed it to Toby and watched as he took the bottle. Toby, conscious of his tongue against its warm lip, drank. Gideon's nipple was erect in the blue flicker of the flames.

As Gideon crouched to light his cigarette, drops of water fell from his hair and the fire sizzled. The white shorts across his buttocks were transparent. Colette laughed and pointed to where Toby was already looking.

'Soaked.' Gideon threw the cigarette on to the straight blue flames and stood to retrieve a pack of Marlboro Lights from the mantelpiece. He crouched again to the flickering blue of the fire, his back shiny in the dimness. 'C'mon,' he said, standing and puffing on his cigarette. Taking the bottle from Toby he led the way into a dark forest. The forest floor was soft underfoot and golden birds thronged the trees. Then they were in the kitchen, they crossed the cold, dim space. Chinese lanterns glowed red on either side of the black marble bed. The mattress shone white, vast and somehow obscene. A blank canvas. Toby felt ashamed. Gideon was fiddling at the window. He located a rod under the heavy black curtains and began twirling it, his cigarette hanging from his lip.

'None of anyone else's business,' he said as the curtains jerked across mock Elizabethan windows. They swung shut. Colette cast Toby an anxious look. He smiled. She smiled and from the adjoining room came the gurgle and hiss of a large quantity of water. Gideon opened the door. A welter of heavy cloud rolled out and he disappeared into it. Colette and Toby waited for it to disperse a little before entering.

Clothes littered the black marble floor. The mirrored walls were steamed up and in the black marble tub knelt Pamela. Like the woman on the seaside lighter, she'd tied her hair in a knot at the back of her head and was delicately sipping from a champagne bottle which she grasped with rosy hands. Black straps showed above the raging torrent. Colette, flapping her hand in front of her face, picked a delicate path between the islands of clothes to her friend. Gideon, bottle of champagne pressed against his hip, was twisting out the cork.

'Get in,' hissed Pamela.

Colette looked at the bubbling water. 'What are you wearing?' She crouched beside the bath to whisper. The hem of her coat trailed on the floor.

'Gotta fag?'

'What are you wearing?' Colette peered doubtfully beneath the water's turbulent surface.

'Get in,' hissed Pamela. 'It's fuckin' lovely in here.' A giggle and a hiccup.

Despite the saturated atmosphere, Gideon's cigarette remained alight. He took it from his mouth and handed it to Pamela and climbed into the tub. Toby lowered one of the the black marble toilet seats. It was square and wet. He sat on it and bent to take off his socks.

'Miss me?' asked Gideon bending to Pamela's upturned lips. He lowered himself beneath the churning surface of the water.

'Get in,' Pamela urged Colette while Gideon made himself comfortable beside her.

Colette looked at Toby. 'OK.' She pulled her hand from the water and shook off the excess. Something cracked as she stood up. Her knee perhaps. The hem of her coat was wet. And barefoot she picked her way back to the door and to where Toby sat. 'Come here a second,' she said, beckoning and opening the bathroom door. He followed her out into the corridor. It was cold and dark and the door closed behind them.

'Colette!' Pamela's shriek rose above the roar of water. 'I know what you're like, Colette. Get the fuck back here Colette Carol Kray.'

They could hear the tub bubbling fiercely. Colette tiptoed purposefully along the corridor, her white coat stiff and unmoving.

'Colette Carol Kray!' It rose in pitch and volume.

'Kray?' asked Toby. 'As in twins?'

'No,' said Colette. 'As in fish.'

Back in the ballroom, both fires blazed.

'Your coat's wet.'

Colette, hand in her pocket, bent to look. She wrinkled her nose. 'If I'm going to get in that bath then I am going to need some of that charlie.' She jabbed her coat pocket in the direction of his own. 'If that's alright, I mean.' Her pointed chin rose. Defensive against her politeness.

With his British Library card, which surprised him by appearing from the pocket of the strange trousers, Toby set up four lines on the black marble mantelpiece. He folded the remainder back into the paper. He rolled a twenty-pound note and Colette stood on tiptoe to see on to the marble top. Toby laughed, Colette couldn't reach. She drew her coat around her and tiptoed over to her neatly paired shoes. She squeezed herself into them and clicked back across the floor to Toby. The four inches of heel afforded the girl access to the cocaine. She held the rolled note. She paused, took off her coat and handed it to Toby. He hung it on a picture hook. She was wearing a dark blue dress which rose high at the neck. Toby liked the way it squeezed at the waist and swelled out across her hips. Her pink heel rose out of her shoe as she leant forward to reach. She finished and turned to see him staring at her rounded calf.

'Have another.'

She rubbed her nose. 'What? With my other nostril?'

'If you like.'

She laughed, stood upright, rubbed her nose and sneezed. She snorted the line and stood back down in her shoes. She wrinkled her nose and looked from left to right.

'I want to ask you something,' said Toby.

'Got a fag?'

Toby shook two from the packet on the mantelpiece. 'Can I ask you something?'

Colette took the cigarettes, her dress tightening above the twin points of her heels as she bent to the flames. She stood, puffing on both cigarettes. 'As long as it's nothing to do with maths,' said the girl, frowning at the ends of both cigarettes. She handed one to Toby. 'Or sex.'

'It's nothing to do with maths or sex.'

'Good,' said the girl. 'Where's that champers?'

Toby turned to pick up the bottle which stood behind him and handed it to her. As she drank he asked, 'Have you ever seen a dead body?'

The girl brought the bottle down. 'You what?' She burped then laughed. She wiped the back of her thumb across her chin and the smile faded. 'Have I ever seen a dead body? How d'you mean and why?' She handed him the bottle.

How did he mean and why? The champagne was not so cold and not so fizzy. He drank deeply and handed the bottle back to her. 'I thought I saw one.'

'What do you mean you thought you saw one? When?'

'I thought I saw one only it didn't have a head. It had arms and legs, shoes even, a cardigan. There was no head though. Just a lot of blood.'

The girl frowned. 'Where was it?'

'On a train.'

'Was it moving?' The girl hiccuped, then laughed.

'The train was moving.'

She laughed harder. 'No, stupid, not the train, the body. Was it moving?'

'No,' said Toby. 'It was completely still.'

'It sure sounds like a dead body,' said the girl and drank. She held the bottle upside down above her open mouth. Toby watched the last few drops fall from the bottle's green glass lip. 'You poor love,' she said and stalked on heels back down the corridor, and Toby waited as she knocked on the open bathroom door. 'Only us,' she said as Gideon and Pamela untangled themselves. 'Well pardon me,' said Colette, her toe toying with a black bra discarded on the floor.

'Are you going to join us?' Gideon was somewhere in the steam.

'Right,' announced Colette. 'I am going to take my clothes off now. And I want every single one of you to look the other way.' She reached behind her to where her zip was at the nape of her neck. Toby liked the way her plump arms worked together. He liked the way they felt their way to each other across her back and then together, located the zip. He sat on the bidet and reached for a bottle. It was wet with condensation. The cork popped and a creamy overflow coursed steadily on to Gideon's blue shirt which was screwed damply between his feet. While Gideon watched Colette wriggle out of her dress, he traced a finger lightly across Pamela's collar bone. Encircled by cloud, Colette folded her dress over one arm and wearing her shoes, pale too-small knickers and a too-small bra seemed uncertain of her next move.

'Here,' said Toby holding the bottle out to her.

A grateful hand emerged from steam to snatch the bottle. Toby took the dress and hung it neatly over the empty towel rail. He picked up Gideon's shirt and did the same. Unlike him. It seemed he was turning over a new leaf.

'Here with that bubbly,' Pamela instructed. She was hanging out of the tub, both hands trailing on the marble floor, while Gideon's dark head moved at the nape of her neck. Colette drank and handed the bottle back to Toby. She undid her bra.

'Don't look,' she said, both hands splayed across her front.

Toby took off his jacket. He hung it from the towel rail. As his trousers slid off he was aware of them and the heavy smell of someone else. He loosened the tie and hung it beside the suit. Last his shirt.

'Oh my God.' Colette seemed to have forgotten that she was almost naked. She was facing Toby. The shape and outline of her pale bra, now loose, showed through the fingers that covered her breasts.

'What?' She was staring at Toby's groin, he covered it with both hands. 'What?'

Colette was laughing. 'Oh my God. Let me see.' Emboldened by something – cocaine, champagne, steam – she abandoned her breasts, her bra dropped, to pull Toby's hands away. Surprised, Toby let her remove them. Her breasts were huge and comforting, uneven, one hung lower than the other and the nipples were almost the same colour as her flesh. Blunt and kindly. She held Toby by the wrists. He examined her face. Her brown eyes were round with disbelief.

'Oh my God.' She dropped one of his hands to cover her laughter. Somewhere behind them Pamela hiccuped.

'What?' he asked again.

Colette let go of his hands to laugh more freely. He wished he was with Imogen. Safe and certain, nothing about him a surprise or a shock. He tried to remember the first night with Imogen. He could not recall a similar reaction. He looked down. The small triangular fabric gaped at the sides through which flesh and hair protruded. He bulged from the small taut hammock between his thighs. Orange hair sprouted thickly.

'Sorry,' he said quickly. 'That's obscene.'

Colette stopped laughing and looked into his face. 'At least you got the day right,' she said softly.

Toby removed his hands just enough to enable him to read upside down on the front of the faded knickers the joined up writing which, surrounded by flowers, spelt 'Thursday'.

'You're alright,' said Colette more kindly. Lightly she touched his arm. And made an effort, biting her lower lip, to stem the laughter.

fifteen

Toby's damp clothes added an extra sharpness, a stab of menthol, to the night air. It was cold and Toby regretted having returned the car to Kentish Town. The white moon face of a clock hung bright above the pavement to show a drooped, French, pencil moustache. It was twenty minutes to four. There was a significance in the symmetry of those hands but Toby didn't know what it could be. He dodged a car to cross the road and walk park side. The black velvet depths soothed and, stooping, he made it under the railings to cross the thick sand track upon which the horses – all the King's horses and all the King's men – galloped. On the cyclists' path beside the dark blue of a hedge bordering a secret garden, the air felt softer. Good somehow. Better. The goodness of the earth spawning growth. He dabbed a finger inside a pocket and held it to his nostril. Snotty and clogged it bubbled uselessly. Instead he rubbed the cocaine into the gum above his teeth. He reached out to feel the petals of a summer rose, it brushed his hand and invited him to pick it. He wondered about taking it home.

'Hello Imogen Green.' Down on his knees beside their bed. Her hair crinkly on the pillow, his knees painful on uneven floorboards, the duvet pulled right up over her eyes. He buries his face in the warmth of her neck. 'I picked this for you because I am sorry for what I've done. And for what I haven't done.' He reached into his pocket to ward off encroaching melancholy. He rubbed his gum and almost instantly it receded into the night.

'And Fuck You Imogen Green,' he shouted through the railings and into the park. 'Fuck you Imogen Green, short, no-tit bitch.'

Silence.

The path forked. Toby took the one that headed up towards Marble Arch and Tyburn Tree. Ahead of him astride the path a giant frozen on horseback raised an arm. Black against the indigo sky both man and horse were paused to mark the movement of the air: pock pock pock went the steel-capped heels of Toby's lucky shoes on tarmac, coins clicked as they slid across each other in his pocket. Toby touched his forehead as he passed. The horseman did not acknowledge him but seemed preoccupied with something beyond Toby, something on the other side of the park. Both horse and rider strained in that direction. Listening. Leaning. Towards Kensington and other prizes.

A pall of mist hung over the Serpentine. At a spot between a silver birch and a plaque naming birds, Toby scaled the knee-high fence. A family of ducks fled quacking into the water. He could see the shape of the willow black against the night and made his way to it. He saw the line of its trunk which rode out low across the water, and could smell the thickness of the decades of duck shit behind the gold curtain of leaves. He stood outside and the leaves rustled, lifting slightly from the ground. He found that he couldn't enter. He'd been inside before with Imogen on a picnic blanket on probably the second day they'd ever spent together. He crossed back over the low loops of the fence and rejoined the path for Marble Arch and home.

The sun was coming up and the sky over Oxford Street glowed pink. A murmur reached him through the breaking dawn as he rounded the lake and began his ascent towards the Tyburn Gibbet. A hanging at sunrise and the murmur of a crowd gathering. The air trembled with anticipation. Sixteen hooves struck Oxford Street and a carriage, urged on by the waxing sun, rumbled in from Newgate in the East: 'Stand back! Stand back!' Toby stood on a bench and above the crowd beyond the fountains saw four black horses. The coachman's cloak flew wide.

'Stand back! Stand back!'

'Innocent! Innocent! Innocent!' the crowd roared.

A young man stood on the cart, a slight man, pale and inconsequential, his new suit and shirt barely visible in the scant light. His hands were tied in front of him.

'Innocent! Innocent! Innocent!' called the rapturous crowd. Another innocent who'd galloped the high road to the Tyburn Tree. The carriage was close enough for Toby to see the Squire's face. Betrayed by his lover, betrayed by the Spaniard. The carriage crossed into the park and the women screamed their approval: 'The Squire! The Squire!'

The Squire squinted in the shadow of death. He was searching the crowd for someone. For a moment his eyes met Toby's. They passed on, it wasn't Toby for whom he searched.

'A watchmaker's shop in his pocket!' shouted someone.

'And a jeweller's!' shouted another. Laughter rippled out across the crowd. The air throbbed with excitement. Infectious, Toby's heart skipped a beat. 'Innocent! Innocent! Innocent!' His cries rose above those of the crowd.

The Squire's eyes moved faster as he processed and dismissed faces.

'The Great North Road won't be the same without you, sir,' shouted a man nearby. 'We'll miss you, sir.' A ripple of approving laughter.

'We'll miss you, sir!' Caps snatched off, the crowd lowered its collective head.

The Squire, distracted, didn't appear to notice, he was still searching.

'Hurry up!' shouted someone. 'Hang 'im! Hang 'im! Hang 'im!'

Toby's cries rose on the air. The noose rested on the Squire's shoulders, he looked over the priest's black shape.

'In the name of the Father, the Son and the Holy Ghost.'

'God Save the King!' shouted someone. Toby turned away. The crack was followed by silence and then a roar that filled the whole of London. From the corner of his eye Toby saw sparks from the horses' pounding hooves. The Squire swung at Tyburn Tree without seeing the face he was searching for. Lady Rose Stockport slept soundly some-where in Fulham.

By the time Toby got home the sun was high enough to ripen the black bags of rotting rubbish that lined Frederick Street. The air was sweet with decay. He stood with his key, in the shadow of the house. The infinite possibility of the night replaced by bright nothing. A dis-order of chicken bones lay brittle on the path, a sluice of last night's piss was drying in the strengthening day. Home.

He opened the door. On the fourth step of the red stairs an envelope stood upright: 'Toby'. Not Imogen's writing, in fact no writing he rec-ognized. Green felt tip, joined up, 'b' like a '6' with a deliberate line underneath. 'Toby' written by someone with important information to impart. He picked it up. Uneven and heavy. There was sellotape across the back of the letter. He sat down to open it on the sixth step facing the front door. The sun shone bravely through the dust-encrusted window above it. I must make a note, thought Toby, I must make a note to get these windows cleaned. My, everything in London just gets so filthy. Oh I know. So quickly. Hardly worth doing at all. He planned this conversation with Primrose. It's unbelievable. Well look, says Toby from the garden. She's standing at her balcony. Well look, Primrose, I've got someone coming. Inside and out. Makes sense to send him on to you afterwards doesn't it? Makes a lot of sense, Toby Doubt. He peeled the sellotape from the back of the envelope.

Inside was a folded piece of yellow paper and a ring. A gold ring set with a large, clear blue stone as cold as ice and as large as a sweet. It sat in the palm of his hand and made a bleak effort to sparkle. It looked fake. The gold was orange and the stone missed light. Dull and worn, it looked like a sucked Fox's Glacier Mint. He wondered whether the gypsy bitch in the Camden Treasure Trove would take it back. She stood there wreathed in as many smiles as £400 bought. Congratulations, the notes stiffening between her hands as she counted them on to the counter. That day he'd stood there, the ring in the palm of his hand, looking out on to Frederick Street and further, beyond the wall, beyond the grey bridge and down on to the railway platform. A white plastic bag filled and rose in the bluster of the day above the platform. It had swept up level with the bridge and he'd watched it bob along the top, up and down along the handrail. A sudden gust had lifted it high into the sky. It crossed the road and kept on coming. It touched the window twice and swirled around to show Toby green letters. 'Bravo!' they read. 'Bravo!' And then it was borne straight up into the air, above the window and over the roof of Number 3 Frederick Street. On the other side of the house, she was in the garden thinning lettuces: the chosen and the unchosen in a row beside her on the concrete. It was 10 March, her birthday, and she was thirty.

'Thursday' the letter read in greedy ink which had soaked up paper and bled through on to the other side.

> Dear Toby.
> Iain and I came by with John Pierson (the man who bought it) to collect Mummy's rosewood desk. We were sorry not to see you. Imogen is home now in Cobham. Enclosed please find the ring. We thought you would want it. I hope you are OK, everything considered, and will see you on Friday.
> Cassandra and Iain.

I hope you are OK. Everything considered. I hope you are considered OK. Everything. I hope you are everything. I hope you are everything Iain and Cassandra considered OK. Toby stood up. He put the ring in the pocket of the trousers of the blue suit and wondered how he might go about getting hold of a reliable window cleaner. Perhaps his conversation with Primrose would be better going more like this: 'Hello Primrose,' he tried it outloud. 'Hello Primrose. I was just wondering whether you might know of a *reliable* window cleaner? Well. Inside *and* out. The thing is… [embarrassed laugh] well the thing is Primrose… I realized we hadn't had them done once since we moved in. I know! Not once in three years!'

Primrose, tartan skirt, red jumper, flustered at this admission, goes back inside to find the reliable window cleaner's telephone number. It's pinned butterfly-style, right through the middle, to her cork message board alongside cards for taxis and Indian takeaways and postcards from Ilfracombe.

One two one two, the shoes on Toby's feet climbed the red stairs up to the kitchen. At the landing he stopped to look out of the window. The garden was entirely stripped: a brown square only slightly longer than it was wide. Everything green had been stacked neatly against the white-washed wall. The tools: rake, hoe, trowel, leant dutifully beside the back door. The crazy paving teetered in three neat towers. It was a clean slate, a blank canvas ready for Mother Nature to do her stuff. Toby was pleased to see that the foolish purple flowers that still clustered at the window had started to brown at the edges.

The kitchen was bereft without Imogen's mother's rosewood roll-top desk. A square of dust on the wooden floor marked the place where it had stood. Thick balls of fluff cowered against the skirting board. Cassandra and the Cyclops had kindly thought to leave behind the yellow pages, the phone directory, what might have been an ashtray and a small stack of bills. They were neatly lined up on the table and beside them, the book of evening classes. From the way it had been left – a little distance from the other items, deliberate and orderly – Toby concluded that this was meant kindly. He picked it up. Philately and Pilates, Portuguese and pottery. He wondered which his new girlfriend might attend. He saw her now: a brown-haired unsmiling girl bent over a stamp collection. 'Oh,' said Toby again to Primrose, nodding sagely from her balcony, 'I don't think you've met Jessica.' He thrust forward the girl who wears glasses and has no interest in gardening.

'We met at Philately on Phriday.'

'Tuesday 3 p.m. Imogen. I've missed you. Back soon. Toby.' He read on a square of green paper. He turned it over. 'No,' he said. 'No to the Green Wood Estate.' If it wasn't so early. If it wasn't so late. If he knew anyone's numbers at all, Toby had an idea he'd be putting in some calls. No, you cunt. It's No to the Green Wood Estate.

The absence of the rosewood roll-top desk threw into relief everything that was hers: the Lloyd Loom chairs at the table. Lloyd who? Loom says Imogen. Lloyd Loom. I-can't-believe-you've-never-heard-of-him. The table which she found on the pavement and phoned him to come down the road to fetch with her. All the way up Kentish Town Road, stopping every ten yards, Imogen holding the table behind her, bump bump bump against her buttocks. Up the stairs, Imogen squeezing her way between banisters and table to inspect and direct and overcome the insurmountable. Imogen wearing red wool gloves, a white t-shirt and no bra, with the window open as wide as it can go, leans on folded sandpaper. Up down up down she rides erasing the table's yellowness and its memory of four decades of dinner. Toby doesn't care if the table's yellow blue or green, what's wrong with you asks Imogen, stopping, face slick with sweat. What's wrong with me? There's nothing wrong with Toby. All he wants to do is get on the table and taste the salt on her face and between her breasts.

The bookcase also contained her things, most particularly the fourth shelf. These things had not been here for very long, just since Christmas. The golden owl, the green glass rock, the miniature teapot and teacups and the tiny china dog – the smallest Alsatian in the world. Imogen, barefoot, rearranges these things from time to time, swiping at the duck with a duster. The white duck and her six tiny ducklings. It is six – Toby doesn't think he'll ever forget that it is six because of the time that one went missing. Imogen frantic as she scours the shelf, opens up the golden owl – though how it would have got in there is anybody's mystery – scans the floor. In the end she found it behind some books on the shelf above and Toby makes the mistake of assuming it's safe to laugh. His mistake. 'It was Anne's,' she says coldly. She's been calling her mother Anne ever since she died. 'And before that Gran's and before that her mother's.' A long line of Imogen's forbears arranging and rearranging the duck and her six eternal ducklings. He'd need to clear the shelf in case Jessica Philately had her own things to display here.

He turned his attention to the kitchen. Imogen's red and blue striped scarf hung from a hook near the fridge. An Alice B. Toklas cookery book, a black and red one by Delia Smith. The collage of the silver snake. He began to make a pile on the kitchen floor. He opened a cupboard, a box of Christmas decorations: hers. Saucepan: hers. Three pink champagne glasses. The green glass vase. The coffee pot still dirty in the sink.

Toby decided to start at the top of the house. In the bathroom, her bubble bath and her sun cream and razor blades. In fact everything in the bathroom was Imogen's. Technically even the Imperial Leather soap and the Colgate toothpaste as she was the one who bought them. But certainly the eye repair cream, the chamomile healing mask, the bust firming gel. The what? He examined the tube. He squeezed some into the palm of his hand. It was clear and cold with bubbles in it. It looked like hair gel. Left hand under his shirt he felt his chest. It seemed firm enough. His left hand fumbled with the button on the trousers. It was stiff and unfamiliar but eventually it undid. He could feel the bust firming gel melting in the palm of his hand. He dropped the trousers and with his other hand pulled down the knickers which still said Thursday. He rubbed the cream into both hands and applied it to his buttocks. Cold and sticky, he read the tube. It didn't say how long it would take and he didn't have all day, but already he could feel the gel tightening on his buttocks as they firmed up. He turned and tried to see them in the mirror above the basin. It was too high and even on tiptoes he didn't stand a chance. He pulled up the knickers and pulled up the trousers. His buttocks cold and firm, the tube joined the heap at the bottom of the little flight of stairs. For a moment he was distracted by her flannel. Pink and hard he held it to his mouth. Scratchy, it smelt of mildew. Imogen in the bath, the flannel flaps at her leg. Today it was stiff like card. Everything about it Imogen-free. A fickle flannel with no memory. It joined the bottles, potions, lotions. He jumped down and climbed over it all to get into the bedroom.

It was hot work and Toby felt sweat on his face.

In the bedroom it was not immediately apparent which was hers and which his. The wardrobe bulged with clothes. The fur coat was still there, a red fox, rich and luxurious. Toby pulled it off its hanger and held it to his face searching for a trace of her. Behind it, crushed into a dark corner hung a faded suede jacket. He was happy to see it. Before Imogen he wore it all the time. He was wearing it at the Stone the Crows gig at the Windsor Castle on the night they met. Jane introduced the girl in the green dress with the short tangle of black hair and the freckled nose: Jane was Howard's girlfriend even then. And this was Imogen, a friend of Dan's. Dan, Jane's brother, was the drummer with Stone the Crows. He was also on Imogen's teacher training course, just in case the Crows didn't take off.

It seemed the girl in the green dress found everything funny: 'Hello, I like your jacket,' she'd said, a slight smile on soft lips, a light in those ice-blue eyes. I like your jacket. He'd known straight away that she didn't, however that was beside the point. The first thing he thought was that here was a person with hair curlier than his own and the second thing he thought was how much he'd like to see her without her dress on. Later on when they were still at the stage where they stayed up all night talking rubbish she'd admitted that she'd only said she liked his jacket because she couldn't think of anything else to say. He hadn't worn it much since then. Now its tassels reproached him for this want of character. He took off his new suit jacket and put on the suede one. The suede was stiff as though it bore a grudge. It creaked resentfully when he bent to pick up the box containing Imogen's half-finished shoes. They still smelt of glue. Sloppy, slapdash, gluey. Unlike Imogen.

The doorbell rang, a light buzz. If he'd had the radio or the TV on or the bath running, he would not have heard it. Fortunately it was just him, quiet, alone. He liked the bell like this. Not insistent. A polite request. I am at the door if you want to see me. I understand if you don't. With the shoe in his hand he went to the window. His mother was standing by the gate. Strange in London, unsure, her tweed coat buttoned all the way up. She turned to look over her shoulder, perhaps to make sure she wasn't getting mugged – this wasn't Cambridge now – and turned back, her face in two separate parts divided by the line of her mouth, a cheesewire cutting downwards.

The doorbell buzzed again. Soft, questioning, unobtrusive. His mother didn't move her hand. And then he saw Howard and Jane. Jane behind Howie, Howie looking up at the window. Toby pressed himself against the wall, breathing heavily. He felt Howie's hot gaze on the bedroom window. Again the door buzzed. Then came a sharp rapping. A bang bang bang bang bang on the door. 'POLICE OPEN UP.' He pressed closer to the wall, the paint in front of his nose and mouth wet now with his breath. Again came the rapping, loud and intrusive. Howie in a suit, his mother in a tweed coat, Jane looking serious, he did not like their attitude. By the time his breathing was back to normal there was no one outside, just a stream of early commuters on their way to work. He looked at the clock on Imogen's bedside table. It said 7.30. Early for a social call. That's what he meant. He didn't like their attitude. It occurred to him that it might have been 7.30 in the evening. Of course, that made better sense. 7.30 in the evening. But then he was missing a day somewhere. He sat on the bed and it felt as though his head would explode. It was 7.30 in the evening and he'd just got out of bed. He was just getting into bed? He'd just got in from work? He lay on the bed and rubbed his head. He went again to the window. It looked like early morning. A river of smart people funnelled down the throat of the tube. Howie and his mother. Since when were they such friends? The last time he recalled communication between them was about twenty years ago. 'That's the last time I have that boy in my house!' After they'd taken it in turns to smash the few remaining panes of glass in the dilapidated greenhouse at the bottom of his mother's dark green garden.

It was 7.42. It was getting later. Toby tore the African tapestry from the wall above the bed. He took the turd-like owl that Imogen had made in pottery class and nested it on top of a knot of tights. He couldn't picture her in the towelling dressing gown which hung off the door but it certainly wasn't his. Her bedside drawer was awash with earrings, Nurofen, pebbles. The whole drawer would have to come. He picked a crinkly black hair from her hairbrush. He stretched it straight and considered keeping it for DNA purposes, for cloning. But what would the use of another faithless gardening bitch be? He emptied the chest of drawers. He filled seven black bin-liners with her belongings and lined them up on the pavement outside Number 3 Frederick Street. He slammed the front door and wondered if he could remember the way to The Firs. Cobham, near Guildford, was out past Wimbledon which meant south over Putney Bridge. He could see a roundabout, a Shell garage and a road with tall hedges on both sides which swept downhill. 'My mother,' says Imogen importantly, 'can remember when there were no roads here. At all. It was fields and she could ride her horse anywhere she liked.'

'And I,' said Toby, wondering where the car was parked, 'can remember the way to your house.'

The car was on Plantation Road outside the Dragon. It had a parking ticket underneath the windscreen wiper. It was unlocked. Toby got in and fired it up, he opened the sun roof and managed a six-point turn. The radio crackled into life. It sounded like applause. He drove to the bottom of the street. A Range Rover came up quickly to meet him. Odd thought Toby, to have such a smart car in Kentish Town. He could see the driver's mouth opening and closing behind the windscreen. He was shouting silently and waving his hand. Toby didn't recognize him, just another irate individual. The Range Rover's door opened and the man, squat and livid, dropped to the pavement in white trainers. An overweight tennis coach perhaps. Toby drove up on to the pavement and with a screech of rubber, passed him on the outside. There was no traffic on Frederick Street. He stopped outside the house and, scattering a trail of beads and shampoo, loaded seven bin liners on to the back seat, cramming them against the ceiling. Glass broke somewhere low down.

He got in and pulled out, narrowly missing a milk float which swerved, delicately tooting a melodious horn. If it wasn't for Imogen, Toby would be blissfully happy. Nice car, morning sun, driving out of London to somewhere with trees and cow parsley whispering in a summer haze, to lie in long grass and consider the whole of life. Cigarettes and cold lager somewhere amongst the buttercups on the green bank of some clear river. He was blissfully happy if he ignored the weight that crushed his chest and stopped his breath. He waited at the lights. I cannot breathe, said Toby Doubt. He closed his eyes. The air he sucked was warm and without oxygen, the stale breath from someone else's lungs. Horns honked behind him. He opened his eyes. The light was green, he turned left and joined the traffic heading south.

Slowly, slower than the pedestrians, he passed Steve's Nest. It was open for business. Through the windows of the cafe he saw clearly the girl from Bulgaria and Steve beside her, sporty in a baseball cap. He smiled to butter toast. Outside Woolworth's there had been an accident: ambulance, police car, a short red bus parked at a strange angle and a man lying in the road. Toby lit a cigarette and held it out of the window in the sunlight. The tassels on his suede jacket pattered like rain against the door of the car. With his free hand he reached behind him through the gap between the seats to touch the black plastic bags filled with Imogen's things. The radio was still buzzing between stations. The policeman motioned for him to pass and Toby saw the man's face: white as alabaster on navy blue, at peace.

sixteen

On the road beneath the aviary in Regent's Park, Toby waited for a family of four to cross. It was the perfect family: first came Mum and Dad, holding hands. Behind them came a boy and a girl, larger than life, wholesome and happy, unblemished brown legs from immaculate white shorts. Mother wore a money belt, father had a map and the blond, brushed, blue-eyed children had each other. Their white trainers pattered obediently on the zebra crossing.

Had Alison Doubt decided to make a go of things with John Lambert III and packed her bags for leafy Vermont, perhaps Toby too might be part of such a family. Aw, shucks Mom, look, a gee-raff! A leaf, green and perfect, zig-zagged down through the sun roof to land gently on the seat beside him. He put his hand on it. The family was safely on the other side of the road and the pressure on Toby's chest had eased enough that he could breathe again. Things were making more sense. He put his hand into his pocket and felt the ring, large and angular. He took it out and put it on his little finger. Hand on the steering wheel he was the Pope driving through the Vatican waving faintly to the crowds. It made sense that she'd gone to The Firs. The man that she loved had spent one night with the office secretary and the next with Pamela of Highgate. It made sense that her ex was on his way down there to deliver the last of her things. To see her, to say goodbye. To tell her he could live without her. Things were making more sense and Toby felt better. He knew where Imogen was. She was in the garden at

The Firs, smiling in the swing seat in the sun, reading a book, wearing a hat, drinking lemonade in the shade of the monkey puzzle. Perhaps Rita was with her, the tip of her spoilt tail flicking discontentedly as she laid out her fur in the best patch of sun.

He turned on to the Westway and followed the road which looped down past the gypsy encampment towards Shepherd's Bush and Putney Bridge and the A3, which led to Imogen. It seemed Gideon was wrong. He didn't need to be with another woman to get over Imogen. I brought the rest of your stuff. He'd tell her. It's all here. I don't want a fight. I just want to hear it from you. He might cry but that didn't matter. He didn't really care. I just need to know, he'd tell her. He wouldn't tell her about his new job. Or about Gideon with Daisy or with Pamela. He wouldn't tell her about the Book of Lurve. Or the cocaine, or the flat or the jacuzzi or the fact that he'd been wearing her pants. There was no reason she needed to know anything about that. If Gideon had told her then that was between her and Gideon. In fact the whole of last night was between her and Gideon and everything from here on in was between her and Gideon. Except for this. He needed to hear it from her. He needed to hear her tell him that it was over. If he didn't suspect that she didn't like the ring he might even have told her to keep it. The ring flashed fire on the steering wheel. He might even tell her he loved her. That he would always love her. That he would always love her without demanding any love in return.

The river was brown and busy below Putney Bridge. Going about its morning business. Its Friday morning business. I, said Toby. Love you. And with that he'd go. He'd leave her. With the bags of her stuff on the gravel. In his suede jacket, he'd pretend the past four years had never happened. It's Friday. Perhaps he'd go to the seaside for the weekend. Keep on driving until he got to the sea. How far is Cobham from the sea? Surrey. Did Surrey have a coast? Kent had coast. Hampshire, Dorset. Brighton. He'd go, anyway, to the beach nearest to Cobham, he'd check into a nice hotel and he'd stay there. Some Four Star in Bognor or

Bexhill. That shouldn't be too far. Long walks, fine wine, good food. He'd think about things. He'd like that. For a moment he saw Imogen: 'Toby.' Clear eyes filling with tears, standing barefoot in the shade on the gravel outside The Firs. 'I'm coming with you.' And leaving her things just like that, in their black bags, the bust firming gel, the fur coat, the shoe with the floppy red rose. She'd hot-foot it across sharp stones to jump into the front seat, flicking gravel off the soles of her feet, putting her seat belt on. Rita might appear from the side of the house, stiff on tiptoes. Spitting Imogen, eyes filled with tears, doesn't notice Toby give the cat two fingers as he spins the wheel to spray it with gravel. And when they come back from Bognor and move back into Frederick Street, Rita doesn't come with them. The cat stays at The Firs and, under the tutelage of Lieutenant Colonel John Green, learns how to be nice.

A penitent Rita, grateful, aware of its utter ugliness, seemed unlikely.

The pressure returned to Toby's chest. He pulled over, stopped the car and got out. He tried to fill his lungs. He looked up into the velvet shade of a horse chestnut tree where a thousand golden motes swirled above him, up and down in the shade. Fairies minding their fairy business, going about their fairy lives or some other rubbish that Imogen might have said. He got back into the car and brought out a small, square package. With trembling hands he unfolded it. At last it showed the face: lips parted, dark eyes fringed with long black lashes. It wasn't Imogen. It wasn't Daisy, it wasn't Colette, it wasn't anyone he knew. He cut the cocaine with a brown comb, he moved it across her face and down until it covered her open mouth and waited until his hand stopped shaking. He opened the door of the car and emptied the white powder, it lifted, scattering on the breeze and Toby felt better able to face her at The Firs, to return her belongings. He even felt that she loved him and felt a reciprocal warmth across his chest.

Signposts to Sandown Park showed a cavalier race horse white on brown, legs thrown out, and suddenly the road ended in a roundabout.

The roundabout, the Shell garage and the crisscross of junctions and roads which hadn't always been there and had been, not so long ago – in Anne's lifetime, except of course Anne was dead – fields and fields and more fields. He pulled into the garage. He'd never seen it so busy: cars queued while a smartly dressed woman – black jacket, black skirt, red flower at her lapel – rattled the nozzle inside her petrol tank. Teenagers on their mobile phones clustered the doorway of the shop, two cars were engaged in carefully choreographed three-point turns. A battered white pick-up bounced on to the forecourt and narrowly missed a black Porsche. A handsome man, dark skin, black hair, turned frowning from his car. Handsome man, dark suit, flicking dark hair out of his eyes to screw the cap back on to the petrol tank of the Porsche. Gideon Chancelight walking stiffly into the garage less than one mile from The Firs, taking out his wallet from his inside pocket. Gideon Chancelight hungover, unwell-looking on the other side of the glass making his slow way along the rack of sweets choosing something for breakfast. Toby opened the door of his car and was sick.

He was waiting in a lay-by when the Porsche came past. Slow, uncertain of the way, a black lick of metal, Gideon's eyes on the seat beside him. Toby allowed the Porsche to get some distance before pulling out. The cow parsley shuddered. The new boyfriend, flowers on the front seat, nervous about seeing the Colonel, except of course the Colonel and Gideon go way back. 'He gave me your adress and told me to write.' The Colonel would approve of the Porsche. Perhaps he might even have been persuaded to approve his daughter's pre-marriage pregnancy. Obviously, a quick marriage was to be expected.

A red car overtook the Golf and sat behind the Porsche. The Porsche turned left into the Hundred. Toby slowed so as not to sit on its tail. Slowly the Porsche rolled over the first speed bump. PRIVATE ROAD read the sign. ACCESS ONLY. The Hundred. Private Road. The trees met in a celebratory green arch above and Toby waited until the Porsche had disappeared behind a towering hedgerow before rolling down towards the first speed bump. His heart was pounding against his breast bone. His head throbbed and he wondered if he was going to kill Gideon. Cut his head off. Smash it into smithereens. A crack like a branch snapping. A thud. A deafening animal thud. And then black. Black and silent. The thunder of the train. And the sudden burst out into bright blinding day and sun and leaves and trees high on the escarpment. And there he is as clear as day. There's Gideon on the floor between the seats. Obscene without a head. Messy with bits of smashed chicken and breast and wing and liver and kidney all over everywhere. Even in death he won't do the right thing. He's there on the floor of the train. Oddly curled. Grotesque. And the train rattles on clickety clack clickety clack clickety clack south towards Folkestone and Dover and the place where the ferry leaves from. The curled-up body wears a blood-wrecked green cardigan. Feet in white trainers. Misshapen white trainers, one on top of the other. Follow up from the trainers to the square of leg which is showing beneath the cream trousers and up even as far as the first part of the cardigan and it could be asleep. See those legs and shoes and believe it's sleeping. Hold its hand. Wake it up. Bring it back to life. And still the rattle of the train. And on the other side of the carriage someone screams a million miles away because a little pink paperback has landed on the seat beside them. Who gives a shit? Grow up.

Around the corner in time to see a flash of black as the Porsche made the next bend. And then the houses started. Under the thick canopy of Surrey commuter belt: The Orchard and The Larches then Willow Lodge and Braziers End where Sara grew up. Owl's Hoot and The Limes and then The Firs. The Firs with its two upstanding chimneys sheltering in its perpetual shade. The house where Imogen has always lived. There was nowhere to park. There was, it seemed, some kind of a party going on. The drive was packed with cars — with jeeps and Volvos, red and black ones. Blue ones. There was no room for Toby. The front door was open and there was no sign of the Porsche. He watched from the driveway of The Cedars opposite. A dark figure appeared at the foot of the stairs, it disappeared and then Gideon was standing there in the doorway. Nervous, swallowing, ashen-faced, he loosened his tie. It was the one that Primrose made, the dentist's tie with the customized paint design which Gideon took for an animal: Giraffe? He'd asked. For good luck? He smoothed his hair and looked down at the flowers he held: white lilies. He looked up in Toby's direction and didn't see him. White lilies. He didn't know that Imogen hated white lilies. 'Funereal,' she'd say. 'Flowers for people without imagination.' Perhaps he wouldn't have to kill him after all.

Imogen liked wild flowers. She liked wild flowers planted by a man she used to work with who came in every day on the Folkestone–London line and threw wild flower seeds out of the window every morning, every night. Clickety clack. And now all summer long ten miles of track clatter through a waving meadow of cornflower and spring violet and wild rose and cowslip. And here's Imogen, the window down as far as it will go. White trainers, green cardigan, round arse she leans out of the window to admire the care-less garden that her friend has planted. There's a crack like a branch snapping off a tree and the black roar of a tunnel then blinding light and a new day. The pink book, Small Hotels in France, is miles away on the other side of the train.

Gideon turned and left the flowers on the step outside the front door. They were propped up against the red brick of the house beside the white plastic basket neat with empty milk bottles. He wiped his feet too many times on the mat. His hand, hovering at the doorbell, dropped, only for it to rise up to it to hover there again. He turned to look over his shoulder, face colourless he swallowed, he turned back, lifted a foot and was inside.

Toby got out and walked across the road across the gravel crunching between the cars – how they were going to get out of here he had no idea – up the red steps, past the lilies still in their plastic on the doorstep and through the open door. The hall was empty except for Rufus who lay low in his basket. The dog's tail beat three times in recognition but he didn't raise his head. Toby ignored him and followed the dark parquet to a closed door beneath which came muted noise. Footsteps on the stairs, he turned and saw a delicate white hand on the banister, shiny black leather shoes beneath flapping black trousers and then an impressive expanse of milk-white flesh above more black. It was the Hill. Hello! And then he saw her face. She did not look pleased to see him. In fact Toby was having trouble remembering an occasion when an individual had looked less pleased to see him. She bent to stroke the dog.

'Hello,' said Toby.

'Hello,' she replied without turning round.

Toby waited. Perhaps she wanted to go ahead to spread the word that the man with the monkey wrench had arrived. She showed no sign of stopping stroking the dog.

'Are you alright?' he asked. For some reason he'd thought they were friends.

'Good dog,' she said.

He shrugged and pushed open the door. The quietest party in the whole of Surrey. Surprise! Twenty faces turned to him. Fifty faces, blank. Expressions didn't change. Paper plates, glasses of white wine. Howie was near the door. He put his arms round Toby. Stringy Howie squeezed the breath out of him. He let him go and Toby gasped for air. Howard held his hand: 'I'm glad you're here.' His hand was hot and wet and tight. So tight it hurt. And here was Jane.

'Toby,' she said and took his other hand. The door opened and in came the Hill. Majestic she walked past them, pale nose turned up, pushing glasses further on to her face.

'What's wrong with her?'

Howard smiled. He almost laughed. He squeezed Toby's hand. 'Misunderstanding,' he said. 'She'll be alright.'

Someone standing behind him. Quiet. Patient. Toby turned and saw that it was Alison Doubt. Alison Doubt still in her coat. Alison Doubt holding a paper plate, yellow with food – some crisps, some half-eaten quiche, potato salad, sweetcorn.

'Hello Mum. Where's Mercy?'

'Aunt Mercy couldn't come. She couldn't leave Betsey. She's having her puppies,' she frowned at the watch on the inside of her wrist, 'probably as we speak.'

'Is she really?' Jane, pale, looked at Toby.

Puppies and here came Cassie. Hard dark blue hat and the Cyclops and here was their baby on his hip. It was almost a child now. How time flies. And here came the Colonel. John Green. Red-eyed, upright. Silver comb-over spick and span.

'Toby.' He held out his hand to take Toby's. 'Well well. Well well.' He looked away and Toby could see that he was crying.

The French windows were open and at the bottom of the garden the monkey puzzle stood solidly giving the party a resounding thumbs-up. And beneath it stood the swing seat decked out in finest summer yellow. And here was Howie still with his arm around him. We'll be OK. And there was Gideon Chancelight with Saffron. And suddenly Saffron was pushing her nose into Toby's collar bone. We'll be OK. And then Gideon. A sausage roll fell from a paper plate. It rolled on to the floor.

'Toby!' He looked amazed.

'Toby,' said Saffron, her arm was linked through his. 'This is Gideon, old friend from school.'

'Toby? Fuck a duck.' He looked at Saffron. Something else rolled off his plate. Saffron's arm tightened through Toby's.

'You alright hun?' She looked up at him. He nodded. Rufus snaffled hungrily at their feet.

Gideon looked down at his plate. It was empty. The dog pushed between them troughing at the carpet.

Toby stumbled on the lip of the step which led out into the garden. Howard held him and let him go. The lawn looked good, vivid green and well-irrigated. The swing seat swung gently through the sunlight as though someone was lying on it. Toby waited for them to move up and sat on the side which had the sun. Howard stood in the doorway. He came across the grass. Head down. Head up. 'OK?'

'OK.'

'I'm just inside.' Howard pointed and made his way back across the lawn. Gideon appeared on the doorstep. Lips moving. He disappeared again.

Toby waited until he felt Imogen's head heavy on his thighs in the sunlight, his hand tangled in her warm hair as he watched Sara and Gideon and Cassie through the French windows.

Exhausted to the ends of the earth. Exhausted to the ends of time.

You silly goose, said the wind in the lime trees, the cherry tree and even the monkey puzzle, as far as it could. You silly goose.

Acknowledgements

I would like to thank Barbara Trapido, Mary Alexander,
Marianne Macdonald, Elizabeth Hansen and my family
for their encouragement; James Lever for his invaluable
suggestions and of course everyone at Atlantic,
particularly Karen Duffy and Louisa Joyner.

Most of all my thanks go to my agent,
Rebecca Winfield, without whose perserverance and
enthusiasm this book would never have been published.